"Incoming!"

Soldiers caught in the open dropped quickly to the ground in the hopes that enemy rounds did not land on top of them. The first impacts rocked the ground hard. Sections of Rogscroft's ancient walls buckled, threatening to cave in. Waves of flames burned hotly where each round struck. Clouds of dust and debris choked the air. Every round screamed into the city. Armored men cowered and prayed for the bombardment to end.

"Take your posts! To the walls!" bellowed the senior sergeant once the barrage ended.

The defenders raced back to their positions. Squires dropped off full quivers behind each man. Nerves changed them. Fear danced in their eyes. The attack they had long dreaded was finally under way. It was much preferable than the endless hours of waiting and wondering.

"Put those fires out, lads! Quickly, before the whole damned castle burns down!"

Several buildings had caught fire. Some had already collapsed in on themselves. Flames licked higher. The destruction was comparatively minimal but might easily burn out of control. Orderlies raced with buckets. Litter bearers checked the rubble for dead and wounded. The heavy thrum of catapult fire echoed over the battlefield.

TIDES OF BLOOD AND STEEL

Book Two of the Northern Crusade

CHRISTIAN WARREN FREED

Copyright © 2021 by Christian Warren Freed

Excerpt from *A Whisper After Midnight*
Cover design by Melissa Andres
Cover copyright 2021 by Warfighter Books
Author Photograph by Anicie Freed

Warfighter Books
Holly Springs, North Carolina 27540
https://www.christianfreed

Second Edition: August 2021

Library of Congress Cataloging-in-Publication Data
Name: Freed, Christian Warren, 1973- author.
Title: Armies of the Silver Mage/ Christian Warren Freed
Description: Second Edition | Holly Springs, NC: Warfighter Books, 2021. Identifiers: LCCN 2021912195 | ISBN 9781736804421 (trade paperback)
Subjects: Epic fantasy | Military fantasy

Printed in the United States of America

10 9 8 7 6 5 4 3 2 1

Where Have All the Elves Gone?

'Sometimes funny and other times a little dark, Where Have The Elves Gone? brings something fresh and new to fantasy mysteries. Whether you want to curl up with a mystery or read more about elves this book has something for everyone. Spend a few hours solving a mystery with a human and a couple of dwarves - you'll be glad you did.'

Other Books by Christian Warren Freed

<u>The Northern Crusade</u>
Hammers in the Wind
Tides of Blood and Steel
A Whisper After Midnight
Empire of Bones
The Madness of Gods and Kings
Even Gods Must Fall

<u>The Histories of Malweir</u>
Armies of the Silver Mage
The Dragon Hunters
Beyond the Edge of Dawn

<u>Fractured Universe</u>
Dreams of Winter
The Madman on the Rocks
Anguish Once Possessed
Through Darkness Besieged*

Where Have All the Elves Gone?
Tomorrow's Demise: The Extinction Campaign
Tomorrow's Demise: Salvation
Coward's Truth*
The Lazarus Men
Repercussions: A Lazarus Men Agenda*

A Long Way From Home: Memories and
Observations From Iraq and Afghanistan+

<u>Immortality Shattered</u>
Law of the Heretic
The Bitter War of Always
Land of Wicked Shadows
Storm Upon the Dawn

War Priests of Andrak Saga
The Children of Never

SO, You Want to Write a Book? +
SO, You Wrote a Book. Now What? +

*Forthcoming   + Nonfiction

Acknowledgments

Where do I even begin? So many people contributed to the pages that follow. From my dear cadets at the United State Military Academy- many of whom I am sure grew fed up with my constant badgering to get their opinions throughout the day, to my loving family. I intended Tides of Blood and Steel to be one with Hammers in the Wind, never envisioning that such a lengthy series would evolve. At any rate, you must have enjoyed book one to get this far. Read on, my friends. Read on.

A New War Approaches

The crunch of thousands of booted feet rang across the empty plains. Deer and small animals fled at the sound. Night birds erupted from rocks and broken trees long dead. Stomp, stomp, stomp-stomp-stomp. Hobnails struck the ice-covered snow in a symphony of untamed aggression. Baleful horns bleated over the army, accompanied by the whips of the drivers. Ten thousand voices, cruel and filled with vengeance, were carried on the harsh echoes of long past winds.

They came from mighty Druem, an almost forgotten volcano in the heart of the Deadlands. The small kingdom sat north of the Darkwall Mountains in central Malweir, butted against the harsh coast. It was here doom flourished after the Goblins race conquered the land. Once, long ago, there had been a dragon under the mountain. The dragon was long dead, but the great enemy continued to thrive.

Evil seldom needs much to take hold. The Dae'shan swept into the Deadlands and wasted little time in coercing the Goblin army to march west into the northern kingdoms. Cold promises were whispered among the shadows. Of deposing kings and claiming long-forgotten dreams of power and glory enticed the Goblins from their caves. War had returned to the north, finally. Under the masterful manipulations of Amar Kit'han, the Goblin general Grugnak took his army west across the plains.

They marched for weeks, often grinding a grueling pace from sunup to sundown. Nothing enticed Goblins more than the prospect of killing. They came with axe and sword, mace, and hammer. Scouting parties found villages along way and the army fell upon them with fury. Only bones remained for the vultures to pick clean.

Leagues went by. Ankles were broken. A few soldiers deserted after growing drunk on plunder. Grugnak didn't slow the pace. Those too injured to keep up were killed and fed to the army. Goblins served no master other than their uncontrollable desires. Lesser armies would break, but not Grugnak's. He used whip and spear. Fresh lands needed to be conquered. Lands where man had forgotten the scourge the Goblin nation had once been.

The army crossed mountains and small rivers. Winter deepened, slowing their progress considerably. The Dae'shan returned every so often to check on their progress, berating Grugnak for his incompetence in the process. Each time one hundred Goblins died to satiate their commander's anger. Worse, they knew the war had already fallen on Rogscroft. Two mighty armies were engaged in an all-out war for survival. Grugnak scoffed at the notion of men fighting. Neither side would know what to think when his ten-thousand-strong army came up behind and drove them into the ground.

They marched with audacity, daring any kingdom to rise up and repel them. None did. Word of desiccated villagers and ruined villages found way to the larger towns and cities. Kings ordered their armies to form but only in defense. No power in the north other than the Wolfsreik had enough strength to meet the Goblins head-to-head. Grugnak knew that. He placed trust in the Dae'shan, to an extent. They whispered promises of glory too rich to ignore.

The Goblin army was a long, winding snake rolling across the countryside. Plague and decay followed. They moved at a murderous pace, covering nearly forty miles a day. Those too weak fell away or were killed outright. Ever the whips cracked and the drums pounded a brutal song. The promise of battle sang in their hearts. The time had finally come when the Goblin nation could return to rise again. All it took was a little push in Rogscroft.

An army so large was bound to draw attention, especially one as destructive as the Goblins. Scouts from a handful of kingdoms kept pace from a distance. Careful not to be seen, they counted numbers and whispered prayers to their individual gods. None living could recall the last time such a force emerged from the Deadlands. The portents for the future were ill, indeed.

Hidden among the sparse pines and gently rolling hills, three figures watched the Goblins with unusual scrutiny. They wore pale cloaks that blended with the freshly fallen snow. Leather-plate armor was form fitting and well used. Knee-high riding boots sank into the snow. Swords, lances, and bows jutted from a dozen places. Their sharp eyes peered intently from beneath their hoods.

"This is not good," the tallest said flatly. "What reason have the Goblins for leaving the Deadlands?"

Their leader shook his head, frowning. "I don't know, but no good will come of it. What kingdoms lie in their path?"

"There is naught but empty lands from here to the Fern River. After that is Rogscroft and Delranan."

Cocking his head, the leader replied, "You forget Drimmen Delf."

"The Dwarves will not intervene, despite their long-standing hatred of the Goblins."

"Odd, considering they were once the same," said the taller. "Are you sure we should get involved?"

"No war needs to be fought, or so I've long believed," the leader said. "King Thord has asked for our aid and we are honor bound to give it. The Dwarves are decent enough folk, for mountain dwellers. Our duties lay in Drimmen Delf."

"What of the Goblins? That is a large army."

Giving the enemy one final look, the leader said, "News will spread quickly. They head to attack the world of men and men must fight them. We ride for Drimmen Delf. Our war is separate." *For now, at least.*

Arlevon Gale was a hallowed place, long forgotten by men and gods. It was once a mighty city in an inhospitable land. Priests and holy men traveled across Malweir to come to the sole place of power capable of delivering their prayers successfully to the gods, for here the veil between dimensions was thinnest. Ever receptive of the cries and pleas of the people, the gods relished the attention. After all, how can a god exist without believers?

Now only ruins remained. The surrounding area was overgrown with thick, winter vines and heavy undergrowth. Trees broke through the original layers of stone and rotted wood. Defaced statues stared accusingly; their features long worn away. They once guarded the paths to the inner citadel. Crumbling towers jutted up from the improvised forest. The stone, once an immaculate steel grey, now languished under years of neglect and grime. Empty windows stared out at the world like so many empty eyes, accusingly and sad. Most of the wood had rotted away, leaving a hollow shell of former splendor. Arlevon Gale was forgotten, but sometimes forgotten things refuse to die.

"This place hasn't been used in centuries," Kodan Bak remarked snidely. Concealed in his billowing onyx cloak, the Dae'shan floated inches above the ground. Flat red eyes glared from beneath his cowl.

Amar Kit'han's frown was lost within the solitude of his own hood. "Humans are forgetful creatures, Kodan Bak, but not wholly ignorant to the deeper mystery. Underestimating them will prove your downfall."

"We have stood for ages, unchecked and unhampered by the plodding rituals of the mortals. They are an ignorant race incapable of maintaining any semblance of dignity."

"You forget we were once human."

"A fact I'd do well to keep forgotten. Mortal flesh was a hindrance. A means to an end, if you will," Kodan replied.

Amar Kit'han, eldest of the four Dae'shan, folded his arms across his chest and turned away. He'd endured hundreds of years of counterplotting and subterfuge from his subordinate. There was no doubt Kodan Bak wanted to be in control. His desires bled from his robes like venom from a snake. But what the lesser Dae'shan had for ambition, he lacked in execution. Kodan Bak was a creature of convenience and delay. Thus far the situation to usurp Amar hadn't presented itself.

"Our former humanity is most assuredly a weakness, but can be used to advantage," he said and paused. "If you are wise enough."

Kodan ignored the rebuke. "Wisdom is relative to desire. Why have you brought me here?"

"This is where the final battle will happen. Arlevon Gale was once a place of immense power, rival only to the great nexuses."

"Which have all been either destroyed or closed to us," Kodan reminded bitterly. *Yet another reason to despise the blundering mortals and their determination to remain independent.*

"True, but the power within these ruins is enough," Amar insisted. "There will be only one chance before the moment is lost. We must not fail."

He stared down at the faint blue aura clinging to the ground. The power was ripe, aching to be accessed. With the collapse of the Mages so long ago, a power vacuum emerged. Only a handful could access the true strength of the world. Amar Kit'han knew the advantages lay in his favor. But for one: Anienam Keiss, last descendant of the Mages and adopted son of the great Dakeb. A time of reckoning was fast approaching. A time when Dae'shan and Mage would end their long-running war. Only one would walk away, and even

Amar Kit'han's inflated sense of confidence wasn't enough to convince him that it would be him.

"The pieces are in motion, Kodan Bak. The final game has begun. We must be quick to seize the advantage," he paused, debating whether or not to speak the next thought. "I worry that the last Mage spawn is gathering strength. We must exhaust all possible resources in trying to stop him."

"He should have been dealt with long ago," Kodan sniped. "You leave too many windows open. Your inaction will return to haunt us before this affair is ended. What of Pelthit Re? It has been too long since we last heard word from him."

Amar tilted his head skyward, as if sniffing the cold wind. "He is…occupied in Chadra with the One Eye. All is moving according to schedule, but we cannot delay. I need you to travel to Gren. There are rumors of Gnaals roving the countryside. Find them and send them to Trennaron."

"You think *he* is going to pose a threat?"

"Artiss Gran has been a threat from the moment he abandoned us. The Gnaals must find him and kill him."

"A difficult task. He may no longer be a part of us, but his powers remain," Kodan countered.

"Break him. Expend every resource. He must not live if we are to stop the Mage spawn," Amar snapped.

Kodan nodded agreement. "Where will you be?"

"I must return to Badron. His mind is yet hale and it will take more to break him enough to be usable for my purposes. The northern kingdoms are about to be torn asunder, Kodan Bak. Hatred and enmity will spread through the population like a plague. An unstoppable machine with one true intent."

Amar didn't bother watching as Kodan folded darkness around him and disappeared with no more than a wisp of black cloud. *Yes, my insubordinate friend. All my problems will soon be dealt with appropriately.*

TWO

Thoughts of Revenge

Life seldom follows the path of dreams. Men spend years of their already limited time on Malweir thinking about tomorrow, waiting for the turn of the sun when they might find opportunity to make their move. Fate or destiny never asks for personal opinions, never cares what man wants next. The universe moves to the tune of pre-written plans without consideration of those involved. Each time the sun chases the moon away, a new opportunity arises filled with promise or despair. For as surely as the need for promise, to hope for better days, is vital to the continuation of existence, the utter dread of despair lurks just behind.

Delranan had become a dangerous place in the span of a few short weeks. With the main army gone to war in neighboring Rogscroft, Harnin One Eye assumed control and immediately began executing his will through ruthless aggression. The weak fell quickly, accepting the sudden change and direction in which the kingdom was ruled. Fear kept many others in line, yet it was fear that drove Harnin's actions. He was a man used to standing behind the power, not being the power itself.

Most surprising to the entire kingdom was the rise of the rebellion. Under Badron there'd been no need to turn against the crown. While he was no saint, Badron ruled with enough wisdom to be perceived as fair. Harnin erased it all. Jails filled overnight. Still more disappeared and wound up in the Keep's dungeons. He feared that the only way to hold power was through eliminating his opponents.

Bahr was the first. The forgotten brother of the king had been an ignored thorn in the kingdom's side for far too long. Some residuals of childhood feelings kept Badron from doing what needed to be done. Harnin lacked no such restrictions. His campaign against Bahr began the moment he convinced Badron to hire him to retrieve Maleela. The rest was too easy. Soon Bahr found himself locked in a dungeon cell awaiting torture and execution. The only complications arose when Argis showed his true colors and freed the prisoners.

The orange glow on the near horizon made Bahr sick to his stomach. Occasional tongues of flame licked hungrily over the trees and rooftops. Harnin's first move had been to set Bahr's ship on fire, reducing his capabilities as well as his preferred mode for escape. Bahr had spent so much time on the *Dragon's Bane* that his life was inexorably tied to the aged timbers. It represented all that was good in him and offered him a sense of purpose. And now it was gone. His life would never be the same again. Heavy sorrow settled over his soul. Instincts screamed for him to hunt down Harnin and end this game. Justice could only be served by killing Harnin One Eye.

Rekka Jel, ever the wise counselor, saw his discomfort. "I know what your heart desires, Captain Bahr. I have felt your sorrow in my life as well. There will come a time when you get to play out your revenge. Now is simply not the time."

"If not now, when? I am tired of being told this is not the right time. Harnin must be punished for all of it. For my boat. For what he did to my friends. And for what he is doing to my kingdom." He wasn't sure what made him add the last statement. Ignored by his father and brother, Bahr never held aspirations for the throne and seldom felt akin to his native land. Delranan was his kingdom by birthright, but it offered little comfort to the self-exile.

"He will be punished," she quietly affirmed. "But we have risked much to save your niece and cannot allow ourselves to become distracted until the main task is accomplished. This war is just beginning."

He tensed. "I don't give a damn about the war. All I want is that man's head."

"I promise you shall have it. The way ahead is still dark but make no mistake. It is filled with danger and will be long and arduous. If the Dae'shan are not stopped, all we know will come to an end. The dark gods will have dominance over Malweir. Stopping them must be our primary focus," Anienam added.

Argis leaned close to Boen and whispered, "What are the Dae'shan?"

Anienam answered before the Gaimosian opened his mouth. "That is a difficult answer to give. Once they were the neutral guardians of the will of the gods. They became corrupt, much as the crystal of Tol Shere corrupted the Mages. The Dae'shan allowed an unnatural need for power to consume them until only a shell of what they had been remains. They are altogether evil now. Twisted and wicked. A shame, really, considering what they had once been."

"I thought the gods abandoned Malweir long ago?" Argis suddenly had a bad feeling gnawing at his insides.

Anienam nodded politely. "To an extent. The gods of light abandoned their claim on Malweir, leaving it to us how best to rule and exist. The dark gods, exiled by the forces of good, have never stopped trying to return from their abyssal prison. They subverted the Dae'shan and use them to execute their will. Many great evils have existed over time, but none so powerful and dangerous as the Dae'shan."

"Your words offer little encouragement, wizard," Boen added from his seat a few meters away.

Anienam offered a sorrowful look. "Why should they? We are trapped in desperate times. I had hoped to beat the Dae'shan here, but I was too late."

"What are they after? Why Delranan?" Argis asked.

A shrug. "Their only real purpose is to open the gateway between worlds to free the dark gods. How they plan on doing so remains hidden from me. There were only three nexuses on Malweir. Two are destroyed and the third is heavily guarded, or so I believe. Without one, the dark gods can't return."

Dorl winced and wiped his eyes. "You think that's what this is all about? The war, Harnin, all of it?"

"It makes sense. Look at how much the north has changed in such a short period of time," Anienam suggested and offered Bahr a knowing look.

Sitting across from them, Bahr reluctantly accepted the situation. He'd lived long enough to recognize when a battle needed to be postponed. Harnin could wait. Everything Bahr knew and loved was on the brink of destruction. He was confused, his sense of faith wounded. The orange glow darkened. Bahr closed his eyes and tried convincing himself that it was just a boat.

"You don't think the crew was on board, do you?" Maleela asked.

Rekka cast a stern gaze on her for asking such an insensitive question. "No. I overheard Harnin say they'd been forced into a labor camp for the army. They may be mistreated, but they're safe enough."

For a time. Her knowledge of northern customs was handicapped by their utter foreignness. So unlike were her people and these gruff northerners that she felt out of place. Rekka was groomed to be a fine warrior and strategist, but even that meant little when faced by the blunt force the northern warriors chose to employ. She used finesse and grace, almost a mockery of Dorl's style. Yet the sell sword attracted her in ways she failed to understand. Confused, she sat back and brooded.

The conversation was too much for Argis. Already a traitor, he felt much worse. Bahr and his companions were involved in affairs that went far beyond Argis' own actions. His misgivings would only grow as time went by. Whatever Bahr planned on doing, Argis made up his mind to stay embedded in the underground. Delranan had to come before the needs of any one man. He'd sealed his fate the moment he agreed to conspire with Prince Aurec of Rogscroft and let him sneak into Chadra Keep. *How wrong everything went after that. Killing Badron's son wasn't part of the plan, but then again, nothing that happened that night was. What a fool I've been.*

"There is nothing for it," Bahr finally said. "They were a good crew but, like Harnin, they too must wait until we're in a position that will allow us to help."

"What is our next move then?" Boen asked. He was glad to move on. There was no point on dwelling on affairs they were powerless to change. Gaimosians lacked the sense of place inherent in most others. Boen had already been stagnant for too long and, without a proper enemy to fight, felt restricted. The desire to move on and find new adventure in warmer climes beckoned.

Bahr drank deeply from one of the canteens they'd confiscated. The water was good, but it was not food. Argis promised them food, water, and enough mounts to see them about their task as soon as they linked up with the underground.

Anienam smiled darkly and answered before Bahr could. "We must find the Blud Hamr."

"The what?" Bahr asked.

"The Blood Hammer. It is an ancient weapon that will destroy the Dae'shan and end this rising tide of darkness."

The Sea Wolf didn't know whether to laugh or shake his head in futility. "That's nice, but where are we supposed to find this hammer of yours? I doubt they sell one in the Merchant's Circle."

"We never got to that part," Dorl added from the opposite side of the fire.

Anienam sighed. The smallness of some minds was exceedingly frustrating. He never understood why some people refused to accept concepts that did not originate through them. The world was filled with magical beings and instruments. Malweir was an ancient world and held many secrets, most of which would never be seen.

He leveled his gaze back on the group. "Delranan was once an important land. The king of Averon once used this very port to launch a raid on distant shores. Then came the horrors of the Mage Wars and all that was civilized fell into chaos. There was once a large temple in the center of Chadra. This temple held the knowledge of most of the northern magic. It is here that we will find reference to the hammer."

"There is only one small problem," Bahr said dryly. "Chadra has no standing temples."

"True, but it is not the actual temple that we need. Most of the knowledge was stored underground in massive vaults."

His hopes slipped with the sudden possibility that it might all be gone. The wealth of the old days was destroyed forever. Until this point, Anienam had been so sure of himself. The winds had blown him into Delranan for reasons he hadn't understood. Raw power was gathering beneath the frozen northern kingdom in unprecedented quantities. He might have laughed if the tides were not shifting against them.

"There are tunnels that run beneath Fareth's Mill," Skuld offered. "That's close to the center of town."

The wizard smiled. "Have you been in them?"

Skuld was more than happy to finally be of worth to this group. "That's where I'd go if people, uh…chased me."

Anienam turned to Bahr. "We must go there."

The Sea Wolf scratched the stubble of his beard. "We should split our forces. I'll take Boen, Rekka, and Ionascu, and head to my estate. We need money and supplies, and I have them. You take the others and find this temple. You have until dawn, after that it won't be safe for any of us. We must escape before Harnin has the chance to mobilize his forces against us."

Argis looked around. *They are all crazy. And now I am one of them.* He was left with little choice. It was too late to go back, despite the grim dawn of the future. Argis saw but one way.

"I will lead your people to the mill," he offered.

Bahr fought his reservations and gave a brisk nod. It was time to move, lest the enemy gain on them. Argis waited for the others to rise before leading his group back to the city. The moment left Bahr with an uneasy feeling. A day ago, Argis had been one of Badron's most trusted advisors. Now he was more than willing to betray a lifetime of trust. Part of that didn't sit well with Bahr. Still, there were great possibilities for both parties so long as Argis didn't cross them. Bahr let the thought fade. There was no point in searching for hidden conspiracies.

His thoughts turned towards his own task. It was entirely possible that his estate had fallen under Harnin's thumb as much as his beloved *Bane* had. Material possessions never mattered much to him, none except for the *Bane*. He focused on salvaging what goods he could. Winter was right around the corner and they were going to need as much cold weather equipment as they could lay their hands on. Besides, he had a sinking feeling that this was the last time he was ever going to return to his home.

Nothol Coll looked back over his shoulder and said, "We'll wait for you at Sundin Pond."

Bahr gave him a halfhearted salute. "Sundin Pond."

The plan wasn't much but it was the best they could come up with on such short notice. The orange glow on the horizon stole his attention back. It called to him. Bahr grunted frustrations and tried to put it from his mind. Revenge was a hard thing to postpone when your life was all but destroyed.

"Captain, are you all right?" Rekka asked gently.

"Would you be?" he countered.

She chose not to reply. Her fears had long haunted her. She'd seen destruction on a massive scale before and prayed she never had too again. Fate would not be so kind to her. This was by far the most volatile situation she'd ever found herself in. Not even the wars in her home jungle of Brodein matched what was coming here. Rekka maintained her suspicions of the northlands. These were a violent people who took great pride in their warlike prowess. The Dae'shan had chosen well.

Taking her silence for consent, Bahr marched to his horse. Time was against them. The dawn charged fast. He regretted sending Maleela with the wizard. She'd been through so much already it almost seemed unfair that he had asked her to endure more. Still, Anienam Keiss was about the best protection he could offer.

"A fire that big and no one is investigating it? This is not right," Boen whispered. His right hand rested on his sword. The Gaimosian was ready for a fight.

Bahr agreed. "Harnin must have begun a curfew. The people have been frightened into their homes. Our path is more dangerous than we thought."

"Nothing a strong sword arm can't handle."

Bahr shot him a cautious glance. "I can never tell when you are serious or not."

Boen smiled and shrugged. "It's not hurting my feelings any."

"How far are we from your estate?" Rekka asked.

"Not far. A few hundred meters."

Rekka rolled her almond eyes. "I suggest you both stop giving away our position then. The enemy might have pickets in the tree line awaiting us."

The Gaimosian drew his great broadsword. "Let them come. I am tired of hiding in the shadows like a common thief."

"That old wizard has something up his sleeves," Bahr added. "I think we are going to be knee deep in battle much sooner than any of us want. Even you, Boen."

They rode on. Only Ionascu remained closed. He had become a shell of his former self. Watching his men being slaughtered on the docks had driven him to the brink of insanity. The brutality of his torture in the dungeons had ruined his body and further fractured his mind. He was Harnin's spy no longer. The betrayal ate away at him. Foul memories tormented him every time he closed his eyes. Ionascu drowned in an overwhelming sense of hopelessness.

"Hsst, we are here," Bahr whispered.

The Sea Wolf slipped to the ground and drew his sword. It was time to find out just how thorough Harnin was. The others closed in around him. All but Ionascu were prepared for battle.

"Boen, swing around the right side. The main entrance is directly opposite of us. I don't suppose I need to tell you to kill anyone who gets in the way."

The Gaimosian shook his head with a rueful smile. He knew his role well enough and was one of the best at it. It was a gift of his bloodline. The only friendlies around were standing beside him. Everyone else was fair game. The dungeon beatings flashed, driving his battle rage higher. Vengeance Knight. The title was much more than a simple name designed to inspire terror in the unbelievers. Boen fully intended to live up to the name before the first rays of light kissed the frost-covered land. Boen rolled his shoulder muscles and stalked off into the night like some dangerous beast from legend.

Bahr snatched Ionascu by the collar. "You stay here with the horses and watch our backs. Got it?"

The broken man barely nodded. His eyes were glazed and remained unfocused, staring off into the snow-covered fields.

Oddly satisfied by the lack of reaction, Bahr said, "Rekka come with me. We secure the perimeter and the barn, get what we need, and get out before they know we are here."

The first break of dawn breached the horizon. Time was almost up. Boen made first contact with a pair of enemy pickets guarding the front door. A feral grin lit his face. He attacked with impossible speed and grace. Neither guard had a chance. The fight was over before it really began. Boen punched his sword through the first man's stomach and spun to take the second's head before either had a chance to draw their blades. Boen dropped into a crouch in search of more targets. Old sensations combined with the sudden rush of adrenaline gave him strength, enhanced his reactions. Born a warrior, he lived every day for the prospect of joining battle with worthy opponents. This was almost too easy. He wasn't disappointed when he caught the column of torches coming down the main avenue. *Right on time.*

Bahr and Rekka moved just as quickly on securing the barn. Rekka struck hard, ruthless in her assault. Two guards, almost bored with their assignment, lounged against the snow and ice-covered door. Bahr frowned, knowing even with their inattentiveness he'd never be able to cross the distance before one or both raised the alarm. Rekka held no hesitations and charged light-footed across the snow. Her slippered feet landed so lightly she barely left a track before falling on the guards. Stabbing the closest in the chest, she ripped the blade free and spun around to catch the second across the stomach. Blood sprayed out in a grizzly arc, followed closely by organs and viscera as the body dropped. Both guards died without a sound. Rekka knelt and wiped the blood and clumps of flesh from her sword.

Bahr was impressed. Until now he hadn't seen her in action. She'd only been an idea, not a dangerous weapon capable of slaughtering them all. Her lethality made him nervous and grateful they were allied. "Let's start loading the wagon. Take all of the weapons and supplies you can find."

"Where are you going?" Rekka asked almost too innocently.

"Inside. My safe is hidden within."

Rekka accepted his answer and went about her task. The horses hitched easily enough and then she set to loading sheaves of arrows and other weapons. Bahr slipped out the back door. Using the buildings for cover, he skirted around the house and met Boen on the porch. The bigger man was sitting in Bahr's favorite rocking chair with a flint glare in his eyes.

The Gaimosian pointed down to the flickering torches marching up the road. "Time is almost up."

Bahr cursed. "Go and help Rekka. I'll meet you back there in a few minutes."

Sounds started to come from the road. Angry, purposeful. Boots crunching down the gravel. Metal pauldrons capping shoulders rubbing against breastplates. Bahr guessed they had maybe ten minutes before the soldiers arrived. Out of time, he entered his house for what would be the last time and hurried through the expanse of rooms to his master bedroom. Bahr ran to his safe hidden in the floorboards under the bed and filled the bag he took from the barn with silver and copper coins. Too many large coins would attract unwarranted attention. Lastly, he took a few small pouches of gold coins and tucked them within his inner tunic. A time would come when only gold would see them through.

"Bahr! Come out now you son of a whore!" Harnin's voice bellowed across the front lawn. "Come out and die with some dignity or I'll burn this house down around your worthless head."

Odd, Harnin actually sounded like a man. Bahr snarled. The snake had spent his life in the shadows and now found himself in a position of power. It was almost laughable. Bahr had no false ideations about his estate surviving intact. Venom dripped from Harnin's voice. Hatred sweat from his pores. They'd never liked each other. Harnin blamed him for the loss of his eye. The battle against a band of raiders had been fierce and many men from both sides were killed. Bahr had one moment of lapse where he failed to protect Harnin's flank. A raider managed to get within his guard and swipe a dagger across Harnin's face, ripping out his eye. Truthfully, the loss of Harnin's eye was no one's fault. It was an act of war as unpredictable as who lived and who died. Regardless, the One Eye maintained a simmering hatred for the king's brother.

"I know you are in there. You didn't think you actually stood a chance of escaping, did you?"

Bahr ignored him. The words were nothing but an undisguised attempt to lure him to act rashly. He chuckled. Bahr had played this game for far too long to fall for such a simple trick. He tied off the money sack and slung it over his shoulder. There was still a small window for escape he couldn't afford to waste. Even now guards and mercenaries were moving to surround the estate. Harnin was content with taunts for now, but it would change as soon as he saw the bodies of his men. Then the fun would begin.

Bahr snuck out the back door and dashed across the yard to the barn. "We need to go."

The sudden whoosh of roaring flames confirmed his worst fears. Bahr had officially lost everything. His old life was finished. The *Bane* was gone. His crew killed or imprisoned. Wishing them to escape did little good. They were on their own. Boen, having already abandoned his chair and returned to the barn to help Rekka, tossed the last sack of grain into the wagon bed and collected his sword.

"Do we fight?" he asked.

Bahr reluctantly said, "No. They are too many. We wouldn't last. They've already torched the house. They'll be heading this way next."

"I am sorry, Captain," Rekka told him.

He silently accepted her words. "Yeah, so people keep telling me."

He helped her climb onto the driver's bench and then ran back to the main door. He and Boen meant to cover the wagon while she escaped back to Ionascu in the forest. The long bow in Boen's hand surprised him. Gaimosians preferred killing close up with a sword. Arrows seemed dishonorable.

"I didn't know you knew how to use one of those things," he told the bigger man.

The Gaimosian shrugged, an act he found himself doing more of as he got older. "I like to keep people surprised. Are you sure we can't kill a few more just for principle?"

"You are the damnedest man I have ever met. Let's see what Harnin has in store for us first. I'm expecting him to slip up and we'll be able to duck out without being seen."

"I don't sneak," Boen frowned.

The wagon creaked by. Bahr idly wondered if Ionascu was still waiting or if he gave in to his nerves and bolted. The man was more of a liability now than when he was a spy. He had half a mind to put the man out of his misery. Too bad the wizard said Ionascu had some part to play in the future.

Bahr looked back at the house. "Do you think he brought enough men?"

More than fifty soldiers fanned out in a semicircle around the estate.

Boen tested the strength of the bowstring. "Anything less would be insulting."

One of Harnin's men spied them and gave a shout. Harnin barked orders. His men formed ranks and prepared to attack. Boen fit an arrow and took aim.

"Can you hit that one-eyed bastard?" Bahr asked.

"If you shut up."

He fired. The arrow sped fast and true, but he hadn't taken into account the slight breeze picking up from the massive house fire. Smoke and flames licked into the sky. Harnin raised his sword to issue the charge when the bolt took the man to his right. Blood splashed. The body dropped with a strangled gasp. The order to charge froze in Harnin's throat. He reluctantly held his forces back as his nemesis slipped into the forest. Their confrontation was going to have to wait.

Harnin sheathed his sword. "Burn it! Burn everything!"

He spun angrily, forcing his gaze away from the forest. Bahr won this time and Harnin lacked the manpower to effectively scour the forest. The wagon rolled, reins snapping for more speed. Bahr stayed a moment longer to ensure they weren't being pursued. Flames poured from the windows and doors, licking up to the skies as more furniture caught flame.

THREE

Into the Tunnels

A stray dog scurried away at the sound of their approach. The dead rat it had been chewing on fell to the ground. Argis stepped past the small corpse and marched on. Skuld walked at his side. Together they traversed the back alleys in the hopes of remaining undiscovered, ranging down into the poorer parts of Chadra. Random patrols were already searching Chadra and Stouds for Bahr and his companions. Argis was immediately uncomfortable. As a lord of Delranan he was unused to seeing this part of town. They'd already passed plenty of homeless, further changing his image of what this noble city was supposed to be.

Former lord, he corrected himself with a smirk. There was no way he'd be able to show his face in Badron's court again after tonight. Traitor. He tried his best to beat back the feeling. Death was not going to be kind. History might view his deeds differently, but not today. Today he stood a traitor to crown and kingdom. The very thought threatened to drop him to his knees. He'd lived an honorable life, abandoning his core principles in favor of securing his own future, for whatever time he had remaining, was an anathema. But corruption needed to be dealt with quickly and effectively before it could spread. He felt the rot growing, but it was for different reasons he let Prince Aurec into Chadra Keep. Argis vowed to take that secret to the grave. Too much was at stake for him to betray not only himself, but the one he meant to protect.

"It's not much further," Skuld whispered at his side. The youth knew the streets impeccably, never dithering or hesitating when it came to a turn.

Good. I cannot bear to see my people suffer so. I wonder if Badron knows how poorly these wretches live, or if he even cares. He asked, "How do you know so much about these streets?"

Skuld tried not to laugh in his face. "You high born wouldn't understand. This is the real Chadra. I was born here and live here while you sit in your fancy keep sipping expensive wine and laughing at petty fears. Look around you, Argis. People are starving out here. More than before. This is what your kingdom is really like. But you wouldn't know that, would you? I've spent most of my life on the streets. There are plenty of bigger people lurking so I had to learn the secret places. I'd be dead by now if I weren't good at it."

"Fair enough," Argis mumbled a bit shamefully.

The street thief scoffed but kept his mouth shut. He was silently grateful that Argis didn't ask the obvious question of what happened to his parents. That forgotten spark of normalcy was as alien to him as the hot wind blowing across the desert. The thoughts were disturbing, serving only to distract him from the cold realty his life had denigrated to. Life was hard. Survival was the only important piece and was ever changing. Skuld spent his days wondering when his time was going to come.

He shivered and forced the memories away. Death needn't come sooner. Skuld pointed at a random stack of crates and broken barrels. "Here, this is the entrance to the tunnels."

Argis tilted his head back slightly, deciding to hold his tongue rather than question the youth again. His feeling they'd be stuck with each other much longer than either wanted demanded prudence. Maybe there'd be a time to reconcile later.

"How did these tunnels come about?" Anienam asked as both he and Argis stepped aside to let the sell swords clear the opening. He purposefully ignored his own earlier supposition that the tunnels were once part of the ancient temple, now long fallen into disuse. Experience showed him that letting the others get as involved as possible not only enhanced the possibility of success but allowed him greater leeway in doing what he *knew* needed doing.

This current group, the latest out of several over the course of his life, had potential but stood on the edge of a very sharp precipice. Many were either too self-conscious or lacked esteem. Bahr and Boen were too old to properly handle what was coming, but Anienam needed both. The sell swords were better suited as comedians. Only Rekka Jel held his trust. After all, he'd been the one to summon her to the north. He sighed. They were wasting time.

"No one knows," Argis replied. "There are rumors that this part of the kingdom was once buried under a mountain, long before the days when your precious Mage Council led Malweir to war. Still, if what Skuld says is correct, we should be able to find the temple. If it still exists."

"Much was lost during the war, not least of which the desire for higher learning. I cannot foresee any reasons why it shouldn't be there."

Anienam Keiss ignored the barb about the Mages. He hadn't even been thought of when Sidian the Silver Mage created a schism amongst the Mages. It was that war that led to a new age of conflicts spanning Malweir. Those conflicts ended, for the most part, after his father Dakeb led a small band of heroes into the foul kingdom of Gren to kill Sidian once and for all. The cracked crystal of Tol Shere was destroyed forever and sent into the dimensional prison with the dark gods. With the crystal lost, there shouldn't be any way for them to return, making all of this quite confusing. There were too many questions lacking answers.

Life had gone very wrong for the Mages with the creation of the crystal of Tol Shere. Designed as a vehicle to store and measure the vast wealth of knowledge from all races, the crystal became corrupted under the subtle influences of the dark gods and their Dae'shan puppets. Sidian fell easily, for he was ever the arrogant one. He used his newfound powers to bring the Mage council at Ipn Shal to its knees. The war that followed spanned generations. Tens of thousands were lost in the most gruesome struggle in history before the crystal was broken into four shards.

The dark gods remained banished in their nether realm and Sidian went into hiding, biding his time until he could release his new masters. The order of Mages was ultimately destroyed; less than a handful survived and most of them refused to practice magic again. Their anonymity took hold with most of the populace, but not with Sidian. The Silver Mage sent his agents to hunt down and murder the few remaining Mages until only Dakeb remained. So far as he knew, Anienam Keiss was all that remained of that legacy.

The hatch to the tunnels groaned open as they worked together to pull the heavy, rusted iron and mass of wood. Clearly it had been abandoned for much longer than even Anienam guessed. Ages worth of dust billowed out, choking them. Cobwebs hung limp, the spiders long dead and shriveled to husks. A rat lurched out of the pile of molded leaves brushed into one corner. Skuld shifted through the rubble to produce a handful of torches. Passing a furtive glance around to ensure no one was spying on them, the street thief ushered them inside. The last thing they needed was uninvited guests following them down. Long swords were of no use in the confined space, making it easy for thieves to come upon them in the dark and use their favored short knives.

"Hurry," Skuld whispered.

Argis and the wizard went first. Maleela went next and was followed by Dorl and Nothol. Dorl Theed cast a backwards glance before slowly pulling the door close. Reservations soured his face. Trusting a half-mad crony and a street rat didn't sit well with him no matter how many different angles he tried to rationalize through. He had doubts about what lay ahead, but it was too late to turn back. Darkness choked at him, beaten back only by the thin slivers of torchlight already pushing deeper ahead.

The tiny group pressed on. Soon only Skuld was able to move without difficulty. The tunnel network constricted at an alarming rate, inviting paranoia and the creeping fingers of claustrophobia reaching in. A thin coat of slime and mold coated the otherwise smooth walls. The floor was covered with dirt and the bones of several small creatures. Dead spiders hung from cobwebs. More than once a whisper of shadow crawled across the ceiling only to disappear the moment torchlight searched for it. Time meant nothing here. They carried on with the hopes that the answers they needed were hidden away in the ruins of a place long forgotten.

"It's not far now, just around the corner," Skuld told them.

They managed a few more meters and halted. He kicked a pair of large rats away. The cramped tunnel gave way to a round chamber large enough for them to stand straight again. Dust trickled from the ceiling like the tender kiss of the first spring rain. The air was damp, humid. They found it difficult to breathe. And there was something else: raw power sat unbridled just ahead. The air hummed with electricity. Skuld's face drained an ashen white. Even in the flickering darkness Anienam recognized the look. *Interesting. The boy might have the latent ability to tap into the energies in the air. He might make a powerful wizard someday.* Anienam decided to watch the boy closely. Perhaps the line of Mages was meant to survive after all.

Argis looked around. His mouth had fallen open. "How is this possible?"

"There are many wonders in the world. Not all are explainable. This might be one of them," Anienam offered.

"Doesn't look like much of a temple," Dorl said. His voice was thick with sarcasm.

The building was a ruin. Three empty windows gaped at them in a twisted mockery of a human face. Most of the structure was buried under the countless centuries of rock and dirt. Pieces from a ruined pillar lay shattered around them. Half of a broken face leered up at them from its resting place. Its twin remained upright on the opposite side of the doorway. Artisans had intricately carved a great serpent into the alabaster marble. The quality of work was impressive even after centuries lost to obscurity.

"This was once a grand building in a more elegant time," Anienam replied.

Dorl Theed brushed it off. "What treasures could possibly be here? This place is a ruin. Looters would have picked it clean before we were born."

"It is not treasure we seek, sell sword. What we need is knowledge and if the secret we need remains, it will be buried here."

Anienam stepped past Skuld, pausing to grip his shoulder lightly. "You did well. Escort me inside if you please."

He stopped Argis from following. "No. I cannot do my task with everyone. Wait here and defend the perimeter."

Argis held out his hands to the eerily noiseless surroundings. "Defend against what?"

"There are powerful magics here. Such a place is bound to have guardians. They might be hidden, but rest assured they are here. We might need your sword before this ends."

His words carried a haunting tone. The sell swords drew their swords in anticipation of the horrors to come. Wizardry spooked them. The use of magic had been considered a bane to existence, ever since the Mages lost control and warred with each other. Dorl and Nothol exchanged uneasy looks and established a perimeter. Dorl Theed motioned the wizard on. The quicker the old man finished his task, the sooner they could head back to the surface.

Their clothes clung to them from sweat. The air was stale, a musty smell to it. Only the faint glow of torches offered any respite from the oppressive darkness. Danger whispered from the shadows. Echoes of wind blew down the tunnels in an almost exuberant sigh from being liberated after so long. New life had come, deceitful and intoxicating. The ancient temple stirred.

Argis looked over his shoulder as the last glimpse of the wizard disappeared. "Do you think there is truth to his words?"

"I have no desire to find out," Nothol answered.

The back of his neck itched. Darkness crept closer and it was all he could do to maintain his courage. Some things shouldn't be disturbed.

Anienam Keiss whispered a few words and the inside of the temple sprang to light under a pale blue glow. Together he and Skuld wormed their way around the piles of broken rock and marble that littered the floor. Past rows of near-petrified benches and broken tables. Small books long turned to dust. Effigies of once important men leered from their eternal monuments to the forgotten.

"What do you know of magic, young Skuld?"

The street thief was taken off guard. Truth be told, he never bothered to think about it. Magic was another of those things in life that didn't matter. "Nothing, sir. I don't see what this has to do with anything though."

Anienam smiled. "Consider it an old man's fancy."

"Folks in Delranan don't talk about magic. We don't believe in what we can't see," Skuld explained, quietly hoping to end the conversation. He felt like he was being watched and didn't want to draw unnecessary attention.

"You northerners are a superstitious lot," Anienam replied. "Wise, to be sure, but wisdom often leads to ignorance."

"That doesn't make sense."

A thick eyebrow arched. "Doesn't it? Those who consider themselves wise often close their minds, thinking they know enough or too much already. They lose receptivity to new concepts or otherwise strange information. Magic fell from favor long ago, thanks to the Mages, but it still exists and is one of the most powerful energy forms among the races. Don't be so quick to discount what you lack knowledge of."

They continued on. Anienam was impressed with the scope of the building. At one point, it must have been the largest building in the north. Ages old cobwebs hung from every corner. The air was staler here than in the outer chamber. Skuld found his breathing grow harder with each step forward. A loud snap stole his attention, forcing him to look down. Two skeletons lay stretched out. Tatters of dark robes clung in strips to the dust-covered bones. The street thief wanted nothing more than to leave this house of death. He was no stranger to the tunnels, but this went beyond the depths of his courage.

"How will we know what we're looking for?" he asked. His voice was desperate to take his mind off the present.

"Patience, my young friend. The way will be shown to us."

Skuld stared at the old man's back. He couldn't begin to fathom the sarcasm his elders constantly displayed. He shook his head and continued. The sooner they finished the better.

"Please hurry," he whispered. The walls closed in on him.

Anienam offered a compassionate glance. "We are almost done. A few more moments and we can leave."

Casting another spell, Anienam focused his attention on the far end of the ruin. It took a moment for anything to happen. Then the air heated, grew damper. A steady thumping noise haunted the shadows. It reminded Skuld of a heartbeat. The farther the duo went the louder the sound became. Skuld struggled to maintain what little courage remained.

"What is that?"

The answer drained the warmth from him.

"I don't know." Anienam gathered his power, just in case. "Keep a sharp eye. We are looking for a bright green light."

The thief did as he was told, hoping and praying to find the key to unlock the next stage of their journey. The ruins groaned. He felt tired eyes watching him, but no matter where he looked they remained just out of reach. Shadows transformed into eerie hands creeping forward to snatch him away to some distant catacomb, never to be heard from again. His heart weakened and only found strength when Anienam spied the faint trim of green light.

"There, Skuld! Quickly, go and grab the book!"

The thief climbed over a broken table and found a massive tome alone on a marble pedestal. He hesitated. The book looked new, as if waiting for his coming. Better judgment warned him not to proceed. Nothing good was going to come from this. *Could it be a trap?* He doubted the wizard's ability to protect them. A strange new energy seeped into him, his muscles, his resolve. Skuld reached out and ran his fingertips over the ancient volume. He suddenly realized how wrong he had been.

"Did you feel that?" Argis asked.

Dorl swallowed hard and clenched his sword that much tighter. It wouldn't mean much if they were attacked, but it helped soothe his frayed nerves. He shivered slightly. All the warmth left him. His breath turned to vapors. That old sense of dread flowed through him, offering promises of violent demise.

"What in the…"

Dorl never got the chance to finish. The ground trembled and shook, throwing them violently down. Dust rained down so thick he could barely make out the others. The torches snapped and hissed. Dorl struggled back to his feet and immediately began searching for the source of danger. The far wall exploded outwards as dozens of skeletal hands shot out, clutching desperately at Maleela. Still on her knees, she barely rolled away in time.

Dorl Theed swore to himself. The skeletons pulled and clawed their way free of their eternal tombs. Nothol dropped into a low guard and waited. His eyes hardened. Of the many foes he'd faced over the years, this was a first. The undead continued to break free around them. Dorl managed to overcome his fright and pull Maleela to the relative safety their group offered. Nothol grinned savagely. He didn't know what it was going to take to kill a skeleton but he decided not to wait to find out. He attacked. Within the confined space only one man was able to wield a sword effectively. Dorl and Argis fell back to protect the princess.

Nothol Coll's first strike ripped a broken skull from the neck a moment before he kicked the remains to dust. The skeleton collapsed in a ragged heap, taking three more with it. He swung again, this time splitting one at the waist. More came. And more. The skeletons now numbered more than fifty. Even with Nothol Coll hacking and slashing, the dead soldiers continued to break free. Bones piled around them.

Dorl Theed watched the situation worsen. He desperately wanted to help but there simply wasn't enough space for both men to maneuver without cutting each other. Frustration made him tremble. He watched as a skeleton burst apart from the force of Nothol's boot in the ribs. The skull rolled to rest at Dorl's feet.

"We have to help him," he told Argis.

The former captain stood with his mouth agape. Shock immobilized him. Never in his wildest thoughts could he imagine an army of the dead. His knees were weak. His mind refused to obey his body. Twice he almost dropped his sword. Delranan had had no foe like this, ever. He struggled to comprehend what assailed them, but his mind failed to rationalize any of it.

Dorl snarled and slapped the man on his back. "Damn it, Argis, snap out of it! We're all going to die down here if we don't act."

Recognition flashed in the back of his pale eyes. "What can we do against this?"

At least he still has his tongue. Dorl frowned. "Send them back to the underworld and hope for the best."

Dorl Theed only managed to take a small step forward before being violently jerked backwards. The force made him drop his sword. Bony fingers gripped him tightly, trying to rip him apart. He let out a strangled cry as they dragged him to the ground. Dorl struggled with all his might. He punched and kicked. A bony arm ripped away and became his only weapon. Dorl used the arm to lash out at his attackers. Blood seeped from a dozen scratches, but the skeletons only clung tighter.

The sudden attack finally forced Argis into action. His resolve strengthened, the old man clenched his sword and attacked. Dust and bones flew wildly about the small chamber. The Delranan noble fought like never before. Vague ideations of what would happen to him should he fail pushed him harder. His muscles soon screamed and began to ache. The old man didn't have much left. Skeletal warriors broke to pieces wherever his sword touched them.

Dorl used the distraction and managed to break free. The sell sword rolled to find his sword through the mayhem and unleashed his pent-up fury. Every beating and taunt from Harnin's guards came back now. Hatred, agony, embarrassment, and fear burst from the inner well of his soul. Dorl attacked and attacked, with sword, fist, and boot. He didn't stop until Argis placed a weary hand upon his shoulder.

Dorl looked around. His breath was ragged, clogged with dust and bone matter. The battle was over. All the skeletons were destroyed, sent back to the decay of their eternal death. Argis dropped to a knee. He was much the worse of the two. Nothol leaned against the far wall, head hung low between his shoulders as he struggled to catch his breath. His tunic was shredded in places and smeared with his own blood. Maleela sat huddled in the corner. Even with all she had been through she couldn't bring herself to accept a battle against the dead.

"What just happened?" Argis asked through strained breaths. His body ached from unexpected exertion.

Nothol sheathed his sword. "This place is cursed."

"I have seen much in my life, but never anything so foul. Those creatures should not exist," Argis added softly.

"Should we go and get the wizard?" Dorl asked hesitantly. The rage was gone, leaving him numb. He had had enough of magic and having Anienam around made him queasy.

The ground trembled and shook violently. Huge chunks of ceiling crashed down. The walls shattered and started to collapse.

"Cave in!" Nothol shouted.

Argis forced himself back to his feet. "We must flee!"

Dorl passed a desperate look to the empty doorway. There was no sign of Skuld or the damned wizard. Duty and honor urged him to go and look for them. Reality screamed otherwise. The very walls were coming down around them. Waiting was not an option.

"Run!" he tried to shout above the roar.

He pushed Argis ahead and ran for his life. Dorl Theed gave a last thought to the others and kept running before they all died. Large chunks of the ceiling continued to drop.

FOUR

The War Begins in Earnest

"Archers!"

Piper Joach clenched his jaw in anticipation. He wanted to smile. The simple thought of extracting a measure of revenge on the same enemy who had thoroughly embarrassed him made his blood hot. Prince Aurec deserved an arrow through his heart and more for that alone. This was a matter of pride, but deep inside he knew it wasn't enough. Skirmishers and ambushers were one matter. This was the Wolfsreik's first real test against Rogscroft infantry battalions. His expression soured. Aurec was not on the field.

The battle, which shouldn't have happened, developed over the last week. Wolfsreik scouts hounded the enemy out of their hiding places, forcing them into the open where they'd be vulnerable. General Rolnir used the diversion to push his main body ahead of the retreat, effectively cutting off the disorganized Rogscroft soldiers from reinforcements. Or so they hoped. War was ever a fickle bitch.

Piper failed to understand how Aurec let his heavily outnumbered forces get caught in such a simple trap. Trained to an extent yet hardly seasoned, Aurec's army was better suited to hit and run guerilla tactics. Meeting the enemy on the open field in rank and file was tantamount to suicide. It left Piper with an uneasy feeling. The trap had been too easy to set, as if Aurec allowed it to happen. He briefly contemplated abandoning the field just to see how Aurec would respond.

The battlefield was good ground. Neutral, but good. There was a slight slope of almost negligible grade that would serve a heavy cavalry charge but, as Piper had already learned the hard way, the snows were too deep for the effective use of heavy horse. Fortunately, the Wolfsreik was primarily heavy infantry. Lightly forested hills formed a natural barrier on the right flank and a small river babbled softly on the left. The only way for Aurec's army to escape was straight through the Wolfsreik.

He watched the enemy infantry crouch down behind their heavy wooden shields as the flight of arrows sped down towards them. Piper had been there many times as well over the course of his career. It was an unpleasant feeling. The panic and the fear. The surge of adrenaline as the whistle of incoming arrows built to a screech. It was capped off with a symphony of screams and cries from the dead and dying. An archery assault was, in Piper's mind, the worst fate on the battlefield.

He gave his field commander a tight nod.

"Fire."

The first flight perforated the air. Piper almost wished he'd order the shafts to be set on fire. Fire was much more demoralizing than a simple attack.

"Nock!" the field commander ordered.

Three ranks of archers obeyed. Three flights of arrows sped away. Piper was disinclined to wait for a response from his foes. He immediately ordered a battalion of pike men forward while the defenders were still in disarray. Ranks of swordsmen followed with cavalry waiting on the flanks should the attack stall. Piper Joach dispassionately watched the battle unfold. He had no love of the enemy, but where there had once been nothing, utter contempt had grown. He wouldn't stop until Rogscroft burned to the ground.

The distance between the two armies closed quickly. The defenders were in a simple linear formation. Four ranks sat high on sloping ground. Basic wooden barriers had been hastily erected. They clearly had not been expecting the speed with which the Wolfsreik marched. The underestimation was going to cost them dearly. Piper scanned the tree line on both sides of the enemy position half hoping that Aurec and his murdering army would magically appear at the last moment. Vindication fueled his rage.

"Commander Prost, advance the archers so they can range that tree line. I do not want any surprises once we are fully committed," he ordered.

Prost stopped giving an order to one of the message runners and took a quick glance to where Piper pointed. "Sir, I don't think that is a good idea. It will take away the advantage of our long bows and place them within enemy range."

"Just do it. This needs to end. I accept full responsibility for any consequences."

Prost nodded, against his better judgment, and issued the order. He was about to stalk off when Piper stopped him.

"Never question my orders in front of the men, Prost. Never."

Prost took the warning for what it was worth. He hadn't gained his current rank by meekly obeying every command blindly. That got men killed more often than not. "Sir, what kind of leader would I be if I didn't have the concern of my men in mind?"

Piper cracked a thin smile. "A poor one indeed. We must remember the mission comes first though. It is impossible to bring them all home alive. The campaign must come first."

"I understand, sir."

Roars went up from across the plain. Piper opened his spyglass. His pike men were fiercely stabbing over the barricades. A new man stepped into the gap whenever a man fell. Piper watched his enemy cast spears and crossbow bolts into the lightly armored pike men. He and Rolnir willingly sacrificed armor for speed. Unfortunately, it meant that men would die. There was nothing glorious or romantic about it. Hot blood splashed the once pristine snow. Viscera and body parts flopped down. Screams howled across the air, weakening knees and worse from those not yet engaged. Piper watched the battle unfold and snarled. His infantry was getting mired down.

"Now, Prost. Send in the cavalry. Both wings, double assault. We break them here."

A full hundred heavy horse launched their attack. They were the heaviest forces in the Wolfsreik. Rolnir like to call them his line breakers, and Piper agreed. There were very few formations capable of withstanding a charge of heavy horse. Piper relished the feeling of the ground trembling beneath the charge, silently thanking the infantry for breaking down the snow enough. Enemy commanders caught the incoming riders and frantically tried to shift their defense. It didn't matter. There was small chance of success.

Time slowed. Piper never bothered with the why or how of it. Another twenty meters and the cavalry would make contact. Piper shifted his focus back to the fighting. Men from both sides were steadily dropping, either dead or wounded in the melee, but his forces were getting the better of it. The enemy center was slowly breaking. He allowed a tight smile. Several of the barricades were already lying broken on the ground. He guessed he outnumbered the defenders by at least three to one. The sheer weight of his numbers was driving them back.

The cavalry on the right wing struck a fraction of a second before the left. Rogscroft defenders were trampled and speared. Horses and riders smashed into them from both pincers, each driving towards the center. Piper watched as his counterpart was trampled under the wall of horseflesh. Satisfaction entered his thoughts. This battle was effectively finished.

"Commander, bring me my horse. I am going to the front," he told Prost.

The few enemies alive and unharmed broke free of the press and ran for their lives. Dozens more were either run down or hacked to death before the Wolfsreik calmed down enough to take prisoners. A handful escaped over the low rise. Piper didn't care. Those few would tell others of the defeat and spark the terror for him. The road to Rogscroft would lie open and waiting. He passed a glance at a file of fifty prisoners being escorted away. None of them bore the look of defeated men. He sighed. The capital city was still many weeks away. Until then it was one battle at a time.

Piper frowned despite the ease of victory. Perhaps it was that ease that left him troubled. It didn't make sense. Their stand resulted in heavy losses Aurec could ill afford. He supposed it could be blamed on the vagaries of war, but experience suggested otherwise. He was missing something. Anxious, he struggled to sort through the random bits of information leading up to the battle. Prost found him with a queer look when he returned with the horse.

"The army performed brilliantly," Rolnir congratulated his adjutant.

Piper gave a modest nod. He was not the one to do his job for recognition or glory. He did it for Delranan and the honor. Nothing more. "Thank you, General. I do not deserve such credit, however. Field Commander Prost developed the strategy and led the men. If anything, I was in his way. He should be so honored, not me."

Rolnir feigned a smile. He expected such from his friend. "Ever humble, eh Piper?"

Piper rubbed the stubble on his chin. "They were in a static defense. I doubt they were in position very long. All of the wooden obstacles were fresh cut and green."

"And their numbers?"

"Manageable. They didn't have more than two hundred. We killed or wounded one hundred twenty-seven and took sixty-three prisoner. I allowed the rest to escape to spread the word of our coming."

Rolnir approved though his gaze darkened slightly. "Our numbers?"

"Twenty-four dead. Thirty wounded."

Higher than he had hoped or anticipated. Sadly, there was nothing for it. War was as unpredictable as the direction of the winter wind. Men died and the battles continued. The only way to stop the dying was through ending the war.

Rolnir knew the end was too far away to begin thinking about.

"Why did they stand? Your force was strong enough to wipe them from the field in less than an hour. There must be some ulterior motivation," Rolnir mused, echoing Piper's earlier misgivings.

Piper threw up his hands. "The only conclusion I came to was that we had them cornered. Cut off from Rogscroft, they had no choice but to stand and fight."

"Against impossible odds? They are fine enough fighting behind rocks and laying ambushes, but they're not battlefield quality and you know it," Rolnir scolded sharply. "Could be Aurec just wanted to see the full measure of what he's facing. Even if meant sacrificing a few hundred men."

"Prince Aurec was not on the field," Piper added.

"He is not my main concern. Every day takes us deeper into enemy territory. Our supply lines are getting stretched and more difficult to maintain. At some point we will be forced to take an operational pause for resupply and refit," Rolnir told him. "The prince will be brought to task in due time. I need you to stay focused on the task at hand."

"Does that mean we ignore what just happened? I somehow doubt Aurec is foolish enough to waste valuable resources so blindly."

Rolnir stalked over to the wall map and pointed out a series of positions. "We've engaged and destroyed three enemy outposts in the last day and a half. King Stelskor is no fool and neither is his son. He is not about to sacrifice his men for no reason. I believe these outposts are designed only to slow us down, nothing more."

"I agree. The king must have a plan. Trying to figure it out has been most infuriating."

"Until we know what that plan is, we remain cautious. I share your uneasy feeling about this affair, Piper," Rolnir reluctantly admitted. "My gut tells me Aurec's using these forts to draw us in, but for what I don't know."

Piper waited patiently. They'd worked together long enough to understand each other's moods. Rolnir was clearly deep in thought and anything Piper had to say would only disrupt him. As in any military affair, the campaign progressed through varying degrees. The initial deployment was slow thanks to the treacherous crossing of the Murdes Mountains. Once they managed to get the full weight of the army in the field, the advance moved rapidly, only slowing for smaller fights and shadow attacks. Rolnir didn't know what to expect from Aurec and that unsettled him, so he directed the army to advance with all haste towards the capital. Take the castle and the rest of the kingdom would fold. Or so he hoped.

Finally, the general said, "Their entire defense hinges on Aurec. I must know where he is."

"Headed north the last we knew. He could be anywhere by now. The kingdom is much larger than we anticipated."

Rolnir shook his head. "No. I think he is much closer than we believe. Aurec has all the advantages except strength. He can pick up and move quickly whereas we take time. I think he's going to strike the supply lines. They are our most vulnerable point of attack, and we don't have the manpower to defend them and carry on the offensive."

Piper scanned the map. His combat experience during this campaign was limited to two battles. Pride demanded more. Anger at his initial losses still burned in him. He would not find satisfaction until the prince and he came face-to-face. The guilt from losing so many men in that first battle insulted him, clouding his judgment.

"Are you listening?"

He looked up; cheeks flushed crimson. "Sir?"

Rolnir scowled but kept silent. He understood. He'd been there himself long ago. The best thing for it was to let time heal. He decided to take Piper's mind off the past. "I asked if you were ready to lead the advance."

"Just give the word."

Confident, and slightly cocky. Good, Rolnir mused. The sting of the initial defeat hadn't yet rendered him useless.

"Take a full battalion out and scour the enemy positions an hour before dawn. Secure and prepare for further infiltration. I want to be within sight of Rogscroft proper by the end of the month. We must move quickly. Winter is nearly on us and the last thing we need is to be bogged down and cut off from our supply lines for four months. Hells, it's already snowing. Any longer and we might need to sit tight until spring."

"We may not have a choice. The enemy is unwilling to fully engage," Piper replied quickly. "They will try to delay us for as long as possible and let winter hinder our campaign."

"It would not be the first time such has happened."

"But?" Piper asked. He already knew the answer.

Rolnir raised an eyebrow. "You know exactly what I am talking about."

He nodded emotionlessly. Badron. The king was the single biggest distracter in the whole campaign. He, more than anything else, was hampering the army. The war might easily hinge on his fanciful obsession with King Stelskor. His fervor was already having a negative effect on morale. None of the soldiers knew the true reasons for the invasion, but their king proved more than willing to sacrifice them all for his gains. That didn't sit well with any soldier. It fell to Rolnir to keep as many of them alive as possible for the return home.

"I suppose this is where we come in," Piper said.

"I suppose it is. Go and prepare your men."

Badron paced uncontrollably across his tent. Anger threatened to consume him. Hundreds of enemy soldiers were dead, wounded or captured, and it wasn't enough. He wanted more. More blood, more battles. More victories. King Stelskor mocked him from the sanctity of his castle.

"You are too tense, King," Amar Kit'han hissed from the furthest corner.

Badron scowled darkly. "Ever you come uninvited."

"No man commands me. I have come and gone as I pleased for hundreds of years. Do not presume to demand so much of me."

The Dae'shan sidled from the shadows. Amar towered over the king, a hulking mass of mystery and despair. His very presence sent shockwaves of violence through the tent. Badron struggled not to cringe lest this abomination found advantage in it.

"I come with news," Amar told him.

Badron wearily sat on his field throne, a makeshift bundle of wood and metal. However genuine, he had doubts as to the validity of the Dae'shan's news. "What tidings do you bear? Something to end the war quickly I trust."

Amar regarded the man through the swirl of shadow and repressed the urge to slit his throat now and be done with this affair. "Tidings of blood and steel. Lord Harnin successfully captured your brother and daughter."

Badron reluctantly stared into the darkened hood. "Go on."

"Apparently your One Eye acted overzealously. He had his mercenaries murdered on the docks and your family imprisoned. Both shall be dead soon; I have little doubt of it. He is a cold man."

"How could you possibly know all of this?"

Amar Kit'han hissed laughter. "I know many things. Did you forget that I am not the only one of my kind? There are no secrets in all of Malweir that we do not have access to."

"Harnin has been my most trusted advisor for decades. I cannot believe that he would turn against my wishes now and execute my daughter."

Even as he spoke the words Badron had a sense of foreboding. He had spent his entire lifetime hating. First his brother and then his daughter. Both stole from him, robbed him of the finer things in life, thus making him what he was today. But dead? The thought paled him. He had dreamed of the day when his brother would no longer be a thorn, but now that it had come he questioned whether he had the stomach to follow through.

"All men are corruptible, King. Harnin is not the man he once was. As we speak, your brother's house and boat lie in ashes. Your dearest friend has ordered the executions of your family. He seeks to seize control of Delranan for himself."

"Impossible."

Amar replied casually, "I have seen this with my own eyes. Your kingdom is in upheaval. A rebellion festers in the dark hearts of your people. The world is changing."

"What rebellion? The population was in full support of both this war and me. What could Harnin have done in the weeks since I left?"

"Your questions are valid, perhaps even warranted, though slightly unanswerable. Men dream of power. It is the weakness of the soul that makes the world such as we see. Harnin believes that it is his time," the Dae'shan taunted.

His tone was smooth, belaying a deceptive undertone. Badron was already so far under his sway that it was almost insultingly simple. Amar decided to turn the screw a little more.

"Harnin will be dealt with in due time. Maintain focus on the war. Rogscroft must remain your sole objective. All else must wait for another time. Your path to domination begins here, in this broken land. It is the only way to rise to your full potential."

Destructive visions flashed across Badron's eyes. The future lay open, a future in which he was the supreme power. He licked his lips as the Dae'shan continued to weave his web. Many paths, previously unimagined, were opened. Badron saw a future where he not only ruled Delranan, but all the north. An empire so mighty all Malweir would tremble for generations.

Long lines stretched from the hidden caves as the warriors of Pell Darga clans left their loved ones and went to war. Their ferocity matched their environment. Cuul Ol and the other chieftains relied on the myths told about them to gain advantage over the invading Delranan armies. Fear was sometimes more powerful than the sword. That same fear pulsed ahead of the Wolfsreik wherever the army moved. Anywhere except in the mountains. The Pell Darga held no fear for any race, especially not their own.

Despite rumors and stories, the mountain folk weren't violent at all. They kept to themselves, shunning the lowland societies for their corruption and greed. Kingdoms of lesser virtue thrived in the lowlands, all but forgetting the simpler tribes of men. The Pell thrived in the heights of the Murdes Mountains. Inhospitable on the best of days, their scouts and hunters ranged far and wide for game and fish. Elaborate cave systems were dug deep into the mountains.

Cuul Ol stared up at the cloud-covered sky. His broad, flat nostrils flared as he took in the scents blown his direction. "Wolf soldiers come soon."

"How can you know?" Durgas frowned, trying but not picking up anything unusual. "The stench of our warriors masks the wind."

Cuul studied his friend. Short and powerful Durgas was one of the best. A brave hunter and cunning warrior, he was the only one in a generation to have gone single handedly into the den of a cave bear and come back with a head. Such things were just not done. *A good man. Perhaps my successor.*

"Scouts have returned. Many soldiers on the way," Cuul answered.

Durgas frowned. His thick brows furrowing deeply, reminding Cuul of winter caterpillars. "Why look skyward?"

The chieftain of the Pell smiled, curt and crisp. "To see if it will snow."

More warriors filed by. Each bore their fabled short spear and a dagger strapped to their hip. Most were covered with heavy animal pelts from bears and wolves. Their hair was mangy, hanging down past shoulders in jet-black waves. Their dark brown skin blended perfectly with the aged tree bark around them. Only the sharpness of their hardened eyes gave their presence away.

"We must return to camp," Cuul said after a moment. His eyes never left his warriors. Men who would much rather be left alone with their families. Men who knew there was no choice but to step forward to defend their homes. "The prince is waiting."

"Let him," Durgas said. "He is trouble, Cuul Ol. Our life was peaceful before the lowlanders came. Now we go back to war."

"War would come with or without the prince. He is not to blame. There is great evil stirring in the land. I feel it."

"More reason for the Pell to melt away," Durgas insisted. "Return to our homes and forget the troubles below."

Cuul offered a sad look. "It is too late for that. War has come to us."

FIVE
Dire Times

"Torval has lost another company."

Stelskor pinched the bridge of his nose between thumb and forefinger and winced. He felt lost. Nothing his most trusted leaders and military advisors did seemed to make one damned bit of a difference. A whole company: one hundred twenty men he could not afford to lose. He only hoped Torval managed to extract some measure of vengeance on the enemy before losing the field. The Wolfsreik continued to advance, raising the body count with each engagement.

"What do we have to do to stop them?" he asked. "Hells, at this point I would be happy just to slow them until the first heavy snows hit."

Fengar, a silver-haired man, cleared his throat. "Sire, no one will dispute that these losses are regrettable, but I must say that they are necessary. Each engagement slows our enemy, perhaps enough for nature to run her course. Either way, we simply cannot afford to put our army on the line and fight the way Badron wants. We cannot win a head-to-head fight with the Wolfsreik."

The king did not need to be reminded of his position. He knew all too well the sacrifice he asked of his soldiers. So many would not be coming home to their loved ones, and more did not even know they were already dead. "Have we heard any news from our allies?"

Fengar shook his head. "No, Sire. I fear we might be alone this time."

"Then we cannot stand," Stelskor announced.

"No," Fengar agreed.

The king stalked off. His mind was clouded with too many scenarios and outcomes. He'd sent messengers off to three allied kingdoms when news of the Delrananian army first reached him. Not one had replied. They were either unwilling to commit or afraid of crossing Badron. The hand of the gods was slowly falling on his people, and he was near powerless to stop it.

"None of this makes sense. We did nothing to provoke this invasion. Why would our friends not help?" Stelskor asked. Anger was replaced with sorrow. The first rays of sunlight kissed his brow, warming him against the dawn chill.

"We must look to the inevitable. Badron and his army will soon be here."

"Dark days have befallen us," the king whispered.

Fengar protested. "Not dark enough to make us give up all hope. The men still have a lot of fight in them. We may yet be able to hold out and force terms."

"I appreciate your courage, old friend, but our enemies will be relentless. I am afraid that even time is our foe now. I would like to believe that we have it in us to stop them, but that is unrealistic. I think it is time we begin evacuating the civilians."

"Sire!"

Stelskor stayed his astonished protests with a hand. "We can rebuild our city, but if we lose our people, there will be no tomorrow. Time will pass and memory of this kingdom shall fade to nothing. I am not willing to be the king who lost his people. Begin the evacuation. Send everyone to Grunmarrow."

Never in his life had Fengar considered that it would come to this. He almost refused to believe his king. True, the Wolfsreik appeared unstoppable, but he still had hope. Anything less would be a disservice to the men fighting in the field. Besides, the prince and his men were out there somewhere.

He decided that it was time to bring the subject up. "Sire, Prince Aurec is still fighting. He's working with the Pell Darga clans to strike the enemy supply lines. They cannot continue the invasion without supplies from Delranan."

"A temporary inconvenience, Fengar, nothing more. Where is Aurec now?" he asked. The question was more for his own sanity than his friend's. Truth be told, he half expected that his pride and joy was already dead. "We have not heard from him since the war began."

"Aurec still harasses the enemy. He is out in the field directing the defense, giving us a chance."

Stelskor smiled sadly. "Your statement lacks certainty. Do not seek to please me with idle fancy. I am prepared to know if my son dies. It is the way of the world. No. There have been no messages since Torval lost his first outpost. I cannot base a decision on wants or desires. My order stands unless Aurec returns soon."

Fengar accepted the defeat and walked away. Giving the command to displace the entire population at the onset of winter was sheer madness. The sick and old would not survive the trek to Grunmarrow. The way was long and treacherous. Still, Fengar valued the lives of his people more than his own. He hoped the surrounding kingdoms would lend their support before more had to die. Bowing, he turned and left the king to his troubles. There were times when being in command just wasn't worth it.

Stelskor cradled his head between his calloused palms and blew a strained sigh. He was tired, angry, and had never felt more helpless. The throne room confined him, made him feel trapped like an old badger. He needed fresh air, the cold slap of wind across his cheeks. Perhaps that would pull him from the deepening stupor. Stelskor hadn't felt this helpless since he was a child. The world he had dedicated a lifetime to building was steadily being ripped down around him without pause or thought. Stalking through the cold granite halls, the king emerged onto a seldom-used balcony. Winter was so close he felt its chill. Taking one of the lit torches from the wall, he set the large, opaque brazier alight.

Normally seeing his city sprawled beneath inspired him, but now he couldn't see past the panic and abject horror gripping Rogscroft. Citizens were fleeing in droves, their wagons ambling away through the winding cobblestone streets and thatch-roofed buildings. Those foolish enough to think they'd weather the storm busied themselves securing provisions and preparing their homes. The old and lame languished in the streets, no one interested in helping. Stelskor punched his fist lightly onto the wall and wondered what he could do to save his people. The answer wasn't forthcoming.

Aurec suppressed an involuntary shiver from the cold breeze forcing its way down his back. His eyes narrowed. Dark rings outlined them. This high up in the mountains exposed him and the men to more extreme temperatures than he preferred. The bare trees offered little protection from the angry winds blowing across the Murdes Mountains. He tried his best to ignore the weather and snuck a glance at Venten. The older man seemed to be taking the raw power of the elements much harder.

"This makes you appreciate summer," he murmured with a laugh.

Venten snorted. "It makes me want to find a warm fireplace and a jug of mulled wine. This type of stuff is for the young, not some crazy old man determined to get himself killed by following you around."

"What would my father say if he heard you now?" he asked. His tone was light, almost mocking. Aurec valued humor, especially during times of duress. Laughter and a warped sense of sarcasm often kept men warm and took the sting away from being far from home and in harm's way.

"Your father had his own foolish ideas I once followed. I doubt he'd be enthused with this mission any more than I am."

That's what I've been waiting to hear, Aurec thought. "None of that much matters here, does it? Torval's last outpost fell yesterday. The best way to stop these bastards is to cut their supply lines."

Cuul Ol approached from a stand of fir. Dull green branches drooped under the pressure from the coming storm. The Pell Darga war chief leaned heavily on a crooked walking stick. His eyes bore a feral gleam, making Aurec and Venten uneasy.

"Prince Aurec, many weapons come," he told them and spat. "Soldiers guard them. This will be hard."

"All battles are hard, Cuul."

The wizened little man nodded. A lifetime of constant struggle made him indifferent to the war raging around him. One might say he was born to this.

"Are your men in place?" Aurec asked.

"Yes. Enemy armor is thick. A tough battle awaits, hard victory. Our arrows will be ineffective."

"Just keep them busy long enough for us to get in and fire the wagons. My men will handle the heavy fighting."

Cuul Ol was insulted. "My people will do our part. You need not worry."

The young prince stared down into his counterpart's hardened gaze and almost felt ashamed for assuming. He quickly decided the best way to handle the situation was to deal past it. "You understand that many of your people may get killed?"

The Pell gestured around with his stick. "This is our home. We will fight and die if the Darga Keil demands it."

A nerve twitched in Venten's neck. "What is the Darga Keil?"

Almost reluctant to share his people's lore, Cuul took a brave step forward. "The gods of the Pell Darga. We are their children. The Darga Keil created us. It is through their will that we live and breathe."

Venten stood in total shock. He knew of no race that still believed in the gods. That train of thought had steadily grown obsolete over the course of several centuries, thanks in large part to the rise of magic. People stopped believing.

None of the great scholars across the lands bothered to figure out why. To hear the chieftain of the shadow people freely admit to his beliefs left Venten uncertain about a great many things.

Aurec felt the same uncertainty but lacked the willingness to enter into a theological debate. His focus was war. That the Pell were going to fight was all he needed to know. "Very well. Let us begin while surprise is still with us."

Cuul Ol flashed a toothy grin and slipped back into the surrounding trees.

"I don't know if we can trust him after that," Venten admitted once the little man was out of earshot.

"His beliefs are not our problem. Ready the men. We attack as soon as we're in position," Aurec replied.

Sergeant Haltaf marched at the head of the supply train with a perpetual scowl on his face. He'd been in the Wolfsreik for twelve years and burned at the thought of being relegated to escorting supplies. Piper Joach told him it was due to his seniority and proven combat record. Ha! Haltaf didn't see it that way. He took this assignment with insult and a grain of salt. There was no honor to be had in guarding supplies. He deserved to be on the front lines leading his brothers into battle.

Haltaf signaled a halt. He frowned at the fallen tree blocking the trail. This meant more time in these damned mountains. Further and further from the fighting. As much as he wanted to put that kind of thinking behind him, Haltaf found he couldn't. He desperately wanted to feel the bitter satisfaction of combat again. The sting of steel and the agony of bloodshed. Babysitting a supply train was almost more than he could bear.

"Bring up the breaching team," he snapped. "I want this tree cleared as fast as possible."

"Yes, sergeant."

A squad of engineers armed with axes and rope rushed forward and set about their task. Haltaf watched impatiently. This was the third time he'd been forced to call a halt, all for similar blockages. A hint of movement caught his attention. He turned, finding nothing but the mockery of the surrounding trees. Trees. *Damned things are a nuisance.* Trees with broken ends that were jagged and unkempt clearly had fallen by an act of nature. This tree, he noticed, had the fine edges of being cut down. Haltaf tensed.

"Establish a defensive perimeter!" he barked, drawing his sword.

It was much too late. Arrows whistled into them from both sides of the trail. Most missed their targets, a handful bouncing off the Wolfsreik's thick armor. A few managed to strike arms and legs. Two caught their targets in the throat, felling both with a small torrent of dark arterial blood.

Haltaf snarled. *Finally, a battle.* "Keep chopping that tree! I'll deal with this."

A double squad gathered on him. He gestured with his sword and they charged into the nearest tree line with a terrible roar. Arrows continued to buzz by. Two thudded into a tree next to his head. He smiled. Bloodlust was upon him. Haltaf caught sight of a pair of deer-skinned hides darting away as their position became untenable. The veteran ordered his men after them.

Violent urges oozed from his pores as Haltaf let the battle consume him. They quickened his reflexes. Made him stronger. Faster. His blood rage quietly built to berserker. Disappointment threatened to steal his momentum when he noticed all the enemy in his vicinity broke and ran. He was about to curse his fortune when a dozen of the brown-skinned men burst from nearby cover.

Each Pell warrior launched a short spear and drew swords. Haltaf batted a spear aside as a second pierced his right thigh. He dropped with burning pain spreading through the muscle. Blood pooled on the fresh snow. His sword slipped as he used both hands to staunch the flow. Tears formed at the corners of his eyes as he realized that he couldn't help his men. The lines met. Soldiers from both sides fell. Haltaf passed out before the company surgeon slapped a tourniquet above the wound.

For all their bravery, the Pell Darga never stood much of a chance against the disciplined ranks of the Wolfsreik. A few got lucky, but most fell under the crushing weight of armor and better steel. A scattering of survivors fell back at the clarion of a lone horn. Black smoke billowed into the dwindling daylight.

"The wagons! They are firing the wagons!"

The soldiers quickly fell back to secure what was left of the supply convoy. All of the wagon masters were dead, along with most of the men left to guard them. It was then dozens of armored enemies attacked. The battle quickly turned into a melee. Leaderless, the beleaguered soldiers of the Wolfsreik struggled to survive. It was a fruitless endeavor.

Sharp pain lanced down his leg and into his groin. Haltaf's leg hurt badly, more from the application of the tourniquet than the spear sticking out of him.

"This one is still alive."

He could barely open his eyes. Acrid smoke curled in his nostrils and he knew what had happened. His men had lost and his charge was destroyed. Bodies lay as far as he could see, frozen in their own blood. The stains in the snow reminded him of a merrier time when the family would gather and the children would color with different paints. Haltaf caught himself grinning for no reason.

A young man knelt in front of him. He bore a regality that few men had. Ash and sweat stained his face.

"What is your name, soldier?" he asked. There was no weakness in his voice, despite his young age.

A rough hand prodded his wound. Haltaf groaned.

"Leave him be. We wouldn't want them treating our wounded poorly," the youth admonished. "He may be our enemy, but he's still a man."

An older man stood over the younger one's shoulder with a disapproving glare. "We might as well find another. This one is as good as dead."

"No, Venten. He's just a soldier doing his duty. I'd like to think that not all of them are as vile as their king." He turned his attention back to Haltaf. "There is no harm in telling your name. I am Prince Aurec of Rogscroft. You are?"

"Sergeant," he said, dribbling blood. "I am a sergeant."

"At least he has a sense of humor," Aurec smiled.

"Yes. A dying one."

"Then we had best hurry," Aurec said. "Listen to me, Sergeant. This is only the first attack. I am sparing your life and those of your men who are left. Go back and tell your generals that they are not welcome in my kingdom. You will get no supplies, no weapons, or any reinforcements so long as we and our Pell Darga allies watch the passes. Leave Rogscroft and end this campaign."

Haltaf tried to laugh, but it hurt too much. "I cannot deliver those words. Do you know what they'll do to me?"

"That is not my problem." Aurec beckoned another of his men. "Dress his wound and get all of them out of here. Venten, have the men take the undamaged supplies and fall back. I want to be gone from here before they send a scouting party back."

Prince Aurec left Haltaf and made his way through the battlefield. Burning wagons lit the area. Melted snow pooled with blood. The crows had already started to gather. Half of the bodies lay on their backs, eyes staring lifelessly upward. Accusation sat in all. He'd won a hard victory and more men died. The butcher's bill was rising and there seemed no end in sight. Rogscroft stood on the cusp of damnation whichever way this war turned out.

SIX

Escape

"Anienam! Where are you?"

Skuld coughed and choked from the thick dust. He could barely make out his own hands scant inches from his face. His body ached from dozens of bruises and cuts. At least nothing felt broken. What he could see disheartened him. The cave-in destroyed what had remained of the ancient temple. Their escape route was gone, along with any hope of finding the others. Skuld hoped they managed to make it out in time. Practicality demanded that he had other matters to worry about. He pushed himself to his feet with a groan.

"Anienam, can you hear me?"

Dust prevented any echo. Skuld felt lost when only silence reached out to him. Vague memories of what made him sneak aboard the *Dragon's Bane* mocked him. He'd been naïve, filled with unobtainable ideals. The world was not the semi-friendly place in his inner dreams. It was violent and brutal. He'd seen men die. No, watched them killed in the name of causes well beyond anything he was capable of.

And now he was alone. His friends, such as they were, might be dead. Anienam Keiss, his one true hope for salvation, lay buried in the rubble. Skuld was deep underground and more alone than ever in his life. He fought back the urge to cry. Such weakness wouldn't do him any good. His best chance was to find the wizard's body, recover the book, and try to find his way back to Bahr.

"Anienam, please answer me!"

His pleas went unheard. The old wizard had to be dead. Misery crept into the street thief. Hopelessness gnawed at him. A familiar sense of abandonment settled back over his soul as if a deposed king reclaiming his throne. Skuld recognized that his life was meant to be filled with hardship and pain. He sank to his knees, unwilling to fight any longer. Tears flowed freely.

"Please," he begged.

A dull groan broke his moment of self-indulgence. A spark. It hadn't occurred to him that he hadn't bothered to look for Anienam yet. Skuld forced himself back to his feet. The wizard was alive!

He shouted, "Anienam!"

Another groan, somewhat louder, answered him. Skuld pushed his way frantically through the debris. He needed a sign, just a scrap of cloth. Hope found its way back into his weary heart and he desperately clung to it. His efforts soon paid off when he stumbled on Anienam's prone body. A rotted log lay across the old man's legs.

"Anienam, you're alive."

"Of course I am," he replied with a weak voice. "I am trapped, however. Help me move this log."

Skuld bent down and gathered what remained of his strength. The log didn't budge. "It is too heavy."

"You can do this, Skuld. Besides, there is no one else. Roll it off me if you must."

Skuld cringed. Visions of breaking bones danced in his eyes. Strengthening his resolve, the boy bunched his muscles and went back at it. Sweat dripped into his eyes, streaking the dust coating his face. His efforts were rewarded. The log rolled away. Anienam was freed. Skuld collapsed beside him.

"Thank you, my boy."

He tried to smile. "Anienam, why didn't you use your magic?"

The look he got in return was one of mild surprise, or perhaps just diversion. "Magic? Oh yes, I suppose I could have. Seems that bump on my head rattled my brain a little."

Skuld was too exhausted to think further on it. He also failed to notice the appraising look Anienam gave him.

"Is there another way out of here?" he asked.

The boy thought. "There is another tunnel snaking through the back, unless the cave-in collapsed that one as well. Do you still have the book?"

He wasn't sure why he asked that question. Before the collapse it hadn't felt like it was any of his business. Something had changed. The thought was disturbing and oddly comforting. Skuld felt a part of something more than himself again. Relief washed over him when he watched Anienam pat the tattered leather pouch around his shoulder.

"Right here. All safe and sound," he said. "Let us be gone from this place. The others will already be at the rendezvous." *If they still lived.*

They moved in single file. Anienam insisted on Skuld going first, claiming implicit trust in the youth. The going was tough. Much of the tunnel network had collapsed and was in complete disrepair. Skuld went as fast as he felt was safe. Subconsciously he tried to take account of Anienam's age and injuries and forced himself to move slower than he wanted. Desperation crept back into the corners of his mind. The walls pressed closer. The ceiling dropped lower. It was all he could do to maintain control.

"How much farther do you think?" Anienam asked to keep Skuld focused.

His personal concern went well beyond the traditional boundaries of their safety. Every moment they delayed gave their enemy another chance at final victory. He'd cursed himself a dozen times over for his inability to see the involvement of the Dae'shan for what it was. Arrogance led him to believe that the emissaries of the dark gods were extinct. He foolishly thought that they'd been defeated and Malweir was finally free from their influences. Wrong. Now entire kingdoms suffered for his mistakes.

Skuld didn't really have an answer. Instead, he focused on the conversation. Otherwise, he feared the dark would crush him. "Shouldn't be much longer as long as the tunnels haven't completely collapsed."

"Leave that to me."

The street thief cracked a smile. Anienam had a way of relaxing him, of setting his fears aside and introducing calm.

"What part of the city are we beneath?" Anienam asked.

A good question. It had been a long time since Skuld had been forced to travel through this part of the tunnels. He wasn't even sure which direction they were traveling. They might well be on their way up to Chadra Keep for all he knew. The consequences were dire. They couldn't risk being caught now, not after going through so much. The sheer responsibility of it all daunted him. All hope rested in his hands.

He ventured, "These tunnels run under the main parts of the city, but I do not know which direction we are heading."

"I trust you, lad. You'll make the right choices," Anienam encouraged.

The praise was unexpected and did wonders for his morale. Skuld strengthened his resolve and pushed forward. Hopefully each step brought them closer to the surface and a reunion with their friends.

Dorl Theed dropped to his knees and threw up. All the dirt and debris came flooding out of him, coating the broken cobblestones. Lord Argis sagged against the wall, struggling to regain his breath. Nothol Coll half dragged, half carried Maleela free. He coughed and sputtered but recovered enough to gently ease her down and splash their faces with water from a nearby rain bucket.

"The wizard?" Dorl asked. He wiped the strings of saliva away with the back of his sleeve.

Nothol looked back to the gaping darkness and then shook his head.

"Damn."

Argis spat. "Then it was all pointless. Harnin has already won. We are doomed."

"That's the problem with you people. You're always so quick to admit defeat. We are far from letting Harnin or

Badron from having their way with this kingdom," Nothol admonished sharply.

Argis bit back, "The wizard was our best hope for stopping the coming war. Without him the rebellion will be washed in blood."

"If you don't have the stomach for it, you shouldn't have gotten involved," Dorl chipped in.

"I am a lord of Delranan!"

Nothol replied, "Then start acting like one! The rebellion will go on with or without you. The consequences of your actions will be seen in the amount of blood spilled. Stand now or step aside. This is no time for indecision."

Maleela looked up at them with tears streaking her face. Her heart wept for what was happening around her. "Please, Argis."

Argis stewed silently. No one but Badron had spoken to him so harshly in a very long time. Newly kindled rage colored his cheeks.

"If Anienam is dead then we have lost the initiative," Dorl said before Argis had the chance to answer.

Nothol Coll shrugged. "We've been in tighter spots."

"Not by much."

"There has to be more than a single reference for this damned hammer," Dorl added. "I don't believe that some forgotten temple beneath Chadra is all."

"What hammer?" Argis asked suddenly.

They told him, albeit reluctantly, what they knew of the Blud Hamr. Argis listened intently, deeper conversations forming in the back of his mind. Clearly Bahr and his wizard keeper didn't fully trust him. He balanced on the edge. Should the rebellion fail, he might still be able to get this information back to Harnin in exchange for his life. *Blood hammer indeed.*

Nothol Coll added random bits of knowledge to the tale while focusing on Argis's facial expressions. Not even an accomplished liar could hide his true feelings. Besides, Argis had already betrayed one group. It was no stretch to imagine he would do the same again. Nothol kept his left hand close to his sword. Whether from a growing sense of alarm or just from habit, Argis couldn't be sure.

"Do we go back in?" he asked.

His heart fluttered. Horrors awaited them in the forgotten places of the night. That such evil dwelt within his home city could have deep implications for the future. He doubted the cave-in had permanently trapped the undead.

Nothol looked back at the ruin of the tunnel entrance. "There is no going back."

"If what Skuld told us is right there must be a dozen entrances," Dorl said.

"None of which do us much good even should we find one," Argis added. "They could come out anywhere."

Nothol was forced to agree. "He's right. Skuld was our way in. He alone knew his way around down there."

"Then it is hopeless," Maleela said in a hushed voice.

"No, remember that the boy does have a wizard with him," Nothol said.

"If they managed to survive," Dorl replied.

"There's no helping that. I say we link up with Bahr and the others. Harnin will undoubtedly know we are missing by now."

Argis measured the sell swords. "It may already be too late. Smoke rises from the northeast."

"What does that mean?"

"Bahr's estate lies in that direction. Harnin must have gone straight there."

The news felt like a slap in the face. Not even their combined strength managed to get a single step ahead of the One Eye. All was lost if Bahr had been caught again. Despair threatened to grip each of them in different ways. Not for the first time.

"We should hurry. Bahr might still need help," Dorl added quickly.

"He's right. We are wasting time," Nothol echoed.

Argis was unconvinced. "Has it occurred to either of you that we may be the only ones left? What happens then?"

"We go and return to Rogscroft. This kingdom is no longer safe."

Conversation faded. Arguing only wasted time. They slunk away from the tunnels. Each was eager to leave behind the darkness-inspired nightmares. The hope of reuniting with friends strengthened their will. It pained each to knowingly leave behind companions, but time was against them. Initiative was lost and it became imperative to regain it if they hoped to find success at the end of the day. Too many lives had already been lost. Delranan stood ready to rip itself apart.

Nothol Coll led the way, unerringly weaving through back alleys and seldom used paths. The quiet of the night unnerved him. He struggled to push back a collage of poisoned thoughts. Soon enough they would know who lived or died. Thinking about it ahead of time served no purpose. The city faded into forest. Sundin Pond wasn't far off. The only problem now was who awaited them at the pond, Bahr or Harnin.

SEVEN

Sundin Pond

"I think we lost them," Boen said through strained breaths. His baritone voice was dark, threatening. All this running sat ill on his conscience. He was used to a straight up fight, not slinking around in the shadows. More and more he had to struggle to contain the rage that wanted free. Lust of open battle threatened to consume him. Boen knew it was only a matter of time before he lost and the rage won.

Bahr gestured Rekka to rein the wagon in.

"The wagon will leave them a good trail to follow," Rekka warned in her lithe voice.

The Sea Wolf nodded grimly. "What choice do we have? We need the wagon. It's the only way we can carry the supplies."

Ionascu, broken into a shadow of his former self, scowled but remained silent. This was neither the place nor time.

"We could always dump him and lose the wagon," Boen suggested. "Both are dead weight."

"No. We need Ionascu, if for nothing more than preventing Harnin from learning what we are about. Besides, look at him. That man has suffered far worse than any of us. He stays."

The big Gaimosian shrugged his indifference. Ionascu was a spy and deserved whatever fate awaited. Still, he managed a degree of sympathy. The man had both hands broken and his mind addled. The indignity of it disgusted Boen. Worse, Anienam had been unable to help beyond minor healing spells. The bones were already knitting back together. His hands and feet were misshapen and ruined.

Boen leaned in closer to Bahr and lowered his voice. "He meant to sell us out. A traitor is a traitor, my friend. The afterlife will not be kind to him. As sad a tale as his life has become, we cannot afford to babysit him. Not if we are to make it."

"Right now, it doesn't really matter," Bahr countered. "We are still waiting for the others. I don't think Harnin will be so willing to commit his forces in the dead of night, but if they don't hurry back, it won't much matter. Daylight isn't far off."

"The sands are running out," Rekka agreed.

Her black hair was almost invisible in the night, giving her a ghostly appearance. Once, that offered a measure of comfort, familiarity. Her run-in with the Dae'shan changed that. Rekka came from a peaceful people. That is not to say they didn't practice the martial arts. She plunged into her studies at an early age and earned the honor of being selected to the ranks of defenders at the ancient temple of Trennaron. There she learned of the eternal war between light and dark from the wizened Artiss Gran. The Dae'shan returned shortly after and Gran sent to find Anienam. The rest was up to fate.

Bahr looked up at the slowly lightening sky. "She's right. Harnin won't wait long."

"It is your call," Boen said.

He reluctantly nodded. "Rekka, take Ionascu and get the wagon out of here. Wait for us a league down the trail. You'll find three lone trees beside an abandoned cottage. We'll be along as soon as the wizard returns."

"How long do I wait?"

Rekka already knew the answer. She'd been entrusted to protect Bahr, even at the cost of her own death. Nothing else was important. Bahr had to live long enough to gain access to the Blud Hamr. Artiss Gran never told her why, but then again, it wasn't her business.

"As long as necessary," he replied. "We shouldn't be too long." He paused to smile. "Even when old One Eye shows up."

"There's nothing like a good fight to start the day," Boen added with a giant smile.

Ionascu whimpered. Violent images flashed each time he closed his eyes. His skin paled. Gone was the urge or will to fight. Rekka ignored him and snapped the reins. Instincts screamed for her to stay, to do her duty. She drove the wagon without looking back. Doing so would only break her heart.

"She's a good girl, that one," Boen said, watching them go. "She comes in handy in a fight."

Bahr wholeheartedly agreed.

"Still, she's rather harsh. I have to admit that I find her slightly intimidating," the Gaimosian added.

Bahr arched his eyebrow, but kept his mouth shut. He still couldn't tell when Boen was joking after all of their long years of knowing each other.

"You don't suppose Ionascu will give her any trouble?"

Boen shrugged. "More likely the other way around. We are wasting time here."

"It seems to be habit forming. Come on. Sundin Pond isn't far off and I don't trust Harnin to stay hesitant much longer."

Bahr led the way, both men moving quickly and quietly through the underbrush. An old deer trail ran parallel to the small creek that emptied into the pond. The way was clear and soon they entered the clearing around Sundin Pond. Ragged breath came out in plumes of steam. Bahr spit, his lungs burning. Sweat covered their bodies. Boen scanned the perimeter and drew his massive broadsword.

Keeping in a low guard, the Gaimosian gave in to decades of instinct and experience. He investigated every shadow, every bush or bole. Caution was a master instructor. Gaimosians still had enemies across Malweir. The weak and sloppy died young. Boen was old, much older than he ever thought he'd be.

"Nothing," he said after completing his sweep. "No sign of our friends either."

"It might be nothing. They could have been delayed."

Boen shot him a glare suggesting neither of them believed that. "They could also be dead. We have no way of knowing for sure and asking what if is pointless."

Bahr let out an exasperated sigh. "That was always the danger of splitting up. What choice did we have though?"

"Stop worrying about what you can't control. There's nothing for it."

The Gaimosian's words were short and to the point, typical of his fashion. His eyes never stopped roaming their surroundings. His muscles bunched, tensing for the inevitable fight.

"What do you suggest we do?" Bahr finally asked.

"We wait for as long is prudent and double back to Rekka."

"And the hammer?"

Boen refused to budge. "We'll find another way if it is that important."

The Sea Wolf took issue with how easily Boen was ready to abandon the others, men he had called friends. Faces of crewmen from the *Dragon's Bane* flashed back to him. They were all dead; killed or drowned during some anonymous voyage across Malweir's vast oceans. Bahr remembered every last one. Some were good, others not so much. That didn't matter. All had died under his command.

"Boen, I…"

"Shhh."

Boen eased into a small patch of blueberry bushes. The faint echo of steel scraping against a branch consumed his attention. The battle with Harnin's thugs was about to renew. Death grinned from his face. Bahr quickly followed suit, trusting in the big man's instincts though he didn't relish the thought of another battle so soon.

"Did you hear that?" came a whisper in the dark.

"Hear what?" came the reply.

Bahr wasn't sure, but he thought he recognized the voices. Four slender figures stole into view, giving him the answers he needed. Dorl Theed and Nothol Coll came first, swords raised and ready for war. Argis and Maleela followed. He finally allowed himself to smile. He eased into the open before Boen could object. The sell swords dropped into attack stance, relaxing a split second later as they recognized the captain.

"What kept you?" Boen asked with a genuine smile.

Any sense of relief was crippled by the fact that not all had returned. The wizard was missing. This boded ill for the future. Bahr's heart sank.

"We ran into unforeseen circumstances," Argis told him.

Dorl rolled his eyes. He couldn't understand how the man remained pompous after all they'd been through. "What he means to say is that we were attacked and lucky to escape alive."

The words cut deep. They'd placed all their hopes in the cranky little man. Losing him, and the boy, was going to hurt them.

"And the others?" Bahr asked, already knowing the answer.

Nothol Coll shook his head and stared at the ground. Maleela broke from behind him and gave her uncle a crushing hug.

"Dead," Dorl snapped. He passed by angrily. His pride was wounded, worse than the physical injuries Harnin's goons inflicted. His body was a mass of bruises, his muscles ached. Instinct begged him to abandon this foolish quest while he still lived and head south to a more lucrative future. Delranan proved too much for his psyche to handle. The only thing keeping him tied to the expedition was the bond shared with his best friend.

"We don't know that."

Dorl flung his arms in a futile gesture. "What other conclusion is there? We barely made it out. They were in deeper. They had to have been killed."

"Quiet!" hissed Boen. "We are not secure here. The enemy can have spies everywhere."

Bahr stepped between them. "Boen's right. We are being stalked. Harnin has burned my house and estate. His forces are cautious but dawn is near. Rekka is waiting down the road at the abandoned Horsch house."

Nothol idly scratched his jawline. "Do you think Harnin had the wagon followed?"

"I doubt it, but we can't afford to wait and see. What happened at the temple?"

The sell sword explained as best as he could. Argis and Dorl interrupted as they saw fit. The tale was short, grim, and difficult to believe. Undead and a cave-in. Times had grown perilous in Delranan. Nothol finished and felt as if a great weight had fallen from his chest. The burden was gone, yet the pain remained.

"Well," Bahr drawled. "Anienam is a wizard. There is every possibility he might have survived. We shouldn't abandon them yet."

"What more do you need, Bahr? They're dead and we're not far behind if we stay here," Dorl argued.

Anger flashed in the depths of Bahr's blue eyes.

"Shut your mouth unless you have something to contribute," Bahr lashed out. "I am tired of your bad attitude. Snap out of it and be the man I hired for this."

Dorl tensed. His fist closed, drawing back slightly. Bahr closed the distance and placed a consoling hand on his friend's shoulder.

"I need you on this one. Our hardest times are still ahead of us. This is going to be difficult. Ionascu found that out from the beginning. But the only way any of us are going to make it back is by pulling together. I need you, Dorl."

Some of the fire smoldered away. He reluctantly nodded.

"That's all very touching, but what do you need the rest of us for?" came a raspy voice from the shadows.

Everyone froze. They'd been discovered! A soft blue light pulsed from the night, illuminating a very haggard wizard and the street thief.

"Anienam!"

He gave a crooked smile. "Who else would it be? I hope you haven't been waiting for someone else the whole time."

"We thought you were dead," Nothol Coll said and rushed out to squeeze the man.

"By all rights we should be. The cave-in made us take a longer way out. We very nearly did die."

"There is more to be told than what we're led to believe," Boen commented from the perimeter.

He was right, but there was much more than a simple escape to discuss. Anienam anticipated the round of questioning. Arms folded across his chest, he patiently waited for the next question.

Bahr opened. "Did you get what you needed?"

"I believe so. The text is very old and I had little time to examine it before the cave-in. Still, it is what we need to point us in the right direction. Skuld here was the key to finding the book and seeing us to safety. He is a good lad."

The Sea Wolf gave the boy an approving glance. "I thought the book was the key."

Anienam shook his head. "The book is merely an opening. Consider it a compass of sorts. You see, the ancients had little trust for any of the races. They knew the potency of the hammer and were unwilling to let it fall into the enemy's hands. Good planning to be sure, but difficult for those in need. The answers we seek should be locked in here."

"Can you decipher it?"

The wizard smiled smugly. "I can't see why not. I am trained in most of the major languages. It should be a matter of finding the data."

"That's great," Boen said, "but we have to move. Now. Harnin is coming."

They drew swords, even young Skuld. Only Anienam remained still. Swords were of no harm to a man of his power. He could crush his foes with a thought if he so chose. That strength remained his most potent secret.

Anienam had seen the devastation of that ability unleashed before and he was loath to unleash it again. Too many deaths added up in the name of wizardly excess. He resolved to let his companions choose for themselves. They must find their own light at the end of dark paths.

"Follow me, quickly and quietly."

Bahr took them down the deer trail as the blue wizard light faded. When Harnin's men arrived they found an empty clearing with no sign of their quarry.

EIGHT

Reunion

Dorl narrowly avoided a decapitating swipe by Rekka's blade on the porch of the abandoned house at the end of the lane. Normally he would have had a good laugh at the absurdity of it, but his darkened mood prevented it. He tried to laugh, wanted to find any measure of humor. Like the rest of them, life had become a very dark thing for him.

Rekka Jel offered a quick apology and sheathed her blade. Dorl stopped until his heart dropped back to its normal place. Only Boen offered a chuckle as he strode past. Gaimosian humor was lost on them. The group ate in muted conversation, washing the small meal down with mugs of ale liberated from Bahr's pantry. Boen finished off his ale and found a pallet in the back of house. He was soon stretched out and snoring. The gentle crackling of burning wood soon accompanied him.

"Isn't he the lucky one," Bahr commented.

Taking a bite from a green apple, he tried to stifle a yawn. Only now did he realize how tired he truly was. The rush of adrenaline siphoned off, forcing him to realize just how old he had become. His body ached. The pain of losing everything finally struck. His estate didn't bother him as much as the loss of the *Bane*. That ship had been his life for decades. And now it was gone, reduced to cinders smoldering in the harbor. Emotions threatened to get the best of him. Rage. Pain. Anguish and sorrow. All collided in a deadly cocktail that promised to rip him apart.

"Are you all right, Captain?" Rekka asked upon seeing the distant look in his eyes.

He refocused, noticing Rekka staring nervously at him. Conversation slowed to halt as all heads turned in their direction. Bahr struggled against a surge of helplessness. What was he supposed to say? The very title of captain felt like a dagger thrust into his chest. He was a captain of a rickety wagon and a handful of outlaws. Life as he knew it, treasured it, was over. The only place he had left to turn was to Anienam Keiss and his damned blood hammer.

He feigned a smile. "Fine. Just thinking is all."

"We have all lost a part of ourselves," Rekka told him. "Our only chance for survival is to band together. We need each other now."

Bahr fought to hold back a grimace. He alone had lost everything, not just some small token of memories. *Easy for you to say.* Bahr knew better than to voice his opinions here. Doing so would serve only to foment animosity among the group.

"Something you said bothers me, Anienam," Nothol said.

Anienam smiled patiently as all eyes fell on him. The twinkle in his eye suggested he already guessed what was coming.

Nothol took the silence as consent to continue. "You said that the book was merely a key."

"Of sorts," he agreed.

Nothol sat down, his mind racing through patterns he failed to comprehend. "If that is the case, what you are proposing to send us on is another quest."

The wizard exhaled a slow breath. All of his ideations were falling into place. All but one. Anienam still had no idea why the servants of the dark gods had chosen Delranan and Rogscroft to begin their return campaign. Strategically it made no sense. Both kingdoms were too far removed to be of any immediate impact. That lack of knowledge left an uneasy feeling in the pit of his stomach.

"I am not all-knowing, master Coll. As much as you would have me wave my hand and produce this token of power, it is beyond me to do so. There are rules to this game, even for me."

"Wonderful." Dorl rolled his eyes. "So you've stood by and let us stumble along into this mess."

"Life is about the power of choice," Anienam countered. "What good is a man without free thought?"

Dorl wasn't convinced. "I feel like a puppet, or worse."

"What are you saying?" Bahr asked.

"This. All of this! Can't you see what is happening? He's engineered this entire affair to get us to do his bidding. The only place he is sending us is to the grave."

"I don't think…"

Dorl cut him off with a wave of the hand. "Quests are the sort of thing that most people in this room aren't going to return from."

"Nonsense," Bahr argued. "We have all been sent on adventures. This is no different."

"What makes you so sure?"

Maleela shook her head. It was all falling apart. "How can any of us be sure?"

Anienam Keiss said nothing. Patience and prudence were needed more than all else at this critical juncture. He sympathized with their suffering even though it was more perceived than true. They were all individually strong, but together they posed a threat that might even cause the Dae'shan to balk. Anienam sat back and waited for them to work through this for themselves.

"Too much of this doesn't make sense," Dorl said.

"That's life, kid. I've lived almost six decades and almost none of them made much sense to me, the least of which was last night. There is plenty I don't know, but I can tell you all this: what happened last night was no accident. Badron has declared his war. If following Anienam blindly in search of this hammer is going to help us win, then I am all for it."

Dorl froze in mid-thought, his argument stalled. The breaking point beckoned him and he wasn't so sure he had the willpower to stave it off.

"While we are busy asking each other pointless questions, I would like to know why all of your stories revolve around these dark gods?" Bahr asked the wizard. "What happened to the good ones?"

"The answers you seek might not be found, I'm afraid," Anienam replied.

Nothol looked up. "Why not?"

"No one is really sure what happened to them. There are many ideas, certain theories set forth by the finest theologians and scholars. Some contend the gods of light left once their foul kin were defeated and imprisoned in the nether. Others would argue that they lost interest in Malweir and drifted off into space in search of a new world in need of their presence. Some think the gods of light died, thus leaving a void in which the dark gods found their purchase back in this world. For myself, I cannot say."

"That seems impossible," Dorl said. "How can a god die?"

"Much easier than you might imagine. The fastest way to kill a god is to stop believing."

None of them were comfortable with the direction the conversation turned. Deicide was an alien concept and humbled them all. A few races still clung to their gods. The Dwarves waged war under the watchful gaze of their war god Krug. Even the foul, night-dwelling Goblins had their deities. But men had lost theirs, and the world suffered for it. Malweir stood upon the precipice. Anienam had grave misgivings about the future.

"So we are doomed," Bahr concluded.

Anienam disagreed. "No. So long as we hold hope there is the potential for victory. We just have to find it."

Bahr thought it sounded like a load of nonsense, but he was just one man, not the spawn of wizards or their ilk. "You speak of hope but threaten our end. I do not know what to place my faith towards."

"Always in yourself, Captain Bahr. You have no cause for doubt. The journey is yet before us. Many things can happen between now and the end. There is no reason to despair just yet."

His words seemed sound but for the neglect of the despair gnawing at them. Bahr was ready to give up on the old man. He suddenly felt the weight of his years. Bahr was tired.

Anienam used the pause to press his point of view. "This is the hour where we must decide. Our answers lie in this book. I ask you all to look beyond yourselves. Delranan's no longer the welcome home it once was. Times have grown dark. Only through defeating the Dae'shan do we stand a chance at finding peace. Understand this: once we set upon this course of action, there can be no turning back. It is all or nothing. Success is not guaranteed, but there is a far greater chance of it if we band together. All of our strengths and weaknesses combined will lead us to victory."

"How can you be so sure?" Nothol Coll asked. He was suspicious of the suddenly optimistic nature in the wizard's words. There were too many secrets for his liking.

Anienam grinned. "Consider it an act of faith."

The quip did not go unnoticed. Only Rekka made a weak chuckle.

"All right. If that is the way it has got to be, I say we vote now. Each of us must choose for himself. There is no shame on those who wish to quit." Bahr went to stand beside the wizard. His gaze hardened. "You have not led us astray yet. I shall stay by your side. My brother and his puppets have much to answer for. If these gods do exist, I would see them before I die."

Anienam bowed graciously.

Tension filled the tiny cottage. None of them moved until Rekka Jel wordlessly marched over to stand beside the two. Bahr raised an eyebrow. He had plenty of questions directed towards the golden-skinned woman as well.

Nothol Coll slowly rose and glanced over at his best friend. "It's the only thing left that makes any sense to me."

Dorl Theed followed his friend, just as he knew he would from the beginning. He passed Anienam a sharp look. "This had better work, wizard. I don't want to die for no reason."

"I have a good feeling," Anienam replied calmly.

Skuld watched Maleela move beside her uncle. That left only him and Ionascu. Fear painted his features. It shone in his eyes, a mirror reflection of Ionascu's hatred.

"Go home, Skuld. No one will hold it against you. You need not risk your life for this," Bahr encouraged.

Ionascu held up his broken hands for all to see. "Let the boy choose his own path. Mine was made for me. I want to see Harnin hang from his own gibbet. I'm in."

For all the wrong reasons, Bahr thought.

"I've never been a part of anything before, not even a family," Skuld told them. "Dorl and Nothol gave me my first taste of a meaningful life. I won't abandon them now, though I am afraid."

Anienam felt proud. "It is good to be afraid from time to time. Take heart, Skuld. You will find the depths of your courage before this is done."

"It's about damned time you people figured all of this out. Maybe now you'll shut up so I can go back to sleep," Boen growled from his cot without opening his eyes.

Argis gave them a deadpan stare. Resolution etched his features. "This is not my path. The resistance will need help. They need a leader. I am too old to go running across the world. My place is here, with our people. Perhaps I can find a way to defeat Harnin and make Delranan safe again."

"That is a noble charge," Anienam approved. "I wish you good fortune."

Argis smiled thinly. "I think I am going to need more than that. I shall take my leave when you do. Until then I may still be of assistance in your planning."

The Sea Wolf thought for a moment, as if judging the turncoat standing before him. Traitors didn't sit well with him, despite his intentions against his own brother. A man was nothing without loyalty. For Argis to turn his back on Badron, the man who allowed him to rise this far, said much for his lack of character. Bahr doubted the man had the gall to see the matter through. Even so, he nodded and the group set about their business.

A guard was posted with the instructions for everyone else to bed down. The coming days were going to be long and perilous, making today seem calm, uneventful. Bahr tried to follow his own instructions but found only disappointment. Dark were his thoughts of late. Harnin's face reached out to mock him every time his eyes closed. The insolence of it spurned him.

Bahr shifted uncomfortably and swept his gaze over his companions. None were truly close enough for him to call friend. Boen had known him the longest, but their relationship was sporadic and surprisingly violent. People died every time they got together. That wasn't to say he felt uncomfortable around the rest. The fact was just the opposite. He trusted each with his life, but only Maleela he trusted with his heart. The bond they shared went unparalleled. Though he spent many years pretending his family was gone, Bahr found himself growing more attached to the young woman.

His normally stern gaze settled on his niece and softened. There was a small measure of solace in the purity of her sleeping face. She seemed almost peaceful. Firelight framed her face, handsomely accented by her long dark hair. Naturally angled, her chin bore a softness he could recall seeing in her mother. Bahr found himself smiling. His heart was much lighter, practically forcing a yawn. Perhaps sleep was not his enemy after all.

The Sea Wolf claimed a spot and laid his head upon a balled-up cloak. He drifted off the moment his head touched the fur.

Anienam Keiss glanced up from the book they'd risked so much to find. A wry smile cracked his thin lips. He felt positive about this group of would-be heroes. All were normal people with everyday issues; some suffered from selfishness while others ached with selflessness. The important part was that none wanted to be a hero or a champion of fate remembered in song and tales for generations to come. They did what they did because they had to, and that was a comforting thought.

Too many times in the past he and his father Dakeb had gathered men and women and gone off to combat one of the many facets of evil threatening Malweir. They weren't always the best, but they were the best available. Anienam struggled to find a bright side. Never had the odds been stacked so high against him. Natural doubt crept into his mind.

The thoughts disturbed him so much he failed to see Rekka Jel slink across the shadowed room. She laid her weapons down and eased over to where Dorl Theed slept. His companion and battle buddy, Nothol Coll, had volunteered to pull the first guard shift and was no doubt standing on the front porch freezing right now. Anienam insisted that his wards were enough to protect them against all but the strongest dark magics. No one wanted to be the one who took chances at this stage of the adventure. The stakes were raised much too high.

That was why she was able to make up her mind so easily. The secrets of her coming north continually threatened to get the better of her. It was all she could do to suppress the urge to break down and tell someone, anyone. Tonight there would be no conflict. She knew what she wanted, for it was more desire than need. Rekka had to feel human again. All of those she'd killed begged for release from her eternal self-torment. She lifted Dorl's blanket and curled into him.

"What?" he asked groggily.

She closed her soft brown eyes and whispered, "Shhh."

Neither of them resisted what happened next. The rest of the world could wait.

A soft wind swirled handfuls of dead leaves in front of him but Nothol lacked an appreciation for it. His mind raced. So much had happened he wasn't sure exactly where he stood. His friends were changing daily, forcing him to change with them. He and Dorl had signed on to keep Bahr safe, nothing more. That part was finished. The conditions changed drastically. Their lives were effectively over. There seemed little doubt the pair would be forced to flee Delranan. They weren't even a part of the war and yet it consumed them.

He thumbed the edge of his sword. Many decision points lay before them. He hoped for the strength to keep going. His heart hurt and he didn't know why. Nothol felt the past finally catching up to him. It was all he could do not to cry. He steeled himself against the night and watched the moonlit fields of frost.

NINE

The Heroes Go East

Anienam interlaced his fingers over his head and stretched. His bones groaned and snapped from degenerative arthritis, causing a frown. He hated getting old. Age was the one thing that left him truly helpless. No amount of magic in any language or from any race could prevent the tides of time from washing him away. There was no way of telling how much time he had left and that was the most disturbing facet. His father had spent countless centuries roaming Malweir in an ultimately vain attempt at stopping evil from taking root. He died without ever seeing that dream fulfilled.

Anienam did not suffer from the same delusions. Evil was eternal, a part of Malweir that could not be excised. Neither evil nor good had the ability to outlive each other. They were reciprocal, mocking yet complimentary. Each needed the other to bring forth the best in races. Entire races dedicated themselves to the pursuit of one or the other. That was the true tragedy of life. He'd never met a Goblin with the propensity to commit an act of kindness. They were savage, brutal creatures with deep emotions that thrived on hatred. Conversely, the Fey seemed incapable of doing harm. Too often they'd been slaughtered for those personal convictions.

Doing his best to force the thoughts away, Anienam settled back in his chair and continued reading. The book was dry, a common failing of the period. The author promoted a high opinion of himself. Anienam reached over and took a sip of tea. No wonder this book was lost, he grimaced. *I can barely read it without falling asleep.* He started flipping through the aged pages. The text went on about this god or that and the qualifying factors that made them gods.

He was just about to give up for the night when he stumbled into what he was desperately looking for. Or so he believed. His heart beat a little faster. *This could be it. Secrets lost since the days before Ipn Shal.* He grew giddy and devoured every word with renewed interest. Seventeen pages later he set the book down. His grin bordered on permanent. Secrets opened to him. He'd discovered the truth of the Blud Hamr.

Anienam glanced to his sleeping companions and decided to let them sleep. Exhaustion reached out to claim him as well. It had been a long day. Marking his place in the book, he set it back down and decided to catch a few hours of sleep.

The hearty smell of cooking bacon and roasted late summer tomatoes woke them with growling stomachs. Half felt like they'd just left a tavern. Bahr didn't find anything wrong with that. A cold flagon of ale would have made getting up worthwhile. Boen seemed the only one unaffected from last night's events. The Gaimosian rose to his full height and stretched, a throaty growl accenting it. He'd slept the most and recovered his strength. Boen looked ready to go to war. He smiled at the smells enticing him. That smile froze upon seeing Rekka and Dorl snuggled together.

"These are strange times," Bahr told his friend.

Boen merely shook his head and went into the kitchen. Bahr puzzled him. He was a good friend and a stalwart companion, but he had too many ghosts haunting him. Boen empathized. Gaimosians spent most of their lives being chased by ghosts. He pushed the thought aside as he passed Anienam. The wizard was face down in that dusty old book snoring. Skuld sat behind the old man, staring out the nearest window as if waiting for Harnin to come. Certainly plausible, the thought made Boen frown. He'd love to run his sword through that one-eyed bastard. More, he liked Skuld. The lad showed character when needed. He had a fire in him that often reminded Boen of his own youth. Satisfied, Boen snatched a mouthful of bacon and went outside.

Argis turned at the soft click of the door opening.

"There is hot food and tea brewing," Boen announced more gruffly than intended.

Argis sheathed his sword, frowning at the thin veil of frost coating the blade. "I would rather have sleep. It has been damned cold out the last few nights. Winter is finally here. My old bones don't agree with the weather the way they used to."

"A terrible thing, getting old," Boen agreed.

"Indeed."

Argis stared at the Gaimosian a moment, silently wondering the man's true intentions. He decided to let matters remain unspoken and went inside, looking over his shoulder only once. Argis was surprised to see the Gaimosian stretching out his immense muscles. No doubt Boen meant to practice his sword techniques. Argis was no stranger to battle, but this was not his place. He closed the door behind him.

The pleasant smell of breakfast greeted him. It was the last thing he expected. His companions were a rough lot used to the hardships in life. Simple luxuries were more of a nuisance. He idly wondered how many men they had killed between them. Of course there was no point in wasting his time trying to figure it out, he was just glad they were all on the same side. For now.

"Well, Argis, it looks like we'll be parting company soon," Bahr said between bites of toasted bread.

"What did I miss?"

The Sea Wolf gestured towards Anienam. "The wizard claims he's discovered our destination. We should be leaving shortly."

Argis nodded at the implications. Part of him dreaded going back to Chadra and battling his former friends. There was little doubt his toughest trials were yet to come. Harnin had once been a trusted friend and ally. They knew everything about each other and that made the situation complicated. He tried to take heart from the thoughts of his allies in the underground. It was on those men and women that the fate of Delranan laid.

"You truly mean to go through with this?" Argis asked.

"What choice do we have? Every hour we delay brings both kingdoms closer to an undesirable end. My brother's madness needs to be stopped. Who better to do the job than me?"

Argis sighed. "I do not envy your task. Badron is a hard man and he has the backing of the Wolfsreik."

He reached out to shake Bahr's hand. A variety of emotions collided within him. Part wanted to march with the tired sea captain while the bigger part demanded he remain accessible to his people. The underground stood no chance without his insight. Even then, it was only a slight chance for victory.

"Your path is no less difficult. Harnin is a snake, always has been. He won't be easy to bring down, not with those damned Dae'shan aiding him. Good luck, Argis. I hope you succeed. Our people have suffered enough."

Argis nodded and replied, "Luck be with you. Gods willing, we will meet again when this is finished."

He let the thought hang. It was a certainty that some of this group would not be coming back alive.

Bahr picked up on that, too, and forced a tight smile. "Perhaps we could do with praying to these gods of Anienam's."

"Goodbye, Captain."

Argis collected his gear, what little he had, and left without drawing too much more attention. The others had too much to worry about and his destiny beckoned. The door swung shut swiftly behind him.

Bahr anxiously cracked his knuckles and went back into the kitchen. Anienam watched him expectantly.

Bahr took the bait. "What's the good word? Tell me you found what you were looking for."

"I believe so. At least the answers to a great many questions," the wizard said. There was just a hint of excitement to his tone.

"Nearby I hope," Boen commented.

"Yes and no."

Dorl rolled his eyes, shrugging off the sense of embarrassment at being caught with Rekka, and tossed his hands up. "Here we go again."

"Have patience, mercenary. All is not necessarily as dark as you would have it," Anienam scolded. "The book specifically tells us that there is only one group of beings in Malweir who know where the hammer is hidden."

"And they are?" Bahr asked.

Anienam cleared his throat. "The Giants of Venheim."

A collective gasp of disbelief circled the room.

"What?"

"That is impossible."

The wizard held up his hands for silence. "Venheim is the key to what we seek."

"Anienam, I do not disagree with your book, but even the smallest child knows that the Giants are a myth. Venheim does not exist. There is no forge in the mountains."

"Myths and legends always begin in reality. I've seen more unexplainable things over the course of the last three hundred years than you could imagine. Giants are just as real as any other race on Malweir, the Dae'shan included."

Dorl had had enough. "Something that big would have been seen. How can a Giant hide?"

"Plenty of races choose to remain hidden. Why should the Giants be any different?" Anienam countered.

Bahr saw the conversation quickly devolving into an all-out argument and moved to stop it. "I trust this book tells us where to find these Giants?"

The wizard stared back indignantly. "Of course it does. I did say that they weren't far away, didn't I?"

"Where do we go from here?" Bahr asked.

"To the base of the Murdes Mountains. That is where we will find the pass that takes us up to the forge of Giants."

"It is not that simple," Nothol interrupted. "The Murdes Mountains are treacherous. We all know the stories of the Pell Darga, but they pale when compared to the broken paths of the mountains. Dorl and I have crossed too many times. Even as skilled as we are, it is pure chance that we lived to tell of it. The skeletons of those less fortunate line the passes, judging us from beyond the grave."

"Be that as it may, that is our destination."

Bahr cleared his throat. "Does the book specify just where this forge is? The Murdes Mountains range for five hundred leagues. We could spend the rest of our lives searching."

Anienam suppressed mild anger and read from the book. *"We traveled south, pushing the wagon team to the point of exhaustion. The captain was adamant about haste. He kept telling us this quest went toward winning the war. Day and night, we stopped only to rest the horses. No one was sure where we were going until we chanced upon the shaman.*

"He told us how to find this legendary Venheim. Take the Borgin Pass and ride west. After a day we'd find a row of jagged boulders that spiral both up and down from the overhead shelves of rock. The 'teeth of the dragon,' he called them. They'd be enshrouded in mist and tinged red from the substance of the stone. They marked the entrance to the land of Giants. Find that and we would find what we seek. The shaman disappeared and left us with a dire warning: 'Be careful what you seek, for death is ever its companion.' The captain thanked him and pushed us forward into the mountains of death."

"This will not end well," Dorl whispered.

Even Boen seemed shaken by the tale.

"Ha!" barked Ionascu. "This is madness. You'll lead us all to our deaths."

"The future remains clouded, even to the likes of me. There is no other way. Only in Venheim will we learn where the Blud Hamr rests. We have no choice," Anienam calmly replied.

Undaunted, Ionascu continued, "That is madness and you know it!"

"What's the matter, old man? Lost the lust for revenge after a good night's sleep?" Boen chided. "If you are afraid, don't step up."

"And what fears accompany your dreams, killer?" he snapped back. Venom dripped from his words.

The Gaimosian bristled. "My kind do not know fear."

"Then you are fools."

"Enough of this!" Bahr shouted. "There is business to attend to. Like it or not, we are heading into the mountains. Anienam has shown us the way, now we need to move. Our enemies will not wait."

"My uncle is right. The faster we move the better. Aurec and the Pell Darga are using the mountain passes for war against my father. I do not like the thought any better than you, but I have been there myself. The danger is not the mountains, but the men who use them," Maleela told them quietly. The constant bickering wore her down and she was tired of it.

"I'd still rather go up against the Wolfsreik," Dorl said. "That old bastard has the right of it. This is madness."

Bahr ignored them. He gave his niece a mighty hug, for her words both inspired and shamed him. Shamed them all.

Boen watched, allowing a tight smile. "What is our next move?"

"Supplies and weapons. There's a small trading town about two days south of here. I've got enough money to equip us for a long journey. Something tells me Venheim is not going to be the end of this," Bahr replied.

Anienam nodded agreement. "Tokens of power should not be easily found, lest the keepers be tempted to use them carelessly."

"If you ask me, people need to stop making things like that under the pretense of keeping the rest of us safe," Dorl told them.

Anienam hid his surprise. The sell sword had more layers than he showed. "Such affairs are beyond our control."

"Enough talk. Let's be about it before that bastard Harnin sniffs us out," Bahr said.

TEN

The Hags

Amar Kit'han listened to the wind howl angrily across the open plains like a lover stolen from his home. He scowled from within the shadows of his hood. The Dae'shan did not like that old feeling of hopelessness trying to worm back into his psyche. Not even the daunting span of thousands of years were enough to ease the storm brewing in his mind's eye. He was angry. The fabric of his carefully wrought plans threatened to tear apart.

"They are on their way," Kodan Bak told him as he stalked up behind.

Amar said nothing.

The lesser Dae'shan took that as a sign to continue voicing his compounding concerns. "Why have you summoned them? The situation is still within our control."

Amar Kit'han passed a condescending glare. "Much has changed. The Hags have never failed us."

"I do not understand. We do not need the Hags to manage this. What do you know that you are not telling me?" pressed Bak.

"Delranan is in uproar. Bahr and the princess have escaped." His voice was uncharacteristically flat.

"Without them in custody," Kodan Bak let the thought die on his lips.

Three great winged figures circled high overhead. The wisp of clouds partially concealed them from the ground. The Hags. Kodan narrowed his eyes. Once they deemed the area was clear, the Hags tucked back their ugly wings and dove. The Dae'shan had had a hundred dealings with the Hags over the centuries and each subsequent time seemed worse. One by one they landed. The largest of the three stepped forward on long, clawed feet and bowed her head.

Amar Kit'han waved off the gesture. "Freina, how good of you to come on such short notice."

She hissed. It was a terrible sound capable of destroying a mortal's eardrum. "We come because we have no choice, undead one."

Amar smiled at the memory. The Dae'shan came upon the three sisters long ago and bound them to the dark crusade. The relationship was testy at best. The Hags took every opportunity to rail against their masters. They'd suffered great indignities through the decades. Amar disregarded their grievances. The sisters were nothing more than tools to an end.

Freina and her sisters were Harpies, three of the last from the great northern roosts. Each was over seven feet tall with the head and torso of Human women. Their legs were those of great birds, the soft feathers an ugly brownish grey. Their fingers extended into razor sharp claws. Needlepoint teeth protruded from both jaws. Stringy black hair hung down past their shoulders, littered with old skulls and other signs of past kills. It was the eyes that Kodan hated most. Eyes that were cold and emotionless. Eyes that pleaded for death, either to give or to receive. He had never met another creature so desperate to die and that frightened him.

Harpies had once roamed across the north, but angry kings hunted them to the point of extinction. And for good reasons. Freina and her sisters rained terror down upon every village they came across. They mercilessly snatched up small children and animals for food or sport. Some of the larger kingdoms successfully warded them off while others offered sacrifices to slake their bloodlust.

Freina clenched her claws into ragged simulacrums of fists.

"I have a task for you," Amar said.

She hissed again.

For his part, he refused to gaze into those cold, black eyes. She, like all her kin, was a hideous creature. Freina's face was abnormally long, the chin littered with stray strands of hair. Her cheeks were sunken, giving her face a hollow draw. Amar often wondered what ancient hatred created such creatures.

None of the Harpies wore much clothing. A simple loincloth covered the parts no one particularly wanted to see. Hair and down covered their breasts and stomach. Each wore a necklace of skulls and bones. Perhaps the Hags maintained a more human side than they typically showed.

"What this time?" Freina asked. Her mocking tone was meant to insult.

Amar ignored her as best he could. "There is a person of great importance who has escaped me."

She made a birdlike clucking sound from the base of her throat. "Man or woman?"

"A woman. She is the princess of Delranan. I want her found and brought to me alive and unharmed."

The Hag scowled. She idly fingered one of her skull charms. "A princess would make a fine addition to our trophies."

"Alive and unharmed," he reiterated. "Disobey me and the three of you will beg for death. Do you understand me?"

"Yes."

Her straightforwardness bothered him for reasons unknown. Freina and her two sisters, Garelda and Brom, were not keen on subservience. They killed without discretion and continually struggled to find freedom from the Dae'shan. The sisters were notorious for pushing the limits of his authority. He danced around the thought of striking them dead now.

Amar Kit'han was already tired of the conversation. "Go now. Find the princess and follow her. I want her brought to me. She will be travelling with companions. Kill them as you see fit, but do not harm the girl."

Freina cackled laughter and launched back into the sky. Garelda and Brom followed wordlessly. A score of black feathers drifted down in their wake, leaving the two Dae'shan in solitude.

"They are disgusting creatures," Kodan Bak snarled.

"They serve their purpose." Amar brushed a feather from his robes.

"We can find better and more useful servants on Malweir than that."

"None that can fly. The great dragons are all but memories now and no other race would succumb easily," Amar reminded.

Kodan folded his hands within his robes and began to disappear. "What do we do now? Badron is concerned over the enemy raids on his supply lines. I fear the king might not be our best choice."

"Let the mortals deal with their own problems. Every death serves our purpose. Besides, the Goblin army will be here by the end of the month. Rogscroft and her people will cease to exist and the path will be open for us. If Badron becomes too much of a problem, there is always another one can turn if needs be."

"Damnation!"

Piper Joach cleared his throat of phlegm as his friend and commander raved throughout the command tent.

"That's two supply convoys lost in a week," Rolnir snarled at his commanders.

"Sir, the enemy is well hidden, it is impossible to hunt them down in these bloody mountains."

Rolnir spun sharply on Colonel Harper. "Thank you for that wonderful bit of insight! Don't tell me what I already know. I want to know how we are going to protect these supplies. Or do I need to remind you that winter is nearly upon us and there is only so much we can forage from this damned land?"

No one spoke.

He snorted. "Now you are quiet? What the Hells am I paying you for?"

Piper decided it was time to weigh in and save his peers further embarrassment. "General, our army is stretched thin already. The advance on Rogscroft proper demands more men and resources. I think we all know what needs to be done."

"I'm listening."

"Take a battalion and burn them out," Piper finished.

Colonel Ulaf unsuccessfully tried to conceal a gasp. "You'd declare war on the Pell Darga by doing so."

"Which is nothing less than what they've already done," Piper told him flatly.

Rolnir stared at his friend. His face was more sallow than usual. Dark bags looked permanently entrenched around his blue eyes. He hadn't shaved in over two weeks. Piper Joach was a changed man. His very thought centered on violence. His hatred of Rogscroft and Prince Aurec demanded fulfillment.

"We cannot risk open war on another front," Herger told them. "We are still vulnerable until our full strength is amassed."

Rolnir asked, "What is our current strength?"

"Eighty percent, more or less," Piper readily supplied. "Regular army reserves are being deployed as well. As you know, they are mainly support troops. There are a few infantry battalions, but nothing up to Wolfsreik standards."

The regular army was roughly the same size as Rolnir's army. They had the same natural aggressiveness as the Wolfsreik but lacked the training and logistics structure. That wasn't to suggest they weren't good in battle. They just weren't *as* good. Rolnir admitted that he seldom gave them thought. Never in his long career had he seen them used in front line actions. He had an odd feeling that that was about to change.

Folding his arms across his chest, the general asked, "How soon can we expect them to deploy and in what kind of numbers?"

"No later than the end of the month and roughly with three thousand men. They will more than make up for our losses thus far," Herger answered.

The speed of the answer caught him off guard and restored a measure of faith in his leaders. The disturbing bit was the last part. He did not relish dwelling on the men who were not going to be going home again.

"How many men have we lost?" he asked slowly.

Colonel Mentyl, the army surgeon, answered in a low voice. "Two hundred thirty-one dead and six hundred seventy wounded. Of those injured, nearly one hundred fifty should not go back to their units anytime soon. Forty more will probably be dead in the next day or so."

Damn, Rolnir grimaced. Almost a thousand men. Rogscroft was not even within sight and he had lost a tenth of his total strength. This campaign was much more difficult than any of them planned for. If they continued suffering similar losses he would be forced to retreat, even with regular troops to aid.

"Fix the wounded, doctor. Get those men back to their units. We need them," Rolnir said.

Mentyl sighed. "I will clear the ones that are healthy enough, but I won't let them go as is. They will only compound the problem."

Of course he was right. A man too wounded to fight could only cause more harm than good. The wounded weren't the real problem, however. Rolnir had to find a way to clear the mountain passes and soon. The alternatives disturbed him. He took a deep, steadying breath and made his decision.

"Piper, send a battalion to fire the mountains. I can't have the Pell Darga harassing us without any kind of retribution."

"Yes, Sir." There was no joy or relief in his voice. He was a soldier and soldiers followed orders.

Herger still wasn't satisfied. "General, the Pell will not engage us. They will melt back to their caves when they see us coming in force. They are a cunning foe, unwilling to make sacrifices too easily. They will not engage us in a head-to-head fight."

"Right now, I don't care. I want those trees burned to the ground. Take their cover from them and they will be less likely to go on the offensive."

The idea was sound, but the Pell were not called the Shadow People for no reason. They were savage, entirely unpredictable. Rolnir would like nothing more than to seal them in their damned caves and be done with it, but that was not a possibility. He knew more men were going to die. Unfortunately there was no way around it. He had Badron breathing down his neck for results. The king had never been a soldier and this war was well beyond the scope of his experience.

Rolnir continued, "We march at dawn, gentlemen. Go and get some rest. I know things tend to get heated, but I truly appreciate all that you are doing for our kingdom and our men. Good night."

They saluted as one and wordlessly filed out. Rolnir watched patiently until only Piper remained. The look in his eyes cautioned building hatred. The war was still too young for his senior commander to be so consumed.

"Piper, a word if you don't mind."

Piper Joach casually retook his seat and waited.

Rolnir still wasn't sure how to handle the situation. "How are your men holding up?"

Piper shrugged. "We are at war with a clever enemy. They are about as good as we can expect them to be."

Rolnir expected nothing less. Now came the hard part. "And how about you?"

"There's not much to report. I am focused on the next mission."

"That doesn't comfort me, Piper. I'm starting to think I need to give you some time off, away from the line so you can recollect your thoughts. It will be a chance for you to get right before our push on the city."

Mild anger flashed. "Sir, my men and I stand ready to do our jobs the only way we know how. After everything we have been through I am surprised that you would even suggest taking a break. It is insulting. We are all men of the Wolfsreik. We will do our jobs."

Piper clammed up, straining the atmosphere in the command tent. Rolnir quickly understood the silence following meant the end to the conversation.

"Dismissed."

Piper Joach threw a crisp salute and left.

"Damned stubborn man," Rolnir whispered after him.

Now that he was alone, his attention reverted to the map table. He must have looked at it a hundred times today. The army had made and was still making considerable progress. Enemy emplacements were a thorn, but were being overrun daily, leaving him with little doubt that the main effort was going to collapse on Rogscroft. Damn. He wished there were another way. A nice big battle on the open plain to settle this affair more suited him. The Wolfsreik was strong, but not urban specialists. Rolnir sighed. He supposed it was too much for Stelskor to march an army out in one final defiant gesture and lay it all on the line.

This led him to his next concern: Badron. The king was under the illusion that Rogscroft was an easy target. The last month of campaign had done nothing to assuage his building desires of conquest. Rolnir shook his head. He felt trapped. The king should never have left Chadra Keep. Rage over losing his son had pushed him beyond the point of rationality. Rolnir knew they must be careful lest the king kill them all. Still, that thought did not preclude him from doing what must be done. It was the time of day when Badron expected him. He reluctantly snatched up his wolf-skin cloak and worked his way over to the king's tent.

"A king should not be made to wait on his subordinates," Badron growled once Rolnir bowed.

Rolnir let the threat roll off his shoulders. He had no time for the petty games of kings. "Sire, I finished debriefing the commanders."

"Then I trust you have something useful to report."

"Potentially. I believe we've found a way to break the enemy's hold on the mountain passes."

Badron listened as his general explained in detail. His face was grey from the lack of sleep and the predations of the Dae'shan. Secrets were killing him, but they were secrets that *must* be kept. He shuddered to think what might happen should anyone learn about his association with the emissaries of the dark gods. He soon found himself ignoring Rolnir's estimates of collateral damage. His thoughts turned to his daughter and his hated brother. They were more trouble than either deserved. Damn the Dae'shan for even bringing it up. And now there was Harnin. His most trusted friend had betrayed him.

Rolnir finished and asked, "Do you have anything else for me, Sire?"

"No. You may leave now."

Badron waved him off, his mind already wandering dark corridors. The coming days were about to turn ugly; much uglier than he ever imagined in his lifetime.

ELEVEN

Anienam's Tale

"Well lad, looks like you're going to get the chance to find out about that Pell Darga treasure after all," Boen chided.

Most of the others were sullen, hiding from the reality of what they were about to undertake. The world was changed. They had already dared to enter the growing hostility in what had once been a peaceful kingdom. Along the way they learned much about themselves. Some was good, some bad. And now they had embarked upon the grand quest. It was the culmination of their lives, a point in time that none would ever be able to recreate or relive in more than fragmented memories with declining age.

Skuld looked over at the Gaimosian. "Somehow it doesn't feel right."

"Times like this never do."

"How do you do it?" the boy asked.

Boen shrugged. "A life like mine is not for the weak. I've killed and been hunted. I have no homeland. No family. I have nothing in this world except what you see." He reached behind his back and drew his mighty broadsword. "This sword is my life. Without it I am nothing. Do you understand?"

He didn't.

Boen continued, encouraged by the snort of his horse. "Battle is a Gaimosian's life. To die of old age is an insult to the tradition of my people. We Gaimosians are a proud breed. The world is now our kingdom. There is no point in trying to escape it. Thinking otherwise is a waste of time. We are what fate has made us. Nothing more, nothing less. Be at peace with this and you will finally accept yourself for what you are."

Boen sheathed his sword and swung his gaze back to the road. He knew better than to believe his words had much impact on the boy. Skuld was too young to understand, too impressionable. Maybe that was a good thing. Too many people stumbled through life thinking they knew what was going on around them. Time and again he'd see those same people cut down in the prime of their ignorance. Boen was determined not to let that happen to Skuld. He liked the boy.

"Living on the streets, I used to dream of being a great warrior," Skuld quietly admitted. "Now I am not so sure. The world is not what I imagined it was."

Boen smiled softly. Fond memories of his own childhood drifted back to him. "Our dreams are always more reaching as children. The disappointment of adulthood robs us of that."

"We rescued the princess so shouldn't we be heroes? Aren't those men always revered as heroes?"

"Sometimes," Boen said and nodded. "Then again, it has been my experience that those things rarely happen. Most princesses have the good sense to stay home and live a normal life. Ours just happens to be a bit feisty."

Skuld laughed for the first time in weeks. It did him good, made him feel almost sane again. His thoughts had been much too foul lately. He had nothing else going for himself, and he was smart enough to know better than to abandon his newfound friends. Instinct pleaded with him to leave now and not look back. Skuld couldn't. His friends were literally the only thing keeping him going. He needed them.

Boen took a moment. "Don't wrap your mind on such trivial matters. We'll be in the mountains soon enough. Use this time to rest. You will have need of your strength soon enough."

"Thank you, Boen."

His words were genuine. The Gaimosian was like an older brother to him and Skuld valued his advice.

"Don't mention it. You would have done the same if our roles were reversed. Get some sleep, boy."

Boen urged his horse forward. A light snow drifted lazily across the sky. They were already a day out of Chadra and still hadn't seen any sign of Harnin. Bahr was satisfied with the pace but knew better than to let down his guard. They weren't out of danger yet and were only heading into even more in the days and weeks to come. One more day and they would arrive at Praeg. If Harnin hadn't caught up to them by then, it was safe to assume he wasn't going to.

Praeg was by no means a safe haven, but it was far enough away from Chadra to relax his nerves a little. He planned on staying in the village just long enough to properly equip the team for a winter journey in the heart of the most dangerous mountains in northern Malweir. The mountains were still two weeks away and he wasn't relishing the thought of what they were going to find once they got there.

Bahr glanced over at the wizard. Anienam sat in the back of the wagon rereading his book. He regarded the little man with renewed interest. An oddity was an understatement. The wizard was dangerous.

"Have you learned anything new?"

Anienam looked up. "Eh?"

"I asked if you'd learned anything new."

Bahr couldn't exactly tell, but it appeared Anienam rolled his eyes. "None of this is new, Captain Bahr. This book is over a thousand years old. There are many mysteries in this life. Perhaps if men had better memories we would not be in this position now," he cackled.

Bahr snorted. "All of the damned people in this world, we are stuck with a grumpy old man on the edge of insanity! Can you just answer my questions without the games? I've grown weary of this."

"We all need a good sense of humor after all that has happened and for what is to come. Our test is not going to be easy."

Bahr glowered at him.

"Believe me, I have a feeling that the level of violence we are about to witness is going to leave those of us who have the good fortune to survive scarred forever. Laugh, Bahr. Laugh while we still can."

There was an inherent threat tangled in his words, a threat big enough for Bahr to take notice. "What do you know?"

"Nothing really. The text alludes to cataclysmic events, most of which do not concern us. The war these men fought in was one of the worst in our history. Their words are not encouraging."

"Which war?" Bahr asked.

"The great Mage War. It was the one war that almost destroyed Malweir. The death toll was in the hundreds of thousands. It was by sheer fortune that any survived."

The Mage War. It was well known to every race, a dark time in everyone's past that was almost their demise. Bahr couldn't begin to guess why Anienam was the only one of them with fond memories. The war was the height of human vanity. Mages brought Malweir to the edge of ruin and were wiped out themselves for their sins. He believed it was better that much power should not be allowed to run free as it was clear that no one was able to control it. Bahr found himself with grave misgivings about the future. Anienam was the progeny of those Mages and an enigma. He might turn on them in a fit of madness.

"That war is ancient history. The Mage order is no more," Bahr replied. "What does the book say about the hammer? What is it supposed to do?"

"The book doesn't get that far. I believe these men all died before they were able to use it," Anienam replied seriously. He bore a dour expression. The implications for the future were severe and all but a few were bad.

Bahr said nothing. Best to let the man keep talking while was in the mood.

"The Blud Hamr is a token of power. There have been many such tokens over the course of time. The most famous of which was the cracked crystal of Tol Shere and, of course, the fabled star silver sword, Phaelor. It was Phaelor that finally destroyed the crystal and ended the war. The Elves took it back, you know. They feared it falling into the wrong hands. A shame, really. The sword always chooses its master."

"The hammer," Bahr gently urged.

The wizard snapped back into focus. "The Blood Hammer is rumored to have been made by the Giants on commission by the gods of light back when the world was young. They knew the schism coming and made certain moves to defend themselves."

"What would a god need to defend himself from? Aren't they all the same?"

"There is no reference for an answer. Most of what we knew about the gods and their ilk was lost when the libraries at Ipn Shal burned. I do not know what powers the hammer bears, but the Giant clans will have the answers. There are no finer smiths in the entire world."

Bahr's heart slowed. Hope diminished. "Are you suggesting that we are about to go to war with the gods and we do not know what we are doing?"

"Encouraging, isn't it?"

"Give me a straight answer."

Anienam let out a steady breath. "The future is hidden. I would say there is a very real possibility that we are overmatched."

The words were a hammer stroke. Bahr felt as if a thunderstorm had broken across the horizon, leaving him helpless. "Then we go to our doom."

It was Anienam's turn to be irritated. "Keep that opinion to yourself. We do not know what tomorrow holds. Our future is still in our hands so long as we keep faith."

"Faith is a difficult concept to maintain when you whisper of death," he protested.

"Ha! When did you start listening to me?"

Bahr had to smile at that. Anienam was a crazy old man, about as cracked as Bahr's own father had been. It made this whole affair both easier and more difficult. Bahr waggled an accusing finger. "You are the one who got me into this mess in the first place. Listening to you took us down this dark road. Now if you don't mind telling me, what do we do when we get this hammer of yours?"

"If I knew that the task would be much easier."

Damnation, Bahr growled. *We truly are in trouble.*

Dorl Theed glanced at the two bickering old men and shook his head. "What do you suppose they are squabbling about this time?" he asked.

Nothol didn't bother to look. "Who knows? Both should be on a front porch watching the grass grow."

"Doesn't really say much about us, following them all over the world."

"We are getting paid for it."

Dorl gave his friend a sharp look. "I haven't been paid yet. The job we were hired to do ended with us in a dungeon and being tortured. All we are doing now is running for our lives."

"Bahr is not responsible for that. We didn't know the girl was his niece until it was too late to do anything about it," Nothol reminded. "He will do us right."

"I will keep my doubts about that."

Nothol wasn't in the mood to argue. And, quite frankly, he was tired of Dorl's darkening attitude. The man was slowly breaking down. That change began in Harnin's dungeon. It was by far the worst experience either had ever been through. Nothol had been able to put it behind him, Dorl couldn't. It was the fact he didn't know how to help his friend that hurt the most.

"We are still alive. That is all I can ask for."

Dorl disagreed. "For now."

Nothol finally snapped. "Enough already! You have been wallowing in self-pity and misery since we escaped. Get over it. It happened and is already behind us. Your mood is starting to turn cancerous."

Anger flashed. "You're a real son of a bitch sometimes."

Nothol Coll smiled. "Thank you. Stop trying to change the subject, Dorl. We need you back to form."

He skillfully avoided the budding relationship between Dorl and Rekka. That was strange, though not entirely unexpected. The two seemed to have an instant connection from the moment she boarded the *Dragon's Bane*. Nothol tried to rationalize that it was the stress of the situation and the intensity of their task that forced the pair together. It was weak at best, but he didn't want to think any more on it. The lucky bastard.

"Do you see what Ionascu has become?" Dorl asked quietly.

"Yes," Nothol replied.

"He scares me. Not what he is, but how he became it."

"I don't understand."

Dorl shrugged. "He scares me because I can see myself slipping into the same role. I have hate in my heart, Nothol. I want to kill Harnin. I want to destroy everything he stands for. I am afraid. Afraid I might lose me and become like Ionascu."

"I won't let that happen," Nothol reassured.

"How can you be so sure?"

"Because I will beat you within an inch of your life first," he laughed.

"I'd like to see you try."

Nothol shook his head now. "No. Besides, you'd probably go running to your girlfriend to help you."

His cheeks flushed. "You know about that?"

"I think Bahr might be the only one who doesn't."

Dorl was at a loss for words. He still wasn't sure exactly what had happened between him and Rekka. He'd been tired and trying to go to sleep when she slipped under the warmth of his blanket. He certainly enjoyed the experience, but he still wanted to know why. Making love to the strange southern woman might well have been the greatest moment in his relatively young life, especially considering the fact she had ignored every advance he had made on her beforehand.

"Look, I…" he began.

Nothol held up his hands. "You don't need to explain anything to me. I'm your friend, not your father."

Dorl smiled warmly. "Thank you."

"You could tell a friend how good she was," Nothol said with a mischievous twinkle in his eyes.

"I think it would be safer if I didn't," Dorl replied. "For the both of us."

Both men laughed. It was a much needed break from their desperate reality. Dorl idly wondered if that was what had happened last night. She might have seen the depth of his building despair and acted. The idea was absurd, but he liked it and decided to stick with it until she admitted otherwise.

Nothol continued, his voice lower so as not to be overheard. "Do me one small favor though. Try not to make so much noise the next time. Some of us need our sleep."

"I can't make any promises."

Rekka Jel listened to them from the front of the wagon. Her face remained impassive despite the potential embarrassment. Her actions were for reasons only she would ever know. Perhaps it had been a onetime thing, perhaps not. Time would tell. The wagon rolled on.

TWELVE

Praeg

Praeg was a tiny village of no real importance. Planners once tried to build it up and make it a rival to mighty Chadra in the west. The idea never took off. People had no interest in living in the middle of nowhere. Then the second class, undesirable citizens, arrived. Most sought escape from the attention of the authorities. Cutthroats and criminals, the majority of the village were the sort to stay away from. Bahr could care less. Praeg was far from a natural water source and in a borderland area that no one wanted to claim.

"Bahr, are you certain we need to stop here?" Dorl asked. "There are other villages along the way, ones where we won't draw attention or have to deal with major issues."

"Have you seen our merry group of travelers? We don't exactly blend in," Nothol leaned over and whispered.

Bahr wasn't amused. "No. This is the one place Harnin won't dare send his troops. Not unless he wants to send enough to pacify it."

"It is also the place he'll think to look first. His spies might already be here."

"That may be, but you and I both know what type of village this is. Harnin's spies won't get far."

Skuld's concerns overrode his caution. "Where are we going?"

"To Praeg, boy. A one-road village where your darkest dreams and deepest desires can come true," Bahr said matter-of-factly.

Dorl cocked his head at the embellishment. "Don't you think that's a little dramatic for him?"

The Sea Wolf cracked a grin. "Nonsense. Those are the same words my father told me when I was but a lad."

"Maybe it has changed since then," Skuld offered hopefully. He was almost at the breaking point as far as adventures were concerned.

"No," Bahr answered. "This is the kind of village where you mind yourself and don't ask questions. All of the scum from civilized parts come here. We don't want trouble, not now leastwise."

Boen let out a bellowing laugh. "This sounds like my kind of place!"

Dorl looked at Nothol and said, "This is madness. It's like a race to see who is going crazy first."

"We might as well get it over with then," Nothol replied.

"Boen and I will take care of everything. The rest of you stay out of sight. The last thing we need is more trouble," Bahr told them all.

Only Ionascu and Anienam didn't seem to mind. One had already seen too many horrors and the other wasn't interested in anything but that damned book. That was fine with Bahr. He felt like more of a caretaker than a grown man. His heart longed for the days when he was alone again. Life was more peaceful that way. Still, he had a good group assembled and they offered his best chance of success at stopping his brother. He noticed Maleela's burning glare and cringed inwardly at the similarity between her and Badron.

"Not this time, Niece," he said and stood his ground.

Not the words she wanted to hear. "No, Uncle. I am a princess of Delranan. I will not hide in the shadows while my friends earn their keep. I want to be a part of this."

"This is exactly the type of place where you want to hide," Bahr reasoned. "All of our lives would be forfeit if even one person discovered your truth."

"He's right, girl. You'd be captured and us killed without a second thought," Boen added a little less gruffly.

Flames threatened to burst from her eyes. Her face twisted in silent rage. Boen was almost impressed. She was a good kid but had much to learn if she planned on rising above her father's legacy.

"I am a princess and expect to be treated as such!" she fumed.

Boen walked his horse closer to the wagon. His tone of voice left no room for doubt as to his intentions. "You are about to be slung over my knee and spanked like the brat you are acting like. You want to be a princess? Fine, be one. But you had damned sure better watch your tone when you speak with me."

He circled away, neither caring nor concerning himself with her reactions. Boen felt a twinge of remorse at having spoken his mind, but he saw no other way around it. Regardless of what she did next, time was against her. Even Bahr was forced to close his now gaping mouth. He hadn't expected the uncharacteristic outburst. He suddenly found himself liking the Gaimosian that much more.

"Maleela, this is not the nice world you grew up in." His winced at the choice of words but drove on. "The men and women in Praeg would like nothing better than to get their hands on you. They'd kill us outright and do terrible things to you. We just got you. I am not willing to lose you so soon."

She softened her stance, if only just. Maleela swallowed her pride, but lacked the maturity required of her station. She recognized this despite the fact it did not assuage the mental storm consuming her. When she spoke, her words were careful, measured. "Uncle, all of you, I truly thank you for all you have done for me. You have all risked so much just for me and I can never repay that. But I am just as much a part of this as you are. We all have obligations to each other. I want to feel like I am making a contribution."

"Ah lass, you remind me so much of your mother," Bahr said lovingly. "You are a part of this and I welcome your help. My decision stands though. Praeg is not a friendly place. You'll be in plenty of danger just sitting in the tavern room waiting for us to return."

"We are wasting time and I am getting hungry," Boen growled.

"You think with your stomach too much."

He shrugged. "I am a big man."

At six feet tall and nearly three hundred pounds of solidly packed muscle, Boen was one of the most formidable men Bahr had ever known.

"Wizard, have you got anything insightful to add?" Bahr asked.

He didn't. *Of course he doesn't.*

The Sea Wolf ignored the old man and led the small band down the gently sloping hill towards Praeg. He dreaded coming back here. The last time had almost done him in. At least now he had a well-armed group of proven fighters highly capable of dealing with whatever new dangers lay in wait. The low-level thatch roofs came into sight, forcing Bahr to shrug off a disturbing feeling.

The village was nothing special. A single road split Praeg down the middle. Two score of houses and shops lined the avenue. All were run down and poorly kept. Praeg lacked most of the amenities of a proper village. A handful of wells, built from crudely cut stone, dotted the plain. Most of the buildings were completed with mud instead of mortar. There was a decided lack of quality in the construction. They all appeared crooked, ready to collapse in on themselves with a stiff wind. Grey smoke pushed out of the chimneys and turned the sky a foul color neither black nor white. The smell of burning wood drifted their way.

The people here wore furs and leathers from tanned deer hides. All the men had thick, unkempt beards and the women all bore a hard, weathered glare. Even the children had a hardened edge. Skuld took it all in with disgust. He would not have lived long had he been born here instead of Chadra. Stray dogs snapped and growled at the group the closer they got to the town center. A dead smell hovered over the ground, a cross between human waste and rot. Maleela gagged from behind the heavy hood and cloak wore to conceal her identity

"This is as good as it will get," Boen cautioned. "Remember not to make eye contact and do not speak to anyone. That goes for all of you."

He led the way into the village, past the gawking leers and condescending looks from windows and doorways. Every single person in Praeg was armed and looking for a fight. Most flinched as Boen rode by. His size kept them from acting foolishly. Soon, but not soon enough for most of them, the wagon pulled in front of the sole tavern.

Bahr slid from the saddle. "Dorl, Nothol, secure a room. We'll be back within an hour. I don't want to spend the night here. It is best if we are away as soon as possible."

The sun was already starting to set, transforming the drab sky into an explosion of colors. Reds and purples ripped through swaths of golden yellow and orange, all tinged with a building darkness. Bahr and Boen left the sell swords to their business. Only Rekka remained with the wagon. Her exotic looks attracted attention but the wickedly curved sword at her hip was enough to deter would-be robbers, which was fortunate for them because what she lacked in the zealous lust for battle, she made up for in skill. She had yet to meet anyone in the northern kingdoms that matched her skill in battle.

Nothol Coll edged the tavern door open with a boot, scanning the room before entering. Conversations died abruptly. Heads swung their way. Nothol felt uncomfortable, but that was nothing new. He had been in this type of situation before. Hardening his face, the sell sword brushed the door open and marched over to an empty table off in the corner. He subconsciously picked a spot that funneled potential enemies in from the front and gave him a secure backing. A plump barmaid missing half of her teeth came to take their orders. Her fingernails were broken and dirty.

"What will it be?" Her voice was the sound of steel being dragged over loose gravel and she smelled of rancid food and unclean bedding.

"Ale and whatever the meal is," Nothol replied.

"Deer shank and boiled potatoes. That'll be two gold pieces for you and your friends," she said.

Nothol refrained from commenting. The girl was good. She'd raised her voice just enough so that everyone within a few tables could hear.

"If I had gold pieces I would not have stopped in Praeg." He produced a handful of copper coins and a few silvers.

The barmaid shot him a look of disgust but scooped up his money and disappeared.

"Quality establishment," Dorl commented softly once they were all seated.

"We've been in worse."

Dorl looked around. Smoke clung to the ceiling. The floors were stained with ale and who knew what else. What few windows there were around the walls were dim and covered with grime. A rat crept along the near wall in search of a free meal. "Not by much. I hope the others don't take too long. This place is giving me a bad feeling."

Their drinks came with the promise of food soon after. She had no problem sloshing a good bit of ale onto the table, as if in anger from being cheated. Ionascu struggled to grip his mug, but his broken hands made the task difficult. He managed to bring the mug to his lips with great effort and he drank deeply. The ale was absolutely horrible. It burned on the way down and left an uneasy feeling in the pit of his stomach. The only positive note was how it stole the early winter bite from the air. A few more drinks and the broken man wouldn't be able to remember his name. He smiled at that.

"Take it easy with that," Nothol growled at him, shaking his head disgustedly at the thick trickle running down Ionascu's chin.

Ionascu glared back. "Or what?"

Lovely. This ignorant bastard wants to pick a fight. Nothol frowned, "Just take it easy."

Ionascu continued to glare indignantly, but kept his mouth shut. Not that it mattered. It was already too late. Between his ranting and the barmaid's big mouth, every person in the tavern had a newfound interest in their group. Nothol and Dorl readied for the inevitable fight.

"This is going to get ugly fast," Dorl warned.

Anienam glanced up from the book. "Nonsense. We don't have anything to worry about."

"Says you. That man in the far left corner hasn't stopped staring at us since we came in," Dorl said.

"Same with the pair on the right," Nothol added.

"Just relax. Do not expect trouble and we should be fine," the wizard countered before returning to his book.

The barmaid returned, thumping plates of food in front of them and then stalked off. They looked down at their meals, each silently debating whether they should eat it. The meat was old and gray and the potatoes had a rubbery texture. The dirt was cooked into the skin. Still, it was hot and they were hungry so they ate.

"This tastes more like dog than deer," Dorl said between fast mouthfuls.

Nothol nodded in agreement.

Skuld's mouth fell open. "You've eaten a dog?"

"Who hasn't? Dog actually tastes pretty good when you are hungry," Dorl replied in mild shock.

Maleela pushed her plate away, face blanched and appetite gone. The sell swords chuckled in their private joke.

"Eat your food, both of you," Nothol said. "We don't know when the next time is that we'll have a hot meal."

Skuld reluctantly did, though he couldn't help but wonder if the meat was dog or deer. It was an unsettling.

"Do we bother to get a room?" Maleela asked once her plate was empty. She took no interest in the ale and made the mistake of asking for water instead. The water was brown and had a brackish taste.

Nothol shook his head. "Bahr was explicit in his instructions. We'll head back to the wagon as soon as we finish eating. Make sure we save some food for Rekka."

Not much later a heavyset man ambled up and set a boot on one of their benches. He had greasy black hair and a broken nose. From the look in his eyes it was clear that he was looking for trouble. His eyes were filled with lust, never leaving Maleela.

"She's a pretty one, she is," he leered. Nothol Coll swirled a mouthful of ale around before smiling.

Dorl's hand crept towards his sword. "What about her?"

The stranger took this as a good sign and pressed further. "How much do you want for her? I'd like to borrow her for a spell."

Maleela began to rise. "How dare…"

Nothol's rough hand pushed her down. "She's not for sale."

"Everything is for sale here in Praeg and I want her."

"I said no."

Nothol watched his opponent closely. The man was as drunk as he was nervous. His drunken caution suggested he might lose control at any given moment. His muscles bunched and tightened beneath his deerskin clothes. His face flushed with building rage. Nothol had been in enough bar fights to recognize the signs. This time was going to be different, though. This time the entire village was against them.

The man continued, "I said give her to me. Hand the wench over and we all walk away in one piece."

"And I said no."

That was the spark. He lunged towards Nothol. The sell sword ducked back and to the side. Dorl was quickly on his feet, sword in hand and facing the crowd. Maleela crowded closer to the wizard while Skuld drew his meager blade.

"I told you this was going to get ugly," Dorl barked over his shoulder.

Despite his panicked tone, Dorl was as calm as possible. His heart beat only slightly faster. A handful of men stood before him, not the enchanted remains of those long dead, and he had beaten them. Odds were in his favor.

"Give me the bitch!" the man roared.

He charged again, taking a split second to jerk a cruel dagger from his belt. Nothol needed no further encouragement. Dodging sharply, he grabbed his attacker by the back of the neck and, using the man's momentum against him, slammed him face first into the dirty wooden table. The aged oak plank was unforgiving. Bone and cartilage broke. Hot blood flew in ropes. Three teeth remained lodged in the wood after the man slithered to the ground. Both hands went to his ruined face as his screams drowned out all other noise. A second man leapt to his defense but came up short as the tip of Dorl's blade kissed his throat. A tiny trickle of blood ran down his shirt.

"Go back to your drinks," Dorl warned.

The man snarled, his pupils widened at the sudden prospect of death. The screech of benches scraping back sent a chill down Skuld's spine. Others had risen.

One hand on his broken face, the wounded man snarled, "He is mine!"

Nothol Coll passively waited. His sword was still sheathed. A sardonic smile lent him a more dangerous aspect. Most of the challenge the bigger man presented was gone, lost in the teeth and blood left on the floor. Nothol could easily kill him, but in doing so would condemn Dorl and the others.

"Don't do it, Marq," warned the man at the end of Dorl's sword.

Marq was beyond reasoning. He moved back into attack position. Marq had learned his lesson, or at least he thought he had. He approached slowly, a big cat stalking its prey. Nothol tensed.

"I am going to kill you for this," Marq said through a shower of blood. He waved the dagger tauntingly.

Nothol bit back a laugh. "Get it over with."

His ploy worked. Marq attacked with every ounce of strength he had. Caution disappeared as he let revenge drive him. He wanted, needed, to make this stranger suffer after the humiliation he'd caused. Again, Nothol Coll was ready for him. He lashed out with a strong kick at Marq's stomach. Marq grunted, threatening to double over in pain. Nothol caught him with a rigid hand to the wrist holding the dagger. A loud snap warned the others thinking of attacking. The dagger hit the floor.

Dorl looked at the wounded man with a smile of satisfaction. "See to your friend before he gets himself killed."

Marq was in sad shape. His right forearm was broken. His nose and mouth were bloody ruins. Embarrassed and wounded, his rage refused to abate.

"Kill them!"

The tavern exploded into action. No one paid much attention to Anienam Keiss standing meekly in the back of the room. His lips soundlessly mouthed an old spell. Black flames burst from the floor and forced everyone back. Anienam hid a brief smile. He folded his thin arms across his chest and watched the darkfire disappear.

"I suggest we all sit back down and enjoy the rest of the night. My friends and I did not come here looking for trouble, but I have no problem burning you all to cinders," he told them, using an old wizard's trick to project his voice.

Most of the villagers slunk away, shoulders hunched and fear in their eyes. A few grabbed Marq and dragged him away with them. No one was in a rush to get killed. Dorl sheathed his sword once he was satisfied the threat was passed. He had a newfound respect for Anienam and wondered why the man had remained passive for so long. Up until now he had only been a crazy old man with a limited grasp of reality.

Anienam noticed them all staring at him. "What?"

"Nothing. Nothing at all," Dorl answered as he sat back down.

The confrontation effectively dissolved their appetites so they decided to collect the leftovers for Rekka and left the tavern. All the fun had been had for one day and each was ready for a quiet night. Hopefully Bahr was having less trouble on his part.

THIRTEEN

Fight and Flight

"I haven't been here in a very long time," Bahr admitted reluctantly.

Boen's eyes never stopped scanning. "I can see why."

"Badron tried to clean it up about two decades ago. He sent in a company of his best shock troops. They made the mistake of trying to arrest the villagers."

"What happened?"

The Gaimosian didn't particularly care. Delranan or scum, all these people were the same. It didn't matter who died or how. Boen figured Bahr would feel better talking right now. He'd been jittery since leaving the others at the tavern. Boen was indifferent. He supposed he might feel differently if his blood was involved. Having no family came in handy from time to time.

"Most of them were loaded into wagons in nice little bags. The villagers slaughtered the soldiers," Bahr said.

"Huh," Boen commented. "Badron should have hired a few Gaimosians. That way the job would have been done right."

"He did want the village left intact."

"Villages can be rebuilt," Boen told him with a shrug. "There is something familiar about this place though. I cannot place it."

Bahr glanced over to his friend. "How do you mean?"

"It is the people. Almost as if I have dealt with them before. I wonder if this is where Harnin recruited his killers."

"You'd have to ask Ionascu about that."

Boen frowned. "I'd just as soon tie a boulder around his neck and toss him to the bottom of a deep river. The man is a poison. We should not have brought him."

"That's a bit harsh."

"He is a liability, Bahr. I did not trust him before and I trust him even less now. We should leave him here and be done with this sad chapter."

Bahr wasn't sure why, but he felt Ionascu's part had not yet been played. "He's not an overly bad man. Ionascu just might be of some use yet."

"He doesn't have to be a bad man," Boen argued. "He's broken, twisted. He is going to get some of us killed."

"He was forced to watch all of his men die. Forget about him for now. The people here would rip him apart before dawn if we left him."

Boen's mood darkened but he managed to keep those thoughts to himself. A sudden longing to be alone again sprang to life. The freedom to do as he pleased was consoling and incomparable to anything else. A stiff wind blowing through his hair and no particular place to go was what he needed. That was freedom. His Gaimosian blood called to him, urging him to return to the path. He couldn't, of course. Honor demanded that he stay with Bahr and fulfill his bond.

"Fair enough," he finally replied. "We are going to need good winter clothes. I don't want to go up into the mountains with what we have."

A light snow began to fall as if to emphasis his point. Frost was already forming on the windows and metal surfaces.

"The mountains of death are no place to go this time of year. We must be cautious," Bahr said.

"At least nothing has changed."

Bahr forced a smile. "The trading post should have what we need. I agree that we are going to need heavy blankets and furs for this trip."

The pair entered the run-down trading post fully expecting to be ripped off by the proprietor. They weren't disappointed.

"Why is everyone out here in the stables?" Bahr asked upon their return.

Nothol looked over his shoulder. Most of the others were fast asleep, buried under a pile of horse blankets. He quickly explained what had happened, much to Boen's disappointment. The Gaimosian would have much rather have had some fun in a barroom brawl than the incessant haggling over prices and goods.

"We had a slight misunderstanding," Nothol said. "Did you get what we need from the traders?"

"Not as much as we should have. The place wasn't in too good of shape and we cleaned out what was left." Boen had a disappointed look.

Bahr added, "Let's wake everyone up and get moving. I think it would be wise if we were gone before dawn."

They decided on letting a few stay asleep, Skuld and Ionascu mainly. Bahr lost the protest against Maleela being awakened, and then she defiantly refused to go back to sleep. The others had good sense enough to walk away as she angrily placed her hands on her hips and glowered at her uncle. She won, as if there were any doubt. Bahr backed down and the tiny group got under way.

The Sea Wolf caught Boen smiling and he held up a finger. "Do not say a word."

The Gaimosian ignored the warning and chuckled. "It looks like you have finally met your match, old man."

"Like you could do better," Bahr scolded before breaking into laughter. "She's going to be a spitfire for that Aurec once all of this is finished."

"Better him than me. I prefer my women far away."

Bahr eyed him curiously. "That doesn't speak well for a normal home life."

"In case you haven't noticed, there is not too much of a home for any Gaimosian. We are independent that way."

They rode on, slowly so as not to draw too much attention. The hour was well after midnight and even the hardiest of them was exhausted. None noticed the broken shadow dislodge from the side of a run-down building and slip off into the night. The air was crisp, just chill enough to leave a burning sensation in their noses and lungs. Bahr liked nights like this. They made for good sleeping. Good sleeping in a nice, warm bed, not riding around in a hostile village. The cold now only served to bring out his aches and pains. He almost regretted instructing Nothol not to get a room. It didn't matter. Soon enough they were at the trading post.

Bahr glanced back at Anienam, who drove the wagon. "Swing it around the back. Boen and I will go in to ensure our friends still intend to deliver. We will meet you in a few minutes."

Snapping the reins, Anienam did as he was instructed while Bahr and Boen went inside. The trader was sitting in the same position he had been when they'd left. Boen immediately grew suspicious. He began scanning the area, wary of a trap.

"Back so soon eh?" the trader asked.

His eyes shifted quickly to the rear entrance and then back. Boen, almost missing the move, stiffened instantly. His instincts screamed with warning.

Bahr caught the movement out of the corner of his eye but played ignorant. "We did say tonight. Is our order ready?"

"Most of it. My men have it out back and are waiting."

"What do you mean mostly? You assured us it was going to be ready when we returned," Boen growled. "I don't trust men who don't keep their word."

Bahr used the opportunity to ease forward. "What my Gaimosian friend here is trying to say is that we've contracted with you to perform a service and we fully expect you to be accountable."

The trader visibly blanched. "A Vengeance Knight, here?"

The scrape of metal whisking free from the scabbard filled the tense air. Boen offered a wicked grin. "You have heard of us?"

"Y…yes."

Bahr's patience was gone. "Our supplies, now! I am tired of talk and I cannot promise my friend will keep his temper in check much longer."

They followed the trader, a filthy and diminutive man, out the back door and into the middle of a scene they'd only half expected. Close to twenty armed men had surrounded the wagon. Bahr found it odd that one had a freshly ruined face, but then recalled Nothol's tale. It all fell into place. These men had bucked up and been slapped down. Pride demanded they return to finish things. They were ready for a fight this time. Or at least they thought they were.

Marq pointed his sword at them menacingly. "Our fight isn't with you."

Boen flexed. "I say it is. Those are my friends. If you have a problem with them, you have a problem with me."

Several of the thugs grew fidgety. None expected a serious fight when Marq talked them into following the wagon. The monster of a man that entered the area was daunting, much more than they were willing to risk their lives against. Making it worse, he had murder in his eyes.

Marq remained unimpressed. "I said stay out of this, old man. My fight is with this one. He broke my face and I want revenge."

"He may have broken your face, but I'm going to take your life," Boen growled. "It might do wonders for your attitude."

Marq postured himself for attack.

The trader ran between them, hands waving in the air. "Stop this! He is Gaimosian! We'll all die."

The thugs paused.

Bahr lashed out, snatching the trader by the throat. They had been compromised and announcing Boen for what he was sealed their fate. "Friend, that just cost you your life."

He threw the trader from the dock. The man landed in a crumpled heap, whimpering to himself. At least one rib had snapped. Still, he knew better than to get up and flee.

Bahr glared down at him. The Sea Wolf cursed the betrayal. Perhaps if he had been thinking straight they might not be in this situation. Praeg was violence, her people scum. They should never have come here.

"Whatever happens next, you die first," Boen told Marq matter-of-factly.

The thug swallowed hard. He was a big man unused to people challenging him. All his instincts said attack, told him to meet destiny with the measure of his worth. His friends whispered caution, fear. Going head-to-head with a Gaimosian was pure suicide. All it took was a second, a singular moment of indecision and Boen made up their minds for them.

"Go back to the tavern and your drinks," Nothol offered a final warning.

Dorl added, "No one needs to die tonight."

Marq raged. "You do! Look what you did to my face! You both must pay!"

His actions spurred the thugs into action. Swords and truncheons swung with wild enthusiasm. Boen burst into action with unparalleled speed and ferocity. He leapt off the dock, driving his blade down through the trader's spine. The man died with a blood-spattered whimper. The violence of action stunned the thugs. They'd come expecting a relatively easy kill. Boen and Bahr changed those odds. Both older men moved with the grace of experienced killers.

Blood sprayed from arterial wounds. Horses neighed and bucked. The band of thugs never had much of a chance. Rekka and Boen accounted for most of the kills. They worked swiftly and efficiently. Rekka's slender blade ripped through one man's throat as he attempted to flee. Survivors were more dangerous than if they stayed and fought. One of his partners lashed out, catching Rekka in the upper right arm. She let out a strangled grunt and backed away. Hot blood trickled down her sleeve. She snarled, raised her sword in a high guard and attacked. Rekka moved so fluidly that she appeared as a blur. Her blade took him just below the sternum. Pain twisted his features even before his body told him he was dead.

"Come on! Let's get out of here!"

Marq shook off his friend with a violent shove. "You run. I am ending this."

By now most of the thugs were dead or mortally wounded. Only Marq was still on his feet. His anger flowed so hotly he failed to notice his opponents were purposefully ignoring him. He pointed to Nothol. "This is between us. Tell your friends to back away."

Nothol shrugged as nonchalantly as possible. "It's your life."

Marq was beyond caring. His veins burned with venom. It was a small victory that he managed to maintain his poise as long as he had. The rest stepped back and gave the duo room to fight.

"Are you sure you do not want me to step in and take care of this for you?" Dorl demurely asked.

Nothol smiled with a malevolent gleam. "He wasn't much of a problem before. This won't take long."

Marq charged, tired of waiting and being humiliated. It was a fatal mistake. The sell sword stepped back, letting his opponent rush into him. Marq judged wrong and thrust too deep into Nothol's defenses. Nothol blocked the blade down and slashed upward. Steel ripped across Marq's unprotected chest. Dark blood poured out from a ragged line. The bigger man staggered and dropped to a knee. His breath came in sporadic gasps. The steam clouded around him. He looked up with pleading eyes. Nothol Coll obliged him, driving his sword through Marq's heart. The body collapsed in a bloody heap and Nothol bent down to wipe his blade clean.

Maleela threw both hands over her mouth, more to cover the gasp of shock than for the level of violence. Blood and death bothered her little now. The nightmare at Chadra Keep, all those weeks ago, started it. This was practically nothing. She shifted her gaze from the body to Nothol. He was already sheathing his sword. She found it odd that he showed no emotion.

"This isn't over," Bahr warned.

He was right. The thugs might have been beaten, but there was an entire village against eight. It was only a matter of time before more came.

"Load the wagon quickly. Take whatever you think we are going to need."

"That is robbery!" Maleela protested and immediately regretted her comment.

Boen stepped over the dead trader. "I do not think he will mind. The bastard sold us out. He gets what he deserves."

"Hurry up," Bahr hissed. "They'll be back soon and I want to be long gone before they do."

This time there were no protests. The tiny band moved as fast as they could, denying their foes the use of necessary equipment should they decide to follow Bahr. Soon the village of Praeg lay behind them.

FOURTEEN

Deliberations

The wagon rumbled on into the dying night. Bahr pushed them as hard as he thought they could take. It was only a matter of time before they were ridden down, either by the villagers of Praeg or by Harnin's men. Dawn wasn't far off and that meant they would be easy targets for anyone close enough to see them. Bahr trusted that the horses could take it. The adventure was still young enough that both men and beast were relatively fresh.

Most of those aboard the wagon stayed silent. No one was rightly sure what to say after the brief battle at the trading post. Violence was no stranger for the warriors flanking the wagon on horseback and that was of small some comfort. The princess, the thief, and the wizard were not warriors and needed the others if they were going to successfully find the blood hammer and save Delranan. Maleela watched Dorl and Nothol the most, curious about their relationship and their inability to emotionally involve themselves in the art of killing.

"You know you got lucky back there," Dorl chided.

Nothol shot him an exasperated glare. "I don't believe in luck. You of all people should know that."

"It doesn't really matter what you choose to believe. You got lucky," Dorl countered.

"That man never had a chance, not from the moment he tried to take the princess."

Dorl shrugged. "He could have had you if he had taken his time."

Nothol rolled his eyes but continued the argument for the sake of passing time and killing boredom. "All right, tell me, wise one, when exactly was his chance?"

A rueful smile. "When they first attacked. He shouldn't have talked so much."

"Oh please! You don't know what you're talking about."

"Nothol, we were outnumbered and taken completely by surprise. They could have easily filled us with arrows."

"Sometimes I wonder if you have lost your mind," Nothol replied. "Besides, that would have been cheating."

"There is no cheating in battle. You fight to win, nothing more," Boen rumbled from behind them.

"I don't understand how men can so casually talk about killing," Maleela said after they had fallen silent.

Anienam smiled endearingly. "They talk about what they know. Sometimes those of us who do not partake in that lifestyle fail to properly understand the impact."

She wasn't convinced. The answer was too easy. "Did you see how fast Nothol killed that man? It is not natural. No man should be that comfortable taking life."

"Such things are not for us to decide. We alone cannot change the face of the world. We must look beyond the fragile borders of our morality and see the world for what it is."

"Anienam, that does not make sense. How will Malweir ever change when the cycle of violence keeps perpetuating itself?" she demanded.

"Life on this planet has existed for thousands of years. Some might argue longer," he replied. "There are times of peace and times of struggle. You were born into a world at struggle."

She shook her head, almost angrily. "That means nothing. How many civilizations have been destroyed because people would not stand up and do what is right? I refuse to believe we are inherently violent despite this seemingly endless cycle of self-destruction we are bent on. Shouldn't we strive to better ourselves?"

She was right. Next to Goblins and Dwarves, man was the most violent race on the planet. Greed was often the spark. It was the drive to constantly want more that fueled the fires of aggression and kept the world mired in one war or another. Not even Anienam could fathom why though. He'd spent centuries roaming the world on a never-ending quest to do good and vanquish the agents of the dark gods. That quest finally brought him here, to the frozen northern kingdoms and what he believed was going to be the last war.

"What you say is undeniably true," he admitted. "I am most impressed by your reasoning, but that does not mean we do not have redeeming qualities."

"Such as?"

He sighed. Even a wizard had a limit to patience. "Unquestionable loyalty is a good place to begin." He gestured to the sell swords. "Take them. What keeps them together? One wishes for a normal life filled with a wife and children. The other is undecided and content. They remain by each other's side out of loyalty. Do not think for a moment that they take pride in any of the killing they do. Violence does not make the measure of a man, Maleela. I have walked Malweir for centuries and have done just as much bad as good, and all from good intentions."

"Yet by your own admission good and evil are subjective."

"Good and evil are indefinable. We are all given the opportunity to choose which paths to follow. That is the greatest gift from the gods."

She fell silent. The old man had given her much to consider. She'd never placed much emphasis on such things until now. All she knew was that life was hard and her father hated her for what she had done. It was a pain she had never gotten over and now she doubted she would ever get the chance. Maleela was almost certain that one of them, perhaps both, was going to die before this quest was finished.

Skuld moaned softly and rolled over. Dawn was breaking over the distant Murdes Mountains in shades of crimson and violet.

Bahr finally called a halt not long after. He judged they'd ridden far enough out and could afford to rest.

"Rein in the wagon," Boen called out when he caught Bahr's nod. "We take one hour."

Nothol and Dorl knew their jobs and didn't hesitate to wheel their horses about and ride back the way they'd just came.

"Are they leaving us?" Skuld asked groggily.

Boen smiled at his innocence. "No, boy. We wouldn't be so lucky. They're going back to sweep the area and ensure we are not being tracked."

"But why? There is no one following us," Skuld said. He felt like everything happening was beyond his scope of understanding. He was a common street thief thrown into a world more dangerous and predatory than his imagination was capable of grasping. It was enough to keep him restless.

Boen offered a warm smile. He liked Skuld, but the boy was no Gaimosian. One of the biggest issues Boen had in dealing with others was that he often forgot they did not come from the same bloodlines as he did. Gaimosians were proud, natural-born warriors. That eventually led to their downfall, but it was the stuff of legends. Boen took things for granted that were difficult or daunting to most others. He didn't consider it a shortcoming, but it was enough to slow him.

"Just because we killed a handful of brigands does not mean the others will sit back and accept our success," he explained. "Revenge is a powerful thing. The ones who live will want revenge for their friends."

"How can you be so sure?"

"They will come. It is natural. Men are predictable beasts, Skuld. Think no more on this. Battle will find us in its own good time. Go and stretch your body. Endless hours of riding, even on a wagon, have a way of twisting your back. Perhaps I will teach you how to use a blade properly."

Skuld beamed. He enjoyed talking to Boen. The man was like the father he'd never known. He felt part of something, a new and mysterious feeling. It was the simple prospect of learning how to use a sword that bolstered his confidence.

"Go on," Boen shooed him off.

"The boy has potential," Bahr commented once Skuld was out of earshot.

Boen shook his head ruefully. "He should not be here. This quest goes beyond the limits of his strengths."

"The same could be said for all of us. I'm not looking forward to crossing these mountains in winter."

Boen glanced at the sky. The grey was oddly soothing, reminding him of the trials in his life. He breathed deeply. Moisture dampened the air. "The snows are not far off. Our biggest concern is the wagon. I do not think it will hold up if we run into a bad storm."

"Hopefully the passes will stay open long enough for us to find this forge and get back."

"Assuming the Giants have the hammer. This might be the beginning of a long journey."

The Sea Wolf frowned. The first few snowflakes splashed on his dark green riding cloak and dissolved. Another winter, he thought. Bahr hated winter.

"How did we get entangled in this?" Boen surprised his friend. "Gods and Giants. I never would have believed such things a season ago. There has got to be an easier life than this, Bahr."

"I am sure there is but you and I both know that neither of us would know what to do with it. Like it or not, this is our life. It is all we are." He forced a shiver. "Dorl and Nothol should be back soon."

Boen snorted, his breath shooting a plume of mist into the air. "With the enemy close behind no doubt."

"Ha! Like you would have it any other way." He clapped Boen's shoulder playfully.

They walked back to the wagon to snatch a quick meal of dried venison and dark bread. Bahr dug into a sack and produced a quarter wheel of yellow cheese and cut two large chunks, one for each of them.

"This is horrible," Boen grimaced between mouthfuls.

"No one said you had to eat it."

"I will take it if you do not want it," Anienam offered cheerfully. He rounded the wagon with a smile almost as large as his stomach.

Boen stayed him with a hand. "Hold yourself, wizard. I'm a bigger man with a bigger appetite, despite the quality of the food."

Anienam waved him off. "Oh bother. Eat your own food, Gaimosian. Just remember to slide any uneaten tidbits my way."

They laughed. Humor was the one thing men needed on a campaign if they expected to maintain some measure of sanity. Dark hours lessened with the wonders of humor, even if most people did not quite understand the quirks in it. Only Ionascu remained silent. His narrow eyes never stopped watching them with a growing cloud of disdain. These were not his people. He desired to be back in Chadra, enjoying the spoils of his efforts.

Boen pulled the stopper from a flagon of ale they'd confiscated in Praeg and drank deeply. "Tell us, wizard, what is so damned important about this hammer? How can we be sure it even exists? It has been my experience that such tokens are naught but legend and myth."

Anienam took the offered ale to wash down the last of his bread. "The Blud Hamr exists, I assure you. It is the one thing capable of destroying the curse of the dark gods. Or so I recall reading."

"Is this from that book you risked our lives for in Chadra?" Maleela asked. She drew her knees up and wrapped her lithe arms around them.

"That and the royal libraries down in Averon."

Rekka Jel busied herself by sharpening her sword. She occasionally looked up when a certain word or phrase caught her interest. Rekka was a pragmatic woman. Her people did not bother with what if or why. They focused on the now and the events they could control. Life was too precious to be spent worrying about potential futures. The jungles of Brodein were harsh, unpredictable. Death was just as easy to find as life.

"I have a hard time with placing my life in the hands of some mythical weapon," Boen stated aggressively.

"Phaelor is real enough. That is the sword young Fennic used to kill the Silver Mage in Gren. Sometimes all we need is faith, Boen."

"Easy for you to say. I have never seen this sword or heard of the hammer. I need more to go on than whims and dreams. When was the last time anyone saw it?"

Anienam paused, if but slightly. "Phaelor was last used by the Elves close to one hundred years ago."

"And the hammer?" Boen was growing impatient. The old man was stalling.

"The hammer has not been seen since the time the book was written."

Bahr did not like the sound of that. "Which was when?"

"Longer than any of us can recall. My guess would be hundreds of years at minimum. The Mage War has been over for a long time."

The ensuing silence was almost frightening. Their quest suddenly become a lot less clear. Uncertainty and doubt gnawed at their reasoning. Hundreds of years. Not even the fabled long lives of the Elves were enough to remember those days.

Bahr attempted to wipe the stress from his face. He supposed they were fortunate the sell swords weren't back yet. Dorl would have exploded. They still will, he surmised. Things had gone from bad to worse.

Anienam felt the balance shifting away. "We have no reason to believe that it does not exist or that it is not being well cared for."

"In Venheim?" Maleela asked.

"Possibly, but who can say for sure? The Giants keep their secrets closely guarded. I still have much to read. The authors do not jump to conclusions. Keep hope in your hearts," he told them with as much confidence he could muster.

"We're doomed," Ionascu chuckled eerily from his perch.

FIFTEEN

A Rebellion Born

"How? That is all I want to know. How can one old man and a cripple escape from this dungeon so easily?" Harnin fumed at his captains.

Silence was the reply. Technically Harnin had no authority over the others. They were all captains of Delranan, but since Harnin had fallen under the subversive influence of the Dae'shan, he had risen above them and secured power. He had become a far greater tyrant than Badron ever dreamed of. Harnin wanted power, raw and unadulterated. A thousand deaths were not enough to slake his thirst. He was a man in need of death.

"We believe they had assistance from inside the keep," Jarrik answered. He had been one of Badron's staunchest supporters and was easily converted by Harnin.

Harnin's gaze hardened. "Thank you for stating the obvious. I want the guard purged. Find out who the traitor is and have him executed."

"There is little doubt who it is, Harnin."

"Who?"

Jarrik cleared his throat. "There is but one of us who is not here. Lord Argis must be the traitor. How else can he explain his rash of absences?"

The weight was removed and had served a dual purpose. Jarrik was glad to finally get Argis's name in the open. He also saw a sliver of space for advancement and the possible replacement of Harnin. Jarrik quietly plotted, patiently awaiting the day when Delranan would be his.

"Badron should have taken him on campaign. He would be more fortunate to find a Rogscroft arrow in his heart than with what I have in mind," Harnin cursed. "Ulfdane, step forward. I have a task for you."

A young blond man slipped between the others. He had the sharp look of a wolf on the hunt. Huge muscles bunched beneath his leather jerkin. His arms were thickly corded and veined. He was every bit the symbolic champion Harnin needed.

"My lord," his deep voice rumbled.

"Find me Argis. I want his head."

Jarrik spoke up. "Why should he remain here in Chadra? Argis has to know that we will have guessed his involvement by now. He surely would have left with Bahr."

"No. He is still here. There is more for him than the blind devotion to the king's daughter. Argis is in Delranan."

Heimdol rubbed his chins. "If what you say is true, perhaps he has a hand in this rumored rebellion."

Harnin grimaced at the fat redhead. Rebellion. He hadn't thought much of those rumors until now. Nothing had happened publicly and no public credence was being given to the rumors of some underground movement. People complained about raised tariffs and the amount of supplies being diverted to the army, but that was their right and it was common enough. No ruler had ever had the full support of the population.

"Who witnessed the escape?"

"The sergeant of the guard appears to be the only one," Jarrik replied.

Harnin hissed. "And he is dead. There must be another."

"All of the guards have been questioned."

"Then we interrogate them harder." Harnin's voice turned bitter. He contemplated setting the Dae'shan on his own people. The only thing that mattered was finding Argis and crushing the building rebellion. It was the only way he could see to solidify his power.

Heimdol protested. "You ask too much. We cannot begin a war against our own people based on rumors. What will Badron do when he learns of this?"

"The king is not here! I rule in his name and stead. Mind your own affairs before I suspect you of treason as well," Harnin spat.

Heimdol begrudgingly backed down. His cheeks burned crimson.

Harnin turned back to Ulfdane. "Go. Find the traitor and bring us any rumors of this rebellion."

Ulfdane nodded sharply and left, glad to be away from the plotting and backstabbing of the king's court. His passions lay in the hunt, making his task perfect for his talents. Ulfdane marched through the wooden halls of Chadra Keep with thoughts of murder on his mind.

Harnin hid an evil grin as the youth disappeared. "I want agents in the city and port. We must stop this rebellion before it gets out of control."

"Let us hope Ulfdane finds Lord Argis and puts an end to this nonsense," Heimdol added, eager to be back in Harnin's good graces.

"The rebellion might prove more dangerous than we think," Jarrik cautioned. "If Argis is involved, he might be successful in bringing the population to a full-blown revolt. He has been a favorite among the masses."

"I will not hesitate to burn this city to the ground," Harnin affirmed. "Leave me. I have much to think on."

"Matters have changed drastically," Argis said dourly.

Murmurs circled around the underground leaders. Many watched the fires in the harbor and the orange glow of Bahr's former estate burning to the ground. There were increased street patrols. Tension threatened to choke the city. Reports poured in of a rising tide of violence against the people. Chadra was becoming a dangerous place.

"We have every reason to believe that you had a hand in bringing all of this to bear," said Joefke, a young man with hard eyes the color of flint.

The assembly broke into a dozen voices.

"Wasn't his fault."

"…risked his life for us."

"Doesn't matter. He's one of Badron's men!"

Argis could not remain silent. The time he'd spent with Bahr and the others had shown him the level of strength necessary to combat Harnin. He doubted these men and women had enough strength. Argis raised his hands and bellowed, "Silence!"

One by one they fell quiet. Satisfied, Argis turned on the speaker. "Joefke, I have pledged what remains of my life to ending the horror Delranan is becoming. What more would you ask?"

Joefke refused to back down. The fire in veins was contagious, though misguided. "You could have stood up to the One Eye. All of this might have been averted."

"We can argue what if until the dawn and it will get us nowhere. Bahr and his companions had to leave the kingdom immediately. I was the only one in a position to help them escape."

A raven-haired woman with a forceful face countered, "Captain Bahr should have stayed. He has been a hero of the people for many years."

"You all saw the fires. Harnin was already moving on Bahr. He'd be back in the dungeons or worse if he had stayed. What happened did so for a reason. I can make no accurate excuses or assumptions."

"What then does the mighty lord of Delranan suggest?" Joefke seethed.

Argis was unaffected by his youthful temper. "Harnin will move quickly. He knows that I am involved and will be relentless in his hunt. We need weapons and the able bodies to use them."

"None of the guards have deserted," an old cooper said.

Argis found that disheartening but not entirely unexpected. "What about weapons? How many do we have?"

Joefke shrugged. "A few swords and some farmer's tools. We have plenty of people to fight most lack weapons."

"We go get the weapons then," Argis proclaimed.

The woman asked, "From where?"

Argis smiled. "There is a small arms room down by the docks in Stouds. Give me twenty men and a cart and we will have weapons before dawn."

A collective gasp circled them. Even Joefke paused. For all his talk he hadn't expected much of anything to happen so quickly. The leaders of the underground made a quick vote, faster than they anticipated. Truthfully there wasn't much of a choice. The only chance they had for survival was to move now while Harnin wasn't prepared to stop them. Joefke volunteered to lead them, at Argis's side. Argis nodded approvingly and took his band out into Chadra. Too much had changed too soon, leaving the former lord with an uneasy feeling that refused to go away.

Argis stepped over the dead guard. A sliver of blood ran down the edge of his sword. It felt good to swing his blade against nature powers again. He looked down into the man's unseeing eyes and shrugged off the silent accusations. The bustle of activity behind demanded attention, forcing Argis away from the dead.

Men had formed a chain and were emptying the arms room quickly. Time was already short. It would not be long before a patrol came by. Argis decided to abandon caution. Secrecy wasted time and put them all in jeopardy. Men unceremoniously dumped swords, daggers, and quivers full of arrows into the small wagon bed. Most of the men did not know how to properly handle such weapons and those who did were on a small perimeter Argis had established for security. Argis, his sword drawn, made the rounds from point to point. The harbor master surely had sounded the alarm already. The underground would prove no match for the trained and disciplined city guard.

Argis rounded a building corner and found Joefke. The younger man was in mild shock. Blood stained his hands and dull yellow beard. He looked up at the taller Argis unbelievingly and then down at the body of a solitary guard at his feet.

"You did well," Argis told him.

Joefke held up his hands. "Did I?"

He nodded. "That is how it is done, boy. Take no pleasure from killing. I do not believe it is a natural act, but do not dwell on it much either. It was his life or yours. Put it behind you. We have to leave before reinforcements arrive."

Argis all but dragged the youth back into the action where they helped load the last of the weapons. Satisfied, he collapsed the perimeter and the band of rebels stole off into the night as the sound of hobnailed boots echoed across the pier.

SIXTEEN

Final Days

"I don't think we have anything capable of stopping them," Aurec told his father.

He was upset that his father forbade him from returning to the front lines. The danger was acceptable considering the situation, so far as Aurec was concerned. Enemy pickets were less than a kilometer away. Aurec quietly thought his father acted too conservatively.

Stelskor stared at his overzealous son. He wanted to say how proud he was, but this was not the place. All of the senior commanders were present and he wasn't about to embarrass the boy.

"The Wolfsreik is almost upon us. You have done more than our people could expect from you, Aurec. All of you have. Your actions have given us the opportunity to evacuate our people from this city. A tunnel is nearly complete that should aenable most of our defenders to escape once we deem the city is lost. Badron will pay dearly for his aggressions. My question to you, my advisors, is what do you need from me?"

Aurec glanced at the commanders. This was their campaign as much as it had been his. Their needs must come before his. Venten spoke first.

"Sire, I believe I can speak for us all when I say that we do not need anything. The defense of Rogscroft has been our first priority from the start of the war. Aurec's campaign was designed to buy us time and he has done so. We are ready to meet the Wolfsreik."

"Thank you, Venten. Keep up your performance and I might draft you back into service for me," Stelskor smiled. "We must keep in mind that each day we delay the enemy costs them in supplies and manpower. I hear that the Pell Darga are fulfilling their promise to you."

"Yes, Father. Cuul Ol and his people have been attacking the supply caravans coming through the mountains.

This has forced Badron to double the resources needed to ensure they get through. Even so, the Wolfsreik is almost at full strength now. They will be ready shortly to make their advance on us."

The king nodded glumly. "How long can we expect to hold?"

"Not long. We are down to almost half strength. Their casualties are more than twice ours, but their numbers promise our defeat."

"I am not willing to throw away our strength so willingly. We continue with the original plan," the king told them. "What remains of the outer defenses?"

Venten pointed at the map. "We have ambushes set up here in Edgeson Vale and another in the Martis Forest."

"How can you be so sure the enemy will go into the forests? It is almost two kilometers from the main road."

Aurec answered. "We have a handful of volunteers willing to draw them in."

The king frowned. He didn't condone suicidal gestures, even if it was for the good of the kingdom. Every life was precious. Worse, the sacrifice of one man was a waste and took from the overall defense. "This is foolish. You'll only waste valuable lives. Our enemy is not so foolish as to follow a handful of random men into an obvious ambush. Their heavy horse will be able to ride those men down at will long before they gain the safety of the trees."

"Sire, we have the road mined with caltrops. There is a heavy stream to the immediate west and a small swamp to the east. The enemy will have no choice but to take the secondary road into the forest," Venten added.

Stelskor studied the map. He soaked in the terrain features he'd spent a childhood exploring. The memories were saddening. All that he knew and loved threatened to be wiped from the world. The long days of his life were nothing compared to impending demise. His kingdom was going to burn and he was powerless to prevent it.

"Perhaps it will work," he said slowly.

"It is the only clear chance we have. All of our primary fortifications have been overrun," Aurec said. "The enemy has paid dearly for each one."

Stelskor clasped his son's shoulder. "You have brought great honor to your name, my son. Gentlemen, I am spending the night here. I wish to see firsthand how the battle goes in the morning."

Aurec bit back the feeling that it was an unnecessary risk. Nightly skirmishes were often chaotic and violent. He failed to see the need for both king and prince to be on the front simultaneously. That time was fast approaching and it would be on the walls of Rogscroft. Not here in the wild.

Wisely, Aurec held his tongue. "My quarters are yours, Father."

"Thank you."

A young scout poked his head into the command tent. Raste, if the king recalled correctly.

"A small enemy force is approaching from the rocks to the west of our lines," he said after a nod from Venten.

Aurec's eyes lit up. "How many?"

"Just over a score."

"That is no attack force," Venten cautioned.

"Possibly engineers?" Aurec suggested.

Stelskor added, "Or a reconnaissance for a coming assault."

"Either way we need to stop them. Assemble the men. I will be there shortly."

Raste nodded and offered a slim smile.

The sounds of fully armed men rushing by drowned out the murmurs from the field commanders. Another night with another battle. Aurec was tired, bordering on sheer exhaustion. All of them were. They'd been going nonstop for nearly a month and there was no end in sight. He got less than four hours of sleep a night and hadn't eaten half as much as he should. Rations were running low and there wasn't much game left in the valley. Water was the only thing they did not lack.

Stelskor gave his son a curious look. The boy had a hollow look, his skin greyish and tight. His eyes seemed darker from the perpetual bags beneath them. "You mean to lead the attack?"

"I am more comfortable that way." Aurec slid his now well-dented armor on and then his greaves.

"Armor at night is not good for ambushes."

Aurec smiled. "Delranan iron is hard, Father. We learned that early on. I will back as soon as this is finished."

King watched prince leave. A large part of him left as well. Stelskor longed to be young again, to have a sword in hand and to meet the enemy in an honorable contest. Only there was no honor in this war. All that left was survival. Losing meant death.

"Luck in battle, my son," he whispered after Aurec.

Mahn slowly pulled an arrow from his quiver and nocked it. He slowed his breathing, exhaling in long, drawn breaths. The first enemy soldier eased into his line of sight. At first he was naught but shadow, a figment in the tired scout's imagination. Then came the smell. Mahn scrunched his nose at the odor the man gave off. It was the smell of a soldier who had not been able to bathe after weeks of light fighting.

Three more emerged in line behind him. Mahn smiled. Provided he did not miss, this was almost too easy. He took aim and waited for the natural pause between breaths. Mahn drew a bead on the center of the first man's chest. He blinked and let go. The arrow sped true and struck his target. A strangled gasp rang out as he fell. Mahn already had another arrow in hand before the soldier hit the ground.

"Where did that come from?"

Confusion gripped the Delrananians. One knelt to check their point man.

"He's dead."

"Who shot him?"

Mahn fired again. The second arrow achieved the same results, only this time giving away his position.

"Over there! Archers in the trees!"

Mahn clutched his bow and ran. The enemy advanced recklessly, hungry for revenge on the man who killed their comrades. Mahn might have been impressed if it weren't for being so fearful for his life.

"Take him alive! I want answers."

Mahn snapped at himself. He fought the urge to stop and fire on the sergeant in command. That would certainly alleviate some of the command functions. Cut the head from the beast and watch it die. He couldn't risk it. The enemy was much too close to take the chance. The old scout really didn't feel like dying or being captured tonight. Still, he admired their brazenness. Most soldiers would not rush a bank of unknown archers in the middle of the night when two of their own had already fallen.

"Hurry, don't lose him!"

Dread pounded in his heart. Every footstep was the sound of thunder. The enemy was getting closer. Mahn pushed himself harder. Thoughts of the prince and his force disappeared in the name of self-preservation. Decades of soldiering had honed his muscles, trimming away the unnecessary fat, but he was running out of breath. The Wolfsreik might easily catch him well before he reached the safety of his mount.

A sudden blast of air brushed past his face, followed closely by the telltale zip of an arrow being shot. A cry came from behind. Mahn looked up and smiled. Raste was there, sitting on his horse and drawing aim.

"What took you so long?" Raste asked after firing another shot.

Mahn pushed through his heaving chest. "Damnation. That was too close. You could have hit me, boy."

The younger Raste took insult at the comment. "Did you get a good look at them?"

Mahn climbed into the saddle before answering. "They're not scouts or engineers."

"Assassins."

He nodded. "A Wolfsreik termination team."

Raste struggled to fight the surge of rising panic. "We must warn the prince."

The sounds of battle suddenly erupted from the night.

"Too late for that," Mahn murmured.

Aurec and his men had engaged the enemy. The ambush quickly turned into a melee. Bodies slammed into one another. Blades hacked and slashed. The men of the Wolfsreik were more than a match for anything Aurec had to throw at them. Outnumbered and overpowered, the Wolfsreik fought like men possessed. Men fell amidst their screams. Slowly, ever so slowly, Badron's assassins began to gain the advantage. Raste watched apprehensively, sword drawn.

"We're not made to battle assassins," Mahn cautioned.

Raste pointed angrily at the battle. "Neither are Aurec's men. We need to help before the prince is killed."

He was right. Mahn held extreme doubts about rushing into a pack of men intent on killing. They might easily be killed by their own men. Both scouts were competent enough swordsmen, but they were unarmored and ill-prepared to fight some of the Wolfsreik's best at night.

"Mahn, you can sit here and debate your morals, but I will not sit by and watch my prince get killed. Sit here and figure out how to tell the king his son is dead."

Raste charged into the fight, leaving the older Mahn cursing and hurrying to catch up. Their horses spooked in sudden fear of the fight, for they were not trained war horses. Raste tightened his thighs and used the horse as much as his wildly slashing blade. His sword ripped down an exposed back. A spray of hot blood accompanied the savage screams as the assassin fell in a twitching heap. Rough hands reached up to drag Raste down. Mahn was the only thing that saved him. He barreled his horse into the assassins and gave Raste time to break free.

"Kill the horses!" bellowed a sharp voice.

Mahn recognized it as the same one who had led the hunt against him through the forest. Mahn tried to pierce the scene and find the sergeant. Nothing could demoralize a unit like the loss of its leadership. His efforts were cut short. Lashing out, he took a hand at the wrist. His horse bucked up and thrashed wildly. Hooves struck multiple men, including one of his, and broke bones.

His horse screamed in sheer horror. An enemy blade plunged deep into its throat. Blood poured from the wound, painting the white hair crimson. Mahn was thrown to the ground. He managed to kick away before the horse's weight crushed him. More hands tore at him. Mahn struggled and fought but it was of no use. Blow after blow hammered into him. He bit back a cry when the loud snap accompanied his nose breaking.

"Leave him! I want that bastard."

Alone, Mahn forced himself to get up. His body ached from the beating and he was fairly certain his nose and at least one rib were broken. He couldn't see his opponent but the voice was enough.

"You killed two of my men," the sergeant growled.

Mahn spit a mouthful of blood. "A shame I didn't get you."

The first blow caught him in the jaw and nearly succeeded in knocking him flat. Knives of pain lanced behind his eyes. Mahn swung wildly but missed. The assassin grinned savagely. He smelled weakness and knew it was a matter of moments before the old man took his last breath. He made a feint to the right and kicked Mahn in the right knee. Mahn fell and tried to roll away, but the Wolfsreik dropped down on him and wrapped his massive, calloused hands around his throat. Mahn punched up, driving the slim dagger he'd snatched from his boot into the sergeant's neck.

The body hit the ground with a squishy thud. The battle was over. None of the enemy remained on the field. Mahn just lay there and tried to catch his breath.

Aurec was on his knees, breathing hard and leaning on his sword for support. Dark blood stained his face and hands.

"They are all dead," Venten announced. The older man was in worse shape.

Aurec glanced at his friend. "We should leave before more come. Their entire line will have heard the noise."

Venten immediately started to round up the men. Thirteen were dead, another dozen sustaining major wounds. In all, Aurec's tiny band had been fortunate. They should have been dead to the man. A light snow began to fall, almost as if nature wanted to conceal the horrors of what had just happened. Aurec tilted his head to the sky and breathed deeply. The night air was crisp yet moist. He felt a deep joy and fought to regain his composure. It felt good to be alive.

Instantly refreshed, the prince rose shakily to his feet and went to check on his men. So many bodies being loaded onto horseback sickened him. Each man in his command was a friend. When he came across Mahn, his heart fell. The old man had become a boon companion during the early campaign and he valued Mahn's experience.

"I'm not dead yet," Mahn growled.

Prince Aurec dropped to a knee and laid a gentle hand on his friend. "You look terrible, old man."

"It comes with trying to keep up with you." He tried to laugh, but it hurt too much.

"Can you get up?"

He shook his head slowly. "Just pull me up."

Aurec did. His howl of pain echoed across the boulder-strewn area.

"Another outburst like that and you'll bring the enemy down on us in force," Venten cautioned.

The prince passed a sidelong look. "Be thankful he can still make that sound. Help me get him on a horse."

"That was reckless of you, Aurec." Stelskor's eyes were sad, as if he knew that his son should have been lost this night.

Aurec tossed the remains of his pear down on his simple cot and filled a goblet with water. He'd already wiped the dried blood away and pulled off his boots. Until now he hadn't realized how exhausted he was. Dawn was not far off. Aurec finally collapsed onto his cot and addressed his father.

"It had to be done. I didn't see any way around it, Father."

The king scratched his jaw. "You are a prince of this kingdom. If I die, you will rule our people."

Aurec smiled. "If that is the case you should probably hurry back to Rogscroft. This is a far too dangerous place for a king and we are not sure who those assassins had come to kill."

He was proud of the retort and hoped he finally matched his father in wit.

Even Stelskor chuckled. "You are lucky I am so old, otherwise I would have taken your place out there. The problem with age is you forget what it feels like to hold a sword in your hand. To be alive again. Never get old, my son."

"The other options don't enthuse me much," Aurec said and drank deep before setting the empty goblet down. "We did well tonight."

"What kind of casualties did we sustain?"

Aurec didn't want to answer, but his father was the king and deserved the truth. "Thirteen dead and the same wounded. Father, they sent in an assassin squad. The Black Guard. We got lucky."

"The Black Guard," Stelskor whispered. "Could they have known I am here?"

The thought was disturbing. The implications even more so. Stelskor didn't want to think that there might be traitors in the camp. It was certainly possible. The kingdom was on the verge of collapse. Most any man would be tempted to sell out his people for the promise of security and extended life. He personally doubted Badron and his captains would hold to such promises. A traitor once never stopped being one.

Aurec's response came hard and decisive. "It is a real possibility, father. I think we need to get you out of here before they try again. Badron won't hesitate to launch a full-scale assault if he learns we are both here instead of in the city. It would be too easy for him."

"I agree. Take care of yourself, son. This is one of our darkest hours, but more are coming. Our people will have need of both of us before the end. Use your forces wisely and know when to retreat."

Father and son hugged, if only briefly, and then broke up. Stelskor exited into the night, leaving his son with more questions unanswered.

SEVENTEEN

A New Threat

Dawn was hardly a prickling of light on the eastern horizon. Snow drifted down lazily. Rolnir and Piper soon had their cloaked shoulders spotted with snow. The general of the Wolfsreik shivered against the chill wind. The fierce look in his eye remained unaffected, however. This was to be his finest hour. Weather could not dampen his spirits. His army was so close to breaking the enemy lines.

"It is time to break their backs, Piper," he said. "Once we do that the road to the city will be uncontested."

"The Black Guard failed to kill their king," Piper casually pointed out.

Rolnir grunted. "It is a small matter. Stelskor is only a figurehead. The real power lies with Aurec. We need to defeat him to make war on the city."

Piper Joach nodded. There were times when he enjoyed his job and others when he was glad to not be in charge. He knew Badron would be enraged when he learned of his private killers' failure. The king of Delranan was becoming increasingly violent. Piper almost felt bad leaving Rolnir to suffer that madness, but such was the privilege of rank.

"End this, Piper," Rolnir commanded.

Piper saluted with a brazen smile and marched off.

The thunder of five hundred horses echoed throughout the valley. The lightly armored defenders watched the advancing battalion and readied to hold the line. Thousands of Wolfsreik foot soldiers marched forward in rank after rank. A few hundred meters away the Delrananian catapults opened fire.

Piper dispassionately watched as dozens of rounds exploded in gouts of flaming pitch across the Rogscroft lines. A few more salvos and there won't be any lines, he mused.

Men and trees caught fire. Men ran screaming through the valley.

"Now!" Piper shouted at his adjutant.

A deep bugle note sang over the army. The men raised a great cheer. The battalion of heavy horse broke into a trot, lances lowered.

"Retreat!"

The command was almost drowned out beneath the barrage. Piper watched the enemy line snap, bending slowly until the stress became too much. Enemy soldiers turned and fled for their lives. Piper smiled. Aurec's men were brave, but not foolhardy. Their mission had been to harass, not engage the Wolfsreik in pitched battle. They fled, and rightfully so.

"Have the infantry sweep the tree line for archers. I don't want any surprises waiting for us when the king comes through."

Another horn blast.

Piper mounted his horse, satisfied with what he saw. "I am riding forward to see for myself. Maybe we got lucky and killed the prince."

He didn't believe it for as long as it took to say. Lady Fortune would never be so kind to any man trying to kill another. Soldiers knew this as well but enjoyed the image it gave their commander. Respect rose as he dared to laugh in death's face.

"Inform General Rolnir where I am."

Piper gained the tree line, or rather what remained after the artillery bombardment. Flames climbed the blackened trunks. Acrid smoke reduced his visibility to scant meters. His biggest worry was the fire spreading across the canopy. Forest fires were notorious for flaring up and spreading through the treetops at uncanny speeds. Fortunately, winter had come, leaving the trees barren.

Charred bodies lay in twisted angles across the area. The early snows had melted under the inferno. Piper shook his head. This was madness. War was going to claim what remained of his morality if he didn't fight it. The carnage around him made it easy to imagine all of Rogscroft burning to the ground. The cavalry had already charged past. Their task was to destroy the enemy, not secure territory. Infantry and follow-on forces had the charge of securing what was taken in battle. Piper had given the battalion commander free reign to pursue the enemy to the banks of the Driml River. Aurec would be trapped if Piper's men gained the bridge first.

Piper guided his horse around a burned corpse, doing his best to ignore the stench. Most of his desire for revenge was gone. A hole in his heart grew in its place. His entire focus had been on revenge for so long he had forgotten everything else. Any embarrassment his men had suffered at the beginning of the war had been repaid a hundred times over during the course of the campaign. Piper felt much older than his thirty years. He wanted to go home lest his humanity was stolen.

"Sir, we've found something you need to see," a burly sergeant said. His face was gaunt, eyes sunken.

Piper asked, "When was the last time you got some sleep, sergeant?"

He adjusted the axe resting on his shoulder. "I will be fine, sir."

Piper reached down and clapped him on the other shoulder. If this sergeant was indication, he needed to order an operational pause before the final push. Casualties went up tenfold when men were exhausted. Piper made a note to bring the subject up with Rolnir the next time they met.

"Show me," he told the sergeant.

Sergeant Egliff pointed down into a small ravine. Piper looked and blanched. Over a dozen bodies lay heaped in a bloody mess of broken bones and tangled limbs. All wore the Black Guard uniform, Badron's famed special forces. The ambush was still a closely held secret, but the senior commanders all knew of the defeat. Ambush was one thing, these men had been butchered.

"One of the scouts found them not long ago. It looks like all of the bodies were dumped here before dawn. The poor bastards," Egliff said. Any sorrow he might have felt was washed away with anger.

Piper forced himself to unclench his jaw. "Secure a detail and have them buried. Oh and Egliff, get their names. Their families deserve to know."

"Yes, Sir," Egliff saluted and set about his task.

Piper hated feeling like a heartless bastard, but his position demanded it. There would be time to weep for the dead later. He needed to keep his men focused on the moment. Nothing could be done to bring the dead back.

Crossbow bolts ripped from the nearby tree line. Men and horses fell screaming to their deaths. A second flight followed while they were still disorientated. Piper shouted, too late. Rogscroft was but a day away and the way was becoming increasingly dangerous. This was the third ambush in the last day. Prince Aurec was determined to hold every foot of land. The Wolfsreik would have no easy passage.

"Form ranks! Attack!" Piper bellowed.

A squad of light cavalry, skirmishers, peeled off from the rear of the formation and slashed into the trees. Enemy archers turned and fled before the riders managed to reach them. The squad leader, a wily veteran named Thenn, knew to halt his men before they ran into a secondary assault line. Heavy horse in trees was a recipe for disaster under any circumstance. Three ambushes and he had not managed to kill a single defender.

Piper slammed his helmet down when Thenn and his force returned to the column with dejected looks. The game was getting old. Piper was more than exhausted by the time they occupied an abandoned farmstead just before nightfall. He saw to the men, ordering the horses taken care of first and then made his way to the surgeons to visit the wounded. Satisfied, Piper went in search of Rolnir. He slumped down on a field stool across from the general. It took every ounce of energy not to collapse.

"How many?" Rolnir asked without looking at him.

Piper shifted his gaze from Rolnir to the dancing flames. "Too many. They refuse to meet us in a stand-up fight. They know better. All we get is ambush after ambush. It is growing tiring."

"Aurec is a smart man. He knows Rogscroft does not have the strength or skill to meet us in the field. I think we are going to have to settle in for the long campaign. This type of warfare is going to hound us all the way to the city gates."

Piper spat into the fire, wiping his chin of the thin sliver of spittle. "We should burn them out, force them to retreat and give us the road."

"No," Rolnir replied too quickly for Piper's liking. "King Badron doesn't want any more destruction of the countryside than necessary. We're trying to conquer the kingdom, not destroy it."

"There is a steep price for that command."

Rolnir sighed. He already knew where the conversation was headed. Piper had not been the same since his first stinging defeat in the opening days of the war. His mood was constantly sour, ever dwelling on what should have properly been shoved to the recess of memory. "The men will do what any good soldiers must. Death is a small price to pay for the immortality of our deeds. This isn't the first time we have had to order men to their deaths."

"No, but each death here takes me a little further from myself. I am afraid of what I might become, Rolnir."

"Go and get some food and rest, Piper. We will speak of this later over a warm mug of spiced wine in Rogscroft. The army moves at dawn."

Piper reluctantly rose, not because of lament, but exhaustion.

"Your boys did good today," Rolnir called to his back.

Piper kept walking.

"Perhaps you could explain to me why I am still sitting in a damnable tent in the middle of the Rogscroft wilderness, General?" Badron accused. Venom dripped from his tone.

The king fumed with misdirected rage. He'd never been a brilliant tactician or showed any martial prowess on the battlefield. His father called him mediocre at best when it came to warfare, despite the time spent learning in the royal Averon war college. None of that mattered this night. Badron had no faith in his commanding general.

For his part, Rolnir resisted the urge to strike his king in the mouth. "Sire, the campaign is progressing as scheduled. This is no small task we have set upon. The Wolfsreik is attempting to subjugate an entire kingdom in the middle of winter. This will take time."

Badron's nostrils flared. "Do not make excuses. I left this campaign to you and you are failing miserably. I…"

"What exactly do you want from me?"

The question stung just the way Rolnir intended it to. He may only be a general, but he had no intentions of being berated by a lunatic with a crown. The general of the Wolfsreik had had enough and hoped he knew how far he could get away with pushing Badron.

Badron jerked back into his temporary throne. Silence choked the tent. Everyone waited to see how the king could react. When he spoke, it came in slow, measured tones. "I want you to do your job and capture that city."

"This is what your army is doing. War is not a precise event, Sire. Let me do my job without being constantly hounded for fast results and we will be at the city gates in a matter of days."

The answer almost satisfied Badron. He dismissed Rolnir with a careless wave, his mind already racing ahead to future possibilities. He despised Stelskor and his people but recognized that he needed the army's full support if he was going to depose the old king. Brooding, he failed to notice Rolnir's growing smile as the man exited the tent.

"You play a dangerous game with that one, king."

Amar Kit'han's voice rasped like ice breaking a window.

Badron scowled. "It is my game to play, demon."

"Rolnir is dangerous. Do not trust your general lest he betray you."

The king almost smiled at the irony. "Of course he will. Rolnir is my best general. There will come a time when he makes a bid to remove me. I wouldn't have him if he weren't planning on it."

The Dae'shan shuffled closer in a mass of swirling shadows. Badron still couldn't believe that the creature walked. "It does not sit well. All you have done is about to be undone. Caution is required."

"Caution!" Badron barked. "Why is it that all of my counselors whisper caution? My army is diseased by the word. What I need are more men with the desire to attack."

Amar stepped into the glow of firelight. His black robes absorbed the light, sucking darkness into the tent from places Badron did not wish to know. The tent seemed...lifeless. "You have no allies in the world of men, king. It is time to look elsewhere."

The irritable hiss caused Badron pain. "Your words offer little encouragement."

"Patience, king. Even in the darkest hour of the night came hope be found."

"What are you saying?"

"Events are in motion that cannot be undone. Help is coming to you. Another army marches from the east. They move quickly and will be here by the time you are ready to assault Rogscroft."

Another army? "You just said that I have no friends. Where then is this army coming from?"

Amar Kit'han shifted minutely. "I said no allies in the world of men."

The king of Delranan jerked back in shock for the second time. Suspicion laced his next question as if he were afraid to know the answer. "Where does this army march from?"

An unnatural pause.

"From the Deadlands. An army of Goblins comes to your aid."

"Goblins!" Badron roared. "They are a stain on the face of the world. Each should be killed and burned lest they plague future generations. I will have no part in it."

The Dae'shan was nonplussed. "You let emotion cloud your judgment. The Goblin army is a valuable asset if you choose to use them wisely."

"They are filth, a scourge destined for extermination. What possible use could I have for such creatures?"

The lack of conviction in his voice gave Amar the opening he was waiting for. "Think. Why waste important lives when you can throw away wave after wave of expendable soldiers? Use the Goblins until they break and leave the vaunted Wolfsreik standing strong, ready to occupy as conquering heroes. You will be invincible with this second army under your command."

Badron's shoulders slumped. The fire had been drained from him. His train of thought took him down dark paths that all ended with his eventual victory. The demon had a point, reluctant as he was to admit it. A Goblin army might turn the tide irrevocably in his favor, and they had more than one use. Badron held no compunction towards unleashing the Goblins on Rogscroft. Let them spend their strength. The more dead, the better. Visions of empire entered his darkened mind.

Badron turned his gaze to the nightmare standing before him. No matter how hard or how many times he looked, there was no penetrating the shadows under the hood. The Dae'shan was as much of a mystery now as from the first time his eerie presence drifted into Badron's bedchambers. Secrets within secrets, mused Badron. Curiosity was not strong enough to override caution, so the king let the question lie.

"These beasts might come in handy," Badron spoke with false confidence. "I shall think on it. What you propose is no easy fact to accept. But enough of this. I wish to know of my brother and daughter. What news do you have?"

"Sadly, none. My spies have yet to cross them. Bahr is crafty. He and his group of troublemakers know how to hide, but it will not last. Sooner or later they will make a mistake and we shall have them. Worry not about this, king. They pose no threat to your conquest of Rogscroft."

Badron smiled politely. He held a sinking suspicion that his once beloved family was on the precipice of causing more trouble than Amar Kit'han could possibly predict.

EIGHTEEN

Ambush

Freina knelt beside the wagon tracks and lifted her snout to the frigid air. A slight breeze ruffled her black feathers, making their natural darkness ripple. She traced a clawed finger around a hoof print in the mud. The Hag almost smiled. They had found their prey at last. Freina rose to her full seven-foot height and faced her sisters.

"What is it you have found, sister?" Garelda screeched.

Freina narrowed her sharp eyes. "The humans are less than a day ahead of us and moving slowly."

Brom, the shortest of the three, flexed her wings. The bone necklace jingled with movement. "Which direction do they move?"

"East, towards the mountains."

Garelda's mood darkened. "Do we tell the demon?"

Freina considered the repercussions of each action. Amar Kit'han was powerful, easily capable of destroying the Harpies. They were an ancient evil that few could master. Kit'han's displeasure once bothered her, but no more. The thrill of the hunt was far too alluring to allow any fear to take root. Either path offered grave consequences. They must proceed with caution.

Finally, she answered, "No, we follow first. The demon will want to know where the humans are going."

"But the Murdes Mountains are not safe, even for our kind. Let the demons deal with these creatures themselves," Brom cautioned.

Freina flared angrily. "We follow the humans."

The Harpies leapt into the air. The hunt had begun.

Rekka Jel abruptly stiffened in her saddle. Her senses warned of a latent danger moving closer, as if stalking them. It was a familiar feeling. The sense had developed when she was still a child. Strange beasts often came from the depths of the great jungle in search of an easy meal or just to cause carnage before disappearing back into the thick canopy. This time felt much the same. She knew they were being hunted.

Maleela was the first to notice. "Rekka, what is it?"

The diminutive warrior woman had a faraway glaze. "Something is coming for us."

"More thugs from Praeg?" the princess automatically asked.

"I do not believe so. Those men weren't dangerous, despite their numbers. This is a feeling of something far worse, sinister. We must be cautious until we know what it is."

Maleela suppressed an involuntary shudder. Rekka's warning combined with the looming Mountains of Death churned her stomach. The world she had grown up reading about closed in on her. Invisible walls made her feel small. Too much death and despair danced ever out of reach yet close enough to torment her dreams. She wanted to be back in Aurec's arms. The singular thought of him already being dead because of her father brought tears to her eyes. Her father. The man was a menace to all of Malweir. She struggled inwardly to keep from screaming at the top of her lungs.

Forcing herself to stay focused, Maleela asked, "Have you ever been in the mountains before?"

Rekka shook her head. "No. I followed the river almost all the way north before crossing overland to your kingdom."

"How far away is your land?"

"Almost a full moon cycle provided the weather stays agreeable. The jungles of Brodein are far away."

Maleela suddenly had romantic notions of what the green jungle must be like. "Is it beautiful? I would very much like to see a world where the cold of winter does not kiss the lands."

"The jungles are beautiful and dangerous. It is green and humid. Snow never comes. Even if it did, the canopy of branches and leaves would catch it and keep it high enough for the sun to melt. There are flowers of every color and beasts that are best left unmentioned."

Rekka continued at great length, discussing the wonders and horrors of her jungle home. Maleela was left daydreaming of an alien world for the rest of the day.

Boen took a seat on a small tree stump, humming as he pulled out a sharpening stone. The crisp crackling of the fire provided all the company he needed as he began sharpening his sword. He, like all Gaimosians, was a relatively solitary man, neither needing nor craving the company of others. Some considered this to be a severe social dilemma though he cared less. Boen lived the life his people had been forced to live for all the generations since the fall of Gaimos.

He often wondered how his blood had fallen so low. Gaimos had once been prosperous. It was called the jewel of the west, filled with a proud people who saw war as a profession while the rest of Malweir struggled sluggishly through petty conflicts. It was the combination of that pride and prowess that sparked a mighty coalition of nations to gather and make war on Gaimos's very steps. When the smoke cleared, his people were scattered, his kingdom ash. Gaimos was no more. Those who survived went on to become the world's best mercenaries. Some were also the founders of the order of Mages so long ago. A wild form of magic ran through their veins, allowing their select few to rise above the misery of the world around them and make a positive difference. He snorted. Magic. It was a useless tool that had burned itself out of Malweir. Today the few Gaimosians remaining in their bloodline were known as the Vengeance Knights.

Soft footsteps made him pause and look up. "You should be sleeping."

Skuld eased into the light. "I have too much on my mind. I can't sleep."

Boen grunted and resumed sharpening his sword. "You are much too young to carry so many worries."

"I can't help it. All I ever wanted was a better life than what I had. This isn't it. There has been so much killing that I do not think I can go on."

"Malweir is not the world in the romance stories. It is dangerous."

Skuld looked up expectantly, hopefully. "How do you do it?"

Boen held up his mighty broadsword. The blade was made from lost technologies. The integrity of the steel was far superior to the weapons produced now. He admired the way the melted snow dripped down the length of the blade.

"This blade gives me the strength I need. This blade and the fire in my blood," he answered mystically.

Skuld had no idea what he was talking about. The spell of warrior and combat had broken in Praeg when he saw the true face of battle, though it surely was more of a slaughter than a battle. His thoughts drifted to what little Boen had said of his ancient homeland. He was amazed at the inner strength the Gaimosian constantly displayed. He was quite sure he didn't possess that same kind of strength. He'd only fostered dreams of greatness, not attempted to realize them. Sneaking aboard the *Dragon's Bane* was perhaps the most important and foolhardy thing he had ever done.

He looked into the flickering flames. "How much of that strength is the sword and how much is what you have inside?"

Boen was impressed by the boy's wit. "We are different people and cannot be so compared. You have much ahead of you, young Skuld. I think this life has more in store for you than what you are willing to believe. Do not abandon hope. The past cannot be undone."

"I wish I could be so sure."

"Patience, lad. A flower does not bloom in a single day. You have already learned much of the path, but not enough just yet."

Skuld cocked his head. "The path?"

"Aye. The path is the way of the warrior. It is the unending road that we forever follow. The only way to leave the path is through death's gates where you will be judged by your ancestors. If they deem you worthy, you will be accepted into their mighty company." A twinkle entered his eyes. "I shall be glad when it is my time."

Skuld had raw potential. Boen and the sell swords took turns trying to refine it into a useable tool, but it took years to make a warrior. Any fool could swing a blade. An artist used it properly.

He smiled as the boy yawned. Cold ate away at their strength, making them more tired than usual. "Go and get some rest. The hard part has not even begun yet."

Skuld barely heard him as he stumbled back to his bed roll. Boen ensured the boy tucked himself in before going back to his sword. Neither of them noticed the three birdlike figures drifting in high circles overhead.

Nothol Coll rode hard back to camp shortly before dawn. A worried look strained his face.

Bahr pulled up his breeks. Steam rose from where he had just relieved himself. "What news?"

"We are in for a fight."

Dorl reached up and took the reins. "You always say the nicest things in the morning."

"How many?" Bahr asked.

"Twenty, maybe thirty with scouts."

Bahr winced. It was not what he needed to hear so early. Reservations from their battle in Praeg were returning to haunt him. Worse, they had been gone from that town for more than a week now. Being chased so far was troubling.

"I thought we would have lost them by now," he said and frowned. "How much time do we have?"

Nothol slid from the saddle. "An hour at the most."

The Gaimosian, disturbed awake, drew his sword with a wicked grin. Old fires flared back to life at the prospect of battle. Maleela stared back at him, an incredulous look of fear etched on her face.

"What?" he asked after noticing the others all staring at him.

She said in her most diplomatic voice, "We should be running, not fighting."

"No. That is what they want us to do. If we run they will hunt us down and set upon us like wolves once we exhaust ourselves. We fight now or get slaughtered later."

Dorl ducked to the back of the wagon and returned with a long bow. "Let's be about this if there is no choice. I don't like to feel hunted."

Bahr reluctantly agreed. His old nerves could only stand so much and he was well past the breaking limit. The mountains were still a few days off and, with the wagon and building snow, he knew they would never make it. The choices had all been taken from him.

"Take Dorl and Nothol," he told Boen. "Slow them enough and get back here before dusk."

"What about the rest of us?" Maleela asked.

"There is still a defense to be prepared. Boen is right. This is the only way."

She glowered as the trio quickly saddled and raced off.

The snow fell a little harder once the sun rose. It was heavy and wet, just foul enough to make the day miserable. Heavy flakes landed in Boen's grey hair and instantly melted. He failed to notice. His hawkish eyes focused on the path ahead. An arrow hung loose in his bowstring.

"Shhh," he hissed. "They are coming."

He halted the line and directed them into the thin tree line. The first few riders came into view moments later. Boen snorted. There was no order amongst their enemy. Men moved in a disorganized rabble that suggested no formal military training, or common sense for that matter. The Gaimosian smiled brightly. Advantage was his. He patiently drew back and took aim as the unsuspecting riders came on. Boen slowed his breathing. He let fly when the first rider was fifty paces away.

Boen wasted no time in seeing if the arrow struck his target. He nocked and fired again. A pair of thrums joined him from the right and four enemy riders toppled from their saddles. There was a natural pause as horses bucked and men tried to figure out what just happened. Boen fired again. A high-pitched cry told him his aim was true.

"Over there! Get him!"

The Gaimosian pushed his mount hard, not waiting for the sell swords to fire one last salvo and follow. The ambush worked better than expected. It was a simple "L" shape, a tactic used by most civilized armies and perfected by Gaimos. The success of it against a score and a half of peasants heartened him. More than ten men were dead before the three defenders disengaged and scampered off into the light forest. The first raid proved more successful than Boen had hoped. He led them towards the second ambush position.

Boen dumped cold water on his head. Blood and water ran down his armored shirt. His breathing was erratic. The muscles in his arms and back spasmed uncontrollably. The big man reluctantly admitted that he was finally growing too old to swing his sword with much regularity. He even felt old. Damn. But at least he wasn't dead. Five corpses lay steaming in the snow, growing pools of blood cooling in the early winter chill. A quick glance showed him that Nothol and Dorl were in the same position.

"That was too close. Is anyone injured?" Boen asked.

Dorl cursed and spat. "One of the bastards got my thigh."

Bright red blood oozed from the top of the muscle. Nothol pulled out a field bandage from his pack and began treating the wound.

"Relax, it's just a scratch," he chided as Dorl jerked at his touch.

Dorl narrowed his eyes menacingly. "Easy for you to say."

"I've seen you cry more from a tavern whore's bite. Keep quiet while I dress this. I'd hate to tie it too tight," Nothol laughed.

It was an easy sound, one that lightened the mood.

"If you two are done flirting, we should leave now," Boen grumbled.

Dorl looked over the battlefield. More than a dozen bodies lay at broken angles in a wide circle. Arrows littered the tree trunks and the ground. A broken spear shaft dug into the ground less than a foot from where he stood. Dorl shook his head ruefully; seemingly amused any of the three were still alive.

The enemy had come into them with a thunder of hooves and violent intent. Earlier losses spurred them on and fueled their hatred. Vengeance stained their eyes as they collided with Boen and his fellows. The battle was hard-fought and furious. It lasted just a handful of minutes. The survivors not only broke contact, they fled. All the fight had been drained. Twenty-two of the thirty brigands lay slaughtered across a little more than a league.

"Do you suppose that is the last we'll see of them?" Dorl asked. He was still in mild shock from what they had done. He, Nothol, and Boen butchered their enemies without remorse. And for what? All for the revenge of one man, a man who happened to be one of the first ones killed before anyone had left Praeg.

Boen shrugged. "It is hard to tell. We bloodied their noses well enough to make most men quit. They might have given up or they could be on their way back with every man they can possibly find. Either way we should get back to Bahr."

"We should fleece the dead. Take what we need and leave the rest," Nothol suggested.

"Agreed."

The rest of the day passed uneventfully. Boen led them unerringly back along the trail the wagon had taken earlier. No one bothered to speak of events that had passed. Battles were only a small part of a greater saga being sung. Each felt they were being pushed into a direction beyond their control. Boen saw no problem, though he did constantly look back over his shoulder. They entered the camp less than an hour later.

"It didn't take long for them to lose heart," Boen said between bites of roasted meat from a pheasant Dorl had managed to kill along the way back. The meat was juicy and, more importantly, it was hot.

Boen's explanation was enough for Bahr. He'd been through enough scrapes to know when not to ask questions. Both sell swords bore haunted looks. Whatever had happened, it was violent and messy.

"None of their actions make sense to me," Anienam interjected.

"Plenty of things on this trip haven't made sense," Boen countered.

The wizard waved him off. "Think about it. Why were these villagers, who have already seen your battle prowess, so eager to throw away their lives? There must be more driving them on than simple revenge."

"Possibly, but what?" Bahr asked.

"If I knew that the hairs on my neck would stand on end."

They finished eating in silence and broke camp. The mountains beckoned.

NINETEEN

Winter's Kiss

The first true storm of the year was heavy and hit during the night. Horse and rider were battered mercilessly as sheets of snow and ice drove into them. Bahr pushed the group harder. They'd been caught in the open and couldn't afford to stop. Shelter was elusive and the storm worsened with time. He cursed. A sailor should have been able to read the weather better, but battle and fatigue distracted him. Hours into the worsening storm, Bahr decided to take a risk and send Dorl and Nothol ahead to scout the land. They had to find some sort of shelter or the whole group would freeze before dawn.

Anienam aided him some. The wizard cast an old tracking spell that prevented the sell swords from getting lost in the snow. They glowed in a haunting shade of green to any friend that looked upon them. The pair exchanged dubious looks but left as Anienam began one of his minor rants. Two hours later they returned with good news. Shelter was less than a league away. The wagon ambled on and eventually arrived at a small copse of pine trees.

"We couldn't have done this in the middle of summer?" Dorl grumbled. He trembled from the cold. Not even the heat of their fire did much for him-yet.

Boen laughed. It sounded more of a bark than anything.

Snow still in his grey hair, Bahr dropped an armful of wood and added another log to the fire. A quick look of their faces told him all he had missed.

"What is Dorl complaining about this time?" he asked with a small smile.

The sell sword held up his hands in defeat. "I need new friends."

"He thinks it is too cold," Boen said, stifling a yawn.

Bahr shook his head. "This is nothing. I can tell you stories about being on the deep ocean in the middle of winter. Compared to that, it hasn't even begun to get cold yet."

"This is my kingdom," Dorl bit back. "I know when I'm cold. This is cold."

Boen laughed again. Winter had only just begun and the tiny band hadn't made it into the foothills yet. Boen knew winter as well. He cared less about the elements than for the enemy. The Gaimosian had fought in the desert, under the triple canopy of the jungle, and here in the frozen northlands. Each terrain possessed unique challenges and hardships and he cared for none. But war was war, and he went where the combat was.

"If my skin was the same as old leather, I would be just as comfortable as you, Gaimosian," Dorl told him.

"I doubt it," Bahr answered before Boen had the chance to grow angry. "Besides, you are the humor on this trip. We need that."

Dorl bobbed his head slightly. "Humor. I'm going to try and get some sleep."

"Try not to freeze," Boen chided with a grin.

"We are all going to die anyway," Ionascu snorted from the back of the wagon.

They looked up at the hastily constructed shelter on the wagon bed. The broken man lay buried beneath a swath of bearskin cloaks. A wild look entertained his usually lifeless eyes, as if he knew a secret no one else did.

Boen pointed a dagger at him. "Mind your tongue, old man. I'd forgotten you were among us. Let us keep it that way."

Ionascu laughed at him. "You don't understand a thing, do you?"

"Understand what? That you are quickly proving to be useless?"

"This is merely a diversion. Harnin won't stop. We already died back in those cells."

Boen scoffed and sheathed his dagger. "You are insane. Bahr, we should not have wasted our time bringing him."

"He may yet be of some use to us. He knows Harnin better than I ever did. That knowledge will come in handy if the one-eyed bastard is still after us."

"I'll believe that when it happens," Boen remained unconvinced.

Bahr looked back at Ionascu. He had no pity. The man plotted to kill them all from the very beginning and only changed his mind after being betrayed. Ionascu held the potential to be a powerful ally with his knowledge or a terrible foe with his silence. Bahr couldn't take the chance.

"Help us," he asked.

Ionascu glared at him sharply and buried himself in the cloaks.

Boen grunted again. "Let me know when you want him dead. I can dump the body in a ravine and no one will be the wiser."

"Maybe later," Bahr countered.

The Gaimosian shook his head, ill with the decision. "Whatever you say. Don't make me regret this later though. The mad are just as dangerous as traitors."

"We'll be fine with or without him. Argis is the one we need to worry about. He needs to find the underground and keep Harnin busy."

Joefke watched from the protective cover of darkness. The city patrol marched past without noticing him or the others. Their grey and black furs hid their bronze armor plates and sword belts. Not a one of the six guards appeared alert. Twenty men and women, all loyal citizens of Delranan, hid alongside Joefke. They were eager to get any measure of revenge on Harnin's men. Joefke frowned. Matters had not progressed the way Argis and the council envisioned since the raid on the arms locker. More than fifty rebels had been captured or killed through a series of strategic raids. People said the screams could be heard deep into the night.

"There's only six," Amendeas hissed.

Joefke kept from smiling. The youth Amendeas was eager, an eagerness that had left Joefke. There'd been too many deaths for him to find any excitement in this task.

"Quiet, there may be more," he whispered.

Amendeas shot him a foul look. "They killed our friends."

"They will kill us if you don't shut your mouth."

The sudden call of a night raven jarred their nerves. Joefke looked up to the second floor window of the chandlery down the street. A single candle flamed to life. The enemy patrol was entering the ambush area. Joefke felt his heart quicken. It was time. He drew his sword and moved. Half of his force split off and sprinted down the alley while he took the rest and followed the patrol. Timing was everything. They had the numbers, but the patrol had the training. Only by attacking from three directions at once could he hope to defeat the patrol. *Those the archers haven't already killed or wounded.* Startled cries announced the beginning of the fight. Joefke cursed and pushed his men into a sprint.

They arrived in time to prevent the patrol from escaping, if barely. Four guards ran into them, eager to flee the hail of arrows behind them. Joefke's rebels fell upon them with unmetered enthusiasm. Though surprised, the patrol was comprised of seasoned professionals. Once the initial shock wore off, they attacked. Joefke ducked under a wild swing and brought his own sword up. Steel sank into flesh. The soldier grunted and fell dead.

Joefke looked for another target, but the battle was already over. With their sergeant dead, the other guards quickly became disorganized and fell apart. The rebels cut them down without skill. Only one of the rebels lay dead. Joefke walked over to the body and turned him on his back. Sadness welled in him. Amendeas lay skewered on a guard's sword. Light blue eyes stared up accusingly.

Joefke knelt and gently closed the boy's eyes. "Get his body out of here. He deserved better. The rest of you take the weapons and armor. More soldiers will be on their way. Hurry."

"Six dead and we lost one," Joefke replied. His voice was distant, withdrawn.

Argis, hands steepled in front of his face, offered a sympathetic look. All of the differences between them had been settled after their first skirmish together. "When was the last time you got some rest?"

"Last night." Joefke was taken off guard by the randomness of the question. How could anyone think about sleep after one of their friends had just been killed? The concept of war was still as harsh as it was alien to him. He didn't understand the unfeeling nature of it.

Argis nodded. "Go and get some sleep. You and your men did well tonight."

"Thank you, but it doesn't change the fact that Amendeas is dead."

Argis watched him go and sighed. The rebellion was taking a heavy toll on them all, the young most of all. Joefke appeared to have aged decades over the last month. His shoulders slumped and deep creases lined the corners of his eyes. Defeat was not far away. It was up to Argis to figure out how to keep it from happening.

"Damnation," he muttered.

The elder noble eased over to where a detailed map of the city hung on the wall. The chamber was small, befitting their clandestine activities. A single, round window barely allowed enough light in for the leaders to see by. A pair of torches burned on the far wall near the doorway. The floor was coated with dust. Ragged cobwebs clung to the corners, the spiders long since gone. This was the command center, a far cry from the polished wooden halls of Chadra Keep.

Argis studied the map, doing his best to forget how far he had fallen. The city polarized quickly once first blood was drawn. The burning of the iconic *Dragon's Bane,* as well as Bahr's estate, fueled a budding rage. The people were not happy. Half supported the rebellion while the rest stayed loyal to the throne. Stalemate gripped them all and the body count continued to rise. Argis reluctantly admitted that his best efforts to avoid an all-out confrontation were failing.

Fenning, an elderly farmer and council leader, entered the chamber. "You seem troubled tonight."

Argis nodded. "Matters are not progressing as I had hoped."

"Wars are fickle. There is no way to control what happens over the course of one," Fenning replied. He gathered his brown robes and sat closest to the map.

Argis hadn't expected much in the way of military brilliance from the farmer, but his words offered a measure of comfort.

"Did the battle go well?"

"Well enough," Argis said. "We took out another patrol and lost only one."

"Harnin will be furious."

"He should be. That brings the total to forty soldiers since we began." Argis traced a line down the main avenue. "I think he is going to try to force our hand soon. Look here. So far all our attacks have been focused in and around the central market area. He knows this. If I were him, I would set a trap and try to end this rebellion before word travels back to Rogscroft and the king."

Fenning leaned closer to get a better look. "It makes sense, but how can we be sure? Harnin edges closer to depravity. Too many have already been tortured and murdered on his witch hunt. There is no way of telling what he might do."

"Our freedom comes with a heavy price," Argis agreed. "I have no desire to shed more of our people's blood but Harnin is not giving me much choice. He will stop at nothing to achieve his ends."

"Meaning we might well lose."

"Such can be said about every engagement."

Fenning poured himself a mug of water. "What are you thinking?"

"I honestly do not know. I can't go up against well-trained soldiers with poorly trained civilians, despite their good intentions. We are not prepared to pay that butcher's bill. The only way we stand a chance is by sticking to our same tactics. We need to adjust our focus. Harnin cannot be everywhere at once."

He wasn't sure if he believed himself or not. Too many already lay dead as price for the arrogance of a single man. Where did it end? Argis hadn't a clue.

Sleep remained elusive to Joefke. Amendeas's face leered at him from the chasm of death every time he tried to close his eyes. The reluctant warrior tossed and turned in a fit. Amendeas had never been a friend. They hadn't even met until a week ago. But to Joefke, the younger lad's death had been pointless. There was no reason for it. The why of it continued to torment him. Joefke hated the word. He'd never been a soldier and was firmly convinced he wanted no part of it. Killing wasn't natural. Argis and the others might think differently. Fine, let them. He had no intentions of becoming one of *them*. Unable to take anymore, Joefke rolled out of bed and went to find Argis.

"I thought I told you to get some sleep," Argis reminded him once he entered.

Joefke pulled his cloak tighter. The hilltop Chadra Keep sat on was off in the distance. Mists shrouded most of the ancient building. "How do you do it?"

Argis turned. "Do what?"

"The killing. The fighting. It is not what I imagined."

"It never is."

Joefke was confused. "Then why do it?"

He shrugged. "Some men are born for it. The only reason I keep going is for our people. A leader is nothing without his people."

"Was this war necessary?"

"King Badron has lost his way. He's forgotten what it means to be a king. Harnin is no better. They have allowed a rot to fester in the heart of Delranan. If we do not step forward to combat this evil now, we stand to lose our very way of life. I fight, and kill when I have to, in the name of my people."

Joefke's heart stirred, though he wasn't entirely convinced. He'd lost friends and slain countrymen. Neither sat well on his psyche. A terrible weight settled over his soul. He looked to the older man and asked, "When does it stop?"

"It has been my experience that it never does," Argis sadly admitted. His dark eyes narrowed at the unspoken prospect.

Howling winds whipped through the sleeping city streets with the ferocity of a demonic predator. A bad omen.

TWENTY

Council of the Pell

Cuul Ol warmed himself in the last bit of sunlight. Normally he would have smiled, for this was his most favorite time of day. Times were anything but normal. The war was already over a month old. His people had done their part, but he still doubted it was enough to stem the fury of the wolf soldiers. The Pell protected the mountain passes as much as possible until the snows came. Now it was all but impossible for Delranan to send in reinforcements by land.

The war had moved beyond his people, and for that he was grateful. The fires of battle raged deep in Rogscroft's heartland. Cuul continued to track the Wolfsreik's progress. Occasionally fleeting dreams took root. What he could do with such a force at his beck and call! Cuul Ol would become the terror folk whispered his people were. He sighed and looked down at the massive army spread out below, wondering how much longer he could keep tracking them. An uneasy feeling gnawed in the pit of his stomach. It was almost as if the enemy king wanted to lure them into ineffectiveness.

"I never thought to see such numbers," said a familiar voice from behind.

Cuul looked back at Sintl Ap. "Impressive, yes."

The taller Pell folded his arms across his massive chest. "Would that be ours. Then we need not hide in the mountains."

"Dreams, Sintl Ap. Nothing more than dreams. Let us focus on now."

Sintl Ap eyed him aggressively. "New leadership might be necessary."

"You should have spear if you wish to challenge," Cuul Ol growled.

Both warriors flexed and postured but did no more. Sintl Ap knew he could not best the Pell leader in single combat and the thought died there.

"What do we do now? The alliance with Rogscroft remains. We cannot abandon them."

The question was more valid than any recently asked. The Pell Darga had done their part, but at great price. Forests had been burned. Trails and favored hunting spots destroyed and lost. Many Pell warriors fell under enemy blades and arrows. The Murdes Mountains were safe again. Winter had come and no one was foolish enough to attempt a crossing. The people of Rogscroft were not so fortunate. Whole villages were erased from existence by the Wolfsreik. The entire civilization teetered on the brink of extinction.

Cuul Ol scratched the thin stubble of his jaw. "Prince Aurec has been a strong friend. We need his support. Only he found the courage to seek us. We cannot leave them to the wolf soldiers."

"We owe them no loyalty, Cuul Ol. The people of the Pell must come first."

"At what cost? We are no more than barbarians to the world. Long ago our people turned from the rest of Malweir. We were once violent yet vowed to change. Do we sacrifice what humanity we have to maintain this image?"

Sintl Ap grunted and spat. "We are more kin to the Dwarves than Men. Let the wolf soldiers do as they will. The Pell must come first."

"I hear your counsel, but it does not feel right."

"I do not…"

Cuul Ol snapped his hand up angrily. "No! I have spoken. Summon Durgas, I have a task for him."

Moonlight lent a haunting chill to the snow-covered rocks and trees. Durgas crouched behind a broken boulder, staring out at the eerie landscape. The Pell Darga were a superstitious people and he found much ill with this night. His face was painted grey with chalk and ash. Twenty of his best warriors hid behind him, each painted similarly. They wore dark vests of bear and deer hide. Each was armed with a brace of short spears and enough provisions to last them for two days.

Durgas paused to drink from his leather canteen. He'd been pushing his men since midday. They had one simple task. Cuul Ol was specific: scout the lands south and east to find access to the routes into the heart of Rogscroft. His company was to be the scouts for the rest of the Pell army. They'd spent that time marching through difficult terrain. The first pass was entirely shut off due to snow. Durgas led his company on to the next, where they now sat and waited. Pell warriors were among the more patient in Malweir. They often spent days stalking their prey, striking only when victory was assured. The path before him made him pause.

He turned to young Phin Ga. "Take Unt and Telor and go east. Move one thousand paces and swing north."

The three youths sped off and were quickly swallowed in the half darkness. Durgas didn't say it, but he was nervous. They had seen no sign of enemy forces since descending the mountain peaks. Ten thousand soldiers with supplies and animals had disappeared without a trace. Durgas didn't understand. He'd been a hunter his entire life and never once had seen anything comparable. A savage chill danced the length of his spine.

He silently tightened the cap on his canteen and was about to replace it in his pack when a blood-chilling scream shattered the calm. The sound was too human to be mistaken. Durgas clutched his spear tighter and readied for battle.

"Something comes!" hissed another warrior.

Durgas narrowed his gaze in the direction his warrior pointed. His heart froze. An unnatural darkness came rolling across the plain straight for them.

"Run! We cannot fight this!"

Courage fled his voice as panic took him. He knew the darkness was evil, the forbidden taint he had felt since arriving. No weapon of the Pell could halt such monstrosity. They fled. Pure hatred overtook them one at a time. Darkness touched the last man not fast enough to escape. Flesh melted from his bones and he screamed in such misery the moon wept blood. Durgas pressed on. He knew that he was dead if he stopped running. The darkness did not give him a choice. It swirled around the survivors, enveloping them in a tightening ring.

"Hold!"

The command barked across the tiny clearing they were in. Durgas lowered his slightly spear slightly as two nightmarish figures began to take shape. His warriors clustered together, more from childhood instinct than the urge to combat this new terror. The two figures were wrapped in cloaks of the darkest night. Waves of terror pulsed off of them, creeping into the Pell hunters and crushing their once proud resolve. Durgas watched in horror as the figures unfolded their arms and… waited. The Pell hunter had but one choice.

"Kill them!"

Two words and the fate of his command was sealed. Vogen, the youngest of the bunch, leapt at their foe. Another hunter dropped to his knees. Blood streamed from his eyes, nose, and mouth. White froth bubbled on his lips as his body began to convulse. The man fell dead, his face forever locked in a visage of agony. Durgas swore he heard an evil hiss from the dark figure. The rest of the hunters charged. They never stood a chance. Vogen died instantly. The figure on the right lashed out with a pulsing wave of power. Lances of dark light tore through Vogen's flesh. He died without a sound.

Durgas watched as a temporal *essence* was jerked from Vogen's body. He swore he saw his friend's face turn to him in a silent scream before being absorbed by the darkness. "No!"

He looked around in despair. His men fell dead all around and he was powerless to stop it. Soon only four remained. Neither of the enemy figures carried weapons. They didn't need to. Every moment was an economy of motion. Hundreds of years of experience, imbued with dark powers, made them the perfect killing machines. Death came swiftly whenever they struck. It was a small mercy.

Durgas recognized that he was already dead. The taller figure let his deceptive cloak open just enough to allow the terrified Pell a glimpse of his shadowed face. Durgas wet himself. He looked upon the face of evil and quailed. Death could not come quickly enough. Still, he managed to resist the urge to drop to his knees and succumb freely. It took the last measure of strength to break away from the malevolent stare of the darkness.

He tried to shout but his voice came out weak and broken. "Run!"

The survivors fled into the night in different directions. The second figure moved to follow but was held back.

Kodan Bak snapped. "They will reveal us to the others."

Amar frowned at the insubordination. "They will not live so long."

"How can you be sure?"

"I allowed their leader to see my face. He knows that death stalks them all."

Kodan Bak bit back a retort. It was not his place to openly criticize, however. "What do you propose?"

His voice measured, Amar concealed his emotion. "We hunt. Our foe is brave, yet foolish. I wish to see the well of their strength before they die."

"You plan on attacking their tribes?"

"Only if they prove worthy."

Amar doubted his own words. The ample corpses littered around them suggested their enemy was not as strong as either had believed. The Pell would make excellent sacrifices when the dark gods were finally freed.

"Few mortals prove worthy for the hunt. This is a waste of time. Let me finish them so that we may be about our business."

"Give them a moment more," Amar whispered. "I want to drink their fear when we drain their essence."

Durgas ran as fast as his body would take him. His breath came out in dagger-like plumes on the cold night air. He had dropped his pack and all but one of his short spears in the hasty retreat. Shame assailed his sensibility when he realized that none of the other three survivors were in sight. He had lost them. Guilt ridiculed him with each new step. So many dead in the same number of heartbeats. His mind groaned under the strain. Sanity threatened to abandon him.

He desperately wanted to live. That instinct drove him on when all else fled to dust. Every step should have taken him further from the lingering death. Should have. Instead he felt icy fingers reaching out to tickle his nape with promises of a violent demise. Desperation followed. It was a new and terrifying experience for the Pell warrior. Durgas pushed himself harder with the grim knowledge that it was not going to be enough. He was a dead man.

A pair of screams shattered the night. His heart sank. Dead. They were all dead but him. Hopefully the four who had run would make it back to inform Cuul Ol and the others. Hopefully, but he doubted it. Sorrow gripped him. These were men he had known his entire life. Friends, companions through a host of trials. And now they were gone. Durgas finally understood what failure meant. Resigned to his fate, he stopped running, turned, and hefted his spear. There was no point in running. The wait was short. Black mists crept out from the shadows. Durgas clutched his weapon tighter. The mists coalesced into the shape of a man.

"You should not have stopped running," the Dae'shan hissed.

Durgas shook his head. "No more running."

Amar Kit'han took a step forward. Murder gleamed in his eyes. "Do you not fear me?"

"I know death for what it is."

Amar cocked his head. Interesting. *This mortal still clings to courage*. He idly toyed with claiming the man's soul and making him a brother, absurd as it was. The dark gods would not tolerate such blasphemy.

"Death I am."

Durgas had time to scream once.

TWENTY-ONE

Preparations for Siege

"Our scouts have ranged to the city walls. The enemy is ready for siege."

Piper Joach listened as the captain spoke. The excitement in the junior officer belied relative inexperience. Piper knew sieges were no easy feat and the king was continuing to place pressure on the army. He shook his head. The Wolfsreik's strength was speed. Momentum won wars. Right now they had anything but.

"What is the strength of their defenses?" he asked.

The captain moved to the stained map he had already laid out. "They have lines dug along three avenues of approach. My men report pitch being emplaced here, here, and here."

Piper studied the map. All three areas were vital for trade and commerce but not necessary for his army's approach. "Do they mean to fire the city?"

"We think so."

Damnation. The smoke and flames would slow their approach as much as crossbowmen in the buildings. Piper made a quick note and motioned for the captain to continue.

"All of the roads and alleys are mined with caltrops. We believe it will be like this all the way to the castle walls. The enemy no doubt will have archers in the second story windows. The way will not be easy, even for the heavy infantry."

Piper frowned. One thought swirled through his mind. Casualties. He suddenly had a sour taste in his mouth. Perhaps they should think of letting Stelskor burn his city and wait for winter to do the rest. Doing so would certainly make life easier for the army and it would save so many lives. Sadly, he knew Badron was not going to let that be. The king had something in mind that he was keeping to himself. Piper didn't like it.

"What else?" he asked with a sigh.

"That is it, sir. I have scout teams creeping through the city to learn as much as they can before we assault."

Piper heard the pause and said, "But?"

"Sir, I do not think the enemy is going to make this easy. We are going to lose a lot of men trying to take it." He fell silent and lowered his gaze to the ground.

Piper placed a comforting hand on the captain's shoulder. "We most likely will, which makes your intelligence reports all the more important. The more you can tell us beforehand means the more lives you will save. Go and get something to eat. You have done well."

"Yes sir."

He saluted and left Piper to his ruminations. Piper stared at the map with a frown. The initial report was not to his liking. He'd known from the beginning that taking the city was going to prove more trouble than it was worth, but this was nearly disheartening. Badron wasn't going to want to delay either. He was going to waste lives because of some sort of bloodlust that no one really understood. The potential for disaster sickened Piper. Throwing on a cloak, he stormed off to find Rolnir. A quick stop in the mess tent was also in order. Perhaps it would settle his uneasy stomach.

The mood around camp was generally high. The Wolfsreik had yet to lose a major engagement in the campaign and that buoyed the soldiers' spirits. Several ambushes and smaller skirmishes had gone against them, but the bulk of victories were on their side. Soldiers laughed and traded stories that more than likely had not happened quite the way they told them. Others sharpened swords and axes. The vast majority had already bedded down for the night for sleep was a luxury often missing from campaign. Piper made small talk with a few. He laughed and joked, projecting an air of confidence.

"What can I do for you, sir?"

Piper offered a warm smile to Borlin, the head mess sergeant. "Something cold with plenty of bubbles."

Borlin shuffled to the back and returned with a tall pewter mug of the best field ale they had left. "Here you go, sir. It's not much but it is damned sure cold."

Piper drank deep, the ale burning a trail to his stomach. "Damn. This has got to be the worst ale I've ever drank. Do they sell this back in Chadra or did your boys brew this up from old combat boots?"

"Ha! Piss water has less of a bite, sir."

He laughed. "Maybe, but at least it sates the thirst."

Borlin nodded, a twisted smile on his lips. He took the empty mug and refilled it.

Piper eagerly accepted. "What are the men saying?"

"The usual. Nothing seems to bother them unless they're in the middle of a fight or hungry."

Piper somehow doubted Borlin spoke true. "You're not telling me much. You're the mess sergeant, you know more than even I do I suspect."

The older veteran rubbed his chin wryly. He'd hoped to avoid this topic altogether. Leaders had more important matters to worry about than the rumors circulating camp.

"The men are worried. We've got those Pell bastards ranging behind us, raiding the supply lines and picking off our scouts, and that damned Aurec is having his way to our front. Hard times are coming. Rumor has it the city is going to be a hard one to crack."

"They've had plenty of time to get ready for us," Piper agreed. "You and I have been doing this long enough to know that no city is ever easy to take."

Borlin snorted and shook his head. "Doesn't make it any easier to swallow, sir."

"No. I don't suppose it would."

"You've got a lot of worry on your face, sir. The men will do their jobs. Don't you worry about that. We'll take that damned city and be back in Chadra before the end of winter."

Piper admired Borlin's attitude. The sergeant was a man to hold his tongue when things went south. He was also a friend. They'd been on numerous campaigns together and

Borlin had consistently proven to be the man you wanted at your back when times were bad.

"These are difficult times," he said. "All we can do is our best."

Piper didn't say it. He didn't have to. Both understood the number of live troops they brought home depended on the king. An old northern proverb claimed that madness had a way of spreading so it was best not to mention it. Piper had no intention of provoking such a chance this late into the campaign.

"Aye. It seems like they are. Would you be wanting any more ale, sir?"

Piper grimaced. "Are you trying to kill me?"

Borlin took the mug back and bit off a laugh. "Have a good night, sir. Trust the men to do their jobs. It will all work out at the end."

"Good night, Borlin."

Piper left the mess tent and stalked his way through the camp. A strange calm settled over them all. Piper was thankful for it. The men needed to relax. War was taxing in many ways. Waiting was one of the worst. Piper shook his head slowly. He never considered himself a necessarily strong person. He was good with a sword and had a good head for tactics, but that was about it. What he lacked was emotional control. Twice already in this campaign he found himself at extremes. The initial disaster at the outset of the invasion took him to undiscovered lows while the string of victories bolstered his desire to fight. Far from foolish, Piper realized his emotional stability depended on Prince Aurec's success or failure. Piper was the sort to hold grudges; he very much wanted that man dead.

"What troubles you tonight?"

He looked up, startled and embarrassed at being caught off guard. Rolnir emerged from the night, hands clasped behind his back. The darkness made him look much older than his forty-four years. The war did not sit well with him either.

"Our lead scouts have returned." Piper's voice was bland.

Rolnir gently bit his bottom lip. "Come inside. I assume you have much to tell me."

"None of it good."

King Badron eyed his two senior officers with a snarl of contempt. He listened to as much of their initial assessment as he could stand, which wasn't much, before waving them silent. Piper and Rolnir might have thought their concerns were valid, but they lacked the foresight of being king. Badron was sorely tempted to have them flogged for incompetence. The king was many things. Patient was not one of them. Dark circles permanently scarred his eyes. He'd lost weight and didn't sleep well anymore. Nightly visits from the Dae'shan filled his mind with dark nightmares. Badron knew he bordered on losing control and he felt powerless to stop it.

"All I ask is that you do your jobs," he said in a carefully measured voice.

"We are, Sire."

Rolnir regretted the words almost as soon as he spoke them. This was not the first of Badron's childish temper tantrums they had sat through. The one constant was that the end results were unpredictable. A junior captain had already been executed for having the spine to talk back to the king.

"Are you? Why do you keep bringing me petty concerns while my bastard enemy mocks me from the safety of his walls? Do I have need of a new general?"

Anger flashed across Rolnir's face. He had gotten away with lashing out at the king once but doubted success a second time. Instead, he composed himself. "Sire, the Wolfsreik has never let down any king in our history. Rogscroft will fall, but I will not commit thousands of lives due to impatience. Too many will die. Those are lives we cannot afford to lose this far from home."

"Losses are not my concern, general."

Cold laced his words. Both military men felt like they'd just been slapped. Never would they have believed that a king of Delranan could act so callously towards his own men.

"Their lives are all we have!" Piper shouted.

Rolnir shot him a stern glare. Piper backed down, ashamed of his uncharacteristic outburst.

"Forgive him, Sire. He speaks out of place. He is right, however. The more men we lose, the less effective we are. I can't condone any action that will only waste lives. I won't." Rolnir lifted his chin slightly, almost daring the king to challenge.

"Calm down, Rolnir," Badron said and held up a staying hand. "I have no intention of throwing my army away."

The emphasis on *my* did not go unnoticed.

"What do you mean?"

"Help is marching to us. We will not assault Rogscroft alone."

Badron struggled to contain himself. He had no way of telling how receptive his officers would be to the news that it was a Goblin army en route. He still had mixed emotions about the situation. His one hope came from the thought that many Goblins were going to be killed in the assault.

Rolnir immediately grew suspicious. "What army? We have few allies here in the north. What land does this army come from?"

A pause. "The Deadlands."

"Goblins!" hissed Piper.

Badron nodded. "Yes. An army of Goblins."

"You have damned us all. Goblins are a blight on the world. What madness led you to this?"

"You yourself said we can ill afford to waste lives," Badron began to explain quickly before their anger grew. He deliberately left pertinent questions unanswered. No one needed to know how the Goblins had been contacted. In the end, Rolnir seemed partially satisfied. The key selling point was the ultimate betrayal of the Goblins once Rogscroft fell.

Cold winds bit into Rolnir and Piper as they left the royal tent.

Piper pulled his cloak tighter. "I don't like this. We shouldn't make this deal."

"What choice do we have? Badron has already committed us. The Goblins are on their way."

"Don't you want to know how he made the alliance?"

"No."

Fifty leagues away, the terrible Goblin army marched. Whips lashed them on at a frenzied pace. They'd already covered five hundred leagues in four weeks, stopping only for a few hours of rest a day. Grugnak watched his army with pride. It had been a long time since last they went to war. He salivated with the thought of sinking his fangs into human flesh. His hatred for mankind was almost unmatched. The Goblin lord only hated Dwarves more. The army continued to march.

TWENTY-TWO

Dreams

Maleela startled awake. Her heart raced. A light sheen of sweat covered her body. Her normally soft brown eyes were widened with fright. Just a dream, she tried to convince herself. She slowed her breathing, willing her body to respond to practicality. She felt lost and confused. A wide range of emotions collided within her. Maleela had never been overly close to her uncle, but her dreams were becoming more disturbing, horrifically vivid. Most of the men in her family alienated her, Badron most of all. Nothing she did was good enough for him. The guilt from her mother's death was hard to suppress even though it wasn't her fault. Badron thought otherwise. Maleela was entirely expendable. Shaking her head, she wiped her face off.

Bahr glanced up from the flames of their small fire. "Bad dreams again?"

"How did you know?"

His gaze softened. "I heard you. I'm surprised you didn't wake anyone up. What was it that made you worry so?"

"I dreamed of fire and pain."

She fell silent. The horror of it still felt real. Maleela closed her eyes and found herself standing in a maze of thorns. Each bush was over ten feet tall, an impenetrable mass of menacing spikes. Greenish mist swirled across the base, adding a haunted look. A full moon hung threateningly over the horizon. The sky itself was pitch black with not a cloud in sight. Even the stars seemed to have disappeared, eclipsed by a nameless menace.

Maleela froze, desperately trying to open her eyes again. She trembled and shook, but no matter how hard she tried, her eyes refused to obey her. Heavy footsteps marched closer. Gouts of flames sprang up in a constricting circle. She heard the menacing roar of faceless monsters in the unseen miasma beyond the flames. Her knees almost gave out. Her heart quickened. The ground shook with each new footstep. She knew it was death and was powerless to escape. Waves of pain spread from the approaching figure. She screamed.

"Your screams are like the sweetest wine."

The voice boomed across the world. All her darkest thoughts came to life with the sound. At last the nightmare came into view. Maleela screamed again as a beast of indescribable horror crept through the flames.

"Will you continue to scream as I tear you limb from limb? Flense your frail human form until you wear nothing but blood?"

She tried to run, tried to figure out where her uncle had gone. Maleela was frozen in place. She couldn't defend herself. The shadowed face leered closer, strange yet oddly familiar.

"You didn't think you could ever escape me, did you?"

Darkness seethed. She cried out as her flesh burned where it touched her.

"Look into my eyes and you will find the truth of your existence."

She did and screamed at the top of her lungs.

Bahr reached out to pull his niece close, whispering that it was all right.

"It was so real," she whimpered. "That face…"

Bahr struggled not to cry. The pain of not being able to help her hurt worse than anything else he had experienced since this nightmare began. "Whose face did you see?"

She pulled away slightly. "My father's."

Bahr felt as if he'd been punched in the stomach. He was speechless. Bahr was unskilled in dream reading and lacked the emotional development to be much more than empathetic. His initial impulse was to tell her to forget about it, that it was only a dream. Doing so might serve to make matters worse. What he really needed was Anienam. The wizard would know exactly how to treat this situation.

"It was nothing but a dream, lass. Shhh."

He did his best towards comforting her, but he had never been a father. This was as alien to him as growing crops. His words felt empty. Bahr almost felt lost. Maleela glanced up at him, shifting to avoid scraping her face on the stubble of his chin. Her eyes were filled with diminishing fear.

"Uncle, I know what I saw. My father is involved with sinister forces. This dream was much too real to be otherwise."

"We should not jump to conclusions. Wait for Anienam to read the truth in your dream," he cautioned.

"What if he tells us what I already believe?" she asked.

Her voice cracked. Bahr looked up. Dawn broke across the horizon. The others stirred and slowly came awake. Anienam was the first to the fire, as if he expected to be needed. He rubbed his tired hands over the fire. His liver spots were darker, making him look much older than he was. He met Bahr's stare.

"Long nights in the field never agree with me," he said and smiled.

Bahr offered a warm smile. "It is not an easy life. I much prefer being on the ocean. Things are less complicated on the deck of a boat."

Anienam grunted. "If you say so. I prefer a warm room in the local inn with down blankets and mulled wine."

"You'll get no arguments from me."

Maleela couldn't take it anymore. "Wizard, may I speak with you in private?"

His gaze danced between Maleela and Bahr. The Sea Wolf nodded.

"Of course."

She explained her dream, at least what she could of it. The visions were too real. The hurt was too deep. Anienam sat silently and drank it all in. His brow furrowed at the mention of her father. Maleela finished speaking and waited expectantly for Anienam to solve all of her problems. He only wished he could. The wizard traced his moustache idly while trying to figure out what to say. The dream was not an easy one to decipher. Any number of possibilities might come from it. Still, a cold sense of dread settled over him.

"I know that look in your eyes," she said. "What is it you know?"

"Most of the dream is meaningless. Riddles that we might go crazy from trying to decipher."

An eyebrow arched. "Most?"

He gestured wildly with his hands. "Yes, most. I think this was more than dream. What you had was a vision of sorts. Flames and thorns mean nothing from your past. Not unless you've got dark secrets none of us know."

She smiled despite herself. "No flames or thorns."

He nodded absently. "The part your father plays disturbs me. He is no great charitable figure, but his visage as some demonic being suggests an influence we do not know of. There is darkness loose in the world. The Dae'shan that hunted Rekka when we came to rescue you was but one in four. Three are known. They have been active players since the night your brother was killed, if not longer."

She flushed. Her brother's murder was unintended and pointless. Her selfish desires robbed him of a long and potentially meaningful life. She had never really needed rescuing. The love shared with Aurec went beyond any other feeling. That love had been torn apart and now his kingdom stood upon the brink of destruction. The possibility that she might never get the chance to tell him she loved him ever again tore at her heart.

Maleela tried to push those dark thoughts from her mind. "Do you think my father has anything to do with the Dae'shan?"

"It is possible, but hard to tell. The Dae'shan are almost timeless. They manipulate to facilitate the will of their masters. Badron may well be under their influence."

A new fear clutched at her. "Perhaps they seek to turn him to their will."

Anienam nodded. "It is a thought. Unfortunately, right now there is no way for us to be sure."

His answer was too much for her to take. "Anienam, we must learn the truth. My heart tells me that we are heading into a horrible time."

Bahr coughed from near the fire. "How do we do that? I am in no rush to go back to Rogscroft and confront my brother, not with ten thousand soldiers of the Wolfsreik at his back."

"We may have no choice," the wizard countered. "Confronting Badron may be the only way to end this war. I do need to remind everyone that deciphering Maleela's dream is not our primary concern. Venheim awaits. We must find the forge of Giants and the blood hammer before time runs out. The Dae'shan are cunning and deceptive. It might already be too late to make a difference."

"How do you manage to bring us darkness every time there is a glimmer of hope?" Bahr asked.

The wizard forced a grin. "Live as long as I have and your outlook will be just as sour. Stop avoiding the subject. Venheim remains our best hope for stopping the Dae'shan."

"Does your book give any light to what we need?"

Heads turned as Boen rumbled up from his sleeping bag to warm himself by the fire. Anienam was reminded of one of the big jungle cats ready to attack. The Gaimosian was mankind's predator. A dangerous race, he mused. Perhaps that was a large part in why Gaimos had been annihilated all those years ago. Maleela blushed. She had hoped to keep the conversation between the three of them. Foolish to be sure, for there was little privacy in such intimate company.

"The book contains many secrets the world has long forgotten. I've only managed to get halfway through it."

Bahr had given the matter much thought since leaving Praeg. There were too many secrets and mysteries for him to grasp the central theme. A sudden thought dawned on him, one he hadn't had before. "What if the Giants can tell us about the dream?"

Anienam's eyes narrowed. "How do you mean?"

"The Giants clearly had a part in the writing of this book. Isn't it conceivable that they might have the capability to decipher Maleela's dream?"

"Giants are reclusive. They seldom suffer strangers on their lands. That the men who wrote the book did not survive their encounter speaks volumes, but it does not support your theory. Most of the world has forgotten the Giants," Anienam replied.

Bahr shrugged. "It's not a theory. I am merely suggesting we may find the answers to the dream and the riddle of the Dae'shan with the Giants."

"Whatever," Boen said. "We shall find out as soon as we meet these creatures. There's no point in guessing what if."

Anienam dismissed him and looked back to Bahr. "There is some merit in what you say. We must find the forge first."

Boen nodded. "We are wasting time."

"I agree. We should be moving," the wizard echoed unexpectedly.

Maleela frowned. She was left with the impression that her dreams had just been blown off for other speculation. Enraged, she was unsure what to do. She was outmatched and overpowered by the false bravado of their male machismo. Maleela decided to quietly bide her time. Soon enough she would get the opportunity to prove she was every bit as capable as the blooded warriors. She was the daughter of a king. It was time to start acting like one. Maleela turned to shake off the snow from her sleeping bag before rolling it up.

"Are you well?" Rekka Jel asked.

She'd approached without Maleela hearing her. The question lacked sincerity, almost sounding demanding. Maleela took comfort in the solidarity aspect Rekka offered. The diminutive warrior was easily the best of their group with a sword. Her skill and technique were unmatched, even with Boen's brute strength.

"I don't know," she finally answered after a few minutes of quiet deliberations.

Rekka slipped closer. A concerned look lined her soft features. "I heard your cries last night. I, too, have had nightmares. You must excise these demons before they consume you."

Maleela had no intentions of reliving the night's dreams. The pain of them transcended into horror mixed with moments of blind terror. Putting all this behind her was the best for all of them.

"You have no reason to be embarrassed," Rekka continued. "We all have our pasts to contend with."

"My past has haunted me since birth. My dreams have grown dark and uncertain. I am afraid, Rekka."

The smaller woman nodded and moved so close that only Maleela might hear. "Fear must be harnessed if we are to move forward."

"How?"

Rekka placed a warm hand on Maleela's shoulder. "The answer can only be found in each of us. The way I deal with matters might not work for you. Have courage, Princess. Hope is not yet lost."

Maleela considered it. She knew what needed to be done but was hesitant to do so. She wasn't a warrior, despite being the daughter of a northern king. All children were expected to be able to read, write, and handle a sword. Maleela wasn't particularly skilled with soldiers' tasks, but she could stab someone well enough. It wasn't enough. She decided to take her first steps in a new direction.

"Teach me how to use a sword."

Her voice was rushed, as if her excitement threatened to override common sense. Rekka stared back at her, quietly judging the princess. Finally, she relented. "All right. Your plan will not be easy. Keep that in mind."

"Nothing ever is," Maleela said and smiled politely.

"Let's move out!" Bahr shouted to the group.
The forge of Giants awaited them.

TWENTY-THREE

Ghosts

Cold winds lashed into them, pelting them with ice and snow. Each gust was a painful scream, like a dying animal caught and left for dead. Loose snow underfoot made the worn path treacherous. Rocks broke and slid down the mountainsides in miniature avalanches. The sun was already setting. Darkness would soon be upon them.

Bahr pulled his hood tighter and cursed under his breath. It was snowing so hard he could barely see beyond the end of his horse's nose. The journey grew more dangerous the further they went into the mountains. Bahr was confronted with two options: push forward in the dark with no visibility on unknown terrain or try to find shelter until the storm passed. Both options presented unique and inherent problems. It was not the kind of decision to be made alone.

"Boen!" he shouted over the angry winds.

The Gaimosian reined up beside him. "This damned storm is going to be the death of us."

"Agreed. We will die if we keep going forward."

Boen shook his head. "We have no choice. We can't go back! The only way is forward."

"Forward to where? We can't see anything."

Boen recognized they were walking into a potential trap. He also failed to see another way around it. "What do you want to do?"

Bahr took a quick glance around, knowing it was a waste of time. Visibility had worsened in the short amount of time they spoke. His choices withered. "We need to stop. It is too risky to go on tonight."

The Gaimosian nodded despite disagreeing. The hunger in his blood stirred again. He gave a brief thought to abandoning them and striking out on his own. His loyalties to Bahr extended only so far. The blood demands of his heritage demanded much more and it grew increasingly difficult to suppress them.

"Let me scout ahead. I can find us a path."

Bahr agreed, with skepticism. The chance of becoming permanently separated disturbed him, but not enough to stop the man. They had to find shelter or risk freezing to death in the snow and cold.

"Do it. We will continue on this path until you ride back to us," he said.

Boen set off without another word. A lifetime of being alone in the field took over, freed from the repression of operating with a group less experienced. Boen was a simple man who knew how to get things done. It was the mark of a good soldier. Bahr watched him until his silhouette was lost in the building darkness and wondered if he had just condemned them all.

The path wound up and around the mountainside for another kilometer before Boen was forced to stop. He hadn't seen any deviations or side paths along the way, though that didn't mean there weren't any. Reduced visibility hampered more than just his vision. Boen felt constricted. Winter was his least favorite season. The snow and cold of the Murdes Mountains did not agree with him.

He took a long drink from his canteen and looked around. The wind wasn't blowing as hard as it had been, leading him to believe the crest wasn't too far off. Heartening, but it meant little. The wagon could have easily ridden past the teeth of the dragon. Venheim could very well be lost to them.

"Damned storm," he complained to no one.

Light snow swirled around him without the frenzied pace from the lower levels. Boen almost smiled. If the sun showed itself he might be in a better mood. Might. Boen suddenly made up his mind to head south once this matter was finished. Warmer climates and easier jobs beckoned. He yawned. The cold had a way of sapping even the strongest man's strength with little effort.

He moved to secure his canteen when a dark shadow moved across his periphery. Boen dropped the small container and drew his broadsword. He scanned the area and found…nothing. Whatever it was had come and gone. Boen frowned. His first impulse was that his mind was playing tricks on him. It was cold. He was tired and slightly dehydrated.

Boen clucked softly, urging his mount forward. He wasn't about to be taken off guard so easily. The Gaimosian decided to check the spot he thought he saw the shadow. Rumors of the Pell Darga lingered. If they were half of what Bahr and the others claimed, he was going to enjoy crossing blades with them. A loose rock tumbled from his right. Boen froze. The same shadow whisked by. Boen snarled. There was nothing here either. The Gaimosian circled his horse in the hopes of finding his prey.

"Show yourself!" he bellowed.

The challenge echoed off the tight canyon walls. Snow and loose slate trickled down around him. Hissing laughter taunted him from the mist. Boen was not the one to be frightened by cheap theatrics, but this was different. He tightened the grip on his sword. His ire was raised, only blood would sate it. Three more shadows danced by.

"*Leave us.*"

The voice was waspish, almost strained. Goose bumps prickled his flesh. Boen had long believed that such a voice belonged to the dead.

"Show yourself, coward!" he demanded.

Laughter mocked him. Boen struggled to contain his anger. Such emotion would work against him. The Gaimosian vowed to meet death on his terms. Dozens of figures formed from the mist in a loose circle. He snarled. A handful of opponents weren't much of a problem, but dozens were too much. Boen felt the first touch of despair sink in. He was surrounded on three sides and cut off from help.

"*Leave us.*"

A chorus of wails rose up to the sky. Boen suddenly felt cold. The chill penetrated to his bones. It was unnatural. The mist stung where it touched him. Boen recognized the danger he was in but saw no way out. A thought disturbed him. Ghosts. His attackers were ghosts. They had to be, for they held no physical form.

"Come no closer," he warned through clenched teeth.

They laughed.

"*You hold no power here.*"

His horse jerked against his control. Boen struggled to keep the beast from bolting out from under him. The ghosts, their numbers in the hundreds now, pressed in on him. He made out broken spears, shattered shields. Their armor was rotted leather and riddled with holes. Each had seen his war and been forever damned to haunt the place of his death. Boen was not going to be one of them.

"What do you want with me?"

He spoke only to find a way out, a means to survive.

"*You should not be here. This is a place of the dead.*"

Boen frowned. "The dead do not belong in this world. Go back to your graves and leave me in peace."

"*We know no peace.*"

He resisted the urge to lash out. Steel would have no effect on the surreal anyway. His sword might as well have been a broken reed floating down a river. He had to think fast if he wanted to spare Bahr and the others from this fate.

"I warn you. Leave me be or face the wrath of Gaimosian blood."

The ghosts wailed at his warning. His ears wept at the sound.

"*A son of Gaimos.*"

The words whispered over and over, rippling through the ghosts. Boen had obviously struck a chord, but how?

"*Gaimos is no more. It cannot be.*"

Boen narrowed his eyes. "Our kingdom yes, but not our people. We are few and scattered but we remain."

"We were once of Gaimos."

He froze. Had he heard it correctly? Gaimos had been destroyed nearly four thousand years ago. That was also the last time such a force of Gaimosians had taken to the field. Boen grimaced at the thought. A full regiment of brothers surrounded him. Such should not be possible.

"What evil befell you here?" he asked. For reasons he did not know, he sheathed his sword.

"Betrayal."

Betrayal? Boen ignored the rising uneasiness turning his stomach. He had questions but wasn't sure where to begin.

"Beware the Dae'shan. Ever they seek to destroy us. Leave this place, son of Gaimos. We shall bother you no more."

The ghosts faded back into the mists and were gone. Boen sat in stunned silence as the sun disappeared over the mountaintops.

TWENTY-FOUR

The Siege Begins

"Incoming!"

Soldiers caught in the open dropped quickly to the ground in the hopes that enemy rounds did not land on top of them. The first impacts rocked the ground hard. Sections of Rogscroft's ancient walls buckled, threatening to cave in. Waves of flames burned hotly where each round struck. Clouds of dust and debris choked the air. Every round screamed into the city. Armored men cowered and prayed for the bombardment to end.

"Take your posts! To the walls!" bellowed the senior sergeant once the barrage ended.

The defenders raced back to their positions. Squires dropped off full quivers behind each man. Nerves changed them. Fear danced in their eyes. The attack they had long dreaded was finally under way. It was much preferable than the endless hours of waiting and wondering.

"Put those fires out, lads! Quickly, before the whole damned castle burns down!"

Several buildings had caught fire. Some had already collapsed in on themselves. Flames licked higher. The destruction was comparatively minimal but might easily burn out of control. Orderlies raced with buckets. Litter bearers checked the rubble for dead and wounded. The heavy thrum of catapult fire echoed over the battlefield.

"Incoming!"

"The moment we have all dreaded is now upon us," Stelskor told his senior leaders.

His gaze shifted to each man. They were the best Rogscroft had to offer. The future of their kingdom rested solely on their strategies. Sleepless nights and high anxiety aged them all in the few short months of the war. Stelskor knew the worst was yet to come. Aurec stifled a yawn. He and what remained of his men had ridden into the city through underground passages during the night. Less than two hundred of his original number still lived. Aurec regretted losing so many, but for every death a handful of civilians were given the opportunity to flee to safety.

"What did you spy on the way in?" the king asked his son.

"The Wolfsreik spent much of the night moving their siege engines into position, as we all know." He paused as several of the men chuckled humorlessly. "Their lines are weak at the rear. It is almost as if Badron doesn't plan on leaving any survivors."

"We will make him rue that decision," Paneolus, minister of state, vowed.

Stelskor glanced at the balding, overweight man and gave an approving nod. Part of their plan had always been to lure the Wolfsreik into a prolonged siege in the deep winter.

"Have any enemy units tried closing in on the walls?" he asked.

Venten answered. "None so far. We have snipers positioned to take out their sappers and engineers when they do."

"The walls should hold. Our primary concern needs to be the gates. If the enemy manages to burn them, none of our preparations will mean much."

"General Vajna is right. We must protect the gates first," the king echoed.

Aurec frowned. "The only way to do that successfully is to take out their siege engines, Father."

"We have done that before," Venten remarked. "The enemy will have learned from their past mistakes. Their machines will be heavily guarded and there is no easy path through their lines."

"Can we range them with our own?" Stelskor asked.

Vajna snapped. "I don't know. We should be able to, but to what effect? We have a total of five and no possibility of creating new ones. If those are destroyed…"

He let the rest remain unsaid.

"Our situation should improve once their infantry starts moving into the city. We have enough defenses emplaced to slow them considerably," Aurec added.

He needed to change the subject before potential defeat dominated their thoughts. Victory was realistically out of reach and the best they could hope for was to inflict enough casualties to make Badron lose the urge to continue. Stelskor had no doubt that Badron was the driving force behind the invasion. His old hatreds and lust for power had made him unstable, dangerous. That fanaticism had spread through the Wolfsreik.

"We all know that Rogscroft cannot stand up to the might of our enemy," the king interrupted. "We make our stand here and then retreat to Grunmarrow. From there we can either continue with a guerilla-style war or wait for the Delrananians to grow bored and leave."

"Father, Grunmarrow is too far away to maintain any resistance in force."

Stelskor shot his son an appraising look. Grunmarrow was a refuge of sorts that had served the people of Rogscroft for generations. No enemy had been able to find the secluded village. And for good reason. As Aurec protested, Grunmarrow was nestled into the base of the Murdes Mountains, days away from the capital and a proper army. The boy was still young and full of fire. Keeping his emotions in check might prove difficult, but they had no choice. Survival was the imperative. Stelskor did what was best for his people, not his son.

"It has also served us well over the years," the king said. "It is a small village in the middle of the forest, sheltered by the Murdes Mountains and unknown to any of our enemies. The Pell Darga should be able to provide additional protection if we need it."

Venten doubted that. "As long as any Pell remain. We have had no word from them since abandoning the outer defenses."

"I think it is time to take into account that the Wolfsreik has already fixed the problem of the Pell. The myth is no more," Vajna added.

Paneolus frowned. "Winter is our best ally now."

King Stelskor shook his head, a pained expression on his aged face. "We need more."

"Sire, there is no more," Vajna said matter-of-factly.

The words haunted the council chamber long after their echo faded. Stelskor felt as if the dawn was too far out of reach. He began to despair.

"Let us refocus," Stelskor said. "We must look to the gates. It is not yet time to worry about retreat."

Paneolus scratched his double chin. "The pumps are finally operational. We should be able to pour enough water on the gates to keep them from burning too much."

"That leaves us with the problem of structural integrity," Aurec said. "Wood and iron can only stand so much before the combination of impacts and fire causes them to buckle. We'll have the Wolfsreik inside in no time."

Silence fell over them. Outside, the barrage renewed.

Mahn watched Raste flinch from the latest explosion. The younger scout still wasn't adjusted to the sounds of war. Skirmishing was one thing, but this was a detailed battle and would continue for many days. It had already been over a day since the Wolfsreik began their artillery barrage and there was no sign of letting up. Raste flinched and jumped every time. The older Mahn might have found it amusing under different circumstances. That wasn't to say that he wasn't terrified as well, but he was a seasoned soldier who had been through this all before. There was only so much a man could take before the booms and screams became common and no longer echoed so badly.

"I really wish you would stop laughing," Raste commented.

Mahn tried to conceal his smile but failed. "Quit being so jumpy and I might."

"I can't help it!"

"There is no point in worrying about what is beyond our control," Mahn told him. "The enemy is going to fling rounds at us until they either run out of ammunition or they break down our walls. There isn't a thing we can do to change that."

Raste shook his head. "You have a way of making things worse, Mahn. Have I ever told you that?"

"Several times." He tore off a large chunk of bread and passed the rest. "Here, you need to eat."

"I'm not hungry."

Mahn insisted. "You're going to need the strength. The time is coming when we're all going to."

Raste reluctantly accepted the loaf of dark bread and took a bite. "We should be out there, not caged in these walls."

"I agree, but that is something neither of us can change. Be patient. Our time will come again."

Raste couldn't drop the subject. There was too much pent-up frustration aching to escape. He was in the prime of his youth and had more questions than a normal man his age. "We need to be out there doing our jobs. Aurec is going to need our scouting reports."

"To what end? The city is surrounded and it won't be much longer before the Wolfsreik attacks," Mahn replied. "If we went out there we would be cut off and, more than likely, killed. At least that would end your complaining."

"Funny. You know what I am talking about. Aurec needs to send us where we can do our jobs."

Mahn pointed an accusing finger. "Right now that job is here on this section of the wall."

Snow began falling. Mahn looked up and relished the cool feeling of the tender flakes melting on his face. He'd found it refreshing since he was a young boy. He and his brother used to go out and play in the massive drifts until their mother sharply called them back inside. Those days were long gone, nothing more than shadowed memories dim with time. His mother died of the flux nearly twenty years ago. His brother was lost at sea when his fishing boat got caught in a late summer storm. Mahn enlisted shortly after and had been a soldier ever since.

"What happens when the wall breaks?"

Mahn smiled grimly. "We find a new place to go."

The barrage continued long into another night. The shock value continued to wear down the morale of the defenders. The Wolfsreik was relentless. Winter was here in force and the invaders had limited resources. They had to either force a quick surrender or break inside and kill everyone. Stelskor understood this. His main priority lay in prolonging the siege long enough that Badron ran out of supplies and got desperate.

"I can't see so well at night anymore," he confided in his son.

Aurec watched his father. The flickering torchlight cast almost menacing shadows over the king's face. His father looked much older in the half-light. Aurec hoped he never had to bear the weight his father carried now. "There is not much worth seeing."

Stelskor reluctantly agreed. "I fear you are right. How did we come to this? Were we too blind to see this war coming?"

"Guilt and blame should be placed on me, Father. If I had not gone to take Maleela…"

"Enough of that," Stelskor scolded. "We've had this discussion. Badron is the one to blame. We must focus all of our efforts on stopping his army and retaining our sovereignty."

"I honestly can't see how. Cuul Ol and his Pell warriors did their part, but now they'd just be wasting their lives."

Stelskor placed a loving hand on his son's shoulder. "Winter is here. There may yet be some life for us. Do not give in to despair. Hope is not lost yet."

"I hear your words but cannot see how hope is possible. There has to be a way to break the siege lines."

"The siege is not important. This war is not important. The only thing that matters is the continuation of our people and way of life."

Stelskor resumed his nightly vigil out the window. Fires burned across his city and at various spots along the wall. Black smoke billowed up into the night sky from a dozen places. He sighed. So much destruction after only two days. The old king never imagined his world would be burning down around him.

"I remember you back in your fifth summer," he said softly without turning. "I sent you with your mother to one of the fishing villages. Keinburg, I believe."

Aurec smiled as fond memories returned. "I remember."

"What you didn't know was that a large band of sea raiders had come from the east. They burned and pillaged everything in their path as soon as they hit the mainland. I barely had time to raise a force strong enough to meet them in battle. It was a terrible summer. More than three thousand civilians were killed. The raiders were stronger than I had anticipated."

He paused. Too many bad memories haunted him. "We were outnumbered, and I was forced to flee. I think I only had around four hundred battle-ready men. We fled to Grunmarrow. That is where we mounted a counter campaign. It took the entire summer, but we finally drove them from our shores. They have yet to return."

"Once again the wolves are at our door," Aurec added.

The king smiled. It was the gleam of a warrior unwilling to accept his fate, the unspoken vow to keep fighting when all the odds stood against him. "We will survive this too, my son."

An urgent knock ended their conversation. Stelskor opened the door. Turgin, the house jarl, was leaning against the wall trying to catch his breath.

"What is it, Turgin?"

"My lord, come quickly."

Aurec instinctively slid his hand to his sword. The tone in Turgin's voice suggested danger. "What has happened?"

Terror lingered in his light brown eyes. "Another army approaches from the east."

"Another army?"

"Goblins," Turgin whispered.

That single word was strong enough to shatter the foundations of the world. The hour had grown late for Rogscroft. King and prince hurried off to the wall to catch a glimpse of this new evil.

TWENTY-FIVE

The War Changes

Thousands of Goblins marched under the brutal whips of their masters. Disorganized ranks of the snarling creatures moved as a black stain against the pure white snow. The men of the Wolfsreik watched in disgust while hurriedly preparing to attack. Word filtered through the ranks that the Goblins, once a mortal threat, had come as allies. Few accepted it as a truth. Most of the vaunted army saw the Goblins for what they were, the harbingers of doom. Others took it as the gravest insult. No matter how any man chose to view it, the Goblin army had arrived and in force.

Rolnir and Piper watched with abject disgust as the Goblins continued to surge into positions on the far right flank. Goblins were squat and powerful, barely taller than a Dwarf. Their grey skin was the color of ash. Fangs jutted from their squared faces. Legends said they ate their dead. Rolnir didn't doubt it. Their presence whispered a violent demise for all humanity stood for. A rancid smell choked the air.

"Disgusting creatures," Piper snapped.

More than just his senses were offended. Piper saw their coming as a personal affront to the abilities of the Wolfsreik. Badron had finally broken down and told his senior commanders about the Goblins. His decision was met with rage. The king denounced them for close-minded fools too willing to risk friendly lives during the coming battle. Not one of the commanders sided with the king, but it didn't matter. Badron was king and his decision was law.

Rolnir couldn't bring himself to look away. The Goblin army presented a ferocious appearance well beyond the fur-clad soldiers of the Wolfsreik. He despised them. Emotions couldn't override the natural hatred Rolnir held in his heart for the vile creatures. Goblins had no right to exist.

"Do you find it odd that such a large force was so well prepared and able to march on short notice?" he asked Piper.

He did. "They must have been preparing for this war as long as we have."

Rolnir hesitated. The consequences of that alone might be disastrous for his army. "Then we have been betrayed."

His words were barely a whisper. Rolnir had lived a soldier's life. It never once entered his thoughts that he might be betrayed by his own king. The convenient arrival of the Goblin army combined with their readiness for battle meant Badron must have struck a deal some time ago. The implications sickened him.

Piper stared at his longtime friend. They'd endured countless struggles and battles, many they should not have. Each trusted the other with his life. Whatever decision Rolnir made, Piper would follow.

"What are your orders, sir?"

Familiar confidence colored Rolnir's face. "Not much seems to bother you these days. How can you be so calm in the face of all this?"

Piper stared out at the sea of Goblins. "They are here. Nothing either of us does will send them back. The best we can hope for is that enough of those monsters get killed so that we don't have much to worry about until the city falls."

He held back his private thoughts. Images of what the Goblins were going to do to the men and women inside Rogscroft turned his stomach.

"When do you think Badron will call on us?"

"I do not think he will. Whatever council he keeps, the king does not trust us," Piper replied.

A company of Trolls, huge and carrying double-headed battle axes, marched by. Rolnir blanched. Their skin was almost pure black, their eyes a possessed red. Tufts of steel-tough hair dotted their muscled bodies. Their foreheads were sloping. Horns jutted from beneath their ears, curving over their faces. Rolnir had had the displeasure of fighting Trolls once. Only three of his men returned alive after the ambush. Trolls had iron-tough skin and took several blows before falling. Just two of the beasts killed almost fifty of the Wolfsreik. Seeing one hundred of the hulking creatures here inspired his darkest fears.

"We have nothing that can stop them," he said.

Piper shivered at the sight. Puss-filled lesions covered the Trolls' arms and legs.

"We'd best start sharpening pikes now," he said and half smiled. "I have a feeling it's going to take a lot just to kill one of those bastards."

"Piper, I want you to do something for me."

"Anything."

Rolnir grinned despite himself. "Work up a plan of attack against the Goblins. I have a sinking suspicion they already have done so against us."

They went back to watching the enemy army continue to move into position.

Badron watched as his Goblin counterpart marched up the snow-covered slope towards him. The king of Delranan struggled to keep disdain from showing. His instincts screamed that he should have resisted Amar Kit'han from the beginning. Every decision since had led him deeper into a growing disaster. The army's morale was at its lowest point since the war began. Badron's faith in his general had also waned. The world slowly closed in around him until this was all he could see.

Badron scowled. He knew the war was unnecessary. Revenge for the death of his son had fueled his ultimate decision. It might have easily been settled through a challenge. Instead, Badron used the single death as a spark to invade his longtime rival. Then came the Dae'shan. He wasn't sure how he had fallen under their spell, for surely it must be a sort of magic. They'd come with promises of fulfillment for all of his private lusts. Dreams of power and conquest had led him to this moment.

Amar Kit'han stood behind the king. The Dae'shan had dissolved his form back into darkness in order to remain unseen. The last thing he wanted was for Badron to realize that he had been duped and that both the Wolfsreik and Goblins marched to his manipulations. The Goblin king halted a few paces from Badron. Drool trickled from the corners of his mouth.

"You are king." It was more statement than question.

"Badron of Delranan, Lord of the Wolfsreik."

Grugnak was unimpressed. Natural hatred extended to all men, no matter their station. "Grugnak," he said.

Badron winced. The words sounded like rocks being chewed.

"Your assistance is appreciated, but unnecessary," he continued. Badron tried to exude a calm he did not have.

He'd never seen a Goblin before, at least not this close. Their kind had been relegated to myth in this part of Malweir. Badron cursed his weakness for leading him into this situation, knowing it was too late to send the Goblins away. The best he could hope for was that Rolnir was disobeying orders and preparing to make war on the grey bodies.

"Careful, King. The Goblins are not the sort to take insults well." Amar Kit'han's voice was a whisper only Badron could hear.

Grugnak shot a look of hatred up at him. "We are here to kill Men. Remember that."

"See how single-minded they are? Goblins detest life, yours most of all." Amar's voice held a certain humor, as if he found this scenario amusing. "Best not to upset your new allies."

"Quiet you bastard," Badron hissed through clenched teeth. "Else you can find a new puppet to play your games on."

Amar turned indignant. "Games? How little you grasp your situation. Mind your tongue, King, lest I have it torn from your mouth."

Badron stiffened, causing Grugnak to reach for his short sword.

"All the men you wish to kill are inside the castle walls," he told the Goblin.

Grugnak relaxed, if only slightly. He had no hesitation towards killing Badron. It was the Dae'shan's insistence that stayed his sword arm. "My Goblins want blood."

Badron felt his stomach turn. It took great willpower not to run the disgusting creature through with his sword. Instead, he reluctantly said, "They will have it. We attack at first light."

"No. Goblins do not fight under the sun. We will attack at night," Grugnak said defiantly.

"That is insane! My army does not have the advantage at night," Badron protested.

Grugnak laughed in his face. "You sleep, we fight!"

The Goblin general turned and stalked back to his army.

"I warned you, king. Do not provoke them. Goblins are touchy beings. It will avail none to anger them."

Badron glared back at the shadows in the dark. "Your words leave a chill upon my soul. I should tell you to piss off and be gone. This is my war."

Laughter. Cold, merciless laughter.

"Why do you laugh?"

"This was never your war."

Belkin couldn't believe his eyes as the first Goblin ranks marched into the city he had been born and raised in. They'd come to kill. Axes and rusty swords glinted in the torchlight. More and more came, all with bloodthirsty abandon. They snarled and called foul cadence. Belkin felt a warm trickle run down his right leg. He never dreamed he'd be forced to stand the line against such a dark foe. Instincts begged him to throw down his sword and flee.

"We need to get out of here," Pilin echoed his own thoughts.

Belkin's voice trembled. "No. We have been ordered to hold. Have faith, Pilin."

"I don't think I can."

Belkin understood. He caught the glimmer of another man in the building on the opposite side of the street. It was time. Dozens of arrowheads poked from every window on the street. Belkin did the same, drawing a bead on the nearest Goblin. His heart trembled. The thunder of each beat threatened to rip his head apart. He prayed his fingers kept their strength. A flaming arrow arced up over the city skyline. The signal. Every archer loosed simultaneously.

Goblins fell dead by the dozen. More lay wounded, trapped beneath the dead and the press of bodies still pushing into the kill zone. The archers loosed volley after volley, as fast as they could reload. Others poured buckets of pitch down on the writhing mass of bodies.

"Fire!"

Fire arrows plunged into the Goblins. A few managed to look up in time to see their deaths hiss down around them. The smell of cooked flesh roasted in the chill night air. Screams filled the city.

"Keep firing! Kill them!"

Belkin lost himself to battle, all thoughts of escape dissolved into the madness of battle rage. He and Pilin emptied their quivers well before the order to fall back was given. The handful of catapults on the castle walls barked flames into the night. Projectiles slammed into Grugnak's follow on forces. The Goblin advance stalled. Body parts were flung up into the air. The iron smell of blood choked the defenders.

"Fall back!" came the order. "Get back to your secondary positions!"

Belkin snatched his empty quiver. "Come on, Pilin. We have to leave before Goblins find us."

They ran, joining a large pack of others. The threat of death was very real. No one wanted to die this early in the siege. Mass confusion greeted the pair once they hit the main avenue. Rogscroft soldiers ran for their lives while burning Goblins ran off in despair. Their massed ranks had worked against them. Belkin and Pilin ducked down a tight alley and into another building. Two full quivers were already there. The boys settled down and prepared to kill again.

Rolnir watched the flames lick up into the fading night sky. Screams drowned out every other sound. He sighed. The Goblin assault had failed, miserably. Realistically it never stood much of a chance. The Wolfsreik hadn't the chance to clear any of the traps or obstacles. Snipers remained hidden instead of being routed back into the castle. Rolnir was almost amused. They might never know how many Goblins had been killed tonight, not that it mattered. Each death was one less his men would need to deal with once the siege was lifted. Rolnir watched the scene with a small measure of satisfaction before turning in for the night.

TWENTY-SIX

Harnin's Fall

Harnin One Eye ripped his wooden-handled dagger from the insurgent's chest in disdain. A slender thread of bright red blood splashed his tunic. Frustration caused the veins on his neck to stand out, pulsing darkly. Another prisoner and the same results. Harnin stabbed down hard. The blade lodged deep into bone. He turned and left the cooling corpse for his orderlies to remove.

"Your tactics don't work," Jarrik said.

"I can see that!" he snapped back. "More drastic measures are necessary."

Skaning slammed his fist into the wall. "These are our people! We cannot continue murdering them without cause!"

"Without cause? They started this war! Need I remind you that the king's own son was murdered not two hundred meters from where you and I now stand?" Harnin raged.

Skaning met his cold glare. "By Rogscroft, not by our own folk. You carry this vendetta too far, Harnin."

"Perhaps I need to take it a step further."

The younger Skaning dropped back into a fighting stance. "If you think you can."

"Enough of this!" Jarrik barked. "We'll get nowhere by fighting ourselves. I'm sure King Badron expects better of us."

"Nor would he want us killing his citizens," Skaning replied.

Jarrik stepped between them. "What would you suggest? I'm afraid that Harnin is right. We must try something else if we hope to end this war."

"Find a military target and I will give my full support."

Harnin spat. "This is what we are trying to do! Argis is behind this insurrection. Find him and we end the rebellion."

"Argis is cunning. He betrayed us and no one saw it coming," Jarrik commented.

"He is the head. We need to find and kill him."

Skaning remained unconvinced. "What if he is not?"

"What?" Jarrik and Harnin asked at the same time.

"Hear me out. Argis betrayed us, that much is true. But what if he was turned by someone else? This rebellion is too well prepared to be run by one man. Argis might only be one of several."

Harnin lashed out. His boot made a squishing sound when it struck the body of the man he had just killed. Blood splashed.

"Do not take me for a fool! You cry that my methods are too extreme, but they have yet to make a prisoner talk. You then dare to steal the blame from Argis and place it on any one of us? What you suggest would tear this kingdom to shreds. Perhaps if I begin hacking off limbs I will find my answers."

Jarrik groaned. "Listen to yourself. What you propose will turn the entire population against us, including our own soldiers. Do you want to be the one who has to explain to the king how you lost his kingdom?"

"So long as Argis remains free and alive he is a threat," Harnin said, ignoring him. "Where does it end? With our deaths? His? Or should Chadra Keep be burned to the ground? None of you have the answers. Regardless if Argis is their leader or not, he must die. The others are disaffected peasants following nobility. Kill the nobility and they go back to plowing their fields."

Silence settled over them. Skaning tried not to stare at the One Eye. The younger lord had always been one of Badron's staunched supporters, but he valued Delranan above any one man. The kingdom must come first. Anything less defeated the purpose. He wanted to run Harnin through for his indulgences. Doing so would only serve to brand him a traitor. The youngest captain instead decided to bite back on his pride and bide his time. Harnin would make his mistake soon enough and all Skaning had to do was wait to reap the benefits.

Jarrik cleared his throat. "We need to focus all of our efforts on finding Argis."

Finally, Harnin spoke in more measured tones. "There is another facet that even Badron had not the time to consider."

They looked at him expectantly.

"Argis must be in league with Rogscroft."

Simple. A clear, concise statement with deep running implications. Harnin knew he had them in the palm of his hand now. Delranan and Rogscroft had never been close allies, but they'd seldom let their animosity flare into open hostility. King Stelskor certainly had his share of flaws and prejudices, just as Badron did. The one thing he didn't have was reason to attack Badron. In that context, the attack on the keep made no sense. The death of Badron's only heir was only helpful if they managed to kill the father as well.

Jarrik spoke first. "That doesn't make sense. How could Argis have done so?"

"Think about it. Rumors are that the Pell Darga often come down from their mountains to trade with Stelskor. You were here the night of the attack. You both were. How many Pell short spears did we find in our dead? I believe they made contact with Argis and turned him against the very people he swore to protect."

"If what you say is true, this changes everything," Jarrik replied.

Harnin nodded slowly. "Making Argis more dangerous. He has to die for his crimes against our people."

"We shall double our efforts," Jarrik said after a few moments of silence. His amber eyes narrowed in newfound intent. The curve of his jaw steeled. "If he is in this city we shall find him."

"King Badron deserves no less, Captain."

Jarrik slapped Skaning on the chest with the back of his hand. "Come on, we have work to do."

Harnin watched them leave. His breathing slowed back to normal. Skaning had come close to guessing the truth, and that was of great concern. Fortunately the man was still young enough to be naïve. Otherwise Harnin would have killed him where he stood. Suspicions haunting his conscience, Harnin turned away. His thoughts were already back on the prisoners. The acting lord of Delranan bore no illusions about halting his tortures. A dark part of him came alive with each new scream, each rivulet of dark blood draining from the victims. Half of the time he hadn't even bothered to ask questions. It was enough to watch them die.

Smiling, he looked down at the blood stain on his tunic and left the dungeons.

"You play a dangerous game."

Harnin's heart leapt to his throat as the voice whispered in his ear. The darkness of the throne room was only broken by the half-dead fire in a distant brazier. He panicked. Fatigue had tired him, forcing down his guard. A shadow moved, ever so slightly, from behind the throne.

"All of Delranan's captains are equally dangerous."

Harnin reached for his short sword, knowing it would be of no avail. "Show yourself, assassin."

Wicked laughter mocked him. "Were I an assassin you would already be torn limb from limb and fed to your own dogs. Put away your sword, Harnin One Eye."

Pelthit Re lowered his shadows and became visible. The Dae'shan had been conspicuously absent these last few weeks, enough that Harnin failed to recognize his voice. That in itself was troubling enough.

"Why do you return now? When I do not need you?" Harnin questioned.

"The hour grows late and you have come to the edge of losing all you have struggled so hard for."

Harnin felt a sudden tightness in his chest, like some giant invisible hand trying to crush his life out. The Dae'shan slipped around the front of the ancient cedar throne. His cowled head angled down in silent contempt. Men were so reliant on trivial symbols of power that it prevented them from achieving any true power.

Harnin gasped for breath. "How?"

An impossible wind lashed across the chamber. Dying embers danced in the air as they trailed aimlessly away. Pelthit Re sat himself upon the throne once Harnin fell to his knees. Corporeal hands gently grasped the arms, intricately carved into the heads of wolves.

"Your arrogance has allowed this. Argis is now a hero to the people. They rally behind his name as if he were a legend, a god amongst men. Will you allow him to deliver them from their nightmares? History often forgets villains."

The constriction faded. Harnin glared up with a pinched expression. "Argis is a traitor to the kingdom."

"Yes, one you helped create. Your blind subservience to that decrepit old man you call king has led you into ruin's arms. I fear you might not recover before he returns."

Taunts. The Dae'shan sought the weakness in Harnin and tried to exploit it. The One Eye felt insulted, his pride slapped. He also found a newly kindled hunger gnawing at him. All his life he had been forced to stand in the shadow of a lesser man. Pelthit Re had been delivered to show him how life was meant to be. His life was now stagnant, brackish from the lack of ambition he knew he was *supposed* to have. Harnin wanted it, wanted it all.

"Help me," he begged from his knees. It was a single thread of hope.

Pelthit Re cocked his head. "Why?"

Harnin bowed. "I want Badron's power. I want his life, the glory, and the pride. Argis is a threat, yes, but with your help I can quench his life and turn Delranan into the kingdom it should have been."

"Perhaps," the Dae'shan answered in a harsh cackle. "You should rise, kings do not kneel."

The Dae'shan was gone, faded back into nothingness, by the time Harnin struggled to his feet. All that remained was a hollow glow in the seat of the throne.

"You should mind your tongue," Jarrik scolded.

Skaning spun on his friend, pointing an accusing finger a little too close to his face. "Harnin is out of control. You know I am right. We risk ruin if we sit by and watch him lead us further down this dark road."

"What would you have me do?" Anger flashed behind his eyes.

"Stand up for our people. We are the captains of Delranan."

Jarrik clenched a fist. "Mind yourself. You may have taken the place of Argis on this council, but you have not risen to his level. Above all we serve the king. Do not forget this. Ever."

His warning was thinly veiled. Threats and suspicion haunted every corner in their kingdom now. No one was safe from accusations, least of all the once vaunted captains. Scores of people had been rounded up in a massive purge. The people lived in fear. Friend turned in friend, brother betrayed brother. No one knew who might be taken next, but no one wanted to die for protecting someone.

Skaning took it as an insult. "I have been a captain for nearly two years! Argis has nothing to do with that."

"Of course he does!" Jarrik threw his arms wide. "Argis is the only reason you gained your title so quickly. Harnin is smart enough to remember that. Watch yourself before the One Eye decides to pursue that thought further."

"I am not worried about Harnin, at least not in that aspect."

Jarrik halted. Confusion twisted his handsome features. "Why insist on provoking his ire? He is not an enemy worth having."

"Harnin will be an enemy for as long as he continues this course of action. I cannot control my emotions," Skaning explained. He leaned closer so that no one else might overhear his next words. "I believe there is more. He does not act alone."

"What more?" Jarrik's tone darkened enough to put Skaning on guard.

"Ever since King Badron left, Harnin has become an entirely different man. He craves bloodshed instead of humility. He willingly sacrifices his people chasing shadows. How did this happen so quickly? He was not always such."

"I don't believe you," Jarrik said without conviction. "Harnin is the sole entrusted regent to the throne. Who could possibly be helping him and what is there to gain?"

"I do not know but think about it. He was always the most rational of us. There was a time, even right after the king's son was killed, that he wouldn't have dreamed of harming his own people. What changed? You cannot expect me to believe that Argis is to blame."

"He leads a rebellion, Skaning. The man is dangerous to Harnin and Delranan."

"So much of a threat that he warrants all of our attention? The rebellion did not exist before *we* created it."

"Are you mad? Argis allowed the enemy to breach our defenses and steal the princess. We would not be at war if not for him!"

"You cannot blame it on one man, Jarrik. It took all of us to arrive here. Do not believe, but there is something sinister driving Harnin."

Jarrik began to pace in tight circles. "Who? What? Without someone to pin the blame on, you only offer baseless claims."

Skaning exhaled a deep breath. "I have said my piece. Take it for what you will."

"I want to believe you, I truly do, but our hands are tied unless you can find out who this person is."

The young captain nodded, almost ashamed he did not have the answers. "I will discover the truth in this."

They parted without another word. Jarrik watched the younger man leave. Skaning had an air of confidence, like he felt better doing the right thing. Jarrik spat. Right and wrong were terms that offered little in the changing kingdom. He saw Skaning for what he was, a threat. If the boy did discover his imaginary truths, he would need to be dealt with. Jarrik decided to keep a close watch until then.

TWENTY-SEVEN

The Dragon's Teeth

"This is it."

Boen stepped past Bahr to stand at the center of his freshest nightmare. Disbelief continued to twist his features with concern. He hadn't been the same since his encounter with the ghosts of his forefathers. The big man acted skittish when confronted now with the new unknown. Part of him had no desire to carry on, but his heart demanded that he learn the truth of why so many of his blood had been slaughtered so far from home in such a god-awful place. Or perhaps they'd been drawn here by some unexplainable power?

Boen shook his head. Snow fell from his unruly hair. "Can't be."

A permanent mist concealed the area. He might have easily led them past here if not for his previous encounter and the urging of the wizard. The old man had been locked in a meditative trance when he suddenly leapt up on the driver's bench and shouted for them to stop.

Bahr dismissed Boen's misgivings. "It has to be. Look at the mist. This is the only place we have encountered mist since we got in these mountains. You said so yourself."

"There was one other," Boen replied tersely.

Details of the ghosts remained his private memories. It was too personal to share. He searched every shadow, every crevice partially hidden from view. Boen did not want to see them again; his blood still ran cold from their last meeting. Yet disappointment plagued him. He had been wrong. The ghosts did not reappear. Boen felt… alone? Bahr listened, but thought nothing of it. He was convinced they had successfully arrived at the teeth of the dragon.

"The book says we would come to a place where the rocks are tinged in red and form teeth. It will appear as a mouth," Anienam added.

Boen reluctantly moved towards the nearest rock. He reached out with a gloved hand to touch the porous surface.

Flakes of red clung to the worn leather. The rock was easily twice as tall as a man. He squinted into the mists. More rocks choked the area. There was an ancient feel here. Boen resisted the urge to turn and leave.

"I told you," he said.

Bahr came forward, staring with mouth agape. The rocks were dark red, as if they bled. A hint of a smile shadowed his face. "I'll be damned."

"I knew it!" Anienam shouted gleefully. "This is the entrance to the Borgin Pass!"

Dorl Theed passed a sidelong glance to Nothol. "Great, now what do we do?"

He had a valid point. All their time and energy had been dedicated to finding this mythical marker in the untamed mountains. Now that they had actually succeeded they found themselves at an unexpected crossroads.

"The forge of Giants lies down this road," the wizard continued.

Growing discomfort continued to spread among them. He needed to stop it and restore a sense of order. They had come far and this was not the time to fracture. Cold mist kissed their exposed skin. Anienam finished whispering his spell and the mist parted long enough for the group to stop deliberating and see the area for what it was. Massive, conical rocks were visible. Most sprang up from the ground while others hung from rock outcroppings. Maleela gasped with awe and shuddered. She felt as if she were standing in a giant maw, about to be devoured.

"It is like a dragon's mouth," she whispered.

Bahr turned to stare at her. "What?"

She edged closer. "The rocks, they look like teeth, Uncle."

An odd feeling of doom clung to them. Ancient and malevolent forces gathered here. She wanted to leave now.

"Perhaps these are a real dragon's bones," Nothol suggested.

"Nonsense. There hasn't been a dragon in this part of Malweir in hundreds of years," Bahr scoffed.

Anienam clambered down from the wagon to get a better look. Despite all of his experience and travels, he had never been to the Murdes Mountains. The sights around him were astounding. He tentatively, reverently, reached out to touch one of the razor sharp rocks.

"Incredible," he said admiringly. "Dragons may be rare, but they are not extinct. They are merely sleeping."

"Asleep? Until when?" Dorl asked.

The wizard offered a tight smile. "Who can say? We are but one insignificant race in a grand world."

"That has nothing to do with these being actual teeth," Bahr said, trying to refocus them. "I'm sure the men that wrote your book thought the same things. Wizard, can you be certain this is the correct place?"

"Yes, I believe so. The book is very specific. The mists. The red stones resembling teeth. It all corresponds."

Pleased with the reply, Bahr said, "Good. We are in the right place."

"We should be moving," Boen urged.

Anienam stayed them with a glare. "Not so fast. We don't know what awaits us down this road. The pass might be filled with traps, or worse."

"Worse?" Dorl hissed.

"The men who wrote the book never made it beyond this point. Once we leave here, we will be blind."

"Wizard, those traps will be there regardless of whether we delay or not," Boen grumbled. Specters leered at him in his mind's eye.

Anienam conceded the Gaimosian was right, but Anienam had a lurking suspicion they were heading into grave danger. He sighed but relented. The best thing he could for them all was prepare. Magic might be the only thing that could save their lives in the days to come. He resumed his place on the wagon.

"Stay close to me, Princess. We are not safe yet," he told Maleela.

She nodded absently. The sheer scope of the mouth went beyond her comprehension. "Do you really think these are bones?"

Anienam smiled warmly. "Bones of the world. There are a few recorded instances of dragons being so large. None in the last two millennia. Whether or not they truly are dragon bones, they are not what we need to worry about."

"I don't understand."

"The Giants have had little to do with the rest of Malweir for centuries. No race has had dealings with them. We might not like what we find when we get to Venheim."

Maleela was about to answer when the faint sound of hammers striking steel drifted across the wind. Her heart erupted with excitement. "Did you hear that, Anienam?"

He exhaled slowly. "Yes, child. I hear them. Venheim."

"We are all dead," Ionascu moaned. He threw his hands up and cursed Harnin One Eye for forcing him into this position.

"Be quiet," Anienam scoffed. "We've made it this far. Have faith and it will carry us the rest of the way."

Ionascu simmered hotly. "Faith in what?"

The wizard offered no answer. In what, indeed.

"Close up and move out," Bahr ordered. "These Giants are real. Let's get this hammer and be about our business."

He tapped his heel to his horse's flank and the tiny band lurched forward. Time had run out. All the deliberation and second guessing was at an end. Bahr didn't particularly care to confront a clan of Giants. He'd already been through enough since accepting the quest to rescue Maleela. Doubts racked his mind. The question of whether they had rescued or damned his niece haunted him. Harnin's betrayal led him to believe they had all been duped.

He might have laughed if the moment were not so grim. Here, in the Mountains of Death, he and his small band were on an impossible quest to claim an ancient weapon and destroy an undying evil. Their chances were slim. Part of him wished he had kicked the damned wizard out of his home when he had the chance. Events might have turned out differently, though he somehow doubted it. Bahr shook his head. Things happened for a reason.

"What do you suppose these Giants are like?" he asked Boen quietly.

He and the Gaimosian weren't the closest of friends, but each had come to rely on the other's strengths. Boen had candor and the tactical experience that dwarfed the rest of the group. "We'll find out once we get to Venheim."

"Do you think there will be a fight?"

Boen flashed a toothy grin. "Wouldn't that be fun?"

Bahr didn't know if he was joking or not, but the question was disturbing. Boen had a way of simplifying even the most complex affair. The hammering sound grew louder. Bahr detected a musical quality in it, suggesting master craftsmanship. He never dreamed he might hear the song of the hammers in the wind. He was about to reply when two massive figures broke through the mists and blocked the pass. The mist distorted them, making them seem even larger than they were. Rocks and snow tumbled from the slopes.

"Swords!" Boen bellowed.

He glanced at Bahr, surprised to find the Sea Wolf in shock. The figures marched closer.

"Who dares trespass on this sacred ground?"

The voice was as deep as the crash of thunder. Boen staggered as the ground trembled beneath him. His heart threatened to quail. They wouldn't stand a chance against these two monsters. The Gaimosian snarled and readied to meet death. The mist swirled like angry lovers around the figures. A sharp screech filled the muffled air. They've drawn swords, Boen thought.

"Answer us," the second voice demanded.

Anienam jumped down and slipped in front of Boen. His arms were held up. There was youthful vigor to his words and movements. "Wait! We are not enemies! There is no call for violence here. I am a friend of your people."

"You are violators and must be punished for your impudence."

"I had hoped it would not come to this," Anienam whispered under his breath.

His mouth moved without sound. Anienam clapped his hands as hard as he could. The pass filled with unnatural energies. The air bore a tainted green hue. A sharp wind screamed out from his fingertips. It tore into the mists, shredding the veil around the two figures. Surprise registered across their massive faces.

"You dare!" roared the Giant on the right.

Blue wizard fire cackled off Anienam's hands. The spry man stood his ground. "We did not come here to fight you."

"You should not have come at all." He took a menacing step towards them.

Anienam offered a tight smile. "Come no closer, I warn you."

Both Giants finally understood what they faced. A wizard. "There are no more Mages on Malweir. What trickery is this?"

They had heavy brows jutting over beady eyes. Bahr immediately compared them to men. Aside from their foreheads, the Giants were just bigger versions of his friends. Nearly three meter-tall versions.

"I am Anienam Keiss, son of Dakeb."

The Giants passed an uneasy glance, murmuring to each other in their language. The sound hurt Bahr's ears. It was crude, un-evolved, and filled with harsh sounds.

"The name of Dakeb is known to us," the obvious leader said. "But Dakeb had no son. You lie."

Anienam exhaled his growing frustration. "Do you truly doubt me? I have already shown you what I can do.

Dakeb was my father. I have no reason to lie. He adopted me not long after Gren fell. It was his wish to rebuild the order of Mages once the Silver Mage was vanquished. It is the great shame of my life that I have not been able to succeed in his name."

The answer seemed to satisfy the Giant guardians. The larger one, heavily armored with a more dangerous aura, knelt before the shriveled wizard. Dark eyes searched Anienam for traces of falsehood. The Giant softened after a moment.

"Why have you come?" he asked.

The Giant, Groge, left his partner at the mouth of the pass and escorted Anienam's party back to Venheim. Giant and wizard spoke along the way. Groge ignored the rest. They were nothing more than a bodyguard as far as he was concerned and, therefore, of little consequence.

"My grandfather accompanied Dakeb on a quest once," Groge admitted proudly.

Blindfolded, Anienam feigned a smile. "My father often sought help from many races on Malweir. He understood, as do I, that none of us holds the key to ultimate success or failure. He was a wise man. More should have learned from his example."

Groge nodded, instantly feeling foolish. Blindfolding them was one of the firmest points he demanded if they expected to move on to Venheim. Giants were secretive by nature. They had tribes spread out across the high places of the world. None were so sacred as the mighty forge atop the Murdes Mountains. Groge expected a harsh return with repercussions for violating the standing order not to allow outsiders in. Still, he led them into the main valley with his head high. Several of his kin stopped to stare at the intruders. It had been over a century since one not of their blood ventured into the forge. Several warriors went for weapons capable of rending a man apart in a single swipe. A ring of warriors slowly formed around the wagon. Horses bucked from fright. Swords were drawn.

"These men are under my protection," Groge warned.

"Stand aside, whelp," snapped the obvious leader.

Tensions rose. The Giants inched closer. Bahr and the others could only wonder at what was happening. Death crept upon them without the decency of letting them see it coming.

"Stop!" growled a stern voice. "These people should not be harmed."

Heads turned as the newcomer stalked into their midst. The fate of the quest stood on the edge, leaving all locked in doubt.

TWENTY-EIGHT

Venheim

The two sides stood apart. Hands twitched, eager for the comforting feel of steel while the Giants merely clenched their fists with anticipation. Fighting was almost alien to the gentle beings, but even a glancing blow would kill one of Bahr's friends. Sweat bead across their brows, inspired by the near unbearable heat radiating from the forges. Acidic smells of sulfur and melted iron ore left the sky dusty, contaminated.

"Forgive me, elder," Groge apologized. "But I do not believe these people mean us any harm."

The elder sneered. "Such decisions are not yours to make. They could be harbingers for a thing far worse than what they claim."

Groge moved next to the wagon, ignoring the ring of warriors threatening to attack. "This man claims to be the son of Dakeb."

Hushed conversation broke out. All knew the legend of the last Mage. Dakeb had been considered a friend amongst the Giant clans. An entire army of Giants once fought alongside the Mage and his meager allies during one of Malweir's darkest times. The Mage Wars was the last time Giants had moved freely among the race of Men. Too many warriors had been killed. In the end, it was not a difficult decision. The Giants chose to abandon the rest of Malweir and became myth to all but a few.

Dakeb was one who always came to visit, for he had many friends down through the generations. The Giants mourned his death for many years, as was their custom. His loss became a pained scar across the face of the world. The Mages were finally gone. For all of their good and bad, the once protectors of Malweir came to an end. The world became a lesser place.

None of that factored into the elder's current position.

"Perhaps he speaks true, but that does not give him the right to defile this place."

Another Giant came forward. Immeasurably old, his very presence commanded respect. "Let the son of Dakeb speak. I wish to hear what he has to say."

Groge helped Anienam down from the wagon. Giant elders were elected by popular vote, but the ancient one held respect and reverence from his lifetime of deeds. Anienam removed the blindfold and stared up at the circle of Giants.

The elder frowned but remained quiet. "Very well. Speak, son of Dakeb. Tell us why you have violated our privacy."

The wizard had expected a harsh reception. The Giants had been his father's friends, not his. He spoke with quiet authority, telling them everything that they needed to know. He left certain matters out and emphasized others. Mention of the Dae'shan caused another round of murmurs. Their evil was well known to the older races. Rumor held that a Giant had once been part of that foul group. Anienam clasped his hands behind his back upon finishing his tale.

"The Blud Hamr! Impossible," spat the elder.

Giants erupted in debate. No human was meant to hold the sacred hammer, let alone use it in battle. Anienam concealed his satisfaction. He'd planned for just this sort of reaction. Long nights spent researching had opened doors for the wizard. He knew the hammer's true purpose and the origins of such a fantastical weapon. He glanced back as the men and women he had come to call friends still squirmed under their blindfolds. Only Boen seemed unaffected.

The ancient Giant slammed the iron tip of his walking staff on the ground. "The Blud Hamr has its own destiny. We are forbidden from denying the one chosen. Blekling, I shall take the son of Dakeb and discuss his quest in my quarters. Have the others housed and fed. They are not our foes."

Blekling, the elder, scowled. Clearly struggling with his emotions, he finally relented. "Very well. It shall be as you say, but know this, Joden, if so much as one of them causes trouble, I will have them all thrown from the tallest peak. They remain here only by your good will."

Joden ignored him. He was the greatest forge master in centuries and his word carried more weight than many of the elders combined.

"Untie the others. Groge, they are your responsibility now," Blekling snapped.

The elder stormed off as the circle of warriors dissolved. The novelty of strangers quickly wore off. It wasn't long before the symphony of hammers danced in the air again. Groge did as ordered, leading them back to his massive stone home nestled in a small cut in the cliff face. Most Giant homes were carved from the mountainside. Impressive stained-glass windows reflected the majesty of the dawn sun. Everything about Venheim suggested beauty. The smell of roasting meat clung to the fading daylight. An impressive building much larger than any of the intruders had ever seen took up the entire back of the valley.

Bahr's jaw dropped at the sight of sprawling buttresses and imposing granite walls. "What is that?"

"Our cathedral."

Groge's answer was so simple it was dismissive, as if everyone should know the answer.

"Cathedral for what?" Maleela asked.

The innocence in her tone alone was what made Groge answer. "It is where we go to pray to God. Do your people not have such places?"

She shook her head, suddenly feeling very foolish. "The gods have not been worshipped since before the Mage Wars. They are all but forgotten now."

The implication for the young Giant was staggering. Faith in a higher power kept his people disciplined and provided purpose. "How do you live without God's favor?"

"Perhaps we don't. Malweir is a dangerous place, Groge," she answered. "The only gods we know are the dark ones that now threaten us."

"Perhaps it was that lack of faith that drove your gods away. Malweir was not always as you describe it. At least that is what our priests tell us."

Groge had an almost childish attitude that became evident when he spoke. Maleela found it refreshing and odd for a being so large. Curiosity soon beat out prudence. "How old are you?"

He appeared embarrassed. "One hundred and nine."

She gasped. "Surely you are joking."

"No. I only recently achieved adulthood," he said indignantly.

She paused. "Oh, I am sorry. I did not mean to offend you. I only thought that you were much older."

"Giants are not considered mature until we reach one hundred. Joden, the one who forced Blekling to back down, is almost four hundred years old. He is the oldest Giant ever recorded. I would be lucky to have such a life."

Tension evaporated. Maleela suddenly felt at ease. The Giants had been terrifying to behold initially, but their subtle charms began to wear down her defenses. If nothing else, she knew that they would all sleep soundly tonight. She spared a look to Rekka Jel. The smaller, darker woman displayed no emotion. Maleela made a note to ask her what was wrong once they had time.

"This is my home," Groge announced.

Bahr and Boen dismounted. They were so alike Maleela often had trouble distinguishing between them. She idly wondered why her father had turned out so differently from them. They were strong, dependable men. She had no issue with placing her life in their hands. Her father, on the other hand, might slip a knife between her shoulder blades given the opportunity.

She looked around, dismayed that she was the only one interested in casual conversation. "Do you live here alone?"

"Yes," he replied. "We all do. It is one of the privileges of being allowed in Venheim."

Nothol Coll finally gave in to the urge to know more. "I was under the impression that all Giants lived here."

Groge emphatically shook his head. "No, this is the sacred forge. Only a handful are selected to apprentice here. I was chosen nine years ago to come and learn from the forge masters. My family is greatly honored."

"Where is your family?" Maleela asked.

The question was innocent enough, but Groge was careful with the answer. Some secrets needed to be kept. "They are back in my village."

Nothol had plenty of questions he could have asked, but Groge's answer proved they would be a waste of time. The Giant may be young by their standards, but he was not about to give away the secrets of his people. The implications of his answer were satisfying enough. There must be Giant villages spread across the world. If such was the case, why had no one seen a Giant? Either they didn't want to be found or they were busy preparing for something big. Nothol shrugged the notion off. Superstitions didn't belong.

"You must get lonely here," Maleela commented.

Groge responded like a man who tried not to think on it. "There are moments, but the honor of learning from the great masters is too much to pass up. We go to the chapel to pray when we grow too lonely."

"Faith has that much power?" Nothol asked.

The idea was more than intriguing. The only thing he ever placed faith in was his will and a good sword. Man, even his best friend Dorl, was fallible. He supposed much the same could be said of a sword. Steel was breakable. Still, that left no room for any kind of gods, light or dark.

Groge led them inside.

"Please, my home is yours."

Bahr cleared his throat. He was still upset with not being allowed to go with Anienam. The old man had a way of keeping secrets, secrets Bahr felt he should know. "Where can we stable our horses? They need to be looked after before we are seen to."

"Of course. How rude of me! Though in all fairness there is not an animal on Malweir that is large enough for my kind to ride," Groge laughed good-naturedly.

He really is still a child, Maleela thought and smiled. She found it refreshing after months of torment and troubles. Groge was comparatively about the same age as she was. He was also far more naïve than she ever had the luxury of being. Those who had ridden on the wagon went inside while Bahr and the others followed Groge to a small shed on the far side of the house. Small was a relative term. The first thing Bahr noticed was how big the shed was. It was like stepping into a small barn.

"What do horses eat?" Groge asked.

The sun had just gone down over the western peaks. The air cooled almost immediately. Bahr grunted as the wave of cold collided with the heat from so many forges. The prospect of spending a freezing night on the roof of the world did not sit well with him.

"We have enough feed, but we could use some water. That is the one thing we have in short supply," he said.

"There is a well two houses down. I will fetch it for you."

They watched the young Giant go, an enormous bucket in his hand.

Boen set his tack down on an empty part of the nearest workbench. He noticed the familiar gleam in Bahr's eye. "What are you planning?"

"I want to find out what our illustrious wizard is learning," he replied.

Nothol and Dorl exchanged wary glances but knew better than to comment.

Even Boen disapproved. "You put us all at risk. I advise against it."

"Anienam isn't exactly trustworthy, Boen. He knew where to find this place all along but chose to let us bumble our way through it. I don't like being played for the fool."

"These Giants aren't the sort we need to be troubling," Boen reminded him.

"When did you become the sensible one? You've been Mister Run-through-them-with-a-sword and move on since we left Delranan. Don't change your song now."

Boen forced a smile he did not feel. He'd been through enough challenges over the course of his life to know when not to rise up against the odds. Attempting to anger an entire tribe of Giants bordered on suicide. "I know my limitations, Bahr."

Nothol Coll couldn't remain silent any longer. "He's right. The Giants don't trust us. It is too early to risk going against their wishes."

Anger flashed in Bahr's cheeks. "I don't give a damn about their wishes. What I want, what I need, is to find out what that old Giant has to say about the hammer so we can be about our business. The answers affect us all."

"Doing so only places unnecessary danger on us," Boen said and punched his saddle. "I believe their little threat about being thrown from the highest mountain."

Bahr couldn't understand why they were so adamantly against him. They'd been through enough scrapes and close calls since leaving Chadra the first time that this one shouldn't be any different.

"Regardless of what you believe, I don't wish to die up here. There is no honor in it," Boen's voice was controlled, every word measured before he spoke.

His hand rested precariously close to his sword. It was more instinct that thought. Gaimosian blood was thick with battle prowess. He had no desire to combat his friend but had no trouble in doing so if push came to shove. "Think about the consequences. We are all in jeopardy."

"Don't get in my way on this."

"Why? What is so damned important that you risk all our lives?"

Bahr raged. "I don't trust the wizard! He's hiding something and I want to know what."

"That's it?" the Gaimosian asked. "I don't trust anyone. Get used to it. We will all live a little longer that way."

Boen's comment diffused the situation, at least for now. None of them wanted to fight each other. The urge to take a break from all the troubles and worries of their quest suddenly overcame Bahr and he sank to his knees. Groge reentered a moment later with a bucket full of water and an adolescent grin. If he only knew.

TWENTY-NINE

A Past Revealed

The walk through the Giant village was refreshing, yet mildly disconcerting. The Giants may have been friends of his father, but they remained cold to him. Anienam had a sinking feeling that he should have come here much sooner in his life. Not that it mattered much. His life had been dedicated towards stopping the dark gods until he passed the mantle to the next man or the gods of light returned. The enormous cathedral dominating the far end of the valley led him to believe the culmination of his life's work was coming.

"Your people still believe in the gods," he commented.

Joden nodded. "Since the beginning. We have never lost our faith. It has helped define who we are."

Warmth spread through Anienam's heart. "Would that more races still held on to religion. Malweir might not be such a dangerous place."

"Most of the races are young, yours included," Joden replied. "We Giants were among the first to stride across the world. There is much wisdom to be learned over that much time."

"How old are you?"

The question was too tempting to pass on. He knew nothing of Giants. Most of the collected knowledge had been lost when the Mage fortress of Ipn Shal burned to the ground. A thousand years had done nothing to ease the hurt of such tragedy. Anienam once held dreams of rebuilding the grandeur of Ipn Shal. Time and the lack of magic left in the world slowly forced those dreams away. The ruins were meant to remain just that.

"That is a secret your father never discovered," Joden replied. He broke into a gentle smile. "As venerated as he was among our kind, there are some things that are meant to remain unspoken."

Fair enough, Anienam thought. We all have our secrets. He opted to change the subject. "I would like to see the inside of the cathedral before we leave."

"That might be possible. Blekling and his closest supporters will not sit idle for long. They will seek to expel you from Venheim before long. He is from the newer thinking."

Anienam had a feeling what Joden meant but wasn't sure. "Which way of thinking is that?"

"The one where no one but a Giant is to be trusted. They keep faith only in their own kind. Once, we welcomed visitors here. Those days are barely memories anymore. Now we hide in our mountain villages and waste our lives in quiet isolation. I find it distressing from time to time."

Anienam was surprised. Dakeb once told him that several Giants had been among the ranks of Mages. Despite their massive size, they were among the gentler races. Still, the wizard dreaded the day when they were provoked into war. Latent anger rested just beneath the surface here.

"The other races have much to share. The Elves once had a forge to rival this one," Anienam said.

Most Giants would have dismissed him right there. Joden merely took it in stride. "I have heard whispers of the star silver sword. I cannot deny that my heart has longed to behold it just once before I die."

Phaelor. The star silver sword. Elven smiths wrought the fabled sword during the time of the Mage War. It was the only weapon capable of destroying the crystal of Tol Shere. Anienam shrugged off a chill. The crystal had been meant as a source of unlimited knowledge. Reality proved different. Evil corrupted the crystal and a young Mage named Sidian fell under its spell. His name was forever linked to the most devastating time in Malweir's history. Sidian became a plague lasting centuries. The nightmare didn't end until Dakeb led an ill-fated quest to destroyed his once friend. The crystal and Sidian were both consumed in the destruction caused by the sword.

"Sadly, the Elves reclaimed Phaelor after Fennic Attleford used it to kill the Silver Mage," Anienam said.

Joden grunted softly. "It is unfortunate, though possibly for the best."

"How so?"

"The sword was created for a specific purpose. With that purpose done, it should not be left to the devices of another handler."

Joden, along with most people, knew the story of that final night in the city of Aingaard when Phaelor slew the Silver Mage. Giant smiths saw the sword as a treasure to be used sparingly and with extreme reservations. Magic had its uses and was easily corruptible. The crystal of Tol Shere proved the dangers in higher powers. The constructs of Men were easily susceptible.

"They say the sword can choose who will wield it," Anienam said. "I must admit that the magic imbued in the sword is well beyond my skill. Unfortunately, the Elves are loath to admit their secrets."

The Giant nodded. "As well they should be."

They arrived at Joden's home without ceremony, the conversation ranging in topics. Anienam was greeted by a roaring fire with flames easily as tall as he was. Joden still added a few more logs to the fire though. He then fixed a kettle of water for tea and joined the wizard on the course stone chairs at the table.

"You broke the subject nicely with talk of the star silver sword," the Giant said after a few moments of awkward silence.

Anienam admitted, "I did have a few moments of consternation, especially when Blekling raged."

Joden brushed off his concern. "He means well. The wrong sorts are normally the ones who come searching for weapons like the Blud Hamr. Caution is prudent. Blekling just needs to learn how to speak rationally with others."

"Agreed."

"Tell me what you know of it, the hammer."

The question helped Anienam relax somewhat. "Not that much. I hadn't even heard of it until I discovered the book buried beneath Chadra."

Joden went to snatch the boiling water from the fire. He moves well for an old man, Anienam noticed. He looked down. Joden grabbed the handle, which was just as hot as the kettle, with his bare hands. Decades of iron work had turned his hands into meaty slabs of callous. Joden didn't even react to heat that would sear a normal man's flesh away. He smiled as he poured two mugs. Steam formed beads of moisture on his hardened face and he apologized for having no small mugs.

"The Blud Hamr is…special. It is much like the Elven sword," the forge master began after resuming his seat.

Anienam remained silent.

"Long ago, our greatest forge masters were visited by a trio of men claiming a terrible evil had been loosed upon the world at the time of the dark gods' banishment. These men believed in the gods of light and devoted their lives towards staying evil's hand. Some say the Order they founded still exists."

He left it open, as if wishing Anienam to confirm or deny the rumor.

"If they do, they remain hidden deeply underground. Secret societies all but died out after the fall of Ipn Shal. Mages became as popular as my friend the Gaimosian," Anienam admitted.

"The Gaimosian tale is a grand tragedy," Joden agreed. He stared into the fire. "Regardless, the forge masters consented and created the Blud Hamr. It took nearly ten years to complete. The men of the Order returned and, along with a band of Giant warriors, headed south to deal with the evil. A great war was fought. Many died on all sides. The strength of the hammer was enough to break the dark gods' hold. Their dark tower in an enchanted forest was smashed apart. The survivors returned the hammer and were not seen again by Giants.

"The hammer has only been used twice since its creation. The second time was by a band of my brothers. They went far into the north to kill a dragon responsible for murdering hundreds, mainly women and children. Dragons are not particular about who they slaughter." He sighed. "Those were more violent times. They slew the dragon and returned as heroes."

Anienam's eyes widened with shock. "I have a vague recollection of that. It predates the beginning of the Mage orders."

"By almost a thousand years."

"And the hammer has not been used in all the time following?"

"I told you, it is special. Very special indeed."

Anienam fell silent in thought. Much didn't add up, but, then again, little did these days. He'd lived long enough to realize most scenarios seldom went according to plan.

"Have the Giants made any other weapons like it?"

"No. I am ashamed to admit it, but we have lost the secrets of master craftsmanship. Many of us have dedicated our lives to reclaiming those secrets, but all have come up empty."

"That is a sad tale."

Joden smiled. "It provides focus to our work. Truthfully though, I do not believe Malweir has need of another such weapon."

Anienam couldn't have agreed more. Magical weapons meant dark forces were loose. The less of each, the better. Father must be turning in his grave, Anienam mused. A sudden thought struck.

"Why did you call the Blud Hamr a tool? I was under the impression it was a weapon."

"It is a tool. The forge masters intended it to be a conduit to the gods of light. Their power is channeled through it to the user. We have never been a violent people. We believe in peace and try to live by that simple code."

"Why create a weapon capable of such destruction?"

"As you say, the world is a dangerous place. Nothing we do will change it. Who were we, mere Giants, to refuse the will of the gods?"

Joden shrugged. He was a simple being, despite all of his age and wisdom. He finished his tea with a satisfied groan. "A mug of tea always helps me sleep better during the cold winter nights."

"I would think it is always cold up here."

"You get used to it after a few decades." Joden smiled. "I have told you how the hammer was created; now tell me why you seek it."

Anienam decided to dive right in and get it over with. "The story is…complicated. We have found ourselves embroiled in a much larger war than just Delranan and Rogscroft. I have every reason to believe the Dae'shan have returned and are manipulating key players in the north. For what purpose I cannot guess."

"That name has not been spoken here in a very long time before today. What could they possibly want now, after so long? And in the northern kingdoms? It does not make sense to me."

"Nor me, but the threat is no less real."

"If what you say is true, we are all doomed."

Anienam quickly said, "Not if we manage to get the hammer and stop them."

"The hammer is not in Venheim," Joden said.

The wizard's world crumbled around him. "What do you mean?"

"After the dragon was killed, a delegation from the Order returned to explain a great many truths. They warned that the enemies of light had been defeated, but not destroyed. Agents of doom were dealt a blow, but they would not stop in their quest to destroy all life on Malweir. This sparked much debate amongst my people. We finally relented and allowed the Order to take the Blud Hamr to a more central location to be protected and held in waiting. The hammer has been safe in their temple for the past thousand years. It rests, waiting for the time when it will be called again."

Joden leveled his gaze on his guest and continued. "I never dreamed that such would happen in my lifetime. It is a sad day for all races that you have come to Venheim."

Anienam was speechless. He felt as if his heart had been savagely ripped out and crushed beneath a boot heel. All their plans revolved around retrieving the hammer from the Giants and heading west to Rogscroft to battle the Dae'shan. Now he discovered it was all a lie. The hammer was no closer than it had been at the beginning. Hope began to fade.

"Who was this Order you mention? I've found nothing at all concerning them," Anienam asked in confusion.

Joden sipped noisily from his mug. "The Order doesn't exist anymore, or so I believe. They were hand selected among each of the races for exceptional attributes the rest of the world lacked. They served the gods of light infallibly. I vaguely recall mention of the Dae'shan succeeding in hunting them down to extinction. A shame really. Malweir needs more good souls willing to step forward in dark times."

Anienam felt his strength sage. "And their temple?"

"You wear a look of cold dread," Joden remarked. "Calm yourself. We know where the temple is located."

"Where?" was all he could manage.

"The jungles of Brodein. The temple is in the city of Trennaron. You will find the hammer inside."

More mysteries sprang to life, ones Anienam couldn't possibly hope to unravel. Too many questions were dancing in his head, giving him a fierce headache.

"Calm your mind, my friend," Joden cautioned. "I do not have the answers you desire. Be content knowing the hammer is secured in Brodein."

"We go to the jungle then," came a new voice from the shadows.

Giant and wizard spun. Anienam scowled as Bahr edged into the light, a triumphant smile on his face.

"Bahr?"

Joden rose to his full menacing height. "You should not be here!"

The Sea Wolf ignored the Giant. "The others are with Groge. I am here because I'm tired of being kept in the dark. I want answers."

"Where is Groge? Does he know you are here?" Joden pressed.

Anienam felt matters disintegrate. "Go back before someone realizes you are missing. We are being watched, you fool!"

"No. I am tired of being pushed around and told what to do. It ends tonight. I am the son of kings and refuse to be treated like a serf."

Joden snarled, unimpressed with the outburst. "It does not matter who you are if Blekling discovers you disobeyed his wishes. Go back to Groge, I will not keep your friend much longer and none of us needs trouble this night."

A booming knock trembled the door. Joden closed his eyes in mild anguish. It was already too late. Groge burst in.

"Forgive my intrusion, forge master, but one of the…" He went silent as his gaze fell on Bahr. Fury shook his massive frame. "You will return with me at once. Blekling already knows you have escaped me. He will not be long."

The silence lasted hardly as long as a single breath.

"Joden! Bring out the humans!" Blekling's voice growled across Venheim.

Slivers of moonlight turned Venheim into a haunted place. Light winds ripped over the mountaintops, forcing sheets of powdery snow across the higher altitudes. The Hags huddled in the sparse warmth of their feathery wings and watched the sleeping village below. Dark eyes focused on the cathedral's steeple.

"Should we warn the Dae'shan?" Brom asked.

Freina gave it barely a thought. "We do not know why the humans have come to see the Giants yet. We wait."

The Harpies sat and watched.

THIRTY

Trial

The six Giants surrounding Bahr glared down in raw contempt. There was no mistaking the malice Blekling and his supporters shared. Groge was off in the corner, head hung low in shame. Only Joden remained nonplussed by the event. He knew Blekling's games and refused to play them.

The elder was furious at the subtle betrayal. "You spit on the trust I have given you. Why?"

Bahr flexed his fists. "Trust? Ha! You all but locked us away in a house and expected us to obey blindly. My reasons for what I did are my own. All you need to know is that there was no harm intended, for anyone."

"You expect that to stay your execution?" another Giant scoffed.

Anienam edged closer to Bahr. "There is no call for executions. We have come to stop the Dae'shan, not banter with witless malcontents. Are any of you strong enough to defy the will of the gods?"

The Giants began muttering amongst themselves, confused by the wizard's defiance. Anienam chose his words carefully, knowing the mention of the ancient menace combined with the gods would be enough to spook the Giants into action.

"How dare you invoke the gods?" Blekling raged. Violent thoughts danced in his eyes.

Anienam calmly folded his arms across his chest. "I dare say that we all stand to lose unless you let us go about our business. We need the Blud Hamr to stop evil from reclaiming the world. Do not act so innocent as to not understand. We are not the first humans to have come here recently."

"The hammer! No human could handle the Blud Hamr! It is impossible. Perhaps your scrolls have failed you," Blekling wailed.

Joden nodded, silently confirming the initial statement. "It is true. The Blud Hamr is too large for a human. Only a Giant may wield it."

"That," Anienam said, "changes things."

The elder wore a smug look. The outcome had never been in doubt for him. Blekling decided it was time to make his final argument. "Anienam Keiss, your position as son of Dakeb does not entitle you to misuse our hospitality."

"Is that what you call it?" Bahr fumed. "We've been treated like criminals since we arrived. Have you no courtesy? Or has the roof of the world dulled your personalities?"

"Your life hangs by a threat, little man. I suggest you choose your words carefully," Blekling warned. "Another such outburst will find you sailing to the bottom of the mountain."

Boen beat him in drawing his sword. Several Giants began to laugh.

"Swords can do us no harm," the elder blustered.

Groge suddenly leapt between them. His hands were held out in a desperate gesture. His face twisted in concern. "This is my fault! I allowed the human to go unescorted to forge master Joden's home. He would not have gone against your wishes otherwise."

Blekling paused. "You?"

Groge swallowed hard, but still managed the courage to nod. It was much too late to go back now.

"The boy acted on my summons," Joden finally said to those assembled. "Bahr is the son of a king and the leader of their expedition. I thought it prudent he knows what the wizard and I were discussing."

With Joden's words Blekling lost the wind from his attack and his focus. The situation slowly spiraled beyond his control. Joden continued.

"The Dae'shan have returned. Only the hammer has the power to stop them. Anienam and Bahr need the Blud Hamr. They need our help."

"Help?" Blekling asked. "Their bumbling will bring darkness to our forge fires."

"Give them a chance."

"That is not our job. Why has the Order not come forward to present their pleas in person?"

Rekka Jel slipped to the front of the group. "We have."

All eyes turned sharply on the diminutive brown-skinned woman. She suddenly did not appear meek or humble. Instead, she held her ground, staring back proudly in unspoken challenge. Bahr's eyes narrowed.

Blekling was unimpressed. "What trickery is this? You expect us to believe that you are their emissary? You, who have remained silent until now?"

"I was so instructed."

Bahr felt like he'd just been kicked in the stomach. "I trusted you."

"I have never betrayed your trust, Captain. The entire time I have been among you, I have remained loyal and served your best interests. Did you think it was an accident that I found your ship right before it was to sail?"

He shook his head. "I don't understand. Why now? This Giant bastard has the right of it. Why wait until he is ready to kill us to declare yourself?"

"Forgive me, but my orders were very specific. I had no choice."

Her tone was apologetic, as if she bore a great shame in her heart. These people were complete strangers the day she rode into Chadra. She had been given only a name: *Bahr*. Rekka had been sent as a guardian. It was no accident that the Dae'shan came to her back in the Rogscroft forest. The game was an old one. Good against evil. She was merely another pawn.

The part of her mission that did not go according to her plan was that she had become friends with them all, save perhaps Ionascu. Rekka had genuine feelings for them, Dorl most of all. Emotional attachment was new to her. It went against the Order's teachings. She was meant to be a warrior, not a compassionate lover. Somewhere along the way Rekka discovered what it meant to be human.

"We trusted you," Bahr repeated.

A tear formed in the corner of her eye. "You still can. I have pledged my life to the success of this quest. You have all become like family to me. Please believe me."

The words were hard to speak, but her pride demanded she go on. "The Order had many secrets. The location of the Blud Hamr is the greatest. Even I have no knowledge of where it rests. There has been a real threat that I might be forced to give away the location if captured. That is why I was not told. My task was to escort you safely to Venheim where the Giants would tell the rest. My master was most adamant about security."

"What happens to us?" Dorl suddenly blurted out.

"Enough!" Blekling roared.

Silence edged back into the valley. Not even the occasional tink-tink of an apprentice hammer could be heard. "I am tired of your chatter. You must all leave here at dawn. You will not be allowed to return, for any reason. I have no doubts that Joden has told you all you need to carry on. Take his knowledge and make good use of it. You will never be welcome in Venheim again."

"But you can't!" Groge protested.

Blekling spun on him. "Mind your tongue, apprentice."

"Like it or not, the boy is right, Blekling," Joden interrupted. "They know what I had to tell, but none of them is capable of wielding the hammer. They will need one of us."

With a malicious expression, the elder abruptly answered. "Very well. Groge will go. He was given the responsibility to watch them, now he can do so on their quest. Be gone at dawn."

He left before any further conversation could begin.

Joden placed a warm hand on Groge's shoulder. "I have a feeling that this task was destined for you, lad. Go with all the good wishes of the gods. Use the hammer and return to us a hero."

"If I return at all."

The forge master smiled darkly. "When, not if. You must have confidence if you expect to enact the will of the gods and defeat the Dae'shan."

Groge had too many doubts to be confident. The Blud Hamr. A weapon used only twice in all of creation. Now it was his turn. The third time. The thought staggered him, practically dropping him to his knees. He suddenly felt very small, a minnow lost in the vast ocean.

"I am not worthy of such honor," he stammered.

"That is not for you to decide. These matters are often beyond the gauge of our reasoning. Trust in yourself."

"Look at me, Joden! I am not even a smith yet. How can I be chosen for such a great task?"

Joden tried to sympathize with him but had no words to give. The forge master certainly never had to undergo such an ordeal. Still, he envied the lad. Joden had never been chosen for the great honor. "You ask questions neither of us can answer. Come, let us go to the cathedral. Perhaps the gods will answer our prayers."

The Giants ambled off in search of answers to replace the growing pile of questions.

"This is wonderful," Dorl said. "How exactly did we manage to piss off an entire tribe of Giants?"

Boen shrugged. "Life is funny that way."

He knew what the sell sword really wanted to ask. It was painfully obvious. Why couldn't Bahr just have stayed put? Boen's silent intimidation successfully prevented any of them from asking. Or so he hoped.

"The Giants will not harm us. Joden won't let them," Anienam told them all.

Dorl scoffed. "Getting thrown off of a mountain sounds rather painful to me, wizard."

"Falling is the easy part. The landing will hurt the most," Nothol chuckled and sliced another sliver off a green apple.

"Funny." Dorl shot him a foul glare.

Anienam sighed. "We have other matters to discuss than how fast master Theed will fall to the ground."

"Such as?" Boen asked.

"Such as how are we supposed to find Trennaron? How long will it take? Who is Rekka's master if the Order is no more? Where are we going to get the supplies we will need and what do we do with the hammer once we obtain it? For starters."

Boen rubbed his chin thoughtfully. "Fair enough. It certainly gives us something to do while we sit and wait."

"Hopefully the Giants will let us resupply," Bahr finally said. Small guilt at being the one who instigated this mess gnawed at him. "But what are we supposed to do with another mouth to feed? The Giant can't ride and will only slow us down."

Anienam half smiled. "The strength of Giants is legendary. I believe we might be surprised. Groge is the least of our concerns."

Bahr snapped his mouth shut.

A Giant smith entered and bowed slightly to Anienam. "Joden says for you to take what supplies you need from his personal stores. He is honored to help the son of Dakeb in this quest."

"Please tell Joden that we graciously accept and appreciate the offer. Where might we find him?"

The Giant hesitated, unsure what to say. "He is in the cathedral praying."

"Would it be too much to ask Blekling if I might join him? I would very much like to see the inside of the house of the gods."

"I...I will go and ask," the Giant replied. "Wait here."

Bahr waited until they were alone again before asking, "What is it about that cathedral that steals your thoughts?"

Anienam smiled. "I believe it might hold some of the answers we need."

Bahr fell silent, already deep in thought.

THIRTY-ONE

The Goblins Attack

Company after company of Goblin infantry poured into what remained of the city of Rogscroft. Bodies, men and Goblin, littered the burnt ruins. The fighting had been intense. Every foot of progress was paid in blood. Casualties on both sides were much higher than anyone anticipated. The Goblins suffered worst of all. Thousands were lost, dead or wounded, under the proud glare of Grugnak. He snarled and spit fresh orders. Overseers lashed their cruel leather whips, forcing the infantry ever forward.

Three quarters of the city was destroyed. Aurec's defenders sold their ground at a high price. Streets ran red with blood once the flames melted the snow. Arrows littered the sides of what few buildings remained. Wolfsreik artillery thrummed overhead. The scope of destruction was so vast King Stelskor could not bring himself to gaze out into his once proud city. Each time the artillery barrage ended signaled a new attack. Clouds of dust flushed upwards to mingle with the foul black smoke. He had never seen war this personal. Goblins rushed in, hungry for the taste of fresh blood. Animalistic war cries growled across the savage wind. Wicked-looking blades glimmered harshly in the flames. All that mattered to the Goblin horde was the chance to kill their most hated foe: man.

Aurec crouched behind a pile of rubble and stared into the growing darkness. What used to be a popular fountain square now lay in broken ruin. The enemy's thick stench almost overpowered his senses. Marching sounds of their hobnailed boots striking cobblestones echoed around his position. Aurec hoped his flanks were adequately prepared for the assault, though he wanted the Goblins to come at him head-on. All of his main efforts were focused to the front.

"I don't like this," he whispered.

Mahn shifted his gaze across their immediate front. "Perhaps they know something we do not."

The prince looked appraisingly at his favorite scout. Mahn was so much more than a mere scout. He'd become a friend and mentor to the young prince.

"Order the sergeants on the flanks to prepare for attack. Either side should expect to get hit," Mahn cautioned softly.

Aurec didn't hesitate. The faster they moved, the better chance all the defenders had at surviving. Aurec needed every available man to last the night if his plans to stop the enemy momentum were going to succeed. He quickly issued the orders.

After he said, "Mahn, you know I am going to whatever part of the line gets hit, right?"

"I know."

The old scout fell silent. Disappointment burned him. He wanted Aurec as far away from the front lines as possible, not only for the boy's safety, but to allow him to do his job better. Instead of worrying about the battle, he had to worry about the prince as well. Worse, Aurec had gone against his father's wishes by coming into the city. There was no point in casually risking the heir to the throne.

"I have to do this," Aurec said, trying to defend himself. This is all my fault, he wanted to say. In his heart he truly believed it. His reckless adventure to whisk Maleela from her father resulted in countless dead and his vision of a perfect dream shattered. And it was all for love. A war of complete annihilation sparked by love. Aurec wanted to laugh and cry at the irony of it.

Mahn leaned closer so that no one might overhear. "I understand you. I do, but you need to think beyond yourself now. Rogscroft will have need of a strong ruler to rebuild. Your father does not have many years left on him. This will be your kingdom soon. It is time for you to start thinking like a leader, not just a soldier."

Aurec didn't get the chance to answer.

A shout cried out. "Here they come!"

Goblins broke from cover en masse. Aurec cringed upon seeing the sheer hatred in their soulless eyes as the front ranks clambered over the ruins of a row of merchant shops. The Goblins could crush his men just from sheer weight of numbers. Aurec knew there was little hope in fighting them head-to-head. Fortunately, he had known this and had appropriate traps emplaced.

"Archers draw!" barked the command.

Bows creaked as tension was placed on them. Aurec drew his sword in anticipation.

"Aim!"

The Goblins were either oblivious or they simply did not care. Rank after rank pushed forward towards the makeshift barricades blocking the road. One of the largest Goblins raised his cudgel and bellowed. They attacked.

"Fire!"

Arrows sped over the head of the crouching defenders. Aurec felt the brief sting of a shaft buzz a little too close to his right ear. Grunts and screams told him the archers' aims were true. He snorted. Of course, it was near impossible to miss like this. Aurec grinned. Each Goblin killed increased his chances of success. Goblins leapt and crawled over the bodies of their comrades. They wanted blood and nothing was going to sate them until they ripped into the Men.

Aurec dared to inch his head a little higher so he could get a clear view of the killing grounds. Enemy numbers were high, but a silent alarm chimed in his mind. *There should be more.* Arrows continued to pour into the exposed Goblins. Aurec racked his mind, trying to figure out what was wrong. A new sound erupted from both flanks. Blood drained from his face. They were being attacked from all three sides. His darkest fears were coming true. None of his traps and tricks mattered much now. Aurec had to move before all was lost.

A runner collapsed at his feet. His breath came in ragged gasps. Blood smeared across his face. "My lord, we are beset. The enemy attacks from all sides."

"Calm yourself," Aurec cautioned with a confidence he did not feel. "Now slowly, explain what is happening."

"We heard the battle start here, but Sergeant Harg had us keep to our posts. The Goblins hit us hard at the moment we were distracted. They broke through and are pushing us back. We cannot hold much longer."

Damnation. Aurec pushed away his building rage. He needed a clear head for this. "Go back and tell Harg to pull back to the river. He…"

"Sergeant Harg is dead," the runner admitted ashamedly.

Aurec reached out to steady the boy by his shoulder and calmly said, "Give my instructions to whoever is in command. It is important not to break contact. We all die if you do. Run!"

The boy sprinted off, dodging a handful of poorly aimed spears. Aurec didn't bother watching him go. "Mahn! Send the signal now."

The scout drew his bow and lit an arrow from the small fire at his feet. He aimed high into the sky and loosed. Aurec watched the shaft pierce the night and began counting heartbeats until he saw the reply. He reached seven before scores of fire arrows sped from the remaining two-story buildings. Burning pitch dripped down along their flight path. Goblins in the back ranks paused to look up at the streaks of flame and smoke.

Most of the arrows hit their marks. Enormous canisters filled with pitch and sulfur exploded within the Goblin mass as arrows hit. Dozens fell dead, shredded from razor sharp shards of pottery filling the bombs. More burned to death. The noise was deafening. Roasted flesh choked the air with putrid smell. More arrows fell. More bombs exploded. The front ranks didn't stop to notice; they continued to press into the defenders. The back ranks scattered in a frenzy to escape the growing flames.

Aurec rose and waved his sword in challenge. "Pikes!"

His infantry shot to their feet and leveled the long weapons. They didn't wait long before the first Goblin ranks impaled themselves.

"Manzo," Aurec shouted over the din of battle. "Start pulling the reserves back. We have to retreat or we are all dead."

Manzo, a robust man with a thick beard and round belly, saluted and started barking orders. The wounded went first, helped along by those with lesser wounds. Aurec watched his men struggle to keep from all-out panic. Panic meant death. His thoughts turned to the flanks. They couldn't hold much longer. The battle raged around him. Goblins died on the sword and spear. Men fell to poisoned blades. Aurec turned to the sounds of one of his men falling dead. Then another, and another. Horror etched deeply in his face as he noticed the short black shafts piercing each corpse.

"Mahn!" he cried.

Any hope of victory crumbled. Fighting on the barricade had devolved into hand-to-hand. Several Goblins were already among his ranks. The defense was failing.

Mahn raced over and grabbed the prince roughly by his armor. "We need to leave. Now!"

"No. I'm not about to leave my men like this."

"Don't be a fool. We are lost and I am not going to be the one to tell your father I got his son killed in some damned fool operation that was doomed from the start."

He shoved Aurec back. Men died all around them. More Goblins broke through.

Manzo slashed his sword across a Goblin's throat. Ropes of blood danced through the air. "He's right, sire. I can handle this. Get out while you still can."

Aurec finally conceded. "All right. Withdraw the archers and fall back. I will see you in the castle."

They fought their way through the chaos in the vain hopes of surviving this long night. Aurec wanted to vomit. So much destruction. Bodies fell entwined in death struggles. Goblin and men, Lord Death did not discriminate.

"Do you have any idea what you did?" Stelskor scolded.

His voice bordered on rage. Aurec and Mahn stood humbly in front of their king. Their heads hung low, embarrassed.

"Father, it was all my fault," Aurec said.

"Aurec, you are the heir to the throne. What right do you have to throw away your life so recklessly? Again we have the same conversation. You are the son of kings, not some base soldier from common blood."

"I understand that."

Stelskor slammed an old fist on the arm of the throne. "Then start acting like it!"

Admonished, the prince held his tongue. He couldn't keep his thoughts from drifting back to the men who fought and died desperately trying to hold the line.

"How many casualties?" Stelskor quietly asked.

"Forty-three dead and close to one hundred wounded. Twelve are missing," Mahn reported.

"They are as good as dead. Goblins do not take prisoners."

Mahn reluctantly agreed. "Matters are worse than just numbers."

Stelskor couldn't see how that was possible. "How so?"

"The enemy is using poisoned weapons and appear to have a coordinated plan. The Wolfsreik hasn't attacked yet. The Goblins knew what they were doing."

"We are in more trouble than I thought if this is true. How did Badron come into an alliance with these creatures?" He paced to the huge window overlooking the ruins of his city. The enemy was already at the river. That thin sliver of water and a wall was all that remained between life and death.

"The engineers are almost finished digging the escape tunnels. We should be able to evacuate those who are still breathing when the castle falls," he told them.

Aurec summoned the courage to speak. "How long can we expect to withstand a siege?"

"As long as need be," his father said sharply. "Our first priority has to be the wounded. The sooner we get them safely to Grunmarrow the better."

"Who stays to command the final defense?" Mahn asked.

Gone was the simple scout. Only Stelskor knew Mahn had once been a fine general. One of his last wishes during command had been that no one learned the truth, not even Aurec. Mahn wanted to live the remainder of his days in a simple fashion. Fate intervened to shatter those dreams.

Stelskor held a twinkle in his eyes. "The time is not yet, but I have several potential commanders picked out."

The prince felt like he was missing a vital part of their conversation. Mahn was an exceptional scout and a good friend and mentor, but he certainly wasn't the confidant of a king. It didn't add up.

Mahn knew better than to press. Instead he decided to change the subject and excuse himself. "Sire, I need to see to my scouts. Several were wounded during the last skirmish."

"Of course," Stelskor said and sighed. "We will have need of them soon enough. Please pass the word that I shall be making my rounds in the infirmary shortly."

He waited for Mahn to close the door behind him before turning to face Aurec. "What is it going to take to make you understand how important you are to our future?"

Aurec struggled with shame. "I do not know, Father. It seems as if all my decisions lately have been wrong. I feel lost somehow."

The king was replaced by the father who tended to Aurec's scrapes and bruises when he was but a child. "It is natural to go through times of doubt. The measure of a man is how well he pulls through them."

"I have tried, but even I can't see how we are going to survive."

A tear escaped his tired eyes. Father hugged his son. "I don't either, son. I don't either."

Raste hadn't stopped trying to rub the blood from his hands since he dropped down exhausted next to the small fire. Soldiers passed him without regard. They had their own miseries to contend with. Wars changed men forever. Many already had nightmares from the opening days of siege. Raste knew that many of those same men had resigned themselves to death. Others moved about with a distant look in their eyes. Still more were reduced to hollow shells of what they could have been. Those men were quickly taken away so their condition did not affect the others. Such was war.

"Try dirt," Manzo said from behind.

The older warrior pulled up a stool and dropped down. His upper right arm was drenched with drying blood.

Raste didn't bother to look up. "How is your arm?"

"Just a scratch. I've had worse, believe me. Besides, the Goblin who did it got the worst of it. Ha!"

The scout tried to smile but discovered he no longer had it in him.

Manzo noticed it with concern. "You have got to learn to let go, boy. What's done is done. The best thing for it is to get a bite to eat, wash it down with some good ale, and then sleep it off. Tomorrow the fight begins all over again."

The advice was sound enough, though Raste had never experienced a real battle before. All the skirmishes and raids combined were nothing compared to the horrors of a prolonged siege. He had watched too many friends die. Screams from the wounded kept him up at night. The smell of burnt bodies poisoned his stomach. Raste knew he was not strong enough to keep going.

"Why dirt?" he asked after a long period of silence.

Manzo barked a jovial laugh. Raste's cheeks flushed crimson, but he still snatched up a handful of loose dirt and started to rub.

"I like you, boy. Mahn's trained you well," Manzo said approvingly.

"There is no way he could have prepared me for this. How do you do it?"

"I was born for it."

Raste couldn't tell if he was joking or not and decided not to call him on it. Drums began to beat in the city ruins. Men wearily rose and grabbed their weapons.

"It looks like we're not going to be getting much sleep tonight," Manzo said. His voice snapped with a snarl.

Raste resisted the urge to hang his head. Instead he snatched up his sword and followed Manzo to the wall.

THIRTY-TWO

The Siege Intensifies

Rogscroft burned. The sound was deafening. The smell of putrid death clung to the air with a pall of misery. Casualties were everywhere and mounting. Massed ranks of Goblins lined the far riverbank firing poisoned arrows at the castle defenders. Burning pitch and fragments of brimstone fell down on them as the Wolfsreik bombardment soared overhead to crash into the castle. Thick plumes of black smoke billowed up. It was a vision of hell. An occasional Goblin fell dead when an enemy archer got lucky.

"Never in all my days did I think to see such a sight," Piper Joach said in awe and mild shock.

Rolnir watched his catapult batteries continue to pummel Rogscroft. Scant few rounds came back at them. The battle progressed as Badron predicted. But it wasn't right. The battle for the city had been intense, so much so that Rolnir felt like he was being led into a trap.

"This is war at its worst."

Piper glanced over at him. "We should not be here, Rolnir."

The general's expression softened. "That is not for us to decide. The life of a soldier is never easy. You know that."

"Yes I do, but this isn't right. Why are the Goblins here? Why are we wasting lives and energy trying to storm a castle in the middle of winter? It does not add up. Our planning in Delranan did not include this."

Rolnir looked nervously about. Anyone might be a spy. "Quiet yourself, Piper. The king might have ears among our men. Goblins we can deal…"

"But?"

"A darker force drives this war forward," Rolnir replied softly. "Have you not noticed how different he acts lately? His chambers are cold every time we have council.

There is some evil at work here and I feel it may damn us before the end."

"We cannot fight what we do not see."

Rolnir shook his head. Another salvo exploded against the castle wall. "We must be cautious. Has anyone tried to escape yet?"

"No." Piper took the meaning behind the sudden change of subject. *Stay watchful until the right moment to act.* "I have scouts surrounding the castle. Roving patrols report negative contact. There is no way anyone can sneak out without us spotting them."

"You have been in the Reik long enough to know not to use never," Rolnir laughed.

"One or two at the most, but no great numbers," Piper conceded.

"I say let them go. They have no allies. The ones who escape are only deserters trying to survive. Each one is one less we have to worry about once we get inside."

"At least the Goblins are taking the brunt of the assault. Do you think old Stelskor suspects we plan on hitting the rear simultaneously?"

Rolnir shrugged nonchalantly. "Does it matter?"

"Not in the least."

"How much longer until we have the siege equipment ready?" Rolnir asked. He didn't say it, but he was starting to get worried. The longer the siege lasted, the more dangerous it was for his men. Complacency would set in and that killed men. They all knew the legends and stories of sieges ending in disaster. Rolnir grew increasingly worried the same was going to happen to him, despite the strength of the Goblin army.

"A few days at most. We will be ready long before our artillery can knock down those gates," Piper snarled.

"We are losing almost two hundred Goblins a day. Normally I wouldn't mind, but we need them if we are going to succeed."

"We are better off without them."

Some of the fire left him and his mood darkened. "That is not our call. Continue with the preparations, commander. I don't want those damned Goblins to be the ones who sack the castle. If this is an inevitable task, I would see the Wolfsreik gain the glory."

"Yes sir." Piper saluted and stalked back to his men.

Rolnir watched the battle for many long moments. It was an awesome display of firepower. He damned Badron for starting this war but found an immeasurable sense of pride from watching his men in action. A king like Badron did not deserve such an army.

Badron found himself staring back into the shadows. His grasp on reality was slipping, of that much he was certain. He had lost control. Not over the war, his army was strong enough to manage that. But he was losing himself. His mind was in constant agony from the manipulations of the Dae'shan. Night was the worst. He always dreamed of his son, and the life robbed. Then came his daughter.

The wretched child who murdered her mother, his wife. Anger demanded satisfaction. All of this was because of her! Life would have been much better had she never been born. Maleela was a cancer to his family. First his lovely wife and now his son. Badron raged and cursed his daughter's name. Dark emotions sprang forth from the deepest recesses of his soul. He hated her. Visions of throttling her in her sleep added fuel to his anger. Maleela was the source of every single bad thing that had happened. She had to pay for that crime.

Barely more than a wisp of darkness, Amar Kit'han floated inches above the ground and watched. The taste of Badron's rage was a fine wine to the Dae'shan. The king had been far too easy to corrupt. Jealous men usually were. All it took was a singular moment of trauma capable of pushing a man over the edge. The rest was easy. Badron held more than enough trouble in his beleaguered soul to make his turning possible.

His pain served as an elixir. Misery and torment provided the Dae'shan sustenance. It was not always so. Once they had been neutral, servants of life. Time and the loss of the gods of light turned them into unholy creatures who fed on darkness.

Badron stiffened. "I know you are here. Show yourself, monster."

"That is no way to speak to your only friend."

"Friend? What manner of friend would drive me to the edge of insanity and still demand more?"

"You act as if either of us have a choice in our actions, king. Perhaps you forget my masters dictate the path of the future. We are all puppets."

"Why all of this secrecy? You sow the seeds of discord among my top commanders and they do not know you exist!" Badron accused.

Amar drifted to the ground. "They suspect."

"Of course they do. They are the very best Delranan has."

"Do not be so fast to place your faith in men. They will turn on you before the end," the Dae'shan admonished.

He forcibly shook his head. "You have no faith in men."

"You have too much."

Badron trembled. He was in no mood to trade barbs with a power he still did not understand. He briefly entertained the thought of running Kit'han through. Nothing about the creature was substantial so he stayed his sword. Still, stabbing him would improve Badron's mood.

"Why have you come to me this time?" he asked.

"I felt great pain in you."

Badron's hand instinctively dropped to his sword. "You read my thoughts?"

Amar stared back from behind the security of his hood. "I do not need to. It is evident upon your face, king. Perhaps it is time you became privileged to one of the world's oldest and most closely kept secrets."

Badron's hand dropped, if only slightly. "More secrets?"

"All life revolves around secrets. One might say this is the secret that began it all. Very few men have been given the opportunity to see what I am offering."

He laughed. "Yet I do not trust you. What does that say of you or me?"

"It gives credence to you wearing a crown. Think hard, but quickly. I am only going to offer once more. After tonight you will never be given the chance."

Indecision tore at him but Badron's curiosity was too high. "What will I find?"

"No questions. Yes or no."

"Not good enough. Will this secret help me win the war? I must know."

Amar Kit'han might have admired the man under other circumstances. "Yes or no. Persistence will not avail you, king."

A wall broke within him. Curiosity and anger infused into an original abomination in the king's mind. Gnawing guilt swelled to life. Badron finally gave in.

"Yes, show me."

Amar Kit'han smiled behind his mask of shadows. His constant manipulations ate away Badron's resolve. Very soon now it would be time to advance the dark gods' plans. "Follow me."

They wormed their way through the night and his sleeping army. No one questioned his passing and few would remember it come the dawn. Amar whispered a spell that made the night darker, more sinister. He led Badron into the heart of the night, past picket lines and sentries. Caution abandoned, Badron was lost to burning desire. They finally came to a halt at the foot of a lone elm tree. Enormous, the tree would easily take ten men to circle it. He looked up in awe. Then he noticed the tree was dead. Most of the bark was gone, peeled away through time and decay. Branches were broken and twisted with age. Badron shivered.

"This place feels evil," he whispered. His eyes narrowed as he searched the supernatural darkness for threats.

"It is only evil if you wish it to be so. Good and evil have always been subjective. They are opposite ends of a spectrum that Mankind has subverted to suit his own needs and desires. You must go closer if you wish to learn the secret."

Badron shot him a nervous look. The desire to know was too strong. He reluctantly obeyed. The tree moved the closer he got. He froze. Darkness swelled around him, choking him. Badron dropped to his knees as visions violently swirled around him until they became reality. He bore witness to sights, such wonderful and horrible sights. Birth and apocalypse. Salvation and Armageddon.

Badron screamed at the top of his lungs.

"Fire!"

Catapults erupted. General Rolnir watched his men with pride. The soldiers of the Wolfsreik moved with the precision that only came from endless hours on the training fields. They were completely professional in their approach to war, down to the lowest-ranking man. Not that he expected anything less. These were his boys. The source of his greatest pride. All were sons he never had.

A young captain, Ulf, moved to intercept him when he saw Rolnir come closer. "General, welcome to the Mouth of the Wolf."

He smiled fiercely. The Mouth of the Wolf was the nickname given to the artillerymen by their infantry cohorts for the booming noise and gouts of fire each catapult threw into the night.

"Captain Ulf. I see your boys are performing admirably."

"We try, sir," Ulf replied. His youthful face brightened at the compliment.

Rolnir had never been the sort to flower his men with accolades or warm embraces. He was a hard and unbending master who demanded perfection in everything. Each one of his men would readily lay down their lives just to please him. Rolnir made it a point to know as many of the men by name as possible. It was the least he could do in return for their great sacrifice.

"What is your ammunition status, captain?"

"We have enough for at least another day and a half of constant barrage. The terrain is naturally rocky so there is no shortage of rounds."

Rolnir nodded. "Good. Then we can take the chance to drop a few rounds short and introduce ourselves to our Goblin friends."

Ulf couldn't conceal the joy he felt. "That can be arranged, sir."

"Keep up your fire, Ulf. We have to beat down the men inside before the first scaling ladder goes up. Every round you fire saves one of our men."

Ulf saluted. "You can count on us to do our part, sir."

"I know, lad. I know."

A battalion of heavy infantry marched north. They were heading to join Piper and the main assault force. Piper had told him earlier that nearly three thousand men were being gathered for the attack. Under normal circumstances that number was too conservative, but with the mass of Goblins, Rolnir didn't see any issues. Hate them as he did, there was no mistaking the sheer dominating power the Goblin presence had.

Fresh snow began falling. Rolnir tipped his head back and let the soft flakes kiss his bearded face. Another salvo of rounds roared across the battlefield. It was times like this that made him appreciate being alive.

THIRTY-THREE

The Beginning of the End

Manzo awoke suddenly with the irresistible urge to relive himself. He grumbled quietly at the thought of leaving his warm sleeping bag to brave the freezing temperatures on the wall. It never failed. Each winter night he had gone through this ritual at least once, sometimes twice. Wrapping his heavy cloak around his shoulders, Manzo headed to the nearest section of the wall designated as a latrine. Engineers staked a handful of large pipes into holes in the wall to allow for a run-off so the waste wouldn't get any of the defenders sick. Manzo appreciated the effort. Blood and death were one thing but having to live in the filth of scat and urine was simply unbearable. He unbuckled his trousers and sighed as he let it out.

A new wave of explosions rocked the wall. There was something different this time. The noise was louder. The ground shook longer. Manzo cursed. A full week had gone by since the damned Delrananians began their siege. A week and he still jumped at the sound. He supposed it was more reaction than anything else. Much longer and he wouldn't even notice it. Manzo shook the excess off and pulled his trousers back up.

"The gates! They've breached the gates!"

A bell began ringing. Manzo's blood chilled. Men rolled from their sleeping mats and bunks and hurried to their fighting positions. Rogscroft quickly became alive with rushed activity. Manzo watched the panic set in and struggled to keep his own from overpowering him. This is it, he kept telling himself. *We are all going to die*. Manzo fought against his fears, but the thought that the castle was one big death trap was almost too much.

He took a step towards his sleeping area when horrible pain filled his chest cavity. Winded, he dropped to his knees. His eyes widened in shock. Blood filled his mouth when he tried to yell. Manzo reached up and felt the razor barb protruding from his chest. He mouthed words without sound.

The back wall!

Blood bubbled from his lips and he fell dead. The enemy crossbowman smiled and signaled to the others on the ground. Scaling ladders started to go up.

"What is happening?" Aurec demanded as he slipped into his armor.

Venten held out the prince's sword. "I am not sure, but some of the men claim the gates have been breached."

Damnation. "We need to be there, now."

This was an inevitable moment, but terror still gripped them. Aurec needed to act quickly if they were to have any hope of stopping the attack long enough for Stelskor's plan to work. The rest of their lives depended on the next few moments. He claimed his sword from Venten.

"Send word to my father. It is time for him to escape to Grunmarrow. I will hold the defense long enough for him to be safely away. Then I will follow as I can."

"I will. Hold the gates long enough for me to return. I wouldn't mind a crack at these Goblin bastards myself."

Aurec nodded and Venten ran off to fulfill his task. Confusion and panic awaited Aurec as he took to the battlements. Generations had passed since the last time the castle had been sacked. Aurec held every intention of stopping the Wolfsreik and pushing them back to Delranan in shame. He refused to be the man who lost his kingdom. Outside, the heat from the flames nearly drove him to his knees. The city gates, which had stood for two hundred years, were shattered into a ruin of their former splendor. Gaping holes yawned back at him. Hundreds of direct hits finally tore the wood to splinters. Only a handful of meters of running water separated him from the Goblin hordes.

"Who is in command here?" Aurec called out once he joined the front lines.

Bodies littered the area. A makeshift field hospital was set up under the dubious protection of the wall. A constant flow of wounded was being dragged in. Fires raged uncontrollably all around them. Aurec winced, suddenly very tired of war. Ragged lines of defenders formed behind a barricade. He made his way through the debris field to where a grizzled sergeant awaited. The top of his head was heavily bandaged, spots of blood staining through.

"I am, my lord. Sergeant Thorsson."

Aurec looked at the ranks of scared men. "Where is your commanding officer?"

Thorsson gestured towards a stack of half frozen bodies by the wall. "He had his head crushed during the bombardment."

Aurec winced despite his projected air of confidence. The men noticed. Arrows and catapult rounds were indiscriminate killers. "Report, sergeant."

"The gates are destroyed and will not hold. I have close to one hundred able-bodied men ready to fight once the Goblins cross. We should be able to hold them for a good while."

He hoped so. The harder they fought gave the king more time to escape. Aurec hoped his presence would inspire the men to fight harder. Aurec dared a closer look at his enemy. Archers rained down a murderous barrage into the Goblin ranks from atop the wall. Bodies fell dead into the river to be swept away. Goblins hauled massive rafts towards the banks. The enemy meant to assault immediately. Aurec ducked back.

"Sergeant Thorsson, form the ranks. Pikes in front. Archers behind. We must stop the rafts from reaching this shore."

Thorsson threw a crisp salute. "On your feet, dogs! To the gates! I want a nice thick flank of pikes ready to impale these grey-skinned bastards. Archers form behind me. Move it or you are all Goblin food!"

Aurec found himself easily liking the veteran. He hefted his own pike, taken from a dead man.

"My lord, you are out of your mind if you think I am going to let you stand the line," Thorsson snapped.

He darkened with anger. "I am your prince, sergeant."

The much bigger man folded his massive arms across his chest and shot Aurec a stern glare. "I don't care. This is my battle and I am not going to allow the only prince in Rogscroft to throw away his life so carelessly."

Aurec recognized the same vitality in Thorsson's face that he often saw staring back in the mirror. There was only resolve, no sense of weakness. Aurec silently thanked his father for developing such a strong, noncommissioned officer corps. Men like Thorsson needed to live if Rogscroft was going to stand a chance.

"Fine, sergeant," he relented. "Where do you want me? Keep in mind that you cannot keep me from *all* of the fighting."

Thorsson didn't budge. His face remained impassive, even as screams from the wounded danced around his ears. "You are a leader. You will be of most use to me on the wall directing the battle. I can't see everything from down here."

Aurec glanced longingly at the massed ranks of soldiers as they readied to do battle against the pulsing Goblin horde. Desperation clung to them like a rotted stink. The desire to live gnawed teasingly at each of them. All the while death laughed as it floated across the skies. The prince reluctantly sheathed his sword. His almond-colored eyes bore a subtle sadness. He reached out and took Thorsson's hand.

"Where do you plan on being?" he asked, already knowing the answer.

Thorsson offered a savage grin. "Right in the middle of it, where I belong."

Raste ripped his sword from the dying man's stomach and kicked the body away. Blood stained his hands and jerkin. Sweat trickled down his face, but there was no respite. Another attacker charged. Raste had a fraction of a moment to look around. Men from both sides fell dead or dying in a brutal struggle. The surprise attack was timed perfectly with the Goblin assault. The Wolfsreik now swarmed over the walls, killing and hacking. Raste fought against the urge to throw down his weapon and run.

There was no shortage of enemy. Raste already had three lying at his feet. The younger scout, unused to extended combat, struggled to maintain his strength. Wavering determination echoed in his cold blue eyes. A small cut on the left cheek had already stopped bleeding, leaving him with a painted face. The fight he so longed for had come and he was woefully unprepared.

The man beside him grunted suddenly and fell back with an enemy short sword plunged deep into his chest. Arterial blood, steaming and dark red, flowed freely down his deerskin shirt. Raste watched the man's eyes glaze over. Fury and anger became his conscience and he attacked. His sword cut clean through the elbow in one stroke. The Wolfsreik soldier dropped screaming to his knees. Distracted, Raste couldn't duck in time to keep from being struck in the temple by a mailed fist. He stumbled back as the pain lanced across his head. Unbalanced, he dropped into a pile of bodies. Their escaping warmth was oddly comforting.

"Stay down you fool!" snapped a familiar voice he couldn't place.

An arrow zipped by, narrowly missing the top of his head. Raste's would-be killer dropped, the shaft buried in his throat. Men pushed forward, fresh troops up from the barracks. Unlike Raste, they were fully armored and armed. Rough hands helped him up. Unfamiliar faces looked him over.

"Can you move on your own?"

He nodded, winced from the pain.

"Stay with us. We have been ordered to fall back."

Raste couldn't believe it. So much killing, and now he was being told to abandon what he had bled for. The reinforcements halted the Wolfsreik surge, momentarily.

"We can't leave. The walls will fall!" Raste struggled to shout above the battle.

"The walls are already fallen! We must move and secure the stairs before it is too late!" the newcomer shouted back.

The Wolfsreik already held a forty-meter section of the wall and were expanding with each passing moment. Rogscroft slowly sank into defeat. The defenders fought well, but it was not enough. Half of the kingdom's armies were peasant conscripts unused to the violence of combat. All the heart and love of country they possessed meant nothing against the ten thousand seasoned veterans trying to kill them. Fear would soon take them and all hope was lost when it did. Raste felt like he had been punched in the stomach. All of this was in vain. He spat a mouthful of blood. Manzo's corpse lay nearby. The *ching-ching* of clashing swords seemed an ironic epitaph. Raste's knuckles whitened as he tightened the grip on his sword. If Manzo had fallen, an accomplished warrior, what chance had he? Dawn broke over the eastern approach. It was a violent shade of red.

"We were supposed to win," he whispered.

"Fall back!" bellowed the order over the battlefield. "Fall back to the stairs!"

The defenders collapsed as orderly as possible. Raste knew that had the reinforcements not arrived it would have turned to a slaughter. His heart doubted it was going to end any other way.

King Stelskor struggled to stay calm as he watched his enemies press in from all sides. Companies of Wolfsreik were steadily enlarging their hold on his walls while the Goblin army continued to waste lives at the front gates. He occasionally caught glimpses of his son, his silver armor reflecting the demonic red glow from so many fires. The king bit his trembling lower lip. Hope was lost. The enemy numbers were too much to defeat. Tears softened his once hard face.

"Sire, you must go now," Paneolus urged. "Time is gone."

"I cannot. Not while brave men still stand," he all but whimpered.

Venten shot the minister of state a pleading stare. Stelskor had never looked so old. His regality was gone, transformed by age and wrinkles. His skin was much paler than it once had been. His eyes had lost their luster and now simmered a dull brown. Venten frowned. "You are the city, Sire. So long as you survive, we do. You must evacuate now before the chance is lost."

A flash of old confidence flared. "Have you no confidence in me, my old general?"

The others in the small band stared at him in muted shock. Venten held his tongue. This was no time for secrets and his was the least important. More important issues demanded attention.

"Sire, faith has nothing to do with reality. This city is lost. The only thing that remains undetermined is how many men will die before the end. Sound the retreat. Let us make haste to Grunmarrow with as many men as we may."

"What say the rest of you?" the king demanded.

Paneolus shook his head, excess rolls of flesh jiggling uncontrollably. As minister of state, it was his responsibility to manage all aspects of the governance of Rogscroft. He had failed. "Sire, leave now. There will be no other chance."

Stelskor turned his eye towards General Vajna. The general of the armies folded his thickly corded arms across his barrel chest and looked down at his boots. The shame of defeat wormed deep into his psyche. "We must retreat."

Venten made to talk but was cut off curtly by the king. "I already know your counsel. All of you have provided me and this proud city sage counsel for years. But look around you. Everywhere brave men die, men from both sides. This is a sad day."

He turned, leaving the marbled balcony to sit upon his throne one last time. His hands slid, almost caressed, along the arms. His head nestled into that familiar spot on the cushioned back. Stelskor closed his eyes and sighed from the heavy weight in his soul.

"Very well. Sound retreat. Start with the wounded. I do not want a single man left behind for our enemy's amusement."

Paneolus and Vajna bowed and were gone amidst a host of bodyguards and administrative assistants.

Stelskor stopped Venten from following. "Wait a moment, old friend."

He winced, suddenly afraid of what was coming.

Stelskor stared deep into his eyes, making Venten worm uncomfortably. "Find my son, Venten. Get him out of here alive no matter what he says. Guide him in the coming days. Rogscroft is going to need strong leadership if we're to find a way out of this mess."

The old general nodded. "I shall do my best, Sire."

THIRTY-FOUR

Argis

"We should start with burning down the barracks at the docks. Harnin won't be able to attack us so quickly without a nearby base of operations," Joefke told them.

He tapped the tip of his index finger on the torn and faded map.

"It might buy us a little time, but how much?" old man Fenning said as he casually chewed a mint leaf.

Joefke rubbed his eyes. He hadn't slept in two days. "Harnin isn't going to just walk away or offer terms at the bargaining table, old man. Every little victory gives us more credit and more willing bodies. That will be enough to turn the tide before the end."

Fenning offered an empathetic glance. "Maybe. Maybe it will be enough."

More than anything, Joefke hated being treated like a child. He had already proven himself a dozen times in the rebellion, earning Argis's praise more than once. He very much wanted to quit and go home, but that was impossible now. There was no safe place in Delranan. Innocent people were being abducted, never to be heard from again. Paranoia was out of control.

Inaella, a black-haired beauty who chose to hide behind heavy, burdensome clothing, interrupted. "I think Joefke is right. We can hurt their ability to hunt us by burning the barracks."

"At what cost?" Fenning asked them.

"Sacrifice, Fenning," Joefke answered. "Isn't that what Argis has been preaching this whole time? It is the only way we will win."

The room fell silent at the mention of Argis's name. The former Delranan lord was strangely missing. Joefke was deeply troubled but refused to speak those fears aloud. Argis never missed a council meeting. Never.

The door suddenly burst open. A wild-haired youth of no more than twenty summers slipped past the pair of guards. His face was flushed and he gasped for breath.

"What is the meaning of this?" Fenning demanded.

"They…they have Lord Argis!"

Joefke felt his world shatter. "How is this possible?"

"The city guard raided the house he was staying in. I watched soldiers drag Argis away, I swear!"

Glass walls shattered. The rebellion lived or died with Argis. The future of Delranan had shifted drastically.

"Where is he now?" Inaella asked. The panic in her voice terrified Joefke.

"Up to the Keep, ma'am."

Joefke's blood chilled. "We have to get him before Harnin gets him inside those walls. It's the only chance we have."

"That is exactly what the enemy wants us to do," Fenning warned. "We'll be slaughtered if we move now."

"We owe him our lives!" Joefke protested.

"This is the reason we shouldn't waste them in an ill-conceived rescue attempt."

"He has a point, Joefke," Inaella added. "We risk everything by going to the Keep unprepared. It's what Harnin has been hoping for, to break us and force us to act brashly. Besides, there is no way we can assemble a force strong enough in time. You know this is true."

His features, once pleasant and angular, contorted with rage. He felt abandoned. A good man's life was nothing to these people. Joefke decided that the members of the council had become ineffective. He no longer wanted anything to do with them.

"The only truth is that you are all cowards! That man gave up everything for us, for the kingdom, so that we could build a better future. You repay his efforts by choosing to condemn him to torment and death from the security of an anonymous room while pretending we are not at war. That is not good enough for me. He's about to die for your cowardice. I will not let that rest on my soul."

"Joefke, hear us out," Inaella urged softly.

He spun on her, pointing fiercely. "I am done listening. Stay away from me, all of you. I am done with this, with you. You have shown me you don't know how to lead."

He stormed out, leaving the council submersed in a combination of guilt and shock. The younger man had always been a hothead. This outburst only proved Fenning's point. The older farmer hung his head. His eyes bore a glassy look. Part of him wanted to call the man back, but pride wouldn't let him. The combined loss of Argis and Joefke would haunt the council much more severely than they could understand until it was far too late.

Joefke crept through the shadows. Frost formed under his nose, in his eyebrows. He clung to the trees and buildings lining the main road up to Chadra Keep. His heart struggled to burst free from the fleshy prison of his chest. The sweat forming on his chest threatened to freeze. Sounds amplified beyond reason. Instincts begged him to turn back now. He knew he was going to get caught. Delranan's darkest hour swallowed him.

He pushed forward, trying desperately to stay focused and on task. His conscience whispered for him to abandon this foolish quest and rejoin the council. Like Fenning, pride wouldn't allow it. Joefke swallowed his rising disgust with himself and pushed on. The jangle of steel chains drifted from just up ahead. He surged forward and was rewarded with a fast glimpse of Argis. His heart sank with defeat. A full platoon of guards surrounded the former lord. Hope of rescue deflated, Joefke nearly cried. Heavy infantry. The guards were heavy infantry, not the paltry city guards that had been conscripted to stem the rising violence. Joefke hung his head. Dawn was not coming for the rebellion.

The armored column marched up the hill and into the gaping jaws of Chadra Keep. Joefke leaned heavily against the nearest building and watched helplessly as the gates closed behind the last rank. For the first time since joining the rebellion, he truly felt lost. Pain and horror mocked him. He sank to his knees and stared up at the forbidding wooden walls of the Keep long into the night.

"We finally have him," Jarrik said as smugly as possible.

Harnin One Eye watched him with an evil look. *Finally*. The last obstacle to solidifying his claim on Delranan was about to be removed. Not even Badron and the Wolfsreik were going to return in time.

"Where is he now?"

"Burg escorted him into the dungeons."

Harnin nodded absently. His mind already raced ahead to infinite futures. "Is he unharmed?"

"As far as I know, though not from a lack of want."

Harnin's face hardened. "My orders are not to be disregarded. I was very clear on this matter, Jarrik."

Jarrik struggled with the urge to lash back. "My men understand perfectly. No harm has come to Lord Argis."

"Argis is no longer a lord in this kingdom! He forfeited that right when he turned his back on king and land."

Harnin pulled on a bearskin cloak, cinching the ball tight around his waist.

"What are you planning?" Jarrik asked suspiciously.

Harnin shot him a sharp, almost malevolent smile. "I am going to have him executed from the top of these very walls not long from now."

"What? Why wait?"

"I want the word to spread to every corner of this city. All of Chadra will come to watch the fate of traitors. A new day is about to dawn for us. The rebellion is over."

Jarrik remained unconvinced. "And the king? What will Badron think when he comes home?"

"That is my concern, not yours. See to the defenses. I do not want my gift to the people interrupted by Argis's friends."

Harnin stormed from the room, leaving the younger Jarrik enraged and feeling slightly endangered. Jarrik swore he heard the faint hissing of laughter coming from the darkest corner of the room.

"Open it."

Harnin's voice carried a harsh edge, partially from the unforgiving rock walls lining the dungeons. A pair of guards obeyed quickly lest they earned the One Eye's displeasure. The door groaned open. Harnin took one step inside and waited for his eye to adjust to the gloom. He smiled as Argis came into view. Overwhelming vindication for all the hard work and time he had put into consolidating his hold on the throne threatened to steal this singular moment of joy.

Harnin turned back to one of the guards. "Has he spoken?"

"Not yet, my lord."

"Good. You may leave us."

Harnin waited until the door clicked shut before moving closer to the limp body hanging by chains on the far wall. He used an index finger to trace a line through decades' worth of grime on the wall. "How many people have we put in this cell, you and I?"

Argis barely lifted his head.

"Hundreds? None has been as important as you, my friend."

He wiped his finger clean on Argis's torn tunic. "Have you nothing to say?"

"Friend?" Argis asked. His voice cracked, broken from a lack of water. "That word no longer applies to you and me."

Harnin barked a menacing laugh. "We were never friends, Argis. Only passing acquaintances in the scheme of time."

"Let me go and we can pass one final time."

"You would like that, eh? The great traitor Argis allowed a final folly before meeting his demise at the tip of a sword." His glare sharpened. "The very breath you draw is a mockery to all Delranan stands for."

Argis tried to spit but lacked the saliva. "You should have been killed at birth for the snake you are, One Eye. Delranan bleeds corruption. We are not the men we once were; do you not see it? Decadence and evil run freely across the land."

An accusing finger jabbed in his face. "Propagated by you and your rebellion! We had peace before the king left. His absence allowed your brand to infest the furthest corners in this society and for that there can be no reconciliation."

"Kill me and get it over with then. I am tired of your voice."

"Oh no. Death certainly stalks you, but I will not let it claim you just yet. You are going to be my grand masterpiece."

Argis narrowed his eyes. His heart beat a little faster. "What do you mean?"

"Word is already being spread throughout the kingdom. I am going to have you executed publicly. All of Delranan will see what fate awaits traitors. Your death will be the end of the rebellion and I will have peace."

"No," Argis whispered. "My death changes nothing. All you are going to accomplish is the hardening of resolve. My death will be the spark that turns the kingdom on end. You and your kind will be trampled under the boots of vengeance."

"A vengeance unfulfilled. I will drown the kingdom in blood before I allow your peasant conspirators to rise up."

"Then you damn us all."

Harnin sneered. "So be it."

He turned and stalked away. His rage was so great it threatened to consume him, urging him to run Argis through and be done with it. Harnin snarled. Killing Argis now served no purpose other than instant gratification. The people needed to see him die. It was the only way. Until then he was going to have to imagine Argis dying over and over again in his dreams.

"You tread a fine path, Harnin One Eye."

Harnin didn't bother facing his accuser. A persistent feeling warned him that the Dae'shan was never far away. Tonight should be no different.

"I walk the only path allowed me," he retorted.

Pelthit Re materialized from the darkness. His lidless yellow eyes watched impassively as the mortal continued pouring a mug of mulled wine. The Dae'shan briefly recalled such simple pleasure. The tender sweetness of grape and spices caressed his tongue. The memory faded much too soon, replaced by the unending suffering of his continued existence.

"The day of judgment is fast approaching," he continued.

Harnin waved him off. "We shall be ready. I will make Delranan strong again."

Pelthit Re might have smiled had he lips. "I have no doubt."

Harnin drank deeply from his mug and let his mind dance over thoughts of empire.

THIRTY-FIVE

Badron Triumphant

"Fall back! Fall back to the tunnels!"

Aurec struggled to contain the rising panic in his voice. Most of his men were already dead, their bodies filling the gateway. Sergeant Thorsson had done his best. The burly man was a natural killing force. Scores of Goblins fell under his blade, but it wasn't enough. A dozen more swarmed into the lines for every Goblin killed. The grey tide was endless.

Soldiers dragged the wounded off. Some made it, some didn't. More than one group of soldiers was cut down by squads of Wolfsreik who had already secured the rear stairs. Enemy soldiers completely controlled the walls. Catapults continued to pour heavy fire into the compound, heedless for their own men's safety. Aurec found it reckless and correctly guessed Badron was behind the frantic push. The city and keep had fallen; all that remained was the mopping up.

A heavy hand snatched Aurec's collar. "I thought I told you to get out of here."

He looked into Thorsson's bloody face. A deep cut peeled back the flesh on his right cheek and temple. "The men come first."

Thorsson nodded slightly, wincing from the pain. "That is exactly what I am doing. Now get your royal ass out of my way. I don't need you dead."

"I can't leave them. Not like this," Aurec protested.

"You are damned stubborn all right. Don't make me knock you out and drag you away myself."

Aurec couldn't stop from grinning. "Sergeant, if we make it through this I will gladly let you punch me in the mouth."

Thorsson snorted a laugh. "Deal. Lead the next group of wounded out. I follow with the rear guard. I want to take as many of these grey bastards as we can along the way."

They clasped hands, a final gesture in the face of insurmountable odds. "No unnecessary heroics, sergeant. I still have more work for you to do."

Thorsson grinned savagely. Satisfied he had done all within his power, Aurec went to gather the next batch of wounded to move out. Chaos raged around him. Goblins streamed into Rogscroft, their hobnailed boots marching across a makeshift bridge of their own dead. They snarled and gnashed, eager for the taste of human blood. Their blades were sharp and slightly rusted. Theirs was a horrifying flame poised to sweep across the northern kingdoms. Just a moment longer.

Thorsson turned back to the fight, bellowing orders as he rejoined the slaughter. "Come on you lazy dogs! Send these grey bastards back to the underworld!"

What few defenders remained rallied to his call with the knowledge that the sum of their deeds would still meet with defeat. Thorsson ducked under a wild slash from a spear and stabbed up. A sickly grunt and soft spray of dark blood met his blade. The Goblin slumped down beside him as more Men and Goblins fell. He kicked the corpse away and drew back to swing again.

Thorsson was suddenly knocked back by a bone-jarring impact. The wind forced from his lungs and new pain racked his body. Something dark and sticky flowed down his chest. Damnation, he cursed. The Goblin arrow struck right above his lung. The wound wasn't totally life threatening, but he feared for poison. Thorsson spit a mouthful of blood and struggled back to his feet. He'd just as soon die fighting than running.

Venten led the various lords and nobles in full retreat through the winding halls to the freshly constructed escape tunnels. A signal fire had already been lit atop the highest tower in the castle, signaling everyone to abandon the city. It also served to warn units already in the wild that the king was coming. It was the only way Venten saw getting Stelskor to safety.

"Just a little further," he called back over his shoulder as he pushed on through the near dark.

Embers of flame drifted from his torch and singed the hairs on his hand. He didn't care. The smell of dirt caressed his nostrils. He didn't care. Venten's only drive was to get the king out of the dying city. All was lost without the king alive. Voices and a lot of heavy movement triggered old instincts. Venten immediately drew his sword and wished for a platoon of infantry at his back rather than the lax noblemen. A pair of guards pushed their way through the crowd to join him.

With no hesitation, the trio moved forward. Relief and despair greeted them. Venten watched as dozens of wounded soldiers made their way into the tunnel from a separate entrance. Many would not live to see the dawn. Trails of blood made the dirt slick with mud. Venten cursed. The blood was going to lead the enemy down on top of them. It also meant the tunnel ahead was clogged with men.

"Who is in command here?" he demanded.

Aurec looked up at the sound of a familiar voice. Mixed emotions showed on his tired face. Venten's presence could only mean one thing: the king was here as well. Aurec passed off the wounded man he had been assisting to another and slipped back to his old friend and mentor.

"It is good to see you alive, Venten," he exhaled.

They embraced in relief. "Prince Aurec, I feared the worst when I couldn't get back to your side. The king kept me in council until the decision to retreat was made."

"Where is my father?"

Venten glanced fleetingly back over his shoulder. "He should be right behind the corner with the others."

Aurec felt something was wrong and started pushing through the small crowd of nobles. Desperation gripped him as previously unknown fears forced him into action. His heart pounded, almost ached. Try as he might, he did not find his father. The fear of losing the king sickened him. He didn't know what to think. Tremors in his veins threatened to sink him to his knees.

"Father!" he shouted. "Where is the king?"

General Vajna reached him quickly. "Lad, your father refused to follow us into the tunnels. He stayed behind. There was nothing we could do."

Aurec felt gut punched. "You...you left my father? How dare you!"

Vajna gripped him by the shoulders. Aurec didn't have the strength to resist. "Listen to me. Your father, the king of Rogscroft, explicitly ordered me to move on. We argued, but in the end it was his will that was done."

"So you abandoned him? Your duty lies with the crown."

"And that crown belongs to your father!" Vajna spit back harshly. "So long as he commands, I obey. He deserves nothing less."

"There is no time for this!" Venten shouted at them. "The enemy is almost upon us. We must flee now or forfeit all."

Aurec hung his head. "Why did he not come?"

"He goes to try and make peace with Badron."

"Then he goes to his death," the prince replied.

Venten softened his stance. "His fate is beyond any of us, my prince."

Two men pulled Sergeant Thorsson to his feet and began half carrying him away from what remained of the battle. Perhaps a score stayed to hold off the waves of Goblins. They resigned themselves to death so that many more would survive. The gesture was not in vain, though the Goblin army slaughtered them mercilessly. Thorsson's fight was over, though he was loath to admit it. He begged and struggled to be let back with his men, to die a warrior's death. The pain in his chest burned throughout his body. Soldiers, he grimaced. They seldom did as they were told. That's when Gaml and Yorl snatched him up and dragged him off despite his screams of protest.

"Be quiet, Sarge. Whining like a little baby isn't going to help you none," Gaml scolded.

"S'right, Sarge. You leave it to us. We got your best interests in mind," Yorl added.

Thorsson bit back a moan. Damned brothers. "You pig-headed fools, the least you could do is let me die with my men. I never should have put you both in the same unit."

"That's not a nice thing to say, 'specially after me and Yorl here went through all this trouble to drag your heavy ass to safety."

"Safety? Bunch of damned fools. We are all going to die."

"We'll see, Sarge. We'll see."

Thorsson hoped they were right, for all their sakes.

Alone. King Stelskor sat upon his throne for what he knew was the very last time. His kingdom, his legacy, crumbled to dust around him. Wolfsreik and Goblin soldiers were everywhere, looting and destroying. Smoke and flame licked up into the early dawn sky. Rogscroft was finished. The dream of a prosperous, civilized kingdom was suddenly torn from Malweir and the future. Generations from now no one would even know this land existed. Stelskor wondered if this was how the last Gaimosian king felt during the final moments. Memories of the ancient kingdom remained only through blood and the deeds of less noble children. Stelskor doubted his own legacy would be so strong.

Battle sounds edged closer. The roar of fresh fires and collapsing buildings sounded as the darkest agonies to the failed king. All he had spent his life to achieve was shattering around him. Stelskor was helpless to prevent it, hopeless to find the dawn. He had nothing left to offer. Soon the enemy would break into the throne room and his reign would fade to ash. He resisted the urge to second guess himself, to ask what might have been.

Stelskor sighed heavily. There was no point in asking *what if.* This was the end the Fates had decreed for him and his people. Nothing was going to change it. Death stalked him like an old friend from the shadows. The sudden crashing against the once proud throne room doors made him jump. His wait was over. The old king drew his sword, an heirloom handed down through the generations, and made ready to meet his end. His one regret lay in not being able to give the sword to his son. The pounding grew louder, fiercer. He sneered. Perhaps the Wolfsreik weren't so smart after all. Common sense said that this was the one room that no one was supposed to be in. There was no reason for the king to remain behind.

Stelskor rose, his resolve strengthened by the hopes that he might soon stride into the halls of his forefathers and be welcomed. The doors splintered apart. Chunks of ancient carvings blew inwards across the marble floor. Enemy soldiers streamed in behind. Their weapons glimmered in the torchlight. The lead soldiers froze, surprised at what they saw.

"Come you jackals, come and meet doom," Stelskor growled.

The Wolfsreik edged closer.

"Hold!"

The command bellowed throughout the room, bouncing from the walls. Even Stelskor held fast, so great was the power in the words. An older man moved through the mass of hungry soldiers. His uniform was nearly immaculate. Hardly a stain could be found, as if he had been saving it for just this occasion. Soldiers ringed him in a lazy half circle.

"King Stelskor, I am Commander Piper Joach, Second of the Wolfsreik and loyal son of Delranan."

Stelskor kept his sword at the low guard. "Save your titles. They mean little at this point. Kill me and get it over with."

A half smile. "I am glad we see eye to eye, but your death will not be on my hands or conscience. I arrest you by order of King Badron. You and your kingdom now belong to Delranan."

"You dare!"

A new voice drowned out Piper's response. "No, I do."

Stelskor paled. Badron himself had come to witness the end of this long nightmare. Sadly, he looked nothing like his former self. Stelskor was surprised to see how old and frail he looked, a haunting echo of the past. His once majestic frame was now gaunt and frighteningly grey. A haggard look scarred his bearded face. This new Badron did not belong in the waking world. Worse, he bore a light of pure malevolence in his dark eyes.

"Badron," Stelskor whispered.

"You have no idea how long I have awaited this moment, Stelskor. You killed my son, threw my kingdom into turmoil, and kidnapped my daughter. The fate I am about to bestow on you might be considered a mercy compared to all of the agony you created."

Venom dripped from his words. Hate, pure and dark hate, consumed his emotions. The last king of Rogscroft threw down his sword in defiance and held out his arms. Every moment he delayed gave his men and his son a greater chance of escaping.

"Do it then. Kill me and claim your revenge."

Badron disregarded him with a laugh. "Revenge? No, not revenge. This is justice."

"Delranan justice has no place within my halls."

"These halls are no longer yours. Your army is routed. Your whelp of a son is dead and I am going to burn this castle to the ground. No one will even remember the pathetic kingdom you struggled to rule."

Stelskor had already stopped listening. *Aurec, my son.* He'd done everything within his power to prepare the boy for this moment. Aurec should have been leading what remained of the defenders to Grunmarrow. Why had he stayed? What had he been thinking? Anguish clutched Stelskor's soul. With father and son gone, there was no one to lead. The king was utterly broken.

He raised his weak gaze to the man he once named brother. "Bastard."

"Indeed."

Badron rushed forward. The sound of steel slicing meat, wet and sickening, filled the tiny chamber. Red mist blossomed across the gap between the two kings. Stelskor groaned from the immense pain tearing through his chest and slumped down on Badron's sword. Already weak, he threw his hands around Badron's neck and tried to squeeze. Guards moved to intercept but their king waved them off. His sneer turned into a smile as he twisted his sword around. He laughed as it pierced his foe's back. Dark blood sprayed from Stelskor's mouth. It bubbled on his lips. The last king of Rogscroft fell dead on the cold marble floor.

Badron lifted his arms in triumph. "Victory!"

The Wolfsreik remained silent.

Somehow, and he still wasn't exactly sure just how, Raste wound up leading a column of wounded out of the castle. He'd been reconciled with the need to keep fighting atop the walls, but he had no desire to die so casually. The Wolfsreik hounded his every step. It wasn't until he and a handful of survivors managed to duck inside the main keep that he paused to take stock of his injuries and catch his breath.

Nine men. That was all that remained of his men and the ones who had miraculously arrived to save his life moments before a Wolfsreik sword nearly skewered him. Worse, he appeared to be the highest-ranking survivor. Raste cursed. He knew next to nothing about leadership. All of his dreams of the future centered on fighting the enemy. Well, he grimaced, that hadn't gone so well. Too many of his friends lay dead in the smoldering ruins of the city.

"We should keep moving," he reluctantly told the nine.

One by one the haggard survivors struggled to their feet and continued the long trek to Grunmarrow.

Mahn sat uncomfortably in his saddle, silently watching as rich flames the colors of merchant silks devoured his home. He felt curiously empty. His world, all that he knew, was finished. Reprisal was out of the question. There were too few survivors to make a difference. Any hope was going to come from repeated guerilla attacks throughout the winter, like the Pell Darga had done during the early stages of the war.

"What do we do now? How can we possibly avenge so much destruction?" he asked.

Sergeant Thorsson spat a wad of congealed blood. "We do what the king commanded. Regroup at Grunmarrow and get ready for war."

His shoulder was swathed in bandages. The bleeding had stopped, but the pain bordered on unbearable. Thorsson took it with clenched teeth. A passing medic claimed the arrow wasn't poisoned, but it sure felt like it to Thorsson. Every ounce of focus was on his hatred of the men and monsters who now occupied his home. He spat again.

"Come on," he said with a grimace. "We still have a long way to go."

The older scout pulled his cloak tight. A permanent frown was engraved on his face. Winter was deepening and they were not geared for the elements. Exquisite pain danced on the fringes of his wounded soul. He had failed, in every regard. Years of hard work and dedication amounted to nothing. Mahn struggled with the abject desire to run and hide. The fight had left him.

"All right," he reluctantly agreed. "Let us put this nightmare behind us."

Cuul Ol leaned heavily on his oak staff. The squat, brown-skinned man watched Rogscroft burn in the valley below. He sighed. The war was over. King Stelskor failed to stop the enemy. Some measure of reciprocity might be enacted if the king still lived, but Cuul doubted it. A true king would have died in the ruins of his kingdom. Such was the code Pell Darga tribal leaders lived by. He shook his head. It was time to see to his own people now.

The Pell chieftain could not help but feel immeasurable sadness at the inferno raging before him. There was no love lost for the lowlanders, but their alliance had been with some benefits. The Pell gained trade rights with Rogscroft and the ability to move freely through southern lands. They also gained a new enemy in the Wolfsreik. Badron's uncontrollable lust for power threatened to rip the fabric of northern Malweir apart. Such appetites needed to be culled.

"We should abandon them now."

Cuul looked up at his growing rival. "Do not be so quick to pass judgment, Sintl Ap. We still need them."

"For what? They are all dead. Fire eats their heart," Sintl scowled. "What more is there?"

"There is still war."

"Not my war."

Cuul Ol lacked the strength to argue, not in the wake of a murdered kingdom. "Durgas would disagree."

Sintl Ap paused. Word of the ambush spread quickly through the tribes. The indignation of such cruel murders spurred the Pell hunters into undiscovered rage. No true warrior deserved to be butchered the way Durgas and his men had. Cuul Ol personally led a group of hunters to see the truth for themselves. What they found sickened them. Fresh bile soon joined the eviscerated corpses strewn among the trees. A pile of heads sat in the middle of the slaughter, eyes open and staring into the dark reaches of eternity. Each face was twisted in eternal of agony.

Cuul Ol ordered the bodies burned, a ritual befitting the deaths of such worthy men. The rising desire for revenge clashed with an eerie feeling creeping around his spine. He couldn't shake the feeling that whoever had so casually killed Durgas was still here, watching their every move. Cuul Ol shuddered before urging his men to hurry.

He shut his eyes. "I was there. I saw the bodies."

Sintl Ap persisted. "The Pell should never have gotten involved. This was not our fight."

Sadness welled within Cuul Ol as he desperately tried to push the memories away. "No. The time is too late to turn our backs. Whoever killed Durgas knows too much of our ways. Our mountains are not safe."

"What do you say?"

"The only way to find peace is through war."

Cuul understood that statement might mark the damnation of his people, but there was no other way he could see. A new day had dawned for the Pell Darga. There would be no return from this new life. Gone was the storied isolationist lifestyle. The Pell were now intricately intertwined in the affairs of the rest of Malweir. Cuul Ol prayed his world did not degenerate beyond control.

Sint Ap finally nodded. "So be it. The Pell Darga have a new purpose. We shall be a name that sparks terror for generations."

"I pray you are wrong, for us all."

They stood in silence and watched as the world they once knew burned to the ground.

THIRTY-SIX

The Quest Sets Forth

Bahr enjoyed the rising sun as it made its way across the roof of the world. Mixed emotions assailed his tranquility. He found the concept of faith intriguing, enough to force him into the cathedral to watch the Giants devote themselves to their god. God. Gods. What this entire sad affair revolved around. The stringent belief in one faith or another threatened to destroy the world. Hundreds already lay dead in the name of powers that no one could prove existed.

He snorted. The notion was absurd. It didn't make any sense that a thing so simple could cause so much destruction. Was man so easily lulled into killing others? Bahr wanted to think otherwise. He still had hope in the innate righteousness his kind possessed. He'd seen both good and bad but did not know where the answers lay. Perhaps the long journey to Trennaron would provide the clues to his dilemma.

There came a soft knock on the aged, wooden door. "Come in."

Boen's massive form looked small in the Giant doorway. "It is time to leave."

"So soon?"

His comment took the Gaimosian off guard. "What?"

"Nothing. I've had too much time to think. Is the wagon ready?"

Boen nodded. "Rekka seems to have a gift for motivation. She's just about finished with everything. Good girl, that one."

"Yes. Convenient she arrived in port when she did," Bahr drawled, recalling the earlier admission.

"You don't sound optimistic."

"Like I said, I've been thinking too much."

"I bet you are a depressing drunk."

Bahr bit back a laugh. "You've seen me drunk. If only our problems could be solved by a jug of wine."

Boen entered the room and shut the door behind him. "All right, out with it. Neither one of us is leaving this room until I am confident your head is in the right place. I mean it, Bahr."

"I'm fine."

"I don't believe you," Boen snarled.

The Sea Wolf blew out a long sigh. "Have you ever bothered to wonder what this has all been for? The reasons we left Delranan were false. It was never about Maleela. Nothing has been as it seemed even from the beginning."

It was now Boen's turn to sigh. "This is not the time for a mental break down. We've got too far to go for this. I need you in the fight with me."

Bahr wiped his red-streaked eyes. "Gods. That's what this is all about. How many people have died in the name of some mythical beings? It doesn't make sense. We are about to go halfway across Malweir, risk our lives, and come back in the middle of a war not of our making. All because of gods."

"Gods?" Bemusement laced his tone. "Who cares? Want to know what I think? I think there's nothing to it. We are our own men."

"How can you say that knowing all that has happened so far?"

"What's done is done. I don't care about some imaginary beings intent on screwing with our lives. Show me a god, a real live god, and I will give him a piece of my mind. Maybe even the tip of my blade."

"Somehow I don't see that ending well for you."

He shrugged. "Doesn't matter. These gods of yours aren't important, leastwise not to me. All I can do is live my life with honor. My death will be worthwhile then. The rest is just a waste of time. Now, strap on your damned sword and let's get moving. I am tired of being around these Giants."

"It's not too late to go back," Dorl said.

Nothol Coll just shook his head. "Go back to what? It's not like we have a home to go back to. Harnin One Eye will have put out warrants on us. Home is gone."

"Then we go somewhere else! How many other kingdoms are in Malweir? Harnin's power only extends to Delranan."

"And Rogscroft," Nothol shrewdly added.

"What?"

"I think it is safe to assume that Badron has already conquered Rogscroft, or at least he should soon," Nothol explained.

"My point is there are a whole lot of places the two of us can go once we get out of these mountains," Dorl said, choosing not to expound on Nothol's statement. The implications frightened him to the point he refused to consider them.

"Uh huh. Can you even name another kingdom?"

Dorl snarled. "Doesn't matter. We don't have to go back."

Nothol Coll rolled his eyes and walked away. He, too, was unwilling to explore the dark possibilities awaiting them. His faith in Bahr to see them through these troubles was enough. He only hoped Dorl would come to see the same.

Lightning struck the ground for as far as he could see. Ominous black clouds hung so low a man could reach up and touch them. Dark boulders sat like broken teeth in a dying monster's jaws. The edges of the far horizon glowed a murderous red. Strange creature of indescribable hatred could be seen dancing among the clouds. They beckoned to him. Ionascu wrapped his arms tightly around himself and struggled to hold back the rising bile in his throat. He wished his eyes were as broken as the rest of his body to save him the torment of these images.

"Ionascu, third son of Matescu. Hear our voices."

He screamed and clamped his twisted hands over his ears. Tiny trickles of blood seeped from beneath his fingers. Strength fled and he dropped to his knees. Massive hands, larger than mountains, jutted up from the ground. Stone and rocks showered down, crushing everything beneath. Ionascu felt cold. He felt hatred so pure it threatened to tear the marrow from his very bones.

"Leave me alone!" he shouted back.

The voices laughed, cold and wicked.

"No, broken son. The hour is much too late for that."

A female voice. *"Yes. The time has come for you to fulfill your purpose."*

"I said leave me be!" he shouted again with less conviction.

Lightning struck close enough to sizzle his flesh and knock him backwards.

"You would do well to listen."

Ionascu bowed low, his forehead touching the ground hard enough to draw blood. "Yes. Yes, please no more."

"See, I told you he was agreeable."

"Perhaps."

A large hand, no more than a wisp of cloud, plucked the groveling man up and set him on his feet.

"Heed our words. War is coming. A terrible war to decide the fate of the world. We have need of agents."

The broken man's resistance weakened.

"Serve us and we will grant you revenge against those responsible for breaking you."

Ionascu looked up. Fresh hope sparked to life. "You, you can do that?"

Dark laughter. *"That and so much more. Follow us and the revenge is yours. All of the foulest desires aching in the rot of your heart will come true. It is a gift."*

Fear and desperation lost their hold on him and Ionascu willingly allowed himself to plunge into the enticements. He wanted Harnin dead more than anything and would be a fool to pass on such opportunity. Ionascu quickly decided.

"What must I do?"

"*Nothing for now. We will come to you when the time is right.*"

Ethereal fingers dissolved and he fell. Ionascu woke up confused and bathed in sweat. He screamed.

Skuld warmed his hands, knowing that this would likely be his last chance to stay warm for a very long time. The Murdes Mountains were by far the worst place he had ever been. His initial fascination of the Giants was gone, just as lost as earlier dreams of gold and riches. He wanted to go home and forget all of this. The only problem was home no longer existed.

"What troubles your mind, young Skuld?"

Anienam's voice cracked from age yet managed to keep a comforting tone.

"I've had too long to think about things, Anienam."

The wizard took a seat beside him and smiled tightly. "A very dangerous thing, that. Thinking has been the ruin of a great many since the dawn of the world."

"You are mocking me."

"Perhaps just a little, though what I say is largely true. The power of thought, one of our most basic freedoms, is also a bane. Too much thinking lets a man believe he can do anything. With some it works within the scope of their boundaries, but with others it pushes them into acts of desperation. It is those men who need watching."

The soft crackle of flames soothed the boy.

After giving Skuld time to think on it, Anienam playfully asked, "You're not one of those men who need watching, are you?"

Skuld smiled sheepishly. "No. At least I don't think so."

"Good. I would have hated to turn you into a toad."

He laughed, finally.

"Does what we are doing matter?" Skuld asked suddenly.

"That depends on how you mean."

Skuld shook his head. "I don't know. This doesn't feel right, Anienam. I feel like we are being pushed into a task for someone else. It bothers me."

Anienam passed a worried glance. The boy is quick, he thought. *He just might make a decent Mage.*

"Between you and me, we are caught up in a war of beliefs. Some here in Venheim might argue that the gods have designs on each of us but aren't strong enough to deal with matters themselves."

"That doesn't make sense."

"No, it really doesn't, which makes what we have to do all the more important. The fate of Malweir might rest on our shoulders. Boen should enjoy that," he added as an afterthought.

Skuld forced another laugh, much more strained than before.

"Think no more on this. There is no point in worrying about matters beyond our control," Anienam said and gently slapped Skuld's knee. "Now come on, we are leaving soon and I absolutely deplore traveling on an empty stomach.

Joden stepped back, admiring his handiwork. The hammer was the finest tool he had ever wrought. Dark iron absorbed rather than reflected light. It was powerful enough to meet the dark times. Tight leather straps provided the grip on the handle, strong and reliable for use in combat. Archaic runes were etched into the head, giving it strength, power. The ancient Giant set the weapon down, lost deep in thought.

It was going to take much for Groge to survive the quest for the Blud Hamr. Joden wished the wizard had come a hundred years ago. The forge master would have leapt at the opportunity to become history. Rather than lose himself to fanciful dreams that would never come true, Joden turned to Groge.

"This hammer," he began, "has not been named. I had planned on doing so if I were ever summoned to great purpose. Fate, it seems, has given that task to you."

"I am honored, forge master," Groge replied.

He hesitated before accepting so great a gift. He certainly had no claim on such grand creation. Groge was just an apprentice and unworthy. He had earned no honor.

"May you use this hammer only in the darkest hour," Joden said as he took up the hammer and passed it to young Groge.

"Then I pray I never have to use it."

The forge master nodded at the answer. He rose. "It is time."

The old Giant led the way back to the central square where the rest of the band of would-be heroes awaited. Dozens of Giants were gathered as well. Blekling and his group of sycophants stood in the center. A perpetual sneer twisted his face. His mistrust of their guests heightened since Bahr went against his wishes three nights ago. No strangers had come to Venheim for centuries and he wished to keep it so. Man was a prejudiced beast incapable of true understanding. They killed what they didn't understand, eradicated what they couldn't fathom. Blekling saw his world crumbling even further and vowed to arrest that progress before Venheim became a true legend.

Joden stopped before the warden of Venheim and offered a curt bow. "The Chosen is prepared to undertake his journey and find glory in the name of the gods."

"Is he?" Blekling asked. He rapped his heavy iron staff on the ice-covered ground three crisp times. "Step forward, Groge of the Barish clan."

Mighty hammer strapped across his wide back, Groge obeyed.

"What is going on?" Dorl whispered.

Nothol shrugged. "Beats me. Looks like more song and dance keeping us from getting on."

Anienam passed them a menacing glance.

The Giant elder continued. "Do you understand what is being asked of you?"

"I do."

"Long have our people been the custodians of the secrets of steel. Entrusted by the gods, we have protected that secret here in the highest peaks of the world. Today you embark upon a sacred quest to retrieve the Blud Hamr. Only this weapon has the power to defeat the rising power of the dark gods. Darkness will consume Malweir should you fail. Are you prepared to devote your life, if need be, to the completion of the quest?"

"I am."

"Then go with the blessings of the gods and those of your people." His final words were spoken with venom. Clear disdain was etched across his broad face.

Groge took his place beside Bahr. The company was now complete.

Blekling turned to the Sea Wolf. "I do not expect to see you again. This quest will be dangerous and worse. Know this, should you by chance succeed, you and your kind are not welcome to return to Venheim."

"That's a shame. I was just picturing where my new home would look best," Boen answered gruffly.

The Gaimosian in him begged for a fight. It took much for him to refrain from lashing out at the nearest Giant and issue the challenge.

Blekling fumed, even as Joden struggled to conceal his amusement. The forge master almost admired the smaller Gaimosian. Red-orange glow from nearby forges painted the village, almost making it seem serene and majestic.

"Be gone from here!" Blekling all but shouted and stalked off.

Dorl Theed clicked his lips together. "Huh. He's not the sort to be invited to a party, is he?"

"No. I don't think he plays well with others," Nothol agreed.

Joden moved next to Bahr. "Not all of us are as closed as Blekling. The well wishes of all good people go with you. Bring back the hammer and end the threat of the dark gods for good."

Bahr nodded crisply. "Thank you." He turned to his companions. "Let's go, it's time for us to leave."

The old man swung into his saddle and started to leave. He'd taken all he could of the Giants and their outdated ways. Still, the experience left him with conflicting emotions. Hinder or help, the Giants were divided. The prospect of using the Blud Hamr was clearly more important than he previously believed. Well, Bahr thought, I have no time for that. What had begun as a personal quest to rescue his niece quickly devolved into a nightmare. He still wasn't sure how he got involved with saving the world. He wasn't sure he wanted to know, either.

He glanced over at Maleela and wondered if he was doing the right thing.

High above, the three Hags stirred awake. Stretching their dark wings, they watched the tiny band of heroes amble out of Venheim. They stretched legs and arms, loose feathers drifting lazily down. Hours of inactivity left them cold and hungry. Claws flexed and clenched repeatedly. Sharp eyes strained to make out distinct individuals. The hunt would soon begin anew.

Freina watched the wagon roll with casual interest. She'd been contracted to prevent the old one from reaching Trennaron, but her heart wasn't in it. Her only concern was perpetuating her species. So very few of them remained.

"Do we hunt?" Brom asked. Her scratchy voice reminded Freina of two swords scraping together.

Freina looked to each of her sisters. Both seemed eager to be underway.

"Yes," she replied.

"Finally."

As one the Harpies took flight.

THIRTY-SEVEN

A New Hope

Brackish mists swirled around a glade of muck and refuse, surrounded by trees long decayed. Three figures emerged from the blackest shadows. Robed and cowled, the memories of their mortal lives nothing more than fractured nightmares haunting pathetic existences, they remained hidden from themselves. The powers of the dark gods twisted them into the foulest creatures. The Dae'shan were finally assembled. Lidless eyes stared from their cowls.

Amar Kit'han regarded his peers with unveiled animosity. Neither would hesitate to assassinate him the moment he no longer proved useful or showed a decided lack of power. His authority was the only thing keeping him alive and he wondered if it was enough. The notion of removing the others slowly came into play. Kodan Bak was easily the most aggressive. His lust for power rivaled Amar's though he lacked clarity of vision. Pelthit Re, however, was more devious. Often tending to work alone, Pelthit enacted plans within plans, sometimes contradictory to what the overall group strived towards.

"You play a dangerous game, Pelthit Re."

Re hissed. "No more than you. I do only what our masters wish of me."

"The kingdom of Delranan has already fallen to us," Kodan Bak agreed. "As has Rogscroft. We are succeeding at last."

"Delranan is not yet ready. There is still too much strength left in Men," Pelthit insisted darkly. "Much needs to be done to break them properly."

Amar Kit'han was not convinced. "What of the daughter of Badron? She may yet prove our undoing. The Hags tell me she travels with a knight."

"I have met this knight. She should prove no problem," Pelthit replied.

"Can we be sure?"

"No more than any of us."

But could he be sure? Amar considered their position. A band of mortals, now accompanied by a Giant, was heading south on a quest to retrieve the fabled Blud Hamr. The one weapon capable of defeating the dark gods forever. With them was a knight of the supposedly vanquished holy Order, though the band remained ignorant of her true purpose. The situation was proving much too close for his comfort. Now was the time to act, and he had but one option.

"I believe it is time for us to return to Trennaron," he told them.

"For?" Kodan Bak asked.

"Artiss Gran must remember where he came from."

Pelthit Re snarled. "Traitor. He is no longer one of us."

"He turned his back on us long ago. Death would be too kind."

Amar shook his head. "Irrelevant. He will soon know the power of our full hatred. Gran must be neutralized if we have hope of succeeding."

"There are but one hundred days left before the thousand years are expired."

"Going to Trennaron is pointless," Kodan said suddenly.

The others turned to him. "What do you mean?"

"Artiss Gran is no longer one of us. He is weak, incapable of properly defending the Hamr. The three of us traveling so far would only leave the north open for our enemies to regroup. We would be vulnerable again for no reason."

"He is a threat unchecked. Don't be so foolish as to believe Gran lacks power because he abandoned us," Re snapped. "I agree with Amar. We must go and kill him."

"No," Amar said unexpectedly. "Kodan Bak may be correct. We cannot kill Gran, for he is still one of us. Only our masters can finish him. Perhaps we should focus on the wizard and his disciples. Kill them and the hammer is useless."

"The Hags will hunt them down, but they are only Harpies. Vile creatures with little real strength," Kodan cautioned. "They can track the wizard but will need assistance in dealing with him."

"Leave that to me. Pelthit Re, return to Delranan and break the One Eye's mind. Kodan Bak, you will stay here in Rogscroft and work on King Badron. Both are vital in the coming weeks."

"Where will you be?" Pelthit Re asked. Suspicion twisted his tone. He floated up a few inches, hands crossed in front.

"I have business in the east. A new war brews and I must fan the flames to keep it from blowing out. Go now. I shall summon you when I need you again."

The others drew their powers. The very air shimmered as if trying to escape. Darkness coalesced tightly as two Dae'shan folded in on themselves and disappeared, leaving Amar Kit'han alone. He smiled, the visage one of pure malevolence. One hundred days before their masters returned to take their rightful places as the masters of Malweir.

Artiss Gran stood atop the lone tower and watched as lightning wreathed the skies. The sky had turned a mottled purple, orange and black. His tired eyes witnessed the portents swirling around the sprawling fortress of Trennaron. Time was ending. Another cycle had almost reached conclusion. Yet unlike the ten times before, this time was different. Relevant heroes had stepped forward to challenge the rising tide of evil.

No stranger to dark times, the former Dae'shan struggled to comprehend the danger lurking just beyond reach. His brothers had lost their way, willfully succumbing to ever present desires and temptations. Artiss knew he should be sad but couldn't find the correct emotion. Their order once held so much promise. A glorious age had been envisioned shortly after their inception. Meant to maintain order, the Dae'shan then had roamed Malweir in search of corruption and overzealous righteousness. So much time had passed since their fall.

Malweir had never been a safe place. That level of insecurity worsened with time. Without the Dae'shan to ensure balance, the world plunged into perpetual nightmare. The Mages helped stave off the coming fires, for a time, but they, too, fell into shadow. Artiss wondered if this was simply the way fate meant it all to play out. He had lost hope, but never conviction. He turned to the primitive tribes of the jungle and developed them into great beings. Defenders and guardians had sprung from their ranks and helped keep the tentative balance in order. For a time.

That time was coming to an end. The final conflict was barreling towards them unchecked. Only a handful stood between doom and survival. Artiss wasn't sure there was going to be any victor, even if the dark gods were finally defeated. The magic of creation was gone. An undying spark casually dimmed through misuse and wanton aggression. His soul ached for those unsuspecting across the face of the world who did not know the true depths of the horror approaching.

Artiss Gran rubbed his hands together. He had much to do before the heroes arrived. Much to do indeed.

END

BOOK III OF THE NORTHERN CRUSADE

A WHISPER
AFTER MIDNIGHT

CHRISTIAN WARREN FREED

Preview of Book Three of the Northern Crusade:

A   Whisper   After   Midnight

One

Cold winter winds kissed the broken mountaintops. This part of northern Malweir was a wicked and cruel place; filled with nightmares despair, the perfect place for the Hags to roost. The three harpies were sisters, wretched and cunning. They claimed the broken peaks and forced away smaller animals and other predatory birds. Men seldom came this far north without truly understanding the perils in the mountains. Only a tribe of Giants occupied the valley at the top of the mountains; Venheim, the fabled forge of Giants. It was here the Hags chose to maintain their watch. And wait.

Freina flexed her clawed feet, tilting her head back to enjoy the breeze. Her dark eyes watched the mountain pass far below, focused on the small band of travelers with their wagon. She was surprised they had made it this far with all the odds thrown against them. Amar Kit'han and the Dae'shan seemed intent on killing them all but one yet nothing they had done worked. Freina attributed that to the wizard, Anienam Keiss. The last of his kind, his magics came from deep in the earth and were stronger than anything she remembered encountering before. The wizard made her and her sisters cautious, perhaps overly so. The Hags bristled at their defeats.

Brom crooned, a strange combination of pain and impatience. "We should not have agreed to help the devils."

Freina spread her wings, dark feathers tipped with frost. "These choices are not ours to make. Our kind swore an oath and we are honor bound to adhere. Do not question my decisions, sister.”

“She speaks what we all feel, Freina,” Garelda snipped. Smaller than Freina, Garelda’s heart bled with hatred. “This is not our war.”

“Men are weak,” Freina countered swiftly. “The Dae’shan herald the coming age of the dark gods. It is wise to serve them now so that we are remembered when the proper time arrives.”

“At what cost?”

Freina cocked her head. “Explain your question.”

“Our kind has exhausted itself to near extinction following the corrupt orders of the Dae’shan. So few of us remain it is impossible to rebuild. We are dying, sister, and your blind obedience will see us put in the ground as well. It is time to break away from the dark gods and find our own path.”

Brom jerked back, shocked by her sister’s boldness. Freina clenched her fists, claws digging into the calloused flesh of her palms. “We serve as our ancestors did. There is no greater cause than that given to us by our birth. To do less would be blasphemy.”

“Against what? We do not worship the dark gods, Freina. Is it not time to reclaim our lives and rebuild the great aeries?”

Freina seemed to consider the wisdom behind Garelda’s comment. The thought of building a nest, a place to raise children and become queen of her race enticed her, but not to the point of abandoning her oaths. Honor spoke otherwise. They were Harpies, as ancient and venerable as the great Dwarven kings of old.

“Our kind has never worshipped the gods. We are sisters of sky and mountain, yet we have sworn commitments. The Dae’shan command us now.”

“The Dae’shan will see us all brought to ruin before this ends,” Garelda countered.

“What say you, Brom?”

The larger Hag puffed out her chest, dark feathers glimmering in the moonlight. "The winds have changed. We are not the owners of our lives. Difficult decisions must be made, but all for the better of our kind."

Freina waved her claws dismissively. "Everything I do is for our kind. There is no personal motive, sister."

"I have doubts," and Brom fell silent.

Too much had happened since Amar Kit'han first ordered them to follow the Delrananian princess. They'd been given free rein to kill as many of her protectors as necessary but had yet to come close enough to make this a reality. The desire to sink her claws into human flesh was becoming overpowering. She needed to feel the thrill of a kill, the taste of flesh and warm blood filling her belly. The Hags hadn't killed in so very long, giving her pause to believe this lay at the center of their discord.

Turning to her sisters, Freina said, "We have much to do if our charge is to be fulfilled, but we obey on empty stomachs. Too long has passed since our claws enjoyed ripping flesh. There is a small Man village at the base of the mountains. Let us go and fill our bellies and relieve this tension."

The prospect of hunting again stole away seditious thoughts, for the moment at least. Brom nodded and took flight first. Garelda, ever distrusting of her sister's true intentions, followed suit, leaving the frigid elder sister along on the small outcropping with dark thoughts coursing through her mind. The past remained unchangeable, but the future was locked in doubt. She very much wanted to see her sisters free again but lacked the foresight to discover how. With heavy sigh she launched into the midnight sky and hurried after her sisters.

Far below, the wagon rambled on, unaware of the forces gathering against them. Only the Hags watched their passing.

BIO

Christian W. Freed was born in Buffalo, N.Y. more years ago than he would like to remember. After spending more than 20 years in the active-duty US Army he has turned his talents to writing. Since retiring, he has gone on to publish over 25 military fantasy and science fiction novels, as well as his memoirs from his time in Iraq and Afghanistan, a children's book, and a pair of how to books focused on indie authors and the decision-making process for writing a book and what happens after it is published.

His first published book (Hammers in the Wind) has been the #1 free book on Kindle 4 times and he holds a fancy certificate from the L Ron Hubbard Writers of the Future Contest.

Passionate about history, he combines his knowledge of the past with modern military tactics to create an engaging, quasi-realistic world for the readers. He graduated from Campbell University with a degree in history and a Masters of Arts degree in Digital Communications from the University of North Carolina at Chapel Hill.

He currently lives outside of Raleigh, N.C. and devotes his time to writing, his family, and their two Bernese Mountain Dogs. If you drive by you might just find him on the porch with a cigar in one hand and a pen in the other.

* 9 7 8 1 7 3 6 8 0 4 4 2 1 *